THE BIG AHA

RUDY RUCKER

TRANSREAL BOOKS

Published January 15, 2014
Transreal Books, Los Gatos, California
www.transrealbooks.com

Paperback: ISBN 978-0-9858272-5-0
Hardback: ISBN 978-0-9858272-7-4
Ebook: ISBN 978-0-9858272-6-7

Early versions of Chapter Two appeared as short stories in *Flurb* #13, Spring, 2012, and in *Omni Reboot* in November, 2013.

Heartfelt thanks to the three hundred and thirty-one backers who helped fund the creation and publication of *The Big Aha*. The contributors' names appear in the Afterword.

And thanks to Tim Pratt who encouraged me to try the crowdfunding stratagem. Thanks also to Georgia Rucker for help with the design, and thanks to my proofreaders Lisa Goldstein, Sylvia Rucker, and John Walker.

For my parents,
for Louisville,
for William J. Craddock,
and for Sylvia

ALSO BY RUDY RUCKER

SF NOVELS

Turing & Burroughs
Jim and the Flims
Hylozoic
Postsingular
Mathematicians in Love
Frek and the Elixir
Spaceland
The Hollow Earth
Master of Space and Time

TRANSREAL SF NOVELS

Saucer Wisdom
The Hacker and the Ants
The Secret of Life
The Sex Sphere
White Light
Spacetime Donuts

THE WARE SERIES

The Ware Tetralogy
Realware
Freeware
Wetware
Software

HISTORICAL NOVEL

As Above, So Below: Peter Bruegel

MEMOIRS

Nested Scrolls
All The Visions

COLLECTIONS

Surfing the Gnarl
Complete Stories
Collected Essays
Mad Professor
Gnarl!
Seek!
Transreal!
The Fifty-Seventh Franz Kafka

NONFICTION

The Lifebox, the Seashell, and the Soul
Software Engineering and Computer Games,
Mind Tools
The Fourth Dimension
Infinity and the Mind
Geometry, Relativity and the Fourth Dimension

ART BOOK

Better Worlds

CONTENTS

1: Qwet Rat

"What do you think of this guy?" asked my old pal Carlo. It was a fall day in Louisville. I was slouched in my soft chair at the back of my nurb store. Carlo was holding something he called a qwet rat, pretty much shoving the thing into my face. Gray fur, yellow teeth, and a naked pink tail.

"He's skungy," I said, laughing a little. "Who'd ever buy that?"

"Skungy!" echoed Carlo, flashing his version of a sales-conference grin. "The perfect name." He raised the rat high into the air, as if displaying a precious vase. The rat's eyes twinkled like black beads. His pink-lined ears made small movements, picking up our voices and the all-but-imperceptible buzz of the gnat cameras that had followed Carlo in.

"This rat's really your prototype?" I asked.

Flaky Carlo had managed to get a job in business, working at a startup company run by one of our high-school friends, Gaven Graber. In his new persona as a marketeer, Carlo was wearing a jacket patterned in scrolls and cut from the latest termite-cloth. He'd been getting gene-cleaning treatments, and he had a youthful air.

"First thought, best thought," said Carlo, lowering the rat back to the level of my face. "Especially from a qrude dude like you. Hell, we ought to use 'Skungy' as the name for our whole qwet product line."

"What's qwet supposed to mean anyway?"

"Quantum wetware. Nice buzz phrase, huh? It's a new tech. This woman named Junko Shimano invented it. She works for Gaven now."

"You guys are crazy," I said, addressing the gnat cameras as well as Carlo. I figured Gaven Graber was watching us via the swarm.

I sold odd-looking nurbs in Live Art—my store. My products

had all been enhanced by independent artists like me. Some of us used genemodding to design our own nurbs, others just trained some existing nurbs.

Modifying a nurb's genes was tricky, and it required the use of a genemodder wand. The results of genemods weren't easily predictable, although the wand did provide some semi-reliable feedback about what to expect. The genemodder wands were expensive, as the United Mutations company still held all the patents on them. And—yet another problem—the genemodder wand only worked on certain special kinds of nurbs. Programmable nurbs. Crazy as it sounds, programmable nurbs had tiny antennae on their DNA strands.

So, even though I owned a genemodder wand, I rarely used it. Too much hassle. But there was simpler way to producing artistic nurb products. Nurbs had basic tweaks that gave them web access, and they all had some level of intelligence. You could talk to it via the web. So—even without getting into genemodding—you might coach a nurb into changing the way that it chose to appear or to behave. Not that nurbs always did what you asked. If your art involved reshaping the nurbs, you were a little like a director working with actors.

Nurb boutiques took pains to make their quirky offerings seem friendly and cute. My shop's dog-sized house-cleaner slugs were hot pink, for instance, and they giggled. The bands on my squidskin wristphones were demure, pastel tentacles. My bourbon-dripping magic pumpkins had a jolly, drunken air—drifting in the air like heavy party balloons. The web-linked dreamchairs in my shop had been coached to take on elegant, sculptural shapes. But this rat—

"It's all about product placement," said Carlo, still holding Skungy. "Gaven wants to go for that outrider chic. He's itching to show the world that Louisville can mud-wrestle with the wild hogs. Letting a qrude like you launch the product is a good step." Carlo gave the rat a sharp tap on the crown of his head. "Bring us luck, Skungy! Drag home big cheese."

The genetically engineered rat glared up at Carlo and emitted a series of rapid, reproving squeaks that were—I gradually realized—actual words. I could even hear some insults in there. *Asshole*, maybe. And *stupid turd*. He had a Kentucky accent.

"The fruits of Gaven's quantum wetware tech?" I said, only to be interrupted by a yelp from Carlo. Skungy had bitten the tip of his finger.

"Oh no!" moaned Carlo. Nurb bites could have horrible side effects.

A bright drop of blood welled out, very red. Wriggling free of Carlo's grasp, the nurb rat leapt onto my sales counter, which grew out of my store's floor like a tall toadstool.

"I've got my rights!" shrilled the excited rat, rising onto his rear legs. "I'm every bit as smart you guys. I shouldn't be for sale!"

If I mentally dialed up the listening speed of my ear, Skungy wasn't that hard to understand. Uneasily I wondered if he might be segueing into a lethal rampage. These things happened more often than nurb dealers liked to admit—especially with nurbware tech's rapid rate of change. None of our products were sufficiently pre-tested.

"Calm down," I told the rat. I rose from my chair and drew my genemodder wand from beneath the counter. The wand was a slender, foot-long, tapering cone jammed with tiny components—one of the rare items in the modern world that was an actual piece of machinery. A United Mutations design. I brandished the wand. "I'll break your DNA if you keep it up, Skungy. Turn you into a puddle of slime. I know you're still mod-accessible. Act right. Aren't you supposed to be, like, Carlo's helper?"

The gnat cameras circled us, taking in the scene from every side. Combining a swarm of gnat-cams' viewpoints gave the user an interactive 3D image.

Carlo found a Voodoo brand healer leech on a shelf and put it on the spot where Skungy had bitten him.

"Oh please don't let me be infected," muttered Carlo. "God *damn* this rat. He's two days old and he's running amok. But don't incinerate him quite yet, Zad. Gaven's got a couple of million bucks in this prototype. We'd hate to burn your sparkly quantum wetware, Skungy. Be grateful, you piece of crap. You should think of Gaven as god. And I'm god's promo man." The tiny flying cameras rocked their wings in agreement.

"Eat shit!" said the rat. His tensely twitching whiskers were like insect antennae—constantly in motion, alert for the slightest incursion into his space.

I had to laugh. I liked the nurb's bad attitude. He was wilder than any I'd seen since my very first roadspider—the short-lived Zix.

"You wave on the rat, huh?" said Carlo with a tense smile. "You're a troublemaker too. An artist. That's one reason why we fingered you as our go-to guy. Not to mention that you're one of the only registered art-nurb stores in Louisville. And thanks to our crazy Kentucky laws, you're allowed to sell art nurbs without federal Department of Genomics approval. We'll give Live Art an exclusive on our Skungy line for a month. You'll have a buttalicious high-end market to yourself."

"I'm not sure I'd want to stock this rat, Carlo. What kind of discount would you give me?"

Carlo was ready for this. "Gaven says you could have your first two dozen Skungies for *free*. A test run. You charge what you like, you keep the money. As the inevitable glitches and nurb attitude problems arise, we'll pump out the upgrade patches. Meanwhile United Mutations is hanging back, watching for law suits, waiting for the Department of Genomics to certify the quantum wetware rats for the wider market."

Skungy was pacing around my counter, surveying my shop and sniffing at the faint scents of food that wafted from my living quarters out back. My wife Jane had thrown me out of her fancy housetree condo, so I'd grown a bachelor pad onto the back of my shop. I had my bed in the store, and all of my remaining *Cold Day in Hell* paintings were on the walls.

I'd made these pictures with nurb-paint—which had been a big deal a few years ago. But they weren't selling at all any more. For that matter, the Idi Did gallery on Bardstown Road had dropped me from their roster. I'd had about seven good years as an artist, and I'd managed to marry wealthy, chic

Jane, heiress to the Roller nurb chow fortune. At one point we'd meant to have a baby, but we hadn't gotten around to it. Maybe I hadn't wanted the responsibility. And now the thrill was gone.

Jane had been ramping up her career, doing well with her Jane Says public relations agency. I was on the downswing, somewhat depressed, not doing much of anything. According to Jane I was dead and hollow.

I snapped back into the moment. This nurb rat, this Skungy, he didn't seem particularly task-oriented. He was more like a pool-hall idler, drifting on the tides of his random thoughts. Noticing me watching him, the rat laid a fecal pellet on my counter.

He was nothing but an alley rat, gene-modded to have a standard United Mutations add-on for web access, plus an ability to hold a larger mind. But, yes, Gaven had indeed put some kind of larger mind into him. That was the quantum wetware part. Skungy was the funkiest rat I'd ever seen.

"I don't know," I told Carlo, weighing his pitch. "What if these rats kill a cat or gnaw a baby?"

"Naturally Gaven covers any legal problems you have," said Carlo. He handed me a crisp, folded paper from the pocket of his silky termite-woven jacket. "Legal waiver for you, qrude. Gaven really likes the idea of us three launching his product. Like he's nostalgic for the old times. He scored big as a house-tree developer, and now he's back to Louisville."

Carlo mimed a salute in the direction of the gnat cameras. The iridescent green dots were grouped into a shifting blob near the ceiling.

"I don't think Gaven was all that fond of me in high school," I said, setting down Carlo's waiver. As far as I was concerned, the legal paper could have held hieroglyphs written with smears of excrement. Like I said, I'm an artist.

But Gaven, he was tech and biz. Flashing back to the numerous times I'd disrespected Gaven before, I directed a lurid grimace towards his swarm of spy-gnats—drawing back my chin, putting my tongue between my teeth and puffing out my cheeks. It was one of the faces I used to aim at him in high school. Gaven's gnats zoomed at my head, perhaps meaning this in a jolly, playful way.

"Have you physically seen Gaven in person since he moved back to town?" asked Carlo, not smiling.

"Just the once," I said. "That big welcome dinner at the Pendennis Club in March. Louisville's favorite son. Gaven's gotten all fit and trim. I hardly got to talk to him. You were there too, Carlo. You were drunk. From all the whiskey pumpkins they had bobbing around the room."

"Don't remember," said Carlo.

"The rest of us do," I said, a sharp note in my voice. "Jane especially. I was still living with her then, right?"

"Too bad about you two breaking up," said Carlo quickly. "Sweet Jane. Why are you looking at me that way? Did I say something bad?"

"You asked Jane how it felt to be married to a washed-up loser," I said. "It was the last straw. The tipping point. The next day she threw me out. You're a jerk."

Even though I meant these words, I didn't put all that much heat into them. Carlo and I had been sniping at each other for twenty years. We were comfortable together because we could be as insulting as we liked. He was that kind of friend.

The rat was still twitching his nose towards my apartment in the back. "Your nest stinks pretty," he told me.

"Think of it as a kitchen midden," I said, lightening up. "A future archaeological dig."

"What all's ripe today?" asked Skungy, swinging his tail to bat tiny turds off my counter.

"We have a local specialty," I said, pointing toward a greasy crust of what they called Derby pizza. The cheese on these things was made from the bourbon-scented milk from merry mares. "Jolly pizza," I told the rat. "Nummy num."

Amusing himself with some qwet-brained routine of being world-weary, Skungy flopped onto his belly and dragged himself across the counter, moving like a parched traveler in a desert. When he came to the edge, he leapt off it, did a mid-air flip, and hit the floor running. Moments later he was back on the counter with his prize, a scrap of crust the size of his body. His tail writhed as he began devouring it. Almost immediately, the merrymilk relaxed him. A pool of urine spread beneath his feet, dampening his fur.

"So anyway, no hard feelings about Jane," said Carlo with a vague wave of his hand. "At that party—I'm sure I was trying to help. You don't do me justice. My point is that you need to change your presentation. Upgrade the package you bring to the table. Otherwise—"

"Don't you go bird-dogging Jane!" I cried, suddenly imagining I saw the old hustle in Carlo's eyes.

"*Au contraire*," he drawled. "I'd like to see you two back together."

"Why?"

"Jane's rich. I like having her in my circle of friends. And I care about *you*, qrude. I'm sad to see you going under. Jane's not going to wait. Gaven Graber wants her. And Whit Heyburn's waiting in the wings."

"Not Whit! He's an evil psycho. If it weren't for guys like him—"

"It's all someone else's fault, huh, Zad? Listen to me. One big reason you're having problems is that you're logging way too much time in your dreamchair. Webzombia, qrude. Each era gets their own madness. Melancholia, neurasthenia, schizophrenia, bipolar disorder—webzombia. Let me ask you this. When you sleep, do you dream you're on the web? Key, key danger sign."

I didn't like being called out on my use of my special chair. Webzombia? I'd never heard the word. Clearly a bullshit concept. I liked my busy, convivial hours on the web. Now and then I sold some nurbs or some art that way, or even cajoled a virtual customer into physically visiting my shop. The web was where I lived these days, and I didn't want Carlo trying to drag me out.

"You're the zombie, not me," I snapped. "You and those fountain of youth treatments you're getting. You look like you're eighteen, you idiot."

Carlo cocked his head, giving me a silent, sympathetic smile. And now Skungy glanced up from his pizza—as if finding me pathetic as well. A nurb was sorry for me?

"I should shove that filthy quantum wetware rat down your throat!" I yelled at Carlo, fully losing it.

"Keep in mind that our rat's seeming filth is a marketing move," said Carlo calmly. He enjoyed seeing me crack. He'd scored a point in our never-ending game. "When people see a scuzzy rat they think *New York City*. And that's a plus."

"Skungy talks like a Kentucky hick."

"Well, that has to do with how we programmed him. Unfortunately we had to take a shortcut. But later on we hope to have our qwet rats sounding totally NYC. Manhattan is so luxor just now. The theme park thing."

"Luxor," I echoed, calming down. "Yeah. I'd like to go to Manhattan again myself. It's been two years since I was up there with Jane. Lately I've been watching the New York retrofits from my chair. The honking nurb cars, the flydinos gliding among those classic skyscrapers—*yeah*. An old-school city of the future. When I watch, it's like I'm there."

"I bet it is. You sitting in your dreamchair." The pitying look again.

Something within me gave way. "Okay, yes, I admit it! I'm going nowhere. I need a change."

"He felt a wistful yen for a life that was real," intoned Carlo. "And the answer was—a *Skungy*! A qwet rat that was smarter than his friends!"

"Smarter than you and Reba Ranchtree," I muttered. "That's for true."

"Why are we even arguing, Zad? It's all coming together. Win-win. Did I mention that we're calling our company Slygro? Louisville's moving up the food chain. Enough with the bourbon and the tobacco and the horses and the Roller nurb chow. With Gaven in town, Louisville can productize some radical nurbs. The Slygro qwet rats can be spies, messengers, thieves—"

"What about Skungy being a biter?" I interrupted.

Carlo looked down at his finger. "A little worried about that," he allowed. "Gaven hasn't fully told me what this quantum wetware shit can do. But never mind. We'll be working it all out in the follow-on releases."

I waved my genemodder wand at little Skungy. "Nobody wants a nurb that bites," I scolded him. "And if the biter is smart, that makes it worse."

"I'm no biter," piped the rat, his mouth full of Derby pizza. "Unless I feel cornered. Your pal went and smacked me on the head. He was asking for it. Once we grow us out a decent pack of qwet rats, I'll get some respect."

Carlo glared at Skungy. "Keep it up with that loose-cannon bullshit, and you'll be the very last qwet rat that Slygro ever makes. Gaven and I need to see some willingness to please. Right now, Skungy. Start kissing my butt."

"You go first," said Skungy, laying a fresh turd on my counter. "Clean my tail. Aw, I'm just joshing. Here's something sweet." The rat began rocking his pelvis and singing, his little voice raspy and sweet. "I want to liiiive," he twanged, for all the world like a Grand Ole Opry performer. "I want to raise me up a famileeee!"

A faint odor of qwet rat had permeated the store by now. And Skungy's plangent melody caught the attention of the other nurbs—the bin of floor lickers, the web-cruising chairs, the wristphone squidskins, the buoyant magic pumpkins, and even the stack of flat, leathery house seeds—all of them were nodding and twitching in sympathy. Gaven's gnat swarm was folding upon itself like ghostly dough.

The scene reminded me of those primordial black and white cartoons where all the objects on a farm start jiving to a tune. I was falling under the music's spell too. Skungy had an ability to get all of us into his channel. Was this part of the quantum wetware thing? The rat seemed taller than before, his fur lustrous and beautifully groomed, his motions eloquent and filled with worldly-wise tenderness and wit.

Relishing his power over us, Skungy rasped a final chorus,

then took a deep bow with his paws outstretched. An appreciative murmur passed around the room. We loved him.

Well, maybe not Carlo. "That part about raising a family?" Carlo said, his voice cold. "That's out of the question, Skungy. You're sterile. Like all the other nurbs."

"Man that's harsh!" said Skungy, feigning exaggerated surprise.

"Think about it," I put in, thinking I needed to comfort the rat. "If you nurbs were to start hatching out litters, what would retailers like me even sell? How would producers like Slygro pay their development expenses?"

"Oh, Skungy knows damn well he's sterile," said Carlo. "He's just jerking your chain."

"I'm gonna clone me some copies," said Skungy. "I ain't no simple tool like those other nurbs. They're soft machines. Me, I've got fighting spirit, and I'm qwet, see? A whole new deck of cards."

Carlo sighed and peeled the healer leech off his finger. The wound was gone, with the skin grown back into place. "I keep telling Gaven he should reprogram Skungy's personality," said Carlo, studying his finger. "But he won't. It's like he's too impatient about impressing us local yokels. In a frantic rush to buy our respect."

"Buying is fine. I'm close to tapped out."

"Oh, did I mention your bonus?" Carlo dug into his fancy jacket and hauled out a serious wad of hundred dollar bills. "To help you with transitional issues. While you're distributing and patching the rats."

A thought struck me. "What if I myself had quantum wetware? Could it give me a better personality?"

"We'll see," said Carlo. "Most likely it would make you smarter—at least some of the time. And, yeah, the qwet rats are a warm-up for the personal product. I'm hanging with this new woman who's far into the concept. The one I mentioned—Junko Shimano?"

"Have I met her?"

"Not from Louisville. A Japanese California girl. Talks all

creaky and flat. Went to Stanford? She's the head nurbware engineer at Slygro, yeah. Invented the qwet tech. Didn't even patent it, for some weird idealistic California-type reason."

"No patent?"

"Doesn't matter yet, since nobody but Junko really understands about qwet. Gaven's mostly faking his part. Slygro's got a big head start having Junko on board. We're tiny, you know, working out of a barn on Gaven's farm. I met Junko the first day that I signed on as the marketeer, and I think we clicked. I'm betting I'll get her in bed. Only—she's on a different level than me. Like she's a human and I'm a dog? But I'm playing it all jaded and courtly, and that usually works. I'm hoping for some volcanic geek-girl sex, qrude. I might even capture some video that you could—"

The gnats appeared upset—to the extent that tweaked insects can show emotion.

"What now?" said Carlo, noticing the swarm's chaotic tremors. "You're jealous, Gaven? Them that asks, gits. Learn from the rockabilly qrudes. Stop being a number skull."

"I'm in a dry spell myself," I sighed. "I need to find the big aha. Before I wither and drop like an autumn leaf."

"Everyone's getting so sad and serious!" said Carlo, shaking his head. "Just because we turned thirty? We'll be giving you ten qwet rats on Monday, Zad. Keep Skungy for your helper. I'm sensing a mutual resonance between you two."

I looked down at the qwet rat. As if overwhelmed by the Derby pizza and his performance routine, he was lying limp on my sales counter. Asleep? He didn't look so nasty to me anymore. He looked like he belonged. He wouldn't bite me. I wasn't a jerk like Carlo.

"Deal," I said. "I'll keep Skungy. But I'm warning you that business isn't good. I know you're giving me that incentive fee, but it'll only cover the hassle of housing your qwet rats for—let's say a month. If they're not selling by the end of October, I get more money or Gaven takes them back."

"*Incentive fee*," echoed Carlo, savoring the tasty phrase. "Let me tell you this. If you don't bungle the qwet rat test run, Gaven might let you do trial marketing for more new nurbs. Even better, he might let you market the human qwet treatment he wants to sell. He has a whole bunch of loofy things to spring. Lucky little Louisville. Gaven says we'll be, like, the epicenter of the qwet wave."

"Let me ask you this," I said, uneasy with all these grandiose plans. "Do you remember my first roadspider? Zix? Untested nurbs can get into dark and surreal fail-modes. Tragically inept. Deadly. People know this. A barn-brewed uncertified trial-market nurb is a tough sell."

"Your art shop sells to the fringe," said Carlo. "The eccentrics, the loofy debs, the qrudes among the horsey set. You sell forbidden fruit. And they feel safe getting it from you. You're a society artist. Your shop is in the eleganto old-town district on Main Street, surrounded by red-brick buildings and the up-to-the-minute Gaven Graber highrise housetrees by the river. I can hear the tintinnabulation of ice cubes in the merrymilk highballs from those balconies. You're at the core, qrude. Totally luxor. Like a high-end drug pusher." Carlo's eyes were liquid, sincere. He had a way of getting deeply into whatever line he was feeding you.

"I'm living in the back of a store," I said flatly. "And the best thing that's happened to me today is that I'm feeling this weirdly organic bond of sympathy with a rat."

Despite my spoken doubts, I had a gut feeling that Skungy would be of great value. A rapport was indeed forming. And at this point I realized that Skungy wasn't actually asleep.

"He's using a cosmic mind state to merge his quantum waves with yours," explained Carlo, giving me a perspicacious look. "A qwet rat does that with his new owner. They're kind of telepathic. You're feeling his glow."

I myself was no mind reader—not yet, anyway— but with the qwet rat focusing on me, I imagined I could feel his little breaths, the rapid patter of his tiny heart. I even glimpsed the dancing triangles of his ratty thoughts. Cat noses, rat vulvas, corners of cheese.

"I wave on him," I murmured.

"Here's his special food," said Carlo, handing me a sack of golden brown cubes—addictive Roller nurb chow for Skungy. The chow smelled like tobacco—which was indeed one of its ingredients. As long as I controlled Skungy's chow, I'd be at the center of his life.

Carlo was ready to move on to other topics. "So—with Jane out of the picture, what are you doing for action? Boning a sex nurb?" Carlo swiveled his head, keenly scanning my store. "You still stock them, don't you? Slit spheres, magic staffs, like that?"

"No, you moron. Sex nurbs are over. The Live Art shop is about quality and grace. And when I get antsy, I go out behind the shop and work on my new car. Sublimating randiness into craft. Thereby enhancing my he-man charm."

"Car?" said Carlo blankly.

"I've got an antique show car," I said. "It's the same model as the black convertible where JFK got shot a hundred years ago. That President? Wife wore a pillbox hat? My car's a Lincoln Continental stretch limo from a bankrupt car museum out on Shelbyville Road. Sizzler Jones bought out the museum—you remember Sizzler from school? He's a land developer now. I traded him one of my nurb-paint pictures for this particular vehicle. I let him have *Cold Day in Hell: Why You Believe in God*."

"Always with that same half of the title, Zad?"

"My brand. It still works a little bit. Sometimes. Rack up a fat sale by Louisville's beloved rebel qrude artist, Zad Plant!"

"You said it was a *trade* to Sizzler Jones," corrected Carlo. "Not a sale."

"It's the same," I said impatiently. "Anyway, Sizzler is razing the museum and planting a grove of Gaven Graber housetrees. There's rolling fields and a lake, see, and Sizzler put a few thoroughbreds in the pasture. Nurb merry mares, actually, but whatev."

"Look, I gotta get going," said Carlo, losing interest.

"Let me finish! You're gonna do business with me, we gotta chat, right? Whittle and spit and talk about cars! Like our grandfathers used to do." I was oddly excited, and I was running my hand across the damp fur of the sleeping rat all the while. Picking up traces of his dreams. "My Lincoln Continental has a V8 internal combustion engine and a Turbo-Drive transmission," I continued. "Not that you can get gas these days, but I've got Detroit pig-iron all the same."

Carlo was at the front door, ready to make his exit. "Roadspiders and flydinos are what matter," he said, pointing at the sky. "There's Reba Ranchtree on her flydino right now. Slygro's biggest investor. Yeah."

For a while after high school, Reba had been my girlfriend. She'd been very bitter when I dropped her for Jane. And then she'd started dating Carlo and we'd become friends again. Always the same little circle of people in my life, nothing ever forgotten, all of us endlessly mind-gaming each other. Louisville's like that.

Following Carlo out to the grassy street, I peered up into the swaying housetrees by the river. It was getting on towards the evening of a late September day, a Friday, the sun low and brassy, the temperature bearable, an evening breeze beginning to stir.

Reba's condo was in the same tree as where I'd been living with Jane. I could see Reba lying on her stomach on the back of the oversized leather-winged nurb flydino that she rode. Tiny and far as Reba was, she somehow managed to see Carlo and me, and she gave us a wave. Maybe the wave was cheerful, but I took it to be lofty. Like a queen acknowledging ants.

"Reba and her rhamphorhyncus," I said with unexpected bitterness. "The savage, toothy beak. The walnut-sized brain." Loser that I'd become, I hated anyone who was doing well. I was forgetting that Reba was my pal.

"And Reba's snobby about—*what*?" said Carlo, stoking my resentment trip. "That's what I always wonder when I see her these days. Why does she think she's better than me? Because her parents died and left her a fortune? I mean, both of us were her lovers ten years ago. That should make for happy memories, right?"

"Actually she treats me okay," I had to admit. "But it's like she's sorry for me. Little does Reba realize how nice my shop's spare room is. Little does she grasp that I've attached a giant nurb slug to the underside of my obsolete metal car. The slug is an industrial nurb I got wholesale from United Mutations. I drove my slugfoot Lincoln around the block last week. Did you hear about that?"

"Maybe, yeah, now that you mention it." Carlo was mildly interested again, and he let me draw him back inside.

"My big ride, she slime around so *nasty*," I said, my spirits rising. "Low and slow, qrude. A luxor assassination limo with a slugfoot. I might relaunch myself selling retrofitted cars."

"Screw retro. But a giant slugfoot—that's good. I want to ride in your car. When I have more time."

Skungy was snuggling against my hand. Brother Rat. He rolled onto his back to expose his white underbelly. I caressed him with my fingertips.

"Before you go, Carlo, give me some background. For pitching our qwet rats to the slobbering marks. I mean—what the fuck *is* quantum wetware?"

"Well—wetware is, like, your body's chemistry. The genes and the hormones and the brain cell goo. You're a wet computer. And your brain has this switch that Gaven calls a *gee-haw-whimmy-diddle*. He thinks it's a funny name."

"Huh?"

"The name is a hillbilly thing. It's a wooden toy that, like, your country cousin Dick Cheeks might whittle to sell to the slickers at the Shelby County Fair? You've probably seen one. It's a thin bumpy stick with a tiny wood twirler like a propeller on one end? You rub another stick along the bumps, and you holler 'gee' or 'haw' like you're a farmer talking to his mule, and the propeller spins the one way or the t'other. Fun for the young, fun for the old. Gee-haw-whimmy-diddle."

"Oh, please. And your brain's wetware gee-haw-whimmy-diddle switch does—what?"

"The ultra-nerds say that a quantum system can be smooth and cosmic—or jerky and robotic. Gaven's quantum wetware lets you jam your brain's gee-haw-whimmy-diddle switch wide open. You can stay in the cosmic mode. And if your buddy does that, too—why then y'all get into a kind of telepathy. What we call qwet teep."

"And Skungy the rat can read minds."

"Yeah, like I said. He's better at it if he's around someone else who's got the quantum wetware. A fellow qwet teeper."

"I'm liking this, Carlo. I'd love to have telepathy. And then at last someone might understand what I'm saying. Or what I'm trying to paint."

"The lonely bull. The qwet teep won't be exactly like you expect. According the Gaven and Junko, teepers don't actually *remember* each other's thoughts. Because of some even more complicated quantum mechanics bullshit."

"Oh *man*. It's bait and switch."

"After Gaven hired Junko, he was looking for secret military funding, but when he told the war-pigs that qwet teep won't be any good for sending secret messages, they cut him off. And now our man's on the brink of a financial cliff. Junko and I are saying he needs to be selling people the qwet teep right away. People will enjoy it even if it's not some obvious bullshit secret-messaging thing."

"I don't even know what you're talking about. Can Skungy read my mind or not?"

"Let's just say he's good at picking up people's vibes. Thing is, as long as you're physically near a qwet teeper, you'll get these little brief touches of mind merge with them, no matter what. And if you're qwet yourself, you get the full connection."

"And then?

"As soon as Skungy was qwet, Gaven used teep to copy a qwet guy's whole personality over to the rat's brain."

"So now Skungy's a person?" I echoed, more bewildered all the time.

"Yeah, baby," said Carlo. "And we're rats." He put his hands up under his chin with his wrists limp. He cheesed his teeth at me, nibbling the air.

I held my hands like rat-paws too. Skungy, Carlo and

I looked at each other, our six eyes glittering with glee. A multi-level goof was filling the room, fueled by Skungy's musky odor. It was like we were high. I could feel the rat's scent molecules impacting me—*pow, pow, pow*.

I wrestled myself out of my trance and asked another question. "And where exactly did Gaven get Skungy's particular human personality?"

"Joey Moon," squeaked Skungy. His rough little voice was warm. "I am Joey Moon."

"Moon works on Gaven's farm these days," said Carlo. "Kind of a caretaker. He's twenty-five, has a pretty wife, always broke. A pale guy with big dark eyes. Kind of rowdy. Drinks, gets into axelerate buds. He calls himself an artist too."

" I know him," I said, shaking my head. "He's not exactly the ideal personality you'd want to implant inside a consumer product."

I'd seen Joey Moon around town over the years, riding a scorpion or drunk in a bar. He was about eight years younger than me, and several notches wilder than my crowd had ever been. He was indeed an artist, in his own way, not that he painted. He made weird, confrontational works from nurbs. Bursting sacks of paint, hypnotically droning mushrooms, slug nurbs that left iridescent trails on your walls and, more recently, some paintings that he wouldn't show me.

In a way, I admired Joey. He went far out. But when he'd wanted to hang his latest paintings in my gallery I'd turned him down. Apparently they were portraits of some type, but, like I'm saying, he steadfastly refused to let me see them until they went on sale. He worried that, as an "art star," I might "steal his big idea." From the few hints that Joey dropped, I had the impression that the so-called pictures might be empty frames or glass mirrors. But his stories were always changing. It was like he wanted your approval, but he wanted to completely mock you and prank you—all at the same time.

"I didn't like for Gaven to be using Joey Moon for the rat either," said Carlo. "Like I said, I wanted someone from New York. But Joey was handy. And, hell, we're only in prototype mode. Gaven paid Joey to sign a legal waiver and to give us full mental access, whatever that means. He gave Joey him a nice chunk of founder's stock as well. And then he made Joey qwet."

"I still don't get the point."

"The point is that we didn't have to design Skungy's personality. Joey just teeped it over. Like—here! This is me! He didn't send it as a program or anything. You can't use teep for detailed facts, see. Joey sent himself as a personal vibe. Like an emotion, almost."

"So that's good?"

"Yeah, but the qwetting process has had some effects on Joey. He's not coping. We're still waiting to see how things pan out. Before we start selling qwet teep treatments all over the place."

"Joey Moon sold his soul to feed his ratty little wife," put in Skungy, loading the pathos into his grainy voice.

"And the other Skungies?" I asked. "The qwet rats to come? Will they be copies of Joey too?"

At this, the gnats began buzzing in Carlo's face, and his wristphone went wild with messages.

"That's enough whittlin' and spittin' on the courthouse steps, old son," said Carlo. "More details later. Gaven's throwing a pre-launch picnic on his farm starting about now. You and Jane are both invited—Gaven already messaged her. He messaged Reba too. That's where she was headed on her flydino, no doubt. Come on over soon as you can. Maybe you'll get laid! You're gonna like it on the Slygro team, Zad. We keep our big ole balls in the air."

And then Carlo was in the street, jouncing off on his roadspider.

2: The Coming of the Nurbs

I'd known Jane Roller my whole life—starting in fog and shadows of early childhood. My parents were in the Rollers' circle of friends, even though we weren't nearly as well-off.

I was an only child. Dad was a society painter, turning out landscapes of country mansions and portraits of the elite who lived within. He wasn't above painting bird dogs and thoroughbred horses as well. Mom was a wedding planner, with a sideline in floral arrangements. We had a reasonably solid old house on fifteen acres in Skylight, east of Louisville. It wasn't a working farm, just a big rolling field that flowed into the woods. We had a barn that Dad used for a studio. I attended the private St. Francis school amid the nearby horse farms—as did Jane Roller. We were in the same grade.

So, as I say, Jane was around from the start—at church, at school fairs, at Fourth of July parties, at the Louisville Country Club, and, later, at our high-school blow-outs.

Jane had remarkable hair—more than blonde, it was yellow with a tinge of red. She'd get flushed and shiny when she was feeling lively, which was often. She had a flexible voice—jolly, outraged, defiant, conspiratorial, amused—and she liked to talk in accents. Not that, in the earliest days, I paid much attention to her. The boys played with the boys, the girls with the girls.

Jane's parents owned a downtown company that made feed for livestock. When I was about four years old, they switched to making food for the new United Mutations nurbs. I first heard about this when my mother showed me what she called a bouquet reef. It was something she'd purchased for a spare-no-expense wedding reception. The bottom of the bouquet reef looked like a log, and pale, flexible blossoms were growing out of it—an amazing array, resembling white roses, creamy tulips, and calla lilies.

"They're not regular flowers," Mom told me. "They're

nurbs, with special genes. More like animals than like plants, I think. Here, you can have one." She uprooted a fake lily, bringing a bit of the crumbly log-thing with it. The lily wailed in protest, lashing back and forth.

I'd been hearing talk about nurbs, but in the outskirts of Louisville this was the first nurb I'd actually seen. I was greatly intrigued. I took the lively lily to my room, and for a few days she was my pet. I fed her sips of water and crumbs of what Mom called nurb chow.

"Made by our good friends the Rollers!" Mom told me. "You know Jane. The big secret is putting tobacco in the chow. That way the nurbs get hooked."

A couple of years later, when I was six, I went over to Jane Roller's house for her big brother Kenny's birthday party. I didn't like Kenny—he was the kind of guy who'd carelessly do something violent to hurt you—and then deny that it had happened. But never mind about him for now.

The point is that Jane had been allowed to invite all her classmates from school. The Rollers inhabited a mansion in the elegant Glenview neighborhood, closer to town than Skylight. The house had intricate wooden paneling and moldings, etched glass doors between the rooms, wrought-iron light fixtures on the walls, and ceilings twice as high as the ones in my family's plain country home. Waiters were serving cake and ice cream from tables around the edges of the dining room. It was a blast, a kiddie paradise.

Mrs. Roller was floating around, keeping it all together. She liked my dad, but she didn't like me. Her hair was the same color as Jane's. She had a sharp voice that she used to keep some control over her family.

After awhile, Mr. Roller announced that he had a special show for us. He was a stocky man with short spiky hair, often very reckless. In addition to manufacturing the Roller nurb chow, he'd become a nurb wholesaler. He had access to the all the latest nurbs that United Mutations was putting out.

He opened the door to a room that he'd kept closed off thus far. Something like a giant flat squid was fastened to one of the paneled walls. A nurb, twenty feet across, holding himself in place with tentacles that grew from the edges of his big flickering body. His skin was forming pictures—he was what we would come to call a squidskin display.

What made the nurb squid a little creepy was that he had a pair of large, expressive yellow eyes, and he was watching us kids troop in. He looked as if he were uneasy, and possibly on the verge of lashing out. The tips of his tentacles were in constant motion, fretfully coiling and uncoiling.

Chubby little Gaven Graber was there too—he was in the same grade as me and Jane. He was overly hyper, perhaps overwhelmed at being included in a birthday party. Wanting to show off, he ran up to the squidskin and yanked one of its tentacles so hard that it broke off. The severed tentacle wrapped around Gaven's neck and choked him a little, then dropped to the floor and humped back to rejoin the squidskin. Gaven started yelling curse words—I was kind of surprised that he even knew them. Normally he talked like a little businessman.

To calm things down, Jane's father walked over to the squidskin with a bowl of Roller nurb chow. The nurb had a large, unsettling beak. While the nurb was eating, Mr. Roller pointed at the beak, and then at Gaven Graber, as if issuing a warning. I didn't want to see the squid take a bite out of Gaven. You had to feel a little sorry for the kid.

At this point Jane began clowning. "Oh, squiddy, my dear!" she yelled in a mock British accent. "Do you care for some tea?"

"No tea, thank you, Lady Jane," responded the squidskin. His voice was gassy and unclean. We kids whooped at the sound. The creature talked by vibrating his surface. I could see his skin bucking up and down.

Mr. Roller gave the squidskin an instruction now, and images began to play across his slick hide. We were seeing a photorealistic cartoon adventure of a little penguin swimming deep beneath the Antarctic ice. The water was cool blue with sun-shafts of luminous green. The penguin swooped along lovely, twisting curves. Little chains of bubbles percolated upward, each bubble a different shade of pastel, the bubbles bumpy on the surface of the squidskin. And now the penguin reached the ocean floor, brilliant with starfish and eels and soft corals, an enchanted kingdom.

Softly squawking in a gargly underwater voice, the penguin located a dully gleaming metal chest. He pecked sharply at the lock with his orange beak—once, twice, three times—and the top flipped open. *Yeeeek*!—a cartoon squid darted out, dark purple and dark green. The creature was surely too large to have been inside that little chest, but here he came anyhow, swelling up like a cloud of smoke.

To complete the surprise effect, the cartoon squid grew to the point where he precisely overlaid himself upon the nurb squid on the wall. And now the big nurb detached himself and began chasing us screaming children around the room, with his beak clacking and his tentacles going *flub-flub-flub* on the floor.

Mr. Roller was laughing so hard that he bent over to brace his hands on his knees. He was kind of crazy, kind of a jerk, kind of like Jane's big brother Kenny.

Jane, who was sitting at my side, threw her arms around me. Whit Heyburn, a mean, handsome rich kid, also from Glenview, was sitting on her other side, but Jane had turned to me. The amok squid wrapped a tentacle around her ankle. Jane screamed for help, screaming right into my ear. Straining our puny rubber-band muscles to their utmost, Whit and I managed to drag Jane into the sanctuary of the dining room, still a peaceable kingdom of birthday sweets.

"Do it again, Dad!" cried Jane, and ran back into the screening room with Whit. The giant squid was crawling up onto the wall again. I stayed in the dining room with Mrs. Roller, just the two of us. I took more cake.

"Jane's too good for you," the bright-haired Mrs. Roller said to me out of the blue. "Don't get any ideas." Maybe she was drunk.

My own little family's parade of days marched on, Mom and Dad and me, with the nurbs keeping pace. The nurbware engineers were learning to mod nurb genes in a more systematic way. It was all a little hit and miss but, often enough to matter, they'd get a new organism to doing something people liked.

Mom began using a china bush and a silver stalk to grow plates and cutlery for her wedding receptions. You had to fertilize the hell out of these two nurbs, but they yielded wonderful thin porcelain and delicately scrolled forks and knives. And, around when I was ten, Mom got the idea of letting nurbs provide the wedding buffet food as well.

The first test-run was a shambles. Mom had gotten hold of a new nurb called a magic table. It was a heavily biotweaked fungus. I helped Mom spread the thing's spores in a circle on the ground in a clearing at the edge of the woods.

"It starts out like a fairy ring of mushrooms," Mom told me. "Have you ever seen a fairy ring?"

"Yeah." I tended to pass a lot of my time outdoors. We lived amid farms, woodlands, and abandoned quarries.

"These nurb shrooms will come up fast," continued Mom. "We'll have our magic table ready in time for our guests."

"Who's coming?"

"The Rollers and the Grabers. It's Dick Roller who got me these spores. They're experimental. I'm sure you'll be happy to see your little friend Jane from school. And her brother Kenny?"

"I hate Kenny."

"The Graber's son Gaven is coming as well," said Mom. "They say he's very smart."

"He's faking. It's not like you can actually talk to him about anything interesting."

"Don't be so picky, Zad. Be polite to our guests."

An hour later, the Rollers, the Grabers and another couple arrived. The grown-ups stood around having drinks. Jane's father was already tiddly and Mrs. Roller was flirting with Dad. Kenny wanted to wrestle with me, but I refused. To get him off my back, I untruthfully told him that Dad had boy and girl sex-nurbs in the woods, and Kenny dashed off to look for them.

Meanwhile, I showed Gaven my father's painting studio in our wonderfully creaky old barn. Gaven was fairly bearable.

He was curious about Dad's craft. He liked the idea of people making things they could sell.

When we returned to the clearing between our house and the woods, little mushrooms were sprouting in a circle, growing so fast that we could see them moving. Bunches of the stalks fused together, making nine columns around the edge. The columns opened into red parasols at the top. Wobbling and feeling around in the air, the mushroom caps fused to make a smooth, undulating red tabletop. Kenny Roller returned from the barn and raced around the table, pounding on it like he wanted to break it, idiot that he was.

"That's not the right way," reproved Gaven Graber, who was very interested in nurbs. Gaven went over to the unsteady red table and—*talked* to it, like someone calming an overexcited horse.

I'm not sure if Kenny's or Gaven's actions had any real effect on the magic table—or if its actions were predetermined from the start. In any case, the nurb entered a fruiting mode. A frenzied cornucopia of vittles began sprouting forth. Rows of puffball popovers, a twitching country hammie, a roast turkon, loaves of grobread, thickets of asparagrass, pudding pupas—a dizzying array of toothsome delights, many of them unheard of.

My dad stayed away from the food.

"Spaulding Heyburn told me about the magic table this week," said Mr. Roller, talking with his mouth full. "Had lunch with him at the Pendennis Club. The Heyburns pretty much own the local United Mutations operation, you understand. Spaulding says the nurb food is testing out as top-notch. Organic, nourishing, all that good shit. You know what, Lennox? Before long, you'll be using nurbs to help you paint."

"An artist wants to be alone the studio," said Dad, shaking his head. "And any real chef wants ingredients that don't talk back." Dad was a fuddydud.

New dishes continued to form on the magic table, as if at some out-of-control potluck buffet. Mom called in our neighbors the Trasks to help polish off the feast. Fifteen of us ate like hungry animals for two hours until finally the drained magic table shriveled and collapsed.

And then everyone started feeling dizzy and throwing up—everyone except for Dad and, for some reason, Gaven, even though Gaven had eaten more than his share.

"That damned magic table is using us to spread its spores," muttered Mr. Roller, weakly leaning against a tree. "Have to redesign the wetware. Sterilize the motherfucking nurbs. Don't let them reproduce at all. We can always clone off copies if we want to."

To my poisoned eyes, the sky seemed full of flowing colors. As if the Northern Lights had settled over Louisville.

"Or like van Gogh's *Starry Night*," I told Jane Roller, not sure if I were speaking aloud. Thanks to Dad, I knew a lot about painting. But Jane didn't understand. She was busy retching.

I fetched a wet towel to wipe her face.

"Thank you, kind sir," murmured Jane. "You're nice. Funny thing is—that food tasted so good." She waved her hands in front of her face, watching the trails they seemed to leave in the air. Her familiar laugh bubbled forth and she put on a thick Kentucky accent. "Looks like an all-nurb world, don't it, Zad? Everthaang's alive."

My next big memory of Jane dates from a bit later, when I was twelve. The loofy crowd from our class at St. Francis was at the house of Jane's friend Reba Ranchtree. They were taking a run at having a teenage party.

Jane and her girlfriends huddled together, whispering, and then Reba and another girl ran over and grabbed me by the hands.

"Seven minutes in heaven," they cried, all but choking on their glee. "Jane Roller and Zad Plant!"

They shoved Jane and me into a dark coat closet and slammed the door.

"Well?" said Jane, standing very close to me. Some of the coats were nurbs, and they were twitching. In the dark, I imagined that I could see Jane's voice. It looked like a short length of wide gold ribbon with a filigree at one end.

"What?" I said. I didn't actually talk with Jane very often.

It was more like we just happened to bounce off each other now and then.

"*Kiss*!" yelled the two giggling girls outside the closet door. "Zad and Janie in the closet, see? K-I-S-S-I-N-G! One minute gone, six to *beeee*!"

"We can kiss, yes," said Jane, pecking me on the mouth. At first I held my lips stiff, but quickly I learned to make them soft, and even to poke my tongue into Jane's mouth. A flat, neutral taste, not unpleasant.

I didn't know where to put my hands, so I wrapped my arms around her. A hug. Close up, she smelled like honeysuckle vines and like salt. Time seemed to stop. My penis was stiff. I hoped Jane didn't notice it bumping against her through our clothes. And at the same time I hoped she did.

Loud thumping on the closet door.

"Lovebirds forevva," said Jane lightly. The door opened, and the excited Reba Ranchtree gave me a kiss too. The girlfriends shrieked, the world rolled on.

Heedless as boys tend to be, I pretty much forgot about the seven minutes in heaven and went back to my ordinary life. It never occurred to me to try and orchestrate a second tryst with Jane. Her parents were so much richer than mine. And it seemed like she was mostly going around with boys from the upper grades at school—the sleek, sinister Whit Heyburn in particular.

Senior year in high school, some of the kids were talking about going to college, but not many people did college anymore.

Sure, there was still a winged-ants-mating-flight aspect to higher education. It was a way to find lovers, friends, and future business contacts. But by now we all had squidskin wristphones—and we made a lot of our social connections via the web. As for learning things, colleges still had some intense courses. But the courses were online as well—if you had the patience to channel them, not that many of us did. In reality you could get by with grabbing piecemeal info off the web—or getting little apps to do the work for you. And whatever you forgot, you could find again.

So I nixed any worries about the expense of upper-crust schools and told Mom and Dad I wasn't going there. They were relieved—for about ten minutes. And then they switched to worrying about me finding a career.

Mom suggested that I might help her with the wedding catering. I was, after all, good with the sometimes capricious nurbs. By now all the nurbs had built-in web interfaces. You could give them instructions on the fly. I'd gotten the hang of talking to them. And, unlike most pro engineers, I had a flair for empathy. People and nurbs liked me. But no, working my friends' weddings wasn't a row I wanted to hoe.

"Be an artist with me," said Dad. "We can do the traditional thing. Plant the Elder and Plant the Younger. Lennox and Zad. Louisville's high-society art dynasty. You draw so beautifully, Zad. You have a vibrant, living line."

"Thanks, Dad. But what did you see me draw lately?"

He was a little embarrassed. "Well, you know. Every once in awhile I cruise the social webs. I did a search for you, and I saw some sketches. That one of your friend Carlo wearing a squidskin coat? And the drawing of that dark-haired girl you've been seeing—Reba Ranchtree? Vivid, powerful work."

"Reba liked her picture too," I allowed. "It upped her sexability rank."

"What if, just to start with, you take on some of my horse and dog commissions?" suggested Dad. Catching the look on my face, he added, "And paint some of the estates as well. They're fun. But it'll be awhile until you can handle the clients' portraits." He smiled softly. "These wealthy women—they're very sensitive, very particular in their needs."

"I bet," I said. There was an unspoken suspicion around our house that my father was seducing his tastier patrons. But Mom wasn't pressing the issue. I had the feeling she was up to something herself. She was a pretty woman, and she'd get all loud and giggly around younger men.

These were topics I didn't like to dwell upon. Indeed, I had a phobia that I'd eventually surf into a video of Mom or Dad in action, eyes bright and features engorged. *Ugh*. Not that, by now, anyone was particularly shocked by scabrous revelations on the web—what with the new gnat cameras around. Everyone cursed, everyone drank, everyone crapped, everyone had sex, and most of it was online 24/7. Privacy was gone, and we'd gotten over it. You couldn't bust people for the little human foibles anymore.

Anyway, I took Dad up on his offer and began working in his studio—and I stayed there for three years after high school. Sure, I was eager to leave home and to be an artist on my own. But for now, I could still learn from the old master. And he was getting me gigs. And he had a primo stash of art supplies.

Dad and I got along pretty well. But our paths diverged when United Mutations started selling nurb-paint. It was a variant of their nurb-gel, which was a generic, highly tweakable slime mold, with a web interface and language parser built into the cell colony like with any other nurb. If you wanted to design a nurb from scratch, you might well start with a big slug of nurb-gel.

The nurb-paint had colors in its cells, and the stuff understood a vocabulary of a few hundred words—what you might call an art-programming language. Once you'd slathered your nurb-paint onto a wall, the stuff's brightness and hue was adjustable from spot to spot. You could form stripes, polka dots, nested scrolls, branching filigrees or, if you were into sampling, you could feed it a web copy of some particular image that you liked.

Given that the nurb-paint layer was several millimeters thick, you also had the option of coaxing it to wrinkle up and form embossed patterns. You could talk to the paint aloud or via the web, and you could push it around with a brush or with a gently tingling electric probe.

Quickly I mastered the craft of making pictures with nurb-paint. I sensed that this new medium could be richly expressive. In a few days I was painting vibrant imaginary landscapes—bedecked with thorns, elephant trunks, and the puckered faces of little people. I murmured steadily to my paints while I worked.

Finally, I had a large finished piece that I really liked. This was in the month of March, three years after I finished high school.

Dad was dubious about nurb-paint, and when I told him he should switch to it too, he exploded. "I want that creepy-crawly crap out of my studio," he yelled, his long, fuddydud hair flying from side to side. "It's slimy bullshit! Use the good old ways I taught you, Zad. Go back to oil paint!"

"That'll be a cold day in hell," I said. In silence I began packing up the easel, brushes and canvases that I'd bummed off Dad—also my stash of nurb-paint.

Just then one of Dad's clients happened to meander in—Todd Trask, a social butterfly who owned a Derby-winning thoroughbred. He lived as a bachelor in the exquisitely outfitted mansion on his family farm overlooking the Ohio River. By now Todd's parents were dead. The mansion was separated from our house by a mile of woods.

I'd always enjoyed it when my family and I were invited to the extravagant Trask family dos. One of my very first memories from my youth was of a picnic that Todd's parents had thrown beside a pond with cattails. We'd driven to the pond in our cars across the pastureland. The Trask family retainers had built a bonfire, and I'd roasted a hot dog on a stick.

Todd Trask was between my parents and me in age. He had an amusingly campy accent—the man was a fop, a dandy, a nob.

"I've got my portrait of your friend Jason all set," Dad told him.

"Yes, yeees," said Todd, ignoring Dad to focus on me and my new painting. "The hale apprentice in Master Lennox's workshop. Greetings, Zad. This exultant blare of shape and color is from your brush? *Hmmm*. Nurb-paint? Most excellent." Todd leaned in close to my large canvas. The man smelled of lavender and country ham. "One might fear a cheap, generic effect, but you've made it *elegant*. Polyrhythms, chaoticity, gnarl. Very of-the-moment. I see a nightmare horse, a crowd in motion and—how sardonic—fat snails on the track. *Une belle bizarrie*. What do you call your—your monsterpiece, Zad?"

"*Cold Day in Hell*," I said, giving Dad a cocky grin. "That's the title I'm using for this series. Each painting has a subtitle too." Knowing Trask's interests, I came up with a good fit. "*Cold Day in Hell: Derby Day Winner's Circle.*"

"I shall have it!" cried my mark. "Name your price."

Dad got in on the conversation then. He knew much more about the business side of art than I did. If I could actually *sell* my strange new works, Dad would be on my side. As he'd later put it, so what if he didn't like the taint of my paint. He'd been wrong about art fads before. Come what may, the Plant family painters were a team.

Todd, Dad and I tossed around some numbers, and then I hit on a different kind of deal. "I'm just about ready to move out on my own," I told Todd. "I'm getting serious about my work, and I'll need my own studio. Would—would you have something like a spare tenant's house I could use rent-free for a couple of years? And a car?"

"How about a grown home and a *roadspider*!" exclaimed Todd. "Yes, yes! An outsider nurb artist. Under my wing. I'd fancy being a patron! Very Florentine. Can you promise me first bid on your next few works?"

"He'll be selling through Idi Did's gallery," put in Dad, smooth as silk. "And she'll set the prices. Certainly Idi can give you a right of first refusal, Todd. But what's a roadspider?"

"An ebony tarantula of the night," said Todd, waggling his fingers. "An eight-legged steed." He gave me a conspiratorial look. "We edgy aesthetes must help along the fuddyduds, eh, Zad? I shall hang *Cold Day in Hell* above the mantel and invite my friends for an epic debauch. My Derby party in May! I hope there's no danger of that nurb-paint crawling off the canvas? Sinister slugs slither in shadow, they slime into the sleepers' slits!" He struck a pose, as if seeing a vision.

"United Mutations claims the stuff is safe," I said, laughing. "When I'm done with a painting, I lock the tweak interface. If worst comes to worst, you burn it and ask me for a refund. If you feed the painting a crumb of nurb chow once in a while, it loves you. I'll guarantee it for ten years. Tell me more about that roadspider. Where will you get it? I didn't know they were on the market yet."

"I've got an inside track with your schoolmate Whit Heyburn," drawled Todd. "I know him from the horse auctions. And now his dad got him a starter job at the local branch of United Mutations. In the old Ford plant near the airport? UM is phasing out wheeled vehicles to grow roadspiders and roadhog vans. They've been testing various models on our country lanes, lending them out to local artists."

"Artists!" I exclaimed. "Why?"

"Seems there's a loophole in the Kentucky biotech laws that says a company can deploy an utterly untested nurb—provided the nurb is being developed as a *work of art*. A gift to the United Mutations bizboys from our accommodating state legislators. That's how Louisville got a United Mutations campus. Bottom line? Kentucky's a frontier for nurb innovation, Zad. You're positioned to be a stellar nurb *artiste*."

In April I moved onto a quarter acre of Todd's pastureland, atop a little hill near his house. And Todd got me a grown home and a roadspider from United Mutations.

I thought of my grown home as a *she* because she talked to me in a womanly voice. And she was, after all, something womby that I lived inside. I called her Bel. She wasn't overly intellectual—we only talked about simple, practical things. Bel didn't require much nurb chow—she spread a fan of roots underground to pull in most of the nutrients she needed.

This was in the very early days of grown homes, and Bel was a little funky, even if she did have three rooms. Her walls were damp, and her air smelled—green. Like a jungle. Nice, in a way. Even if her membranous windows weren't fully transparent, they let in plenty of light. And, when I wanted, my grown home's flesh would glow. Some kind of firefly gene in there. As a final touch, one of her inner walls acted as a squidskin, cruising the web in response to my spoken words.

My roadspider seemed female as well—but in the menacing style of a warrior goddess. Her name was Zix. Zix was gorgeous—sculpted and gleaming like a black, chromed racing motorcycle. She had a comfortable seat grown into her back, and her eight legs arched high, strongly fortified by carbon fibers.

Perched amid Zix's living machinery, you'd get a smooth, bouncy ride. Zix could really cover the ground—not as fast as a car, but upwards of forty miles per hour, even without a road.

It was Whit Heyburn himself who delivered Zix—he rode out to the Trask place on a chrome-shiny roadspider, with Zix trailing along.

"The great artist," sneered Whit. He had the same blank, supercilious look as ever. "Are you Trask's butt-boy now?"

"Your family gave you a job, huh?" I shot back. "Do you have an office? Go to meetings? Salute the flag?"

"Don't tell me your Dad didn't set *you* up with a career. I can't believe Trask is actually trading you a house and a roadspider for a painting. Is it any good?"

"Sure," I said. "I'm a genius. You've known that for years."

"Show me the painting."

"I'd rather not, Whit. You'd just mock it. Give me the roadspider and be on your way."

"Fine. By the way, I'm meeting up with Jane tonight. I hear she's wild. And she's rich. Like me." Hatefully he leered at me. How could Jane possibly spend time with this vain, vicious, zero-empathy bully?

"You should leave her alone," I snapped, my voice tight. "She deserves better."

Whit grinned down at me from his roadspider, enjoying himself. "Better? I'm the best! Anyway, I'm supposed to warn you about Zix. Give her a big feed of nurb chow after every ride. If she ever gets too hungry, she'll go off to forage on her own. Not a good thing. Can you keep that fact in your flaky art-poser head?"

"Yes." There was no point arguing with Whit. He was cold and mean all the way through.

"Have fun with Todd Trask!" And with that, Whit galloped off.

Zix had a low-grade intelligence. Her voice was sweet,

with a trace of a lisp. She imprinted on me as her owner, and she called me "Master." A creepy thing about Zix was that the nurbware engineers hadn't yet straightened out the horrific look of her churning arachnid mandibles. They couldn't disentangle the mouth parts from the processes that grew the legs. At least Zix's mouth was on her underside.

It was wavy riding Zix around town. Everyone would crowd around to look at her and to ask us questions. Sometimes Zix would recite a pitch for the upcoming line of United Mutations Roadspiders.

Whenever the roadspider and I got home, she'd go to her trough of nurb chow, and then she'd settle down in a messy funnel-web that she'd spun amid the branches of the maple tree beside my bulgy home.

Wanting to justify the goodies that Todd Trask had given me, I got fairly serious about my art. I did three more pictures with nurb-paint during the month of April. I liked being an artist.

Reba Ranchtree came over to spend the night as often as she could. And my pal Carlo Solera was dropping by as well. My friends dug the vibe of my studio, with my uncanny nurb-paint works on display. Sometimes we'd get high off an online brainwave channel—we had these buzzy little eel-pad nurbs we'd put on our necks to trickle in the stim. No real data, just itchy rhythms. Like music, but without the sounds. I liked to imagine we were as loofy as the NYC qrudes.

Sometimes when my friends and I were riding a channel, I'd be gone enough to let them poke into the interfaces of my paintings. No point being tight, I'd say. Welcome the chaos.

Late in April, Carlo started bringing Jane Roller along. She'd broken up with Whit Heyburn. She'd noticed, thank God, that Whit was possessive and cold.

I loved hearing Jane's lively, malleable voice bounce off my grown home's resonant walls. That voice echoed all the way back to my earliest childhood. Soon I'd admitted to myself that she'd been the one for me all along.

I told Carlo that I was much more interested in Jane than I was in Reba. He wasn't against a switcheroo. But we weren't sure how to swing it. It was like I was too deeply in love with Jane to go ahead and tell her. Put more simply, I was an inarticulate raw youth.

The turning point came the evening of Todd Trask's Derby party, early in May. Around dusk that day, I'd given Carlo a ride to my place on the back of my roadspider. Zix didn't like the extra load, but her stronger-than-metal legs could handle it. When we got to my grown home, Zix was of course very hungry. I mistakenly thought I'd filled her food basket that morning, so without really looking, I went right inside with Carlo.

We wanted to amp up for the Trask do. I was a little nervous about the event—which would involve, I expected, Todd braying at length about my *Cold Day in Hell* painting in the party room he called his great hall.

Jane and Reba showed up at my place in Jane's electric car, the girls like pastel flowers in their nurb dresses, Reba a lustrous brunette and Jane a reddish-blonde. As the sun went down, we four keyed in on a luxor new brainwave channel that Reba had found. It was crypto, off the grid, on the border of epilepsy. Carlo, Jane, Reba and I flubbed around on my soft floor for an hour or three, not really noticing anything in the outer world.

"Are you sure you fed the spider?" said Jane all of a sudden. Her voice was clear and sweet, like a tendril from another world.

I sat up in the gloom, pulling the eel-pad nurb off my neck, and gathering my wits. Down the hill, Todd's party was going full blast. Time to regroup.

In the light of the walls' faint green glow, I saw that we four had gotten naked. Carlo was on top of Reba, softly rocking.

"Yukker," said Jane. "I just hope my dress can smooth out." The sleek, silky cloth crawled onto her lap.

"Now you've got me worried about Zix," I said. "Did you hear something? Is that why you asked?"

"A floppy, dragging sound," said Jane. "A dying neigh. Up high?" Jane's skin was beautiful, milky, her breasts of a perfect, cuppable size. But now her dress flowed over them. Jane stared into my eyes, her face framed by the dark gold straw of her hair. I was at a loss for words.

"Bad to channel such loofy brain waves," said Jane. "Not doing that again, *unh-unh*. You miss everything."

"When I get that high, I always feel like I'm going to find the answer," I said. "The big aha. But then—"

"But then—*oh well*!" said Jane, laughing. "Are you ready to go?"

"Yeah," I said, pulling on my pants. "Did you and I—"

"Don't think so," said Jane. "But it's high time. We've been circling each other for so long. And you've gotten hot. An artist! In high school, you were just, you know, too luxor for the lecture. Now you're on a star-quest."

Saying this, she made a lo-and-behold gesture towards my latest work, *Cold Day in Hell: Two Flights Up*. For this one, I'd painstakingly painted three pictures on top of each other, sampling some Bosch and Bruegel along the way. I'd taught my three batches of slime mold to slowly trade places. The result was a multiplex triptych, with the three nurb-paint pictures cycling through Hell, Eden and Heaven. My waviest work yet.

"The Eve in my Eden is you," I told Jane.

"Sweet," she answered. "And you're my Adam." We kissed for first time since those seven minutes in the closet all those years ago.

"Did you say *dying neigh*?" I said after a bit, mentally scrolling through our conversation. "Why did you say that?"

"What I heard maybe," said Jane. "Up in Zix's tree?"

"Shit."

We went outside with a nurb light, and sure enough, Zix's funnel-nest was torn and trembling. Blood dripping down. The big spider had dragged a colt up there. Zix was feeding on the one-week-old horse. The colt's thin legs were doing a staccato flutter, as if in frightened protest. But his motions damped down as Zix bit his body again and again.

"She's *venomous*?" said Jane.

"Nobody told me," I said weakly.

Music was sweeping up from the Trask mansion, and people were silhouetted on the big, open porches, their voices rising in self-satisfied honks and quacks. I heard someone yelling my name. Todd Trask. The patron summoning his pet artist.

I found a long stick on the ground and poked at Zix, wanting to drive her out of her funnel and away from the colt. I had some half-baked notion of burying the horse's body or at least dragging it off into some underbrush. Maybe Todd would think a fox had killed the colt. This was a very special horse, by the way, sired by a Derby winner that Todd owned, and potentially worth millions of dollars.

"Leave me, Master," said Zix, in her sweet, raspy voice. "I am feeding."

"Get off that horse, damn you. I've got plenty of nurb chow. Just wait and I'll fill the trough. I'm sorry I forgot."

"I like the…horse," said Zix.

Recklessly I poked her again with my branch. With a sudden whirling spasm of motion, the spider popped out the other side of her funnel nest, holding the pathetic dying colt tight with her mandibles, dragging him by the neck. As if frightened of me now, Zix scrabbled down the hill towards Trask's house, her legs arching high, and the colt leaving a trail of blood that glittered dark in the party lights.

Uncertainly Jane and I tagged along. By now the people could see what had happened. Todd Trask was yelling. No more hothouse accent.

"The best goddamn colt I ever owned! Killed by that giant fucking spider!" Spotting me, Todd grew apoplectic. "I want you off my farm, you son of a bitch. I never want to see you again."

Todd was drunk and dangerous. By the time he'd fetched his shotgun from the gun rack in his front hall, Jane and I were back at my grown home.

"Get in my car," Jane urged. "Never mind Carlo and Reba. They're still goofing."

I could hear the gun blasting again and again as Todd wiped out Zix. The music had fallen silent, the guests were mewling in dismay.

"Come back down here, Zad," shouted Todd. No way.

"Why don't we go someplace and have sex," suggested Jane.

"I don't like to leave my paintings behind," I said, getting into her car. "Todd might do something to them."

"Spoken like an artist," giggled Jane as we drove off. "Todd won't hurt the paintings. He's being a drama king and he knows it. This big scene makes your art worth even more."

3: Loofy Picnic

So I had a seven-year run in the art world. Along the way I married Jane. We opened my Live Art shop, and Jane started her own public relations agency: Jane Says. I was hot for awhile and then my star dimmed. By the time this the whole qwet thing started, I hadn't sold a painting for two years—nor had I made any new ones.

After my conversation with Carlo in my shop, I got into my slugfoot Lincoln and headed for Gaven Graber's farm, leaving my current roadspider at home. I was hoping to get a deal to market a whole line of Gaven's experimental nurbs. I had the car's roof down and my qwet rat Skungy was perched on the dash, enjoying himself, now and then dispensing some bullshit Joey Moon advice. Route directions from a Southern hipster rat.

The Lincoln was a dream to drive. With her slimy foot, she rocked and rolled like a luxor boat. I followed the old river road along the Ohio, heading towards the horsey end of town. Even if the ocean levels had risen by thirty feet, this far inland, the river levels were the same.

These days, much of the asphalt and concrete was gone from our roads, replaced by tight, impermeable nurb grass. This might have been a problem for a car with wheels, but not for my slugfoot.

A few people waved to me along the way—the guy running the BBQ stand near the waterworks, an art collector tooling past on her roadspider and a realtor friend of Dad's on a zig-zag-backed flydino. The news about my slugfoot Lincoln was out. Chatty little Louisville. Even if I hadn't sold jackshit for a couple of years, I still had my glamour. That qrude and loofy artist, Zad Plant.

It wasn't until Skungy was guiding me up the long green driveway to Todd Trask's old place that I grasped this was where Gaven Graber lived. Todd himself had died of a nasty flesh-eating disease a few years back. The word was he'd caught it at a debutante sex nurb party in New York. Trying too hard to be a jaded roué.

The nurbs had brought along some new health risks all right. Sometimes a nurb would incubate a human disease, and the bugs would leak back out a thousand times as strong. At first people hadn't realized that could happen. But by now most of us knew better than to fuck nurbs.

Poor Todd. He'd given me my start. Naturally we'd made friends again a few weeks after the roadspider fiasco. And—just as Jane had predicted—the gory death of the thoroughbred colt had launched my career. Todd had managed to buy himself *two* new thoroughbred colts by reselling one of my *Cold Day in Hell* pieces. But now I was little more than a shopkeeper.

Halfway up Graber's driveway, I spotted the guests down by that same pond where we'd picnicked when I was a boy. A rangy security guard waved me to a stop. He looked familiar, and I recalled that he'd been on a basketball team my school had played.

"I'm Zad," I told him. "Zad Plant."

"Right," said the guard. "I'm Artie. Hell of a vehicle you got here. Just drive her on down across the field."

I swung down the gentle slope to join the gang. They were lounging on nurb chairs beneath a big oak tree, with Reba's flydino wallowing in the pond. The flydino was pale purple, with batwings and a slender beak. A graceful, pale green roadspider was wandering around as well. The September sunset was coloring the sky. Very idyllic.

It had been a warm day, and three calf-sized nurb bullfrogs were croaking out cool, dry air—they had icicles in their mouths like white teeth. Iridescent skeeter-eater moths were fluttering around. Bluegill fish with little pink legs were walking around the edges of the pond and its cattails, rooting up worms. I noticed a burrow in the bank of the pond beside the cattails—I had no idea what lived inside.

Gaven was making some amazing shit.

He was standing next to my wife Jane, intently chatting her up. Like all the other guys my age, he'd always admired Jane. She was a star. Meanwhile Reba Ranchtree was talking with Carlo and with a self-possessed California Japanese woman I hadn't seen before—I figured she was the Junko Shimano whom Carlo had been fantasizing about.

What had Carlo said—volcanic geek-girl sex? Didn't seem likely. Junko looked more like the type for bird-watching at dawn, a full day of engineering and an evening singing twentieth-century musicals with a chorus group.

Off to the side, oh God, it was Joey Moon, tending a fire and arranging some food that had spilled from the mouth of a nurb horn of plenty. I hadn't seen Joey for several months, and I was sorry to see him sunk so low. Pale and twitchy. Working on Gaven Graber's farm. Letting them copy his personality onto Skungy the rat. It struck me that Joey and his wife were probably living in that same grown home where I'd started out. Bel.

I didn't much want to talk to Joey. He'd just start running one of his wheedling, superior-sounding cons on me. Talking down to me like I was a fuddydud, a mere gallery owner, and no kind of artist at all. Not to mention the fact that, according to Carlo, the quantum wetware treatment had messed up Joey's head.

I noticed hot dogs on the table. Cool. A nostalgic Trask farms weenie-roast coming up. A full-lipped woman stood behind a table laden with drinks. She had oily skin and what I thought of as a gypsy look. Joey Moon's wife. Now she was someone I *did* want to talk to. I'd seen her around, but I'd never actually met her before.

"Hi," said my wife Jane, walking over to me just then, graceful and composed. "Your weird car's finally working. Very luxor."

"The farthest I've driven it so far," I said. "You look wonderful, Jane. I miss you."

"Oh, Zad. You look nice too. And right at this minute I don't feel like shaking you and screaming in your face until I'm so hoarse that I can't talk."

"We've done enough of that," I said. "Both of us. I keep wondering if—"

"Just as well we never had that baby," interrupted Jane, staving me off. "Makes it easier to split up for good. But I do wish you'd get the vat of nurb-paint off my balcony. I keep asking you to do this, and nothing happens. I'm ready to sell the vat online. I want to put a little garden on my balcony."

"*Our* balcony," I slipped in.

"Zad, let's not keep going back to square one. The Live Art shop is yours. The apartment is mine. A clean break. Now about that vat—are you ever planning to make a painting again?"

"I want the vat, yes. Even if I don't paint with the mold, it's my friend. You know how I can coax the stuff into sticking up dozens of little heads and they all jabber at each other?"

"I do like that trick," said Jane. "But your nurb-paint won't do *anything* for me. I think it's sulking. Look—let's get someone to cart the vat over to your shop and you can keep it in your alley. The rain won't hurt it. You can feed it, it'll grow."

"Fine. And when the vat gets full enough, I'll stick my head into it and suffocate."

"A perfect exit," said Jane. "Your nurb-paint pictures will get a nice bump in the market."

I liked how gracefully she'd sidestepped my bid for pity. It was nice to be talking to Jane, our conversations were like a graceful dance. "Speaking of slimy nurbs," I said, "here comes the big guy."

The creature that had carried my car was wriggling out from beneath it. A twenty-foot yellow mollusk with globular eyes on stalks.

"Eew!" exclaimed Reba, wandering over to join us. "Is that thing safe? You ride the scariest things, Zad Plant." She mimed a comic expression of awe. Her hair had a maroon tint these days, and it was permed into intricate curls.

"Sluggo needs his supper," I said, popping open my old car's bank-vault of trunk and dumping a bushel of nurb chow onto the ground. The big yellow slugfoot was on the stuff in seconds, but not before Skungy had scampered over and claimed a nugget for his own. The slug begrudged this, and he actually went for the rat, but Skungy skittered out of reach and clawed his way up my pants and shirt to find a perch on my shoulder. Finishing off the chow, the slug humped across the grass to join Reba's flydino in the pond.

"Zad's so qrude!" cooed Reba, not snobby at all. I had a feeling she was expecting to hook up with me tonight. Reba and Jane were good friends. Maybe they'd made a deal for Jane to hand me off?

"So you like the qwet rat," said Gaven. He was six inches shorter than me, but he wasn't flabby anymore. He looked taut and toned. Some kind of nurb biohack, no doubt. Injectable fitness like Carlo was using. Gaven wore dark cotton pants and a patterned silk shirt. His wristphone was tweaked to resemble an old-school gold watch with a crocodile band. And he wore a geeky black holster with some kind of nerdly instrument in it. In no way did his small stature make him any the less confident.

"Carlo tells me you're going to be repping us in your gallery," he continued. "On the winning team at last!"

"Me on your team?" I said. "Or you on *my* team?"

"Rude and qrude," said Gaven, with a tight laugh. "Same old Zad. Do you know I own one of your paintings too? *A Cold Day in Hell: Louisville Flood.*"

"That's a good one," I said. "I like when the Ohio overflows in the spring. The mental liberation of a natural disaster. Everything flat and shiny along River Road. Weird junk floating. Like the inside of my head. People go down to the floodwaters and party. Atavistic."

"I never went to many parties," said Gaven. "You know how it was. But Jane's helping me find my way into the qrude Louisville scene at last. I'm a client of the Jane Says agency."

"You're working with Gaven?" I asked Jane, surprised. "I hadn't heard."

"Working like a Trojan," said Jane in a fake perky tone, kind of breathless. "Dumb expression. Never mind. Anyway, yes, Gaven wants to launch a whole raft of high-profile products in Louisville. And I'll be zinging my connections. It was my idea to let you handle the prototype qwet rats, Zad."

"Thanks," I said. "Carlo hinted that I might be test-marketing a whole series of things. Like qwet teep for people? Right, Gaven?"

"One step at a time," said Gaven. "But, yes, the qwet rats are only a start. In a month or two—well, I don't want to rush into things. Non-disclosure!"

Jane laughed, clearly in the know. It bugged me to think of her and Gaven having cozy meetings. It would be just like that grotty little geek to try and get something going with my wife. His day in the sun at last.

"I like the cute rat on your shoulder," Jane told me. She could tell I was tense, and she wanted to cool me down. "You named him Skungy? I hear he's practically human."

"I contain multitudes," said Skungy in a genial tone. "I aim to pee."

"That rat bit me today," put in Carlo.

"I was watching through my gnat cams," said Gaven. "Show me the spot."

"This finger," said Carlo sticking out his right index. "At first I thought it was healed, but, look, it's swelling up."

"Are you feeling any, ah, personality inflation?" asked Gaven. "Any expansion of your psychic boundaries?"

"Maybe," said Carlo. "I'm using the bourbon to damp all that down."

"Soldier on," said Gaven, not seeming very worried.

"I could treat the bite with something," said the engineer woman—Junko Shimano. "But if it's what Gaven and I think it is, it's too late. I say we let it run its course. And learn from the process."

"Agreed," said Gaven.

"Is this whole routine some giant revenge trip?" I asked Gaven, feeling annoyed on Carlo's behalf. "You've come to Louisville to destroy your high-school tormentors? Steal my wife and kill Carlo? You're really that lame?"

"Cool it," snapped Carlo, shoving his rat-bit hand into his

pocket. "Don't blow our deal, Zad. I can take care of myself."

"I do admire you two guys, yes," said Gaven, rocking back on his heels and grinning at us. Like he was watching a video. "You gotta know that. You're the qrudes. Have you met Zad, Junko?"

"Not yet," she said, stepping forward. She had an odd coiffure, with her dark hair up in two flat buns—a little like lacquered mouse-ears. "I'm a fan of your paintings. All the Wet E majors at Stanford like you. Gnarladelic! This man knows that nurbs are beautiful!"

"Thanks," I told Junko, shaking her cool, dry hand. "Carlo was praising you to me, too."

"We all need flattery," said Junko. "Pile it on. I'm very insecure. The bright girl with no social skills. Carlo has scheduled me to be his next conquest—in his dreams." She studied him with a certain fondness. Like the way you might look at a pet animal. "It's so strange coming to Kentucky from California. Like I'm visiting another country. Your secret histories. Social taboos. Folk garb."

"Folk garb!" cackled Reba. "Are you talking about my patchwork-plaid suit with the wiggle beads?"

"I do indeed want to know where you found that outfit," said Junko. "I'd like to take one of those back to California."

"I'll give you mine," said Reba. "We're about the same size. And it's not something I'd wear over and over."

"I wouldn't wear it *once*," said Jane, teasing Reba.

"Those beads," asked Junko. "Are they nurbs?" And then the women got into a conversation about that.

"How's Joey Moon holding up?" I asked Gaven, lowering my tone.

"He's stuck in an overly contemplative mental state," said Gaven, glancing over at Joey, who wasn't doing much of anything right now. "He's orbiting around a psychic fixed point. But Junko and I feel that people ought to be able to avoid that. We hope to develop a very broad user base for qwet teep." Gaven paused, looking me over, assessing me. "It's an increasingly fluid situation. In the end, qwet might be—"

"Joey Moon!" squealed Skungy on my shoulder, interrupting us. The rat wasn't paying attention to our conversations, and he'd only now noticed Joey standing over there. He raised his little voice and chirped louder. "Joey Moon!"

Joey didn't seem to hear. He was staring up into the oak tree as if lost in thought. Seized by enthusiasm, Skungy leapt to the ground and scampered over to confront his template. The qwet rat squeaked shrilly at the distracted hipster, who shook his head and kicked savagely at the quantum amplified animal, even trying to stomp on him. Abashed, the rat retreated to the dashboard of my car. The woman at the bar—Joe Moon's wife—remonstrated gently with her husband.

Wanting to learn more, I went over and asked the woman for a bourbon and water. "I'm going to be marketing those rats," I said. "I'm Zad Plant?"

"I'm Loulou Sass," she said. I hadn't known her name. She had a low, purring voice. "And that's Joey Moon." She frowned at me. "But you know all about us. Thanks to the rat."

"I only just now got the rat," I said, wanting to placate her. "And I certainly don't plan to—"

"You know a good lawyer, Zad?" put in Joey Moon, a little unsteady on his feet. He seemed resentful and pissed off. And he stank like a goat. "Your friend Graber, his experiments messed me up, and they've declared me legally incompetent. It's like a hall of mirrors in my head. With voice. Not voices, exactly. Nudges and winks. And I can vibe what you're thinking about my wife, you poncey son of a bitch. I ought to—"

"Oh, stop it, Joey," said Loulou shaking her head. "Christ!" She set my drink on the table with a clack. "Here you are, sir."

"I need a drink, too," said Joey. His rank smell was invading my nose, and I felt like it was sensitizing me to his tangled, self-referential thoughts.

"No you don't," said Loulou, fed up. "Sit down and stop bothering people."

Before slinking off, Joey addressed me again. "Don't you ever forget that I'm an artist too, Zad. Even though you wouldn't show me in your gallery. I'm not a hot shot who gets everything handed to him on a silver platter. But I'm better than you. I'm the next wave."

"Sure, man. You've had it hard." Anything to calm him down.

Joey went and sat down at the base of the oak tree, glaring at us and making odd little gestures meant to show that he sensed our inner thoughts. As if I was in some weird, flickering teep connection with him. For sure he was accurate about the feelings he seemed to be reading from me. My fear, repulsion, and guilt towards him—and my lust for his wife. Being around Joey was a drag.

Be that as it may, we had a party to do. I knocked back another bourbon and smoked a cornsilk bomber with Carlo. All at once he seemed to be turning as paranoid as Joey Moon.

"I'm wise to your hidden mockery," said Carlo. "And I'm picking up on Junko's low opinion of my intellect. Nobody really likes me. I'm a court jester, a hired fool."

"Oh come on, Carlo. Is Gaven spreading this teep shit like a plague?" I paused, studying the cornsilk's clearly etched tendrils of smoke. I picked up an odd odor in the air. Something from Carlo. "Are you wearing cologne, qrude? That's how far into the salesman mode you are?"

"It's a probiotic nurb skin culture transferred from kangaroos. It's called Tailthumper. Women like it."

"Sure they do. But anyway, can you, uh, tell me about Loulou Sass?" For some reason Reba Ranchtree had fallen into an intense conversation with Loulou. It looked like they were making a deal.

"Loulou's a few years younger than us." said Carlo. "But she's gotten around. Used to be a well-known nurb modder. Started out as a gamer, then got hired for commercial apps. Worked at United Mutations for awhile. I don't know why she's dropped down to working on Gaven's farm, but I've seen her talking a lot with Junko. I'm sure there's some kind of weird twist to come."

"Loulou's deep, huh?"

"Ruthless. At this point, I think she's gone qwet like Joey.

If I even look at her, I feel like I'm going to explode. It's like going into a carnival funhouse." Carlo stared down at his hand, trying to control his careening thoughts. "This rat-bit finger, man, I can't understand why nobody wants to help me. Junko's over there talking to Joey Moon. Why bother? Meanwhile there's something physically twitching inside my finger, Zad. A horrible parasite alive in my flesh."

"You're wasted, man. You're on a head trip."

"Hey you two!" called Reba, very jolly in the wake of her conversation with Loulou. "My two old beaus. I don't usually have this much fun on a Friday night. Eeny meeny miney moe, catch a qrudie by the toe!" She was moving her finger back and forth with the words, and she ended up pointing at me. The gold paint on her eyelids was sparkling. "Aren't you lonely sleeping in the back of your store like a janitor, Zad?"

And now here came the newly trim Gaven, walking with his arm around Jane's waist. His gold-tinted wristphone gleamed in the low sun.

"How can Jane stand letting him physically touch her?" said Carlo, blurting out exactly what was in my mind. He said it loud enough for them to hear. Jane responded with a cretin grunt.

"Shall we dine *en plein air*?" said Gaven, coming on all smooth and baronial.

"You sound like Todd Trask," I told him. "Guy who used to live here. Piss-elegant."

"A good role model for me, no?" said Gaven. "Landed gentry. I'm upgrading my image. Do let's eat." Gaven turned Jane loose and gestured towards the horn of plenty. "Sausages, shrimp, burgers, quail—whatever you feel like grilling. Do it yourself. Or ask Loulou."

"*But don't ask Joey*," hollered Joey Moon, fifty feet away by the base of the tree with Junko Shimano standing there talking softly to him, as if trying to steer him out of his fugue. Joey was way too tuned in.

"If all of our qwet rat template providers experience psychiatric dislocations of this nature, it could pose a workflow problem," said Gaven in a bloodless monotone. "Not to mention the public relations fallout regarding qwet teep."

"What if, for the rats, we just use Joey's personality over and over?" suggested Carlo, wrenching himself back into business mode. "We could copy it across from Skungy. No need to deal with Joey or with any other human template again."

"No need for Joey," echoed Gaven, liking the sound of that. "We can put him into treatment, in a place where he's safe."

"And that way Zad gets a clear shot at Loulou," said Carlo, beginning to enjoy himself again.

"Is that really what you're thinking?" Jane asked me. "You'd go for a slutty climber like that?"

"That's not your business anymore, is it?" I said. "Especially if you're dating Gaven. Or going back to that psycho Whit Heyburn. And Loulou's not slutty."

"That's what you think," said Jane. "You're so unaware, Zad. It's pitiful." She put on a blank, simpering expression. "La, la, la, I'm the unworldly artist."

"Let's scroll back," interrupted Carlo. "Back to Skungy being, like, the standard meter for the qwet rat personalities. My bright idea."

"*I've got your platinum diamond meter stick right here*!" screamed Joey. He was pulling down his pants.

Junko backed away from him—laughing and not particularly shocked.

Gaven was murmuring into his gold wristphone. "Code red, Artie. Calm Joey."

Artie was smooth as silk. He loped down from the driveway and sprayed a nod pod into Joey's contorted face. Joey took a halting step, then collapsed to the ground, his body limp, his pants around his knees. Loulou said something sharp to Artie, pointing her finger. The guard shrugged, then fastened up the inert Joey's trousers. Loulou looked deeply unhappy, indeed she stuck out a finger and mimed shooting herself in the head.

"Time for grub," said Gaven. "I think we're all a little on edge. You can go back up to the driveway, Artie."

"Is Joey going to be all right?" I asked.

"Artie only gave him a light dose," said Junko, rejoining us.

"He'll bounce back in fifteen minutes or half an hour. We've had to do this before. Sadly. Joey's really such an interesting character. Did you know he's an artist? I don't know why he's stuck in such a recursive thought loop. Teeping himself teeping himself. He makes qwet look bad. Do you know Joey very well, Zad?"

"A little," I said. "He's younger than me. Sharp, off-kilter. Maybe he could be a hit. For sure Joey's colorful, especially with his psychiatric issues. The public likes an eccentric artist. But he hasn't learned to crank a steady flow of product."

"So, okay, you should know I'm pushing qwet treatments for everyone," said Junko. "A ninety percent adoption rate, right, Gaven? It's disruptive tech. Like the PC or the smartphone or the nurb."

"And the worry is that lots of people end up like Joey?" I asked.

"Just forget about him," said Junko, her voice rising. "We've tested other people. Joey is an anomaly. An exception. He's only caught in a loop in his head because that happens to be the type of thing he's obsessed with. Basically he's doing it to himself."

"What you're telling Zad is supposed to be a secret," Gaven warned Junko. "You signed a non-disclosure agreement, you know."

"Disclose *what*?" said Junko tartly. "I invented the qwet process on my own, and I chose to make it open source. It's a matter of public record. Not that anyone else knows how to use it yet."

"Open source?" I said. "That means free?"

"Slygro will be marketing installation and maintenance," said Gaven. "At least that's been our plan. But, as I said before, the plot is thickening. A rather different business model that may come into play."

"Whatever that means," I said. "I'm not good at decrypting your sly, meaningful biz hints. I'm an artist."

"I think Gaven and Slygro are moving too slow," said Junko. "And United Mutations is going to eat our lunch. My big-deal founder's stock won't be worth crap." Junko stared at me, and I seemed to feel a tingle from the touch of her alert eyes. "I'm qwet already," she said, nodding her head. "And so is Gaven. We made the change a week ago. It feels good. It's fine for everyone in the world except crazy Joey Moon."

"I think I'm turning qwet too," interrupted Carlo, deep into his own head. "Thanks to that filthy rat biting me. I have this, like, creepy free-floating feeling of empathy? Like I'm a social worker? I hate empathy."

"Not to harp, but am I the only one who's at all hungry?" said Gaven, sounding testy. Whatever biotweak he'd done on his metabolism, he still had the same big appetite. "Why won't you people look at my wonderful food! Open up some of the German white wine, would you, Loulou?"

Loulou took a deep breath and nodded—even though her husband Joey lay unconscious on the ground. My heart went out to her. She was so incredibly lovely.

"I remember my family coming to a cook-out exactly here," I told Loulou, wanting to lighten her mood. "Twenty-five years ago. One of my first memories. I really appreciate your helping out today."

Loulou mimed an expression of extravagant gratitude and interest. Probably sarcastic. She hadn't always been a maid. I wasn't getting over to her at all.

I skewered a hot dog with one of the supple green branches that Loulou had prepared. I held the thing over the fire, enjoying the gentle bobbing of the weighted branch. The big air-cooling frogs made the heat of the flames bearable.

"I see this man knows the drill," said Gaven.

"Be a dear, Zad, and roast some of those divine little sausages for Jane and I." This from Reba, in a *faux* high-society voice. She and Jane burst into laughter.

"And I'll sizzle up a couple for Junko and me," said Carlo, pulling himself together. "Gaven here can handle his own weenie. As per usual." The drinks were making us silly.

The horizon was a dappled sundown maze of gray and gold. Reba's flydino and my slugfoot were peaceful in the pond.

Joey was flat on his back.

"Something I just remembered," I said. "Those cattails—they look like hot dogs on sticks, right? And when we came here when I was five, I was sure that if I could manage to yank a cattail out of the pond, it would roast up just as good."

"I wonder if I can make that happen for you," said Gaven, feeling at the gizmo he wore dangling from his belt. "With my qwetter and a little teep. Junko and I designed the qwetter last month."

"Gaven shouldn't have worked on our design project at all," said Junko. "All of his ideas were wrong. Like he rushed me so much that we used all this kludgy, ridiculous old-time tech. Like you'd see in a United Mutations genemodder wand."

"He's saying he can use the qwetter to turn a cattail into a hot dog?" I asked.

"I don't see why not," said Gaven in a stiff tone. He was stung by Junko's criticism. "After I make the cattails qwet, I'll do telepathy with them. And then I'll ask them to taste like meat. Like tweaking a nurb with a genemodder wand. Seems easy enough."

Junko rolled her eyes, but refrained from saying anything.

The qwetter device had the rough outline of a pistol—a pistol that was cobbled together from a hundred little parts. Fins, tubes, chips, condensers, magnets, mirrors, a superheterodyne unit, and a tiny helium tank—stuff like that. Kind of weird.

Gaven tinkered with the components for a minute, then aimed the pistol at the pond. Unnerved, the flydino and my giant slug splashed to the pond's far end.

The qwetter hummed with no obvious effects. Gaven stared at the cattails for a very long time. His lips were moving. He made mystic passes with his hands. It was like he imagined himself to be hypnotizing the cattails, asking them to turn into meat.

"Mind over matter!" he crowed. "Harvest time, Zad."

"Here, Reba," I said. "Hold my hot dog sticks for a sec."

"I think not. Let Loulou do it. Could you, dear?"

Pouting and wordless, Loulou took over my sticks. Her

hand brushed against mine, and I felt a sexual thrill—followed by guilt at thinking about her that way, with her poor husband all screwed up and lying on the ground conked out by the bodyguard's nod mist. And meanwhile I had the creepy feeling that Loulou knew everything I was thinking.

Oh well. By now I was drunk enough to wade into the pond with my shoes on, and to yank up three of the cattails by their roots. But despite all of Gaven's build-up, the cattail bulges weren't even close to being meat.

"Fluff," I announced, scratching at one of the cattails with my fingernail. "Same as before."

"So okay, maybe the cattails are qwet by now," Junko told Gaven in a flat tone. "And maybe you can do telepathy with them. But, Gaven, the only things we can *genemod* are programmable nurbs. Nurbs that have little antennae on their DNA strands. Not the locked commercial nurbs. Not people. Not animals. And *not wild plants*. You're like a clanking robot trying to hump a junked car. Stick to money. Stocks, deals, licenses, non-disclosure agreements, like that."

"Won't any of you know-it-alls at least *taste* one of my cattails?" said Gaven. Peevishly he tossed the qwetter back to Reba. "Maybe the cattails are meat, but in a downy form? Take a bite, Carlo."

"No way," said Carlo. "Bad enough that my finger's infected."

"Feed Joey Moon a cattail!" whooped Reba. She'd always had a bit of a mean streak.

As if roused by the sound of his name, Joey jumped to his feet and, moving unbelievably fast, pinwheeled over and snatched the qwetter from Junko's hand.

"No!" roared Gaven. "Don't start with that! Guard! Artie! Stop him!"

"Who wants to be first?" cried Joey. "Zad? Jane? Reba?" He was making really horrible faces while he danced around. His mouth was a crooked slash, and his freaked-out eyes were like wobbly, scribbled dots. He waved his arms frenetically, holding them at unlikely angles. One of his legs went back and back in an extreme yoga move until it touched his shoulder from behind, leaving him balanced on the remaining leg like a flamingo.

Artie the guard was almost upon Joey again.

"*Wheenk*," whooped Joey, hopping into the air and whirling around. He sprayed the qwetter at the hapless guard, then focused the full force of his will upon him.

As if hypnotized, Artie dropped to all fours—and began imitating a pig. Joey was teeping into Artie's mind, overwhelming him with bad vibes. The long-bodied Artie rubbed his nose and chin across the ground, as if sniffing for acorns.

Back on two feet, moving slowly and regally as if fascinated by his own weirdness, Joey grabbed a handful of food from the horn-of-plenty nurb and stuffed it into his mouth. Cheeks full, hair spiky, scowling, he leveled the qwetter at us, preparing to—

Cuing on some unseen signal of Gaven's, one of the big cooling frogs flipped out a thirty-foot tongue and glommed the qwetter tool from Joey Moon's hand. Rushing forward, Gaven fixed his eyes on Joey and on the rooting Artie, *thinking* at them, teeping his notion of normality into their heads. And this time Gaven's efforts seemed to be having an effect.

"Undo, undo, undo," cried Gaven, his voice shrill with the joy of winning. I remembered that tone of his from our schooldays—when he'd gloat about his perfect grades.

Moments later, Artie was back on his feet, acting like his old self, more or less—and Joey had collapsed once more to the ground. His limp limbs slid back into their normal alignment. Despair radiated from him like a physical force.

"Put Joey under physical restraints," Gaven instructed Artie. "And call in that psych clinic we've been talking about. Have them send an ambulance. Why do you look so scared, Artie? Don't worry. It's just that you're qwet. It's good. You'll learn to like it."

Artie ran a trembling, big-knuckled hand across his features, checking that everything was in place. He had mud on his nose, and a bit of acorn in the corner of his mouth. "I—I can feel

Joey's mind. And yours, Gaven, and Junko's and—"

But now Artie was interrupted by Carlo screaming bloody murder. Right in my ear.

"What is your *problem*?" I snapped.

"My finger! It's *splitting open*. Oh my god, a tiny rat is crawling out. Shit, shit, shit!" The newborn rat dropped wriggling to the ground.

Skungy snickered. He was perched on my shoulder again. "Carlo said I couldn't make babies. He was wrong. That's my daughter. Call her Sissa. I grew her from a clone cell I put inside Carlo. And now I'm sending my personality into her. I'm making her just like me."

"It keeps getting worse," moaned Carlo, holding his head, with blood dribbling from his split finger. "The sky is singing. And Joey and Gaven and Junko and Loulou—they're like cyclones of colored fog. I'm screwed, I'm qwet. I was hoping I could—oh, shit. Help me, Junko."

Junko wrapped a healer leech around Carlo's finger while he goggled at her, increasingly disturbed by his teep impressions of her mind.

"You're not attracted to me at all?" he asked.

"Just as a friend. *Duh*? Can't you see I'm gay? Am I in Kentucky yet?"

Carlo cursed and stumped across the grass to get himself another a glass of bourbon.

"Carlo has a marginal personality," said Junko. "And so does Joey Moon. At least Joey's artistic. Loulou says he's made some amazing pieces over the years. The art grenades? The painter slugs? And his new mirror paintings are incredible. Loulou herself is very creative, too, in case you didn't know. She used to be a champion at Levolver. That game about making battle nurbs?"

"Impressive," I said. "Carlo mentioned something like that. And he said Loulou worked for United Mutations, too. But now she's here on Gaven's farm being—what? A maid?"

"To tell the truth, she's been consulting with me quite a bit," said Junko. "But I'll end up with most of the credit. Stanford grad that I am."

"Thank god this is a private party," interrupted Jane, wandering over. "I've never seen such a fiasco."

"You like the excitement I'm bringing to town," said Gaven. "Right?"

Jane studied the twitchy, unprepossessing little man. I was picking up her on emotions—not via qwet teep, but via married-couple vibe-resonance. With regard to Gaven, Jane was midway between pity and repulsion. In any case, she meant to play him and get what she could. A strategic plan. It made me jealous, but for now I had to let it go.

Down at my feet, the new little rat Sissa was shaking her body—letting the Skunginess stink in. And now the wised-up baby rat made as if to climb my leg like her father had done. Skungy scampered down my leg and bared his teeth at her.

"Zad's mine," squealed the older rat. "You be *Loulou's* helper. That woman right here."

Loulou was at my side, as if magnetically drawn by my longing for her. "Get me out of here," she said in a low, vibrant tone, twiddling her fingers in a gesture of legs running away. "It's too crazy."

All right, then. I led the mysterious woman to my car, followed by our two qwet rats. The Lincoln's slugfoot was already back in place beneath the chassis.

"We're outta here!" I whooped, an unsteady mania in my voice. "Screw you all!"

And now I was speeding away from the Trask farm with a woman again—just like with Jane, ten years ago. Ah, Jane. The voices behind us rose in remonstrance and complaint. And then Loulou and I were out the driveway and heading for River Road.

We rode in silence for ten minutes, letting the night air beat against our faces, each of us gathering our thoughts. It was a September evening with a low chunk of moon—the air hot, moist, and luscious, boding a night of mystery and promise. I was picking up a musky scent from Loulou, and with it came little pings from her personality. I had the feeling Loulou was qwet like Carlo had said.

"Pull into the next road on the left," she said in her husky voice. "That clearing behind the old Ballard school? Nobody will bother us." She nodded, emphasizing her plan.

Synch beyond synch. The Ballard bower was exactly where I'd gone with Jane on that night I'd just been thinking about. The first place where Jane and I'd had sex.

As soon as we stopped, Loulou started kissing and rubbing on me. Five minutes later we were naked and making love in the back seat of my car. Romantic to be doing it outdoors, behind the Ballard school, a return to the glories of youth.

On the hood of my car our two qwet rat helpers danced in celebratory glee, savoring our rich sensations.

After sex, Loulou and I lay on the smooth old leather of my car seat, looking up at the sky, with Loulou nestled nude on my chest. I felt very close to her, and to the world around us. Close like never before.

It was more than Loulou pinging me now—I was blending with her thoughts, right inside her skin. I was feeling the minds of our qwet rats, and, in some indefinable way, I was feeling the shapes of the gently swaying trees and the scuttling of the insects in the rotting leaves on the ground. Everything loose and impressionistic. Like the hues in nurb-paint before you tightened them up. All the walls were down.

"I see the I's—" I stammered, having trouble with my words. "I see you."

"Please don't freak," whispered Loulou, her lips against my cheek. "Please get used to it."

"You're teeping too? You've been that way all along, right?"

"I caught it from Joey. They switched Joey over to quantum wetware last week, remember? So that he could merge his mind with your rat's."

"And you made me qwet just now? By having sex?"

"It's contagious if you're intimate. You might say that—qwet teep is a sexually transmitted disease?" Loulou let out a warm, two-note giggle, higher on the second note. "Teep is good, Zad. We'll use teep to merge our minds into one."

"A beautiful dream. Are you sorry for Joey?"

"Sure I am. But Joey's stopped making sense. Also he hasn't washed for a week. You're my knight for now. Maybe we'll be right together. Relax into it, baby. Qwet is like a magic power."

Easy to relax, but a little scary. I didn't want to drown, didn't want to be a piece of dust in the cyclone of the minds. I was merged with Loulou, and with our two qwet rats, and now, as if sensing lights in the distance, I was feeling the minds of Carlo, Joey, Junko, Gaven and Artie the guard as well.

Gaven was drooling over Jane. Carlo was putting the moves on Reba Ranchtree, and Joey—he was in a straitjacket inside the shell of a road-turtle about to take him to a clinic downtown. Junko Shimano was studying the circuitry of her and Gaven's clunky prototype qwetter device, mentally paring it down, looking for ways to replace it with a biomodded nurb. Artie was staring up at the sky, wanting to be in bed with his wife. All their little voices were in my head, blurred and unclear. Kind of cozy.

Loulou was right. I didn't have to fall apart. I could still be me. I was reaching into the other mind flows, tasting them, not remembering any real facts, but somehow changing my vibe.

I fell back on the image of cruising the web. As if the other minds were websites I was browsing on multiple screens. The screens were in the flickering zone of my peripheral vision.

Maybe I hadn't been wasting time cruising the web in my dreamchair for the past few months. I'd been getting ready. Ready for qwet.

4: Oblivious Teep

I brought Loulou to the room behind my store and she spent the whole night with me. It was epic. I was with her in my dreams. Like sleeping through a transreal biopic movie.

Let me pause here and say more about how quantum wetware leads to teep. It has to do with what you might call quantum psychology.

If you ever take a serious look inside your own head, you'll notice that you have two styles of thought. We called them the "*robotic*" and "*cosmic*." Robotic thought is all about reasoning and analysis. Cosmic thoughts are wordless. It's easy to be dominated by your endlessly-narrating inner robotic voice. Step past the voice and you can see the cosmic mode. Analog consciousness, like waves on a pond. Merged with the world. Without opinions.

Ordinarily your mind oscillates between the cosmic and the robotic at a rate of maybe twenty cycles per second. You need both modes. The cosmic state is a merge into your surroundings, and the robotic state is when you draw back and say, "Okay, it's me against the world. I'll plan what to do next to stay alive."

Junko's technical discovery was that we have a specific physical brain site that *controls* when our state of consciousness flips between the cosmic and the robotic. And, like Carlo had told me, Gaven liked to call the site the gee-haw-whimmy-diddle.

So, okay, your gee-haw-whimmy-diddle controls when your consciousness flips between the cosmic and the robotic. And Junko's quantum wetware allowed us to lean on our gee-haw-whimmy-diddles and keep our minds in the merged cosmic state for a longish period of time. A loofy thing to do. You *could* stay fully robotic for hours at a time instead—but I personally wouldn't see much point in that.

Now for the pay-off. It's the cosmic mode that leads to

teep. How? Well—from a physicist's point of view, your mind isn't your physical brain. Your mind is a Hilbert space wave function that happens to look like a brain. Matter and wave, one and the same. If you and someone near you are both in the cosmic state, then your quantum wave functions can merge into a single combined wave system that gets gnarlier and more interesting the longer you can maintain the merge. Your brain waves overlay each other like two sets of ripples. And that's teep.

Serious dark beauty, qrude.

I know I'm droning on for too long—like an old-school professor tap-tap-tapping his chalk on a freaky, dusty blackboard.

But I have one more tidbit to tell. According to quantum mechanics, whenever you make a mental note about what you're experiencing, you automatically bust your mind state down into the robotic mode. And your teep connections break. To remain in the teep state, you need to stay cosmic, and you can't be laying down any organized memories.

Putting it another way, qwet teep is *oblivious*. As in *unseeing, unaware, ignorant, forgetful*. This means that when you teep with someone, your memories of the trip will be as vague and flaky as last night's dreams.

"Zad!" It was mid morning, nearly ten. I didn't usually sleep this late. Loulou was up on one elbow, dark and beautiful, twirling a lock of my hair. She waved hello.

It took me a minute to get my robotic mode going. "An intense night," I grated. "I know everything about you."

"That's what you think."

By now my randy cosmic wave function had retreated into the shell of my skull, and everything about our big night was unclear.

"I—I forgot to remember," I said.

"Don't worry. You've integrated it all into your psyche. Stuff's gonna drift up. Flotsam from the crystal ship. Jetsam on the shore. Postcards from the Nth dimension." Loulou pursed her lips and studied me. "Don't look so worried. You've got a new mind! Feel around!"

"You grew up in a horse-drawn trailer in Mexico?" I asked, grabbing onto something that resembled a memory.

"A scavenged split-level in the suburbs of Washington, D.C. But, yes, my mother is Mexican. And my father's a Hungarian mathematician. He's a math professor at Georgetown University, specializing in quantum computation. He did some consulting on the prediction software for the United Mutations biomodder wands. As for the horse, yeah I had a little nurb model of a horse." With one hand, Loulou mimed a toy horse prancing across the sheet.

"Okay." Another recovered memory emerged. "You were raped by a cuttlefish from a UFO?"

Loulou guffawed. "Actually that was a heavy date with the boss when I worked for a nurb modding company called Itchy. I got the job because I won some tournaments in that biomodding game Levolver? I'd be working with a biomodder wand, and I'd keep adjusting the mods on a nurb I'd be building. I'd force a full-body refresh after each new mod, to see where I was at. You know how it works. The competitive aspect of the Levolver game is that there's three or four of you making nurbs at the same time. Battle-nurbs."

"Yeah," I said. "And for the final act, the nurbs fight. Those Levolver battle-nurbs can be very loofy."

"All along while I'd be modding a design, I'd keep an eye on what other contestants were doing," said Loulou. "We'd push each other to new extremes."

I dug into my mind, combing the web. "There you are! *Loulou Sass*! You really *were* the champ."

"Yeah. Papa wanted me to go to college, but I couldn't be bothered, and then I got this hot biomodding job at Itchy. It was great. But then the sleazebag boss had his way with me. Jerk. It could have been okay, but he posted a video of us, and it gave me a bad name. Especially with Mama." Loulou put both hands to her throat, as if choking herself.

My fanciful half-memories of Loulou's life story kept rearranging themselves. "So then you stole a UFO?"

"That would be the Itchy boss's luxor nurb scorpion vehicle.

I muted its tracking unit and I hit the road. I didn't want to live at home anymore—Mom thought I was a slut, and Dad was looking down at me for not being an academic scientist like him. Even though my salary at Itchy was higher than his at Georgetown."

"More to you than meets the eye," I said, admiring Loulou.

"Always has been. I rode the scorpion to Louisville. I wanted to see some thoroughbred horses. The trip took awhile. Since I was on the lam, I couldn't use credit and I'd left too fast to bring enough cash. I got very fond of that scorpion. I kept having to stop and scam more nurb chow for him. Shoplifting, chores, sob stories, and once I even entered a local Levolver tournament. Wiped out my competition with a thing I called the Brr Bird."

"And then in Louisville you worked as a stripper in a funeral home?"

"I was a designer at the Louisville United Mutations campus, out near the airport." She put on a wide-eyed, good-girl face—miming her job-applicant persona. "Once I told them who I was, they wanted me. And they cleared my problems with the boss at Itchy. Made all the charges go away. And then—*eek*—I switched to helping on Gaven's farm. Maybe that's the funeral home part."

"You switched from being a biomod designer to being a maid?"

"Well, I am in fact helping Junko with the qwet stuff quite a bit. We're going to have this new way of modding nurbs, see, and we'll be solving the DNA retrofit problem with this instant-enlightenment qwet mode that I'm calling cosmic logic."

"Whatever that means," I said. "Let me finish with my memories. I see an image of a snarling dog?"

"Joey Moon," said Loulou, smiling. "I met him in a bar on Bardstown Road. He does have a sweet side. He makes me laugh. He was wild about my scorpion. He was making these loofy exploding balls of nurb-paint. Art grenades. We started living together. I got tired of going to United Mutations all the time. I didn't like my boss there either. A guy called Whit."

"Whit Heyburn?" I exclaimed. "I hate that guy. And he's everywhere. Please tell me you didn't fuck him."

"No reason to," said Loulou, studying me, enjoying my reaction. "Not yet."

"Let's get back to you and Joey."

"I was using my Levolver tricks to help Joey with his art. I never had much interest in making it as an artist myself. I'm, like, where's the money? Long story short, Joey got us in with Gaven. But that's enough with the total recall, Zad. I think you have food?"

"Chow for us too!" squeaked our qwet rats, perched on the foot of my bed. Skungy and Sissa. I remembered having fed Sissa a lot last night. The two rats were the same size now. Perhaps they'd been in on the night-long mind-merge? I had a feeling there'd been scuttlers and crawlers within our vision-thickets. Hopefully just the rats.

I got to my feet and opened the locked cabinet where I'd parked the nurb chow.

"Rich toasty goodness!" I said, feeding a couple of the tobacco-smelling cubes to the eager rats.

"It's funny," said Loulou, studying my naked body. "When I see you in teep, you're fat. But you're not. Just a soft belly."

"I have a poor self-image," I said, glancing down at myself.

"Better than Joey's!" said Loulou, making a gesture of slitting her throat. "Could you believe how gnarly he acted at Gaven's farm? It was sick how he bent back his leg."

"Like a contortionist."

"Yeah. He has a high threshold of pain. It bothers me. Don't you be that way, Zad. Respect yourself, even if you're not making it as an artist these days. You're cozy. I could live with you, if you like."

"Uh—*wow*," I said, not wanting to commit. "I'm kind of boggled right now. Coming to terms with qwet teep. Hard to see where everything's headed."

"I see your food nurbs right over there," said Loulou pointing to a little table in the corner of my bedroom. "It's time."

"Right. My endless sausage, my eternal loaf, my coffee

plant, and my rubber chicken."

The rubber chicken wasn't really rubber, we just called them that. She was a hen with no feet, and she had a butt-tube that pooted out whatever type of egg dish you wanted. She required more chow than the other nurbs. The sausage and the loaf were like snakes. You fed chow to their mouths, and you lopped off as much of their tails as you felt like eating. They tasted like salami and like a crisp French baguette, respectively. The coffee plant had green leaves on it, and its stalks were shiny, metallic tubes. Like a tiny refinery. It whistled while it worked. A cheerful tune.

I bustled around, assembling us two breakfasts, and then I sat on the bed with Loulou to eat, happy in the cosmic mode. Sweet morning sun was slanting in through a skylight. Loulou was naked like me. She smelled good. We did some teep, sharing the moment.

But as soon as I tried to analyze our situation, I was robotic again.

"What comes next," I said. "Do I really start trying to sell qwet rats? What if they keep biting people and giving them qwet teep?"

"Qwet will spread no matter what," said Loulou. "Teep's good. And I love the cosmic mode. It's an inner high."

"I can imagine the DoG banning quantum wetware," I said. "The Department of Genomics. I mean—if it's easy to space into cosmic mode, will people still go to work?"

"Work sucks," said Loulou. "My carefully researched conclusion. We're filling the world with miraculous nurbs. Like genies, almost. No need to labor like anxious peasants." She threw her hands out in a lo-and-behold gesture. "The rapture of Saint Loulou. I open my heart to the nurbs. And to teep, to horses, and to sex. My latest dream is that I get a serious wad of money together and own a horse farm like Gaven's."

"You could seduce the man himself."

"Too steep. I'll leave that to—*Jane*." Loulou did a quick teep merge on me, relishing my reaction.

Which was? The same disgust and jealousy as last night.

"Let's talk about us instead," I suggested.

"Talk about Jane," pressed Loulou. "Can you take me to look at her apartment? The place you two used to share? I love seeing fancy homes."

"She, uh, she might be there," I objected, starting to wonder what Loulou was after.

"Call her and find out." She laid on her most alluring smile—and literally batted her eyes.

"Well, all right." I was in fact curious about Jane's whereabouts myself. As I mobilized my wristphone, I worked out a pretend reason for the call.

"Hi, Zad," said Jane's voice. No visuals from her end, no map info. I had my visuals off too. No way did I want Jane to see Loulou in my back room. She'd go wild.

"Reba told me she saw you bringing that Loulou to your shop last night," said Jane, already in the know. "Reba was flying Carlo home to her housetree."

"Lots of excitement," I said as blandly as possible. "I, uh, I called to say I'm ready to pick up that vat you were talking about. I can do it right now."

"Well, fine," said Jane. "Only I'm not in my apartment. But I can tell my door to let you in."

"So you spent the night at Gaven's?"

"Nosy, aren't we? I'll be very glad if that vat's gone before I get home. Bye now."

"Bye." My wristphone went dark.

"Vat?" said Loulou, cocking her head.

"The stuff I use for my paintings," I said. "Nurb-paint."

"Tweaked nurb-gel," said Loulou. "Sure. Each of the modded slime mold cells has color organelles like the ones in squidskin. *Cold Days in Hell*. I know all this."

"I talk to my paint and I push it around," I said, wanting to talk about it. "Or I message it on the web. It can take on shapes as well as making colors. But I don't have to dig all the way down into biomodding. I can't believe Reba told Jane that I brought you home."

"Louisville's a small town, isn't it?" said Loulou. "Chatty,

chatty, chatty. Anyway, I'll be glad to see Jane's apartment. And to get your nurb-paint." She studied me. "You're a big artist with his own gallery. Gaven has one of your paintings. Joey kind of liked it. He said it was camp." She trailed off, not coming up with the full-on compliment I hoped for. I didn't dare teep into her head.

Instead I pointed towards one of the works I had in my room. "Wave on this one. *Cold Day in Hell: Hunter Thompson Versus Muhammad Ali*. Two famous Louisville figures from the twentieth century. The white guy with the swollen liver is a writer, the black guy is a boxer. And because I used the nurb-paint, they're animated a little bit."

"Bobbing and weaving," said Loulou in a flat tone. "Very cute. And the crowd is cheering. You don't think your work is a little—corny?" Strained, fixed smile, slightly pitying.

"I've sold a lot," I said, feeling hurt. "That's more than your Joey Moon can say. He got some buzz from his art grenades and his painter slugs, but hardly anyone ever actually paid him for—"

"Joey says you wouldn't help him get started. You wouldn't show his new paintings in your gallery. He was really upset about that."

"He never even let me *see* those pictures, Loulou. I had no way of knowing what he was talking about!"

"I've seen them," said Loulou softly. "Incredibly stark. But until he gets a show, they have to be secret."

"Oh, god. The mysterioso routine. Beloved by fake artists since the dawn of time." I pulled on my jeans and a red ultra-checked shirt. "Never mind. You want to help me move that vat, or not?"

"I'm guessing it's insanely heavy?"

"I'll rent a couple of mover nurbs from Gurky Movers down the street. Craig Gurky calls them his golems. We'll herd the golems and they'll do our bidding. Come along and you'll get your peek inside my old apartment."

"The lair of sweet Jane. My rival for the Prince's hand." She'd pulled on her striped tights from last night, and now she picked out a dark multi-polka-dot shirt from the nurb clothing I had on display. "I'm up for some looting, yeah."

I looked at Loulou, once again wondering about where her mood was at. "I woke up thinking I'd seen your soul. But now—"

"I'm elusive," said Loulou, wriggling one hand like a fish. "A sneak." And then she leaned forward and kissed me. We had another minute of teep. Glorious.

I could see the cosmic thought mode becoming addictive. It was like a pure and unforgettable first high that you might spend the rest of your life chasing. It was here for the taking now, anytime I liked, thanks to quantum wetware. And being cosmic made me feel smart.

"Keep an eye on the store," I told Skungy. "We might get some customers. Be polite. And use your squidskin link to call me if someone wants to buy something."

"I could just use teep," said Skungy, giving me a touch of his jagged little mind.

"If you teep me I won't know what you're talking about," I said. "You'll want to tell me, like, someone's buying a fancy nurb floor licker, and I'll hear you saying your daughter Sissa is having sex with a plague-infested fully organic river rat and you want me to watch."

"Don't go talking that way about Sissa or I'll rip your damn throat out," said Skungy, rising up to his full height of five inches and baring his yellow fangs.

"*Ooooh*," I said, mocking him. "The cuddly pet rattie-wat. He's a hard guy like Joey Moon. Like Joey Moon who's in a psych ward zonked on nod."

Despite all my teep pleasure, I was in an edgy mood. I guess I was jealous of Joey. And uptight about Gaven and Jane.

"Stop right there," said Loulou. "You don't have to mock Joey when he's down. And you don't have to pick on your qwet rat. You've won. You've got me." Loulou held up one arm and yanked the air, as if sounding a triumphant train-whistle.

"Uh—yeah!" I dug the way this woman moved.

We went outside. It was eleven o'clock of a Saturday

morning, a cider-crisp summer-fall day. Qrudes riding road-spiders and straight citizens piloting the pig-based nurb vans we called roadhogs. People strolling, shopping, socializing. Some of the women had nurb servants tailing them, shaped like pygmy lawn-jockeys—some white and some black—carrying stuff their owners had bought. One of the little nurbs had balanced a chair on his head. I thought of an ant bearing a dead beetle.

"Jane's apartment is over there, right?" said Loulou, pointing at one of the tall trees by the Ohio River. The housetree was like a giant stalk of bamboo, pale green and gracefully curved, with joints separating it into apartment floors. A pair of lifter tubes twined along one side.

"How do you know?" I asked, feeling a twinge of suspicion.

"Duh! From teeping with you all night long? A few actual facts do stick—if you learn how to mine them. It doesn't have to be all cuttlefish in UFOs."

"I've always had a thing for space aliens," I said as we crossed Main Street, sidestepping a roadhog van driven by a chauffeur perched on the pig's head. Instead of being set up for freight, the giant pig was a personal limo, with the window-membranes so dark you couldn't see inside.

Loulou was still thinking about my remark. "If there's aliens at all, the likeliest time to contact them would be when you're in cosmic mind mode," she said as we reached the sidewalk on the other side.

"How do you mean?"

"Sometimes I hear squeals when I'm teeping," said Loulou. "Like there's things outside our space. N-dimensional pigs, maybe."

"I'm still getting used to the idea that we're lovers," I said, not in a mood to get all abstract this early in the day.

"That's my boy," said Loulou, patting my head. "Oh, hi, Whit!"

And there he was, my old nemesis, wearing a white shirt and a herringbone nurb cloth suit. He'd risen in status at United Mutations. As Loulou had already alluded to, Whit was the business manager of UM's local research lab. Not that Whit knew jack-shit about science.

"Loulou!" exclaimed Whit. "It's slow at UM with you working off-site. I got your message about—what was it? Quantum telepathy?" He gave me a calculating nod. Even now, years later, he was still miffed about having lost Jane to me. Very rare for Whit to lose a girl. His usual pattern was to ensnare them, abuse them, and reject them himself. But wait—Loulou was still reporting to him?

"This is Zad Plant," said Loulou, pretending that she didn't know we two had a history. "The guy who runs the Live Art gallery down the street? He's the one selling the qwet rats for Slygro. And they're a test-bed for the quantum telepathy service, yeah."

"Zad," said Whit Heyburn, taking my hand and squeezing it much, much harder than necessary. He had the sleepy low-lidded eyes of a squidskin show idol—and a mouth as mirthless as a mailbox slot. "The former artist."

"Whit here is a screwball," I told Loulou, my words falling over each other. "When he was drunk in high school, he'd lie on the floor of his car and run the pedals with his feet. Carlo would do the steering from the back seat with his belt tied to the wheel."

"Why bring up a thing like that?" said Whit. "Nothing's happened to you since high school? I was sorry to hear about your breakup with Jane." He cocked his head, cruelly vigilant.

"It's true, Jane and I are temporarily on the outs. But—"

"But now you've got Loulou!" said Whit. "Art boys always score. Anyhow, the thing is, my United Mutations engineers are begging for a qwet rat. This qwet stuff will explode. First I thought it was just a new high and a means of telepathy, but now Loulou's talking about cosmic logic and a new biomod installation technique? Qwet will be huge. I was on my way to your store, matter of fact."

"Fine," I said in a noncommittal tone. "But I'm confused. Loulou told me she *used* to work for United Mutations. But you're making it sound like she's still on your payroll?"

"Not a weekly paycheck," said Loulou with a shrug. "It's more like a finder's fee. Whenever I give their research group some good information."

"You're an industrial spy? A mole in the Slygro lab?"

"Zaddy's heating up," said Whit. "Poor impulse control. I can come back later, if you lovebirds need to squawk and peck. But I've got spot cash for a qwet rat right now. My boys at UM want it bad."

"I, uh, don't actually have any of the qwet rats for sale yet," I said, calming myself with a touch of cosmic mode. "There's two beta-model qwet rats minding my store for me, but—"

"Oh, let him take Sissa," interrupted Loulou. "How much, Whit?"

"Pitch me a number, Zad." Whit opened his eyes a little further and gave me a level stare. "See if you can play big league ball." His eyes were blank and dark.

I tripled the highest figure I could think of—and Whit handed me the money right away. With a dismissive gesture, he tendered Loulou half the same amount. "Off the books," he said. "You're *my* people."

"Never," I said, feeling like I'd been had.

"I'll wait here while you boys finish the deal," said Loulou.

I led Whit back to my store and sprang the news on my qwet rats.

"Whit here is buying Sissa."

Skungy was immediately on the offense, shrilling defiant insults. But Sissa calmed him down.

"I'd *like* to get away from you," she told Skungy. "Get it? I want to see new things on my own. Gaven's gonna send Zad more qwet rats anyhow. So clamp your snout, Skungy."

"But you're my family," said Skungy, sounding plaintive. "On account of—"

"*I'm* your owner," I told Skungy, an edge in my voice. "So start being of some use to me."

"Big slob. Bully."

"Incredibly shoddy nurb design," said Whit, studying Skungy. "You have no control over that rat all. Vintage Gaven

Graber. He's been talking to me direct, you know."

News to me. And never mind Gaven's bombast about non-disclosure agreements. But I played it cool. "And you guys want to be marketing qwet yourselves, am I right?"

"Not sure *anyone* will be selling qwet," said Whit in a matter-of-fact tone. He seemed to know as much as me—or more. "Qwet for free is more likely. Good will gesture. Then Slygro and/or United Mutations cashes in with add-ons and product support. We might even buy Slygro out. If the numbers work. Wholly owned subsidiary."

"Fat cats," I said, reverting to childish insults. "Greedy pigs."

"UM would handle qwet better, Zad. Admit it. Gaven is a goob. Remember that fire-breathing dragon nurb he paid Craig Gurky to build in high school, and the fire department had to come? Kind of a shame to see you throwing in your lot with an idiot like that. If you're open to offers, Zad, maybe I could—"

"I have an errand I need to do," I told Whit, wanting to forestall one of his pseudofriendly control routines. "So—"

Whit shrugged, then laid his hand on the counter near Sissa, palm up. "Just look at her," he crooned to the rat. "Little Sissa with her pretty fur. I'll take good care of you. Hop aboard, and I'll set you in my coat pocket. You can peek out from there. We'll take a ride, and I'll find you a nook in our lab. Check back with you on Monday, Zad?"

"You're not gonna dissect Sissa, are you?" piped Skungy. I could feel Skungy's anxiety as clearly as if were my own. Knowing Whit, Skungy's worry was fully justified. But Sissa was simply annoyed by Skungy's concern.

"Chill!" she sharply chirped. She was already ensconced in Whit's coat pocket. Her little pink paws held the edge, with her bead-bright eyes and whiskered snout peering over. Cute as a button. "I can take care of myself," she told Skungy. "This is my big opportunity...*asshole*." A qwet rat's idea of a fond farewell.

"Seems like we're done for now," said Whit. "Fire off a signal rocket when you're ready for help, Zad. And say hi to sweet Jane." He paused and gave me a hard look, continually toying with me. "Or, what the hey, I'll call her myself. I expect she's still a decent lay. Maybe a bit overeager. Living alone and all."

Before I could properly react, a feather-light stingray nurb had wriggled out from beneath the collar of Whit's coat. It rippled in the air like a leaf, flexing its long thorn of a tail, hovering between Whit and me.

"Loser," said Whit, enjoying himself.

And then he was out in the street hopping into the comfortable chauffeur-driven roadhog I'd noticed before. Whit's private vehicle, with a fully enclosed passenger compartment. Strictly speaking, Whit didn't even need to work. His job was like a hobby for him. An opportunity to power-trip people's minds.

So there I was, choking on revenge fantasies. I could have used my genemodder wand on Whit's stingray, but no no, surely that thing had its genes locked. I could have gotten my firepig sausage and flamed the stingray, and then have strangled Whit, or punched him in the face.

Or maybe I could burst into tears. Or I go inside my shop and hang myself. Instead I stared off into the sky and dialed up my cosmic mode. All is one. I was a soliton in Hilbert space, a flick of paint on the canvas, a turd on a limb. In cosmic mode, things were in equal measure comic and pathetic. My life. The greatest spectacle I'd ever see.

After a few minutes, my heart rate had damped back down. And now I thought to hunt down Loulou. My teep connection made it easy to sniff her out. Leaving the disgruntled Skungy in charge of my shop again, I found Loulou in a jewelry shop two blocks down Main Street, spending some of the money she'd gotten from Whit.

"What do you think?" she asked me, palming back her hair to display a pair of shiny nurb earrings. "I'm wearing these for you." Little bunches of golden tentacles waved from cute silvery disks with domes on the top. Toy cuttlefish in tiny UFOs, one in each ear. The two cuttles had watchful, tawny eyes.

"Now that I'm qwet, I can genemod a programmable nurb just by looking at it," bragged Loulou. "Most pieces of jewelry are programmable, and it's actually pretty easy to make them qwet. I used spit. And then I fondled the earrings with the fingers of my mind." Playfully she ran her hand across my crotch.

"I'm feelin' this," said the jeweler behind the counter. Ned White. We knew each other well. He was a smooth-skinned man with a handsome face. "Loulou here is a nurb modder supreme. She buys these earrings, stares at them, and—*whomp*—they ripple and they change shape. Help me out, Zad. Clue me on the qwet scene. You're running with Gaven Graber, right?"

"In a way. I'm distributing qwet rats for his company. Slygro. I'll have some rats in stock in a few days; stop by and buy one. Wholesale rate for you. Get in ahead of the herd."

"Never mind the rats," said Loulou. "Junko Shimano is going to be distributing qwet for people really soon. A freelance giveaway." She studied Ned White thoughtfully. "Qwet means quantum wetware, you wave? It makes you high, it gives you telepathy, it helps you use cosmic logic to find biomod designs without a computer, and it lets you install your mods onto programmable nurbs just by thinking at them. Those last two bits are thanks to me. Advanced qwetology."

"I want qwet," said Ned.

"Try calling Slygro on your wristphone right after we leave," said Loulou in a confidential tone. "Ask for Reba. She can put you on a list. Or make a house call." Loulou flashed her smile. "If that doesn't work for you, I might could turn you on myself. I did Zad last night."

"I can hire you?" said Ned, lowering his voice. "Seriously?" He gestured along his counter of nurb jewelry. "Bring me online and we'll make *all* of this stuff qwet and mod it like a mofo. You can make up the new designs. I'll give you a consult fee, Loulou, or a salary, or commissions—whatever you want." Ned seized her hands like a passionate suitor. "It'd be a *delight* to have you in my shop."

I interrupted. "Don't you think you're getting ahead of yourself, Loulou? We'll catch up with you later, Ned. We've gotta run."

"This man is strait-laced," said Ned, pointing at me.

"Stop stirring up trouble," I hissed to Loulou outside. "You seduce me in front of my wife, you infect me with qwet, you spy on us for United Mutations, you spill the Slygro trade secrets, and you want to give away qwet before Gaven's ready. And why'd you tell Ned to ask for *Reba*? You're driving me crazy."

"I'm chaos," said Loulou cheerfully. "You're riding a whirlwind." She bobbled her head, flashing the qwet earrings. The cuttles waved hello with their tiny tentacles, right in synch with Loulou's mood.

"Let's go get my damned vat," I snapped, fully as fuddydud as my dad. "Gurky Movers is across the street."

Craig Gurky was another boyhood friend of mine, although we'd gone to different high schools—me private and him public. Craig's father had run a gas station and motor repair place down on River Road, living with his family in a riverside cottage on piers. Mr. Gurky was an adaptable man, and when the nurb craze hit, he sold off his River Road properties, bought a warehouse downtown, and got hold of some sturdy nurbs that served as the work force of Gurky Movers. Craig's so-called golems.

Craig had the flaky, unworldly attitude of an artist. As boys, Craig and I had enjoyed making prank assemblages together—I remember a set-up that ignited a tethered balloon of questionable gas when Craig's father opened his bedroom door. A ball of flame, a crispy fart-stench, and Craig's choking hiccups of joy.

Now Mr. Gurky was dead and Craig, anything but a go-getter, was running the family business. Craig had always professed to have a slavering interest in women, but his fantasies were baroque and theoretical, as if he were thinking about imaginary science-fictional beings. He was single, and he shared the family apartment over the warehouse with his Mom, a kindly moon-faced woman with a wart.

"Zad," said Craig, greeting us as we entered his cavernous shop. Nobody was in here but Craig and his idle, heavy-set nurb golems. Craig's plain face always seemed wider than it was high, especially when he smiled. "With a lady friend! Introduce us, dolt. I crave social intimacy."

"This is Craig Gurky," I told Loulou. "He's good guy. Craig, this is Loulou Sass. She's been living on Gaven Graber's farm with her husband."

"That rotten Graber," said Craig, his face darkening. "Like he's going to be the one to smarten up our nurbs? My nurbs are plenty smart already. I mod them right. Did I tell you I taught my golem Gustav to bounce down Third Street like a rubber ball? I adjusted his muscles so they don't bruise. Hundred-foot hops. And for the finale, he flies up past the housetrees, bounces off a girder on the old Clark bridge, bonks into that big black sphere on top of the bridge tower—the place with that sex club called Kegel Kugel? Plenty of she-males there. Anyway, my nurb bounces of the Kegel Kugel and—*sploosh*! Gustav lands in the drink!"

"And then what?" asked Loulou, puzzled by the pointlessness of the feat.

Craig glanced around his space, feigning slyness. "And then? We do it again. I've been running my tests at night. But tell me this. Have you two had sex yet? Do you need to borrow some chains?"

As I said, Craig's notions about women were very cartoony. Indeed, my sense was that, given his druthers, he'd prefer to be gay. But he seemed to have no hands-on experience in that area either. Apparently he labored under some unrealistic hangup about shocking his mother—who surely wouldn't have cared.

"Craig's always been special," I told Loulou. "A genius who acts like he's from Mars."

"Faint praise," said Craig. "Are you here for business?"

"Two of your mover golems," I said. "We'll need them for a little over an hour."

Craig drew a folded, dirty piece of paper from his gray pants and mimed a lengthy written calculation with a pencil, muttering while he worked. "*Base rate, temporal overage, cartage surcharge, cleaning costs, negative discount, rudeness multiplier, fat tax, chintz lien…*"

But this was one of his routines. The rental amount was in fact very reasonable. I paid Craig and he called over two of his golems—stocky, gray-skinned figures like clay men. They were four feet tall, with three-fingered hands, and with stubby tails on their rears. Instead of having skeletons, they were all muscle, and they had an ability to adjust their shapes by flexing themselves in various ways.

"I'm Gustav," rasped the first one, staring at us with flat black eyes. "I da one who bounce like a ball."

"I'm Bonk," said the other, his voice an octave deeper. "I'm strong."

Loulou and I set off towards Jane's housetree with the golems.

"You want me carry you?" offered Gustav.

"No thanks," said Loulou. "You might crush me."

"We got delicate touch," said Bonk.

"Just follow us," I said.

The housetrees were imposing things—verdant, smooth, stretching up towards the heavens, gently curved. Recognizing me, Jane's lifter tube opened for us, and the fine hairs on the tube's inner walls swept us to the eighteenth floor. The apartment door opened and there we were. My former home. A big round room, with a segment divided off for the bedroom. The living green walls were slightly translucent, with transparent spots. The city, the bridge, the river—all at our feet.

"Nice," said Loulou, twirling. "How long ago did you move out?"

"Move everything now?" interrupted Bonk, misunderstanding her.

"You two stand still," I told the golems, and turned to Loulou. "It's been six months."

"I like the shiny old wood furniture," said Loulou, drifting around, touching things. "The fancy vases and the oriental rugs. Silk cushions. In my house we had cheap junk, and then we got cheap nurbs. How was it in the house where *you* grew up?"

"Country casual. Kind of a farm. My mother's a caterer and

my father's an old-school painter. Lennox and Sally Plant."

"I sort of remember that from our dreams. With the memories all warped and inside out. Your mother killing pigs and your father rolling in the blood."

"But exactly!" I said with a laugh. "Maybe I'll take you to meet Mom and Dad sometime."

"You're laying it on thick, Zad." She kissed me. "Should we make love in Jane's bed? Taint her sheets with my scent?" Loulou flashed me a hot rush of teep.

I was tempted, but fuddydud common sense prevailed. "Everything in here is watching us," I reminded Loulou. "You know how nurbs are. They tell their owners whatever they see."

"Fine with me!" said Loulou. "I don't like Jane. Anyway—" and now her eyes went slanty and sly. "I know some nurb maintenance codes from working as a modder. I know how to put nurbs to sleep. It's like a temporary hypnosis. Genemodders and cops use the codes all the time."

For the sake of drama, Loulou moved her hands in a circle, as if casting a spell over the room. But really she was beaming out a rather long string of low-level nurb program code. I paid close attention, memorizing the details.

"You really are putting them in a trance," I said, kind of amazed. "I didn't know anyone could do this. It's like knowing a magic spell."

"Yeah. It lasts for about half an hour. The nurbs won't see or remember anything we do. So come on, Zad. Fuck me on Jane's floor."

What was the word Carlo had used about Loulou? *Ruthless*.

"I've still got a lot of sympathy for Jane," I told Loulou. "So the answer has to be no."

"I'm disappointed," said Loulou, not letting up.

"Come on now, I'll show you the balcony," I wanted to get this errand done. "You too, Gustav and Bonk. Don't bump anything."

"We not clumsy," said Gustav.

The vat of nurb-paint wasn't quite as big as I'd remembered, maybe three feet across and two feet deep. It was two-thirds full with nurb slime mold, gently undulating, cloudy-clear, with inner webs of colored veins. It made me happy to see the stuff.

If Loulou really did come live with me, maybe I'd start painting again. Even if she thought my work was corny. I could kick it up a notch, show her something new, take a further step. Maybe go abstract at last. Even if Dad still claimed that abstraction was a cop-out. Fuddydud that he was.

Bonk walked over to the vat and nudged it, not having much trouble making it move.

"Nurb-gel can be so pretty," said Loulou, admiring the stuff. "I used to love working with it when I played Levolver all the time. How much does the vat weigh?"

"Half ton," said Bonk. "Thousand pound. I can carry."

"And I can balance," said Gustav.

"That's fine, boys," I said. "Bring it to the alley in back of my store on Main Street."

"I could qwet your nurb-paint, do a genemod on it and make it into—I don't know—maybe a nurb ape," said Loulou. "Strong little guy. He could carry us down the housetree's outside wall like King Kong."

"I want to do this my way," I said, feeling stubborn. Nurb-paint was *my* thing. I didn't want Loulou taking it over.

"Suit yourself," said Loulou, still miffed about my not wanting to have sex. "Be an ass-kissing society artist. Too stuffy to learn from the street."

I took a hit of cosmic mode and held my tongue.

Bonk widened himself and hunkered down. His muscles were extremely elastic. His hands began pulling on the vat's closer edge. Gustav lifted the vat from the other side, helping to position it atop Bonk. Bonk rose a bit, resting on his tail as well as his feet, like a three-legged table. His calm, lucid eyes peeped out from beneath the vat.

Loulou was leaning on the balcony railing, taking in the scene. "I love the air up here," she said. "So fresh and high. I've spent my whole life in cruddy shacks. Will you get me an apartment like this, Zad?"

"This teep thing is accelerating the hell out of our affair,"

I said, drawn to letting my mind merge with Loulou's yet again. We were soaring birds, cathedral gargoyles, stars in the sky. Of course I wanted to get this difficult, exotic woman an apartment. But I didn't have the dough.

As we dropped back into the robotic mode of thought, Loulou fully assimilated the knowledge that I was poor. Something she hadn't realized before. Something she didn't like to know. Something that would permanently reduce my standing in her eyes.

"We go now?" said Gustav, standing beside Bonk with his steadying hands on my vat of living goo.

"Uh, yeah," I said. "Before Jane comes home."

"Let's steal something," said Loulou as we passed again through the sumptuous living room. "That!" The little nurb cuttlefish in her earrings waved their tentacles in glee.

She was pointing at a smooth, organic-looking object that sat upon a carved wooden shelf. It was the shape of a baseball, its surface mottled in shades of lavender and mauve. One side of the ball bore a puckered conical indentation. I'd often studied the thing, trying to decipher its origins and its possible significance.

One of the odd things about the curio was that its appearance wasn't fixed. The subtle spots and streaks on its surface changed from day to day. And sometimes the ball would wobble and pulse, with its puckered dimple flexing like the lips of a mouth with no teeth.

Jane had given me this numinous token for Christmas last year. So it was arguably within my rights to bag it. But Jane was very fond of the thing. She called it her amazing oddball. She'd found it walking alone in the woods near her parents' house. I hadn't been with her that afternoon.

Jane claimed the oddball had called her by whispering her name, and I half believed that. We still hadn't fully decided what the oddball actually was. We'd done numerous web image searches for objects resembling the oddball, but we'd never found anything similar. Our best guess was that it was a fungus of some kind, like a puffball. Or an invertebrate animal of some kind. Or possibly it had some connection with Kentucky's ubiquitous limestone caves?

When I'd obsessed on the oddball in the past, I'd sometimes get a feeling it was talking to me, not that I ever understood what it said. And sometimes I'd dream about its mouth. If I could shrink down and crawl inside the mouth—where would I land?

Here in the moment with Loulou, I took the oddball in my hand. It nestled against my palm, and I seemed to feel a faint glow of thought. Now that I had teep, I was more sensitive than ever before. Was the curio synching with my qwet mind? No time to ponder this now.

"Okay, I'll bring it," I told Loulou as I squeezed the slightly yielding ball into my pocket. "Really it's mine anyway. So we're not actually stealing. And tell Jane's apartment to snap out of your trance and let us go."

Loulou broadcast another code and a moment later the door to the downward lifter tube opened.

"We go first," said Gustav, still guiding the heavy-laden Bonk.

"*Oh* yeah." The lifter tube's cilia were powerful, but I didn't want to be in there with those guys tumbling after me.

Within a half hour, the vat of nurb-paint was in the alley behind my shop, right next to my slugfoot Lincoln. Gustav and Bonk had walked back to Gurky Movers. My Lincoln's slug was draped on the car's roof, soaking up the sun. I had a roadspider hanging around back there too. As kind of a joke, I'd named her Xiz in memory of old Zix—I'd had to incinerate Zix after she killed that colt.

"Let's do make my nurb-paint qwet now," I said to Loulou. "The paint will know how I *feel*. Have a sense of my dreams. It'll deepen my work. Make it less corny, right?"

"Oh, Zad, I didn't mean to hurt your feelings when I said that word. Let's not end on a sour note."

"End? We're just getting started, aren't we? Tell me again what you did to make your earrings qwet. Did you really just spit on them? It's that simple?"

"For the spit to be contagious you have to add some psychic *oomph*," said Loulou. "Lean over your vat, massage the slime, drool on it, and imagine that the slime is getting qwet. If you want something badly enough, you can actualize it. And, Zad, you should really start biomodding. Painting pictures isn't enough. We're deep into the twenty-first C. You ought to be making live nurbs. Like—surreal animals with bizarre personalities."

"I'm not really good using the biomodder wand," I muttered.

"Don't play dumb," said Loulou. "You're qwet now. You can biomod without any United Mutations wand. Teep into the target nurbs with your mind."

"How would I figure out the right mods?"

"If you're in cosmic mode, the gene designs pop right out at you, qrude. That's what we call cosmic logic. You find the mods and you teep them right into a nurb without any kludgy wand involved. I'm pretty sure we talked about this last night. Why do you look so blank?"

At some level this stuff did sound familiar, if foggy. "Maybe later I'll try," I said. "But right now I'd rather do things my way."

"Oh fine!" said Loulou impatiently. "Model your gel with your hands. The fuddydud stays in nursery school. Whatfucking-ever. Can I play with Jane's oddball now?"

"Sure," I said, more than ready for her to go away. I handed her the oddball. She carried it into my bedroom.

5: Scene of the Crime

Not really expecting the process to work, I put some spit on my fingers and dipped it into my vat of nurb-paint. As usual, it reacted to my touch with a ripple of pastel colors. But I didn't feel anything like an answering pulse of teep. I'd need to try harder.

I knelt by the vat, rolled up my sleeves and buried both my hands in the gel, waggling my fingers. I liked the smell of the stuff, faintly sour and carrying a slightly intoxicating headiness. Why had I stopped painting? Just because of a dip in sales? Painting was, after all, the one thing that made me truly happy. I'd been a fool to stop. And perhaps Loulou was right—perhaps I could progress into animated sculptures, or hell, why not start biomodding full-fledged nurbs. But for the moment, I just wanted to play.

"I love you," I told my nurb-paint. "I'm qwetting you."

I lowered my face to the vat and licked the slime. It shuddered and bulged, then extended a tongue of its own upwards. I let the tongue into my mouth—cool, smooth, and tingly. But when it made a move to slide down my throat I spit it out.

I heard a giggle. The gel was qwet. We were teeping. I had a new friend. I sent some of my thoughts into it—my worries about Jane, my excitement over Loulou, my longing to resume my career. Bubbles and blocks of color danced in the vat, connected by a network of spiral curves.

"This is good," I happily told the paint. "We'll make some great new pieces pretty soon."

Walking through my bedroom to the storefront, I told Loulou I'd successfully qwetted my paint. "Uh huh," she said, not really listening. She was busy staring at the oddball, turning it this way and that. "From somewhere else," she muttered. "Another world." I'd sometimes had that feeling about the oddball myself. But right now I needed to see what Skungy was up to.

"Did anyone come in?" I asked the rat, entering the front room.

"Losers looking to buy shit," said Skungy, running his tough-guy routine. "I chased them off."

"Thanks a lot. No food for you tonight."

"I'll rip your damn throat out."

"I'll incinerate you." The rat and I were enjoying ourselves. It was like the way I talked to Carlo.

Speaking of whom—a couple of noisy idiots burst into the store just then, yelling my name. It was Carlo and Reba, laughing their heads off, with Carlo beating *bebop-a-rebop* tattoos on the wall and Reba teeping into my head. Her personality felt like a tropical jungle.

"I'm qwet too!" she exulted. "Isn't it dreamy, Zad? The next big thing. And we're launching it in little old Louisville."

"I boned Reba," said Carlo. "If that's not too frank?"

"Speaking truth to power," said Reba. "After we merged, Carlo and I got so jazzed that we staged a Slygro palace revolution. Gaven's great at streamlining production, but he's too fuddydud for a major market splash. I'm the big boss now, and I started marketing the Slygro qwet teep personality upgrade as of noon today." Just what Loulou had predicted.

"Tell me more," I said.

"Carlo and I went out to the Slygro lab in the barn around eleven, and nobody was there," answered Reba. "We found the qwetter lying there on a work bench, and I took it. So that means we've got a service to supply. And while we were at it, Carlo tweaked the Slygro phone tree so that incoming calls go directly to me. Reba the CEO. Buy your qwet from Reba. In fact I already sold a qwet treatment to a jeweler down the street from your store. Ned White? He called me up—that's why we came down here."

"Gaven is okay with all this?" I demanded.

"We didn't actually see Gaven at all," said Reba. "But he knows what's up. He sent this nasty furry thing with a beak to spy—"

"A platypus," interrupted Carlo. "Gaven has two qwet platypuses living in a burrow off the pond. I didn't tell you? It's his latest thing. He's been backing up his personality onto them. An idea Gaven and Junko have been working on. Junko wants to take it a step further and write the backups into her own body's muscles."

"Anyway, yeah, Gaven's platypus was watching us," continued Reba. "The man himself was sulking in his house. He doesn't like that I'm in charge. He's like a spoiled kid. As of today, I own fifty-five percent of the stock, qrude. I paid a pretty penny. But a girl needs her fun."

"Reba bought stock from Loulou at the picnic," reported Carlo. "And I sold her mine during the night. And this morning Reba called Junko Shimano and got her to sell, too."

"Loulou had stock?" I said.

"It used to be Joey's," said Reba. "But Joey's mentally incompetent, and Loulou's his wife. So!" Reba paused, studying my reaction. "Loulou didn't tell you about her little side deal, did she? *Now* do you believe that she's a two-faced whore?" Surely Loulou was hearing this from the bedroom.

"Watch your mouth," I snapped at Reba. "And I don't know what the hell you think you're buying with Slygro. Junko Shimano is the one who invented qwet tech, and she made it open source. That's why she was glad to sell you her stock. It's not worth shit."

My back door slammed right about then. Loulou on the way out.

"Exit the guttersnipe," whooped Reba, gladly throwing an extra log onto my firestorm of emotions. "And, oh-oh, look out the window, there she goes on your roadspider!"

"I'm sure there's an explanation," I said, trying to stay calm. "She's running an errand." But when I tried teeping Loulou, I found she'd blocked me off. And I couldn't contact my roadspider either. Apparently Loulou had disabled Xiz's tracking unit by using low-level nurb maintenance commands.

"You're better off with *moi*," said Reba, picking up on my discomfiture. She was standing right up against me, the smell of whiskey on her breath. "I don't know *why* I've never done a threesome with you and Carlo. Or maybe we did? Hard to remember."

"Qwet teep's in town," said Carlo, wearing a loose, weary grin. "Big fun."

Reba said something else about Loulou, and I yelled at her for awhile, and she agreed to back off on the snide remarks. Obviously she was jealous. Be that as it may, I was starting to wonder if Reba and Jane were to some extent correct about Loulou. For sure Loulou had acted weird in Jane's apartment. And I'd picked up that sharp disappointment vibe when Loulou realized how little money I had. And she'd more or less stolen my roadspider. Maybe she'd been gaming me all along.

Chalk up a fresh heartbreak for tortured artist Zad Plant?

I gave Carlo and Reba some breakfast, and we talked a little more, sitting around my store's counter, enhancing our words with teeped emotions.

Like I mentioned earlier, the brain's natural rate is to switch between the cosmic and the robotic modes at a rate of ten or even twenty times a second. Like rapid sonar *pings*. But now I was slowing the rate way down.

Going slow was a way of harnessing my teep so that I could have a heavy but non-oblivious conversation. I'd spend a second or two in the cosmic state, dipping deep into people's minds and picking up intense tastes of their emotions. And then I'd snap back into robotic mode and lay down some facts. I was tasting the cosmic logic, and waking up every second or two to note down my impressions.

Putting it a bit differently, I was drifting into oblivion, bobbing up to the light, drifting down, and bobbing up again, over and over, creating an offbeat synthesis of the two reality modes.

Reba didn't understand about tuning her vibrations. She'd sit there staring at Carlo and me in a cosmic merge, and then she wouldn't remember anything that had happened for the last ten minutes. Not that Reba's humid, overheated teep was actively unpleasant. She was, after all, an old friend. Even if, psychically speaking, she had a tendency to stand closer to me than I was standing to her.

"Let's see Gaven's qwetter," I said to Carlo. He laid it on the table—it was like an old-time electrical engineer's Christmas stocking, in the shape of a water gun.

"Junko tells me that, thanks to Gaven's input, this qwetter has a hundred times as many parts as it needs," Carlo said. "Not to mention that fact that it's even using old-school tech at all. Being a nerd doesn't automatically make you smart."

"Gaven did have that big score with the housetrees," I said.

"Yeah, but he bought/borrowed/stole the designs from little guys. He's biz. A raptor. Knows how to siphon into the cash stream."

"And every single bit of the qwet stuff is Junko's, right? With Loulou pitching in."

"Junko's saying she'll have much simpler qwetter design by tomorrow. And it's going to be nurb instead of bunch of antique parts. She wants to let the qwetter's new genes be open source too. She's a zealot, an ultrageek. Doesn't even care about getting rich."

"Hell," I said, "Loulou showed me how to qwet people with sex, and how to qwet nurbs with spit. This shit's contagious."

"Loofy times," said Carlo.

"Slygro's got nothing to sell," I said.

"We don't see it that way," said Reba, momentarily snapping out of her trance. "I was already talking to Jane about a business plan today. It's like Gaven says. Slygro can troubleshoot people's qwet teep installations. Offer online seminars. Sell aftermarket add-ons. Do tech support. And make sales on our own. Jane said I should call her back when I'm sober. Did I tell you I just zapped Ned the jeweler with this qwetter? Customer numero uno." Reba rummaged in her hair with both hands. "What a night! I'm Kentucky fried."

"Grab a nap?" I suggested. "You can use my bed."

Despite Loulou's defection, I was feeling high and relaxed. The air shimmered in synch with my slowed-down cosmic/robotic vibration. I was seeing rainbow fringes, motion trails, op-art moirés. My two friends seemed like mythological archetypes. If people learned to handle qwet teep properly, their lives could become incredibly great.

"It's better if I take Reba back to her apartment," said Carlo, bristling with possessiveness vibes. Even if Slygro tanked, Reba was rich.

"Fine." I turned to Reba. "Where was Jane when you talked to her this morning?" I made my voice as casual as I could. "At Gaven's?"

Reba chuckled and wagged her finger at me. "Zad's *jealous*. He's in looove."

"Jane did sleep at Gaven's," said Carlo. "But Reba says it was, like, a platonic thing."

"They had milk and cookies at midnight," said Reba, breaking into snorts of laughter. "Oh Lord take me now. Twin beds. Matching pink and blue jammies. Two toothbrushes. Sinister note: Gaven has a ball in his room, like a wrinkled baseball. He calls it his dirtbubble. It's a little like Jane's oddball, only it's brown and muddy-looking and it smells like, I don't know, like formaldehyde. Somehow it seems *mean*. Gaven keeps it on a cat's bed like a pet and he talks to it. Under a night-table between the twin beds. I bet he uses the dirtbubble for sex."

"And you know all this *how*?" I demanded.

"We girls like to talk in the morning and share the details of our nights with you big bad men," said Reba. "Jane's so mad that you did Loulou. She's talking about all her old boyfriends again."

"I don't see where Jane gets off," I spluttered. "After—"

And right then of course my wristphone chimed. And it was Jane. This time she had her visuals on. The squidskin of my wristphone was percolating signals directly into my nervous system, so it was as if I was seeing Jane through my own eyes—without needing to look down at the phone's display. Jane was standing in her apartment, serious and cute. Standing right where I'd been an hour ago.

"Where is it?" she demanded. She was of course talking about the oddball.

"It's mine," I essayed. I was imagining it was still in my

bedroom here.

"I found it in the woods behind my parents' place last year," said Jane. "And it lives on a carved shelf in my apartment. And I want it back here today."

"You gave it to me for Christmas last year."

"That was more like a *loan*, not a gift. You can't just take it away. The oddball is precious to me, Zad. And now Gaven Graber wants to buy it!"

"How did Gaven find out about it?"

"Well that's the strangest thing. Gaven has this thing he calls his dirtbubble, and it looks like the oddball a little bit. I can hardly believe this, but Gaven says his dirtbubble talks to him, and that it told him about my oddball? Maybe it wants a friend? This is all so crazy. Gaven likes that dirtbubble so much that he keeps it in his bedroom. Even though it smells bad."

"Reba mentioned that to me, actually."

"Oh, she's such a long-toothed gossip. Anyway, Gaven thinks he can use the dirtbubble and the oddball for a special project that he and Whit want to do. Something really big, but he won't tell me what. Not yet. Gaven said that if I'd give him the oddball, or even just lend it to him, he'd give me all the secrets of qwet teep. I said not now. But those secrets must be worth a lot! I'm tempted."

"Gaven is trying to cheat you," I said. "We were talking about this at the picnic. Doesn't anyone ever listen to me? Those secrets are public domain."

"Oh, what does that even mean? I despise tech-biz lingo. Jane Says is supposed to be simple. Promo and buzz. I'm the Aphrodite of access. The Juno of jive. Gaven and I will make a mint off qwet teep!"

"You're the best," I said, smiling. My Jane. It was nice to see her on the little squidskin display, bright and loud with her yellow hair.

"Don't you try and jolly your way out, Zad. Adulterer. Where's our oddball? Show it to me."

And now, *duh*, the full realization dawned. I walked into my bedroom, but I barely needed to look.

"Loulou stole it," I had to report. "And she took my roadspider too."

"She's going straight to Gaven!" cried Jane. "I bet he'll do something to ruin our oddball. He'll crush it, or slice it up, or sell it to someone in China! You run out to his farm—or I'll never ever take you back!"

"I hadn't known that was a possibility," I said, my heart rising.

"I hadn't known I'd care who you sleep with." Jane's face had an odd expression. Maybe wistful.

"I'm going to Gaven's right now."

I ended the call, and right away Reba had to put in her two cents worth. "You don't know for sure that Loulou went to Gaven's. She might have gone to meet Joey Moon. Did I tell you that Joey broke out of his clinic two hours ago? One of their staff called Slygro to tell us. Sounded like a country girl with her first city job."

"Why not call Xiz and ask her where she is," Carlo suggested to me.

As I may have mentioned, if you owned a nurb, you had a built-in encrypted wireless connection to it, like a remote link. You could always check on its whereabouts. But thanks to Loulou's tinkering with Xiz's maintenance codes, calling my roadspider wasn't a current option.

"I'm leaving for Gaven's," I repeated.

Right then Ned White, the jeweler from down the street, came bopping into my store, all excited about the qwet teep treatment that Reba had sold him.

"I keep forgetting what I'm doing," said Ned, beaming at us. "You're all sunny inside, you three. New day."

"I have to go," I told him. "Emergency. Talk to Carlo and Reba if you like. And, Skungy, you watch my store again."

"I want to hunt for Joey Moon," said the rat in a hoarse whisper. "My living idol."

I was nearing a condition of frenzy. Loulou would be at Gaven's by now. With our valuable oddball in her hands. What did any of this mean?

"Just come along with me then, Skungy, I don't care. Clear out of here, you other three. I'm locking the place up."

"We'll talk later," Carlo told me, ushering Reba out the front door. She was in cosmic mode, and wobbly in the knees.

Ned White dogged my steps back through my bedroom, and into the alley. He was holding a handful of nurb earrings, and he wanted an answer to the same question that I'd asked Loulou about my vat of paint.

"How do I make these things qwet so I can try and mod their shape?"

"Use *oomph*," I said, parroting Loulou. "Drool on them or put them in your mouth or piss on them. Actualize. As for the actual modding—Loulou says the cosmos will help you. Whatever that means." Turning away from Ned, I called out to my slugfoot nurb, who was still sunning himself on my Lincoln's roof. "Time to go! Get under the car!"

But the big nurb wouldn't move until I'd fed him a bucket of chow. I felt like my head was about to explode. While I fed the slug, Ned White continued pestering me with questions. He had some wistful notion that he might have a chance with Loulou, now that he was a qwet teeper too.

"You don't want her!" I hollered. But maybe *I* still did.

And then I was on my way, riding my presidential assassination replica vehicle down River Road with Skungy on the dashboard, just like the day before.

Things were quiet on Gaven's farm. Early Saturday afternoon and nobody working. Looked like even Junko had taken the day off. And I saw no sign of my roadspider Xiz.

The excited Skungy skittered up Gaven's porch steps a few seconds ahead of me. His shrill alarm squeak filled my ears as I entered the front hall.

There lay Gaven, his face contorted, his body quite still. His skin was paler than pale, with a cast of blue. He had no teep aura at all. I touched the back of his hand. Although it was a little warm, his utter lack of a reaction convinced me he was dead. Another possible clue: Gaven's hair was slightly damp. Sweat? A painting lay face-down on the floor at his side.

"Loulou?" I called. "Are you here?"

No answer. Everything was still, everything silent—like an enchanted castle. All of the nurbs were in a trance. Powered down by Loulou, no doubt. I teeped out the wake-up codes I'd learned from her.

The house and its furnishings came back online. And I heard a shrill buzzing. Flies on the corpse? Oh, wait, those were Gaven's gnat cameras, circling him, landing and taking off, darting at me. One of the first things the gnats did was to call the cops. I knew because they told me via my wristphone.

"Wait here for the authorities," the gnats shrilled through my wristphone, their voices in my head.

Great, just great. I was the only one at the crime scene. It looked bad. And if I fled, it'd look worse.

I wondered who else the gnat cams might be telling about Gaven's death. Perhaps Carlo. Probably Junko Shimano. Probably not Loulou or Joey Moon. But I was guessing that one or both of them had been here just a few minutes ago.

I had a few minutes to look around on my own before the cops came. I paced to and fro, with little Skungy's whiskers twitching in my aid. We found no signs of Loulou nor of Jane's oddball. No weapons and no blood. The only thing out of place was that canvas on the floor. Even if it meant tampering with evidence, I flipped it over with the toe of my shoe.

How to describe breath-stopping horror? Putting it as simply as possible, the canvas held a squidskin portrait of Gaven. But the image had been tweaked and enhanced to represent a highly repellent version of the man. Had the sight of this terrible likeness jolted Gaven into his final collapse?

The image's nostrils were flared as if smelling something bad. The front teeth were bucked out over the lower lip, miming an expression of imbecility. One side of the mouth was pulled down in a sour frown, the other side was drawn back in a dopey grin. The forehead was furrowed in bestial stupidity, and the eyes were crinkled in a baleful glare.

"A squidskin portrait by Joey Moon," said Skungy, who was of course an expert on the man who'd given him his personality.

"Not that I'm saying Joey was here to make it. My Joey ain't no kind of killer."

Trying not to look at the repellent image itself, I studied the construction of the picture. It was indeed a squidskin, with tiny eyes along the edge. Evidently it had functioned like an interactive distorting mirror, drawing you into a feedback loop. Gazing at the squidskin, you'd be reacting to what you saw. And the image would continue reflecting and exaggerating your expressions until you and the image had reached a sufficiently extreme state. And then freeze on that. Like a predatory paparazzo with a flash.

A simple, loofy idea for an artwork. Now I understood why Joey had been so secretive about his gimmick. It really *would* be easy to rip off the idea.

Depending on the programming of a canvas's squidskin, it might jolly you into a laughing fit, precipitate a crying jag, lead you to a peak of personal pride—or march you towards a brutal baring of your most-feared monster within. And steal away your very breath. I was guessing that's what had happened to Gaven. Judging from the temperature of his skin, it hadn't been so long ago.

But who'd shown Gaven the lethal squidskin? Joey Moon himself? Loulou? Was Whit Heyburn somehow involved? Or—

"Oh shit, there goes my job." It was Artie the tall security guard, drag-assing into the house. "I let the poor guy down." He leaned down, peering closely at Gaven. "We need to call the cops."

"His gnats already did that," I said. "You were supposed to be on duty?"

"I have a house on the property," said Artie. "An old cabin down the hill. I think you lived on this farm yourself about ten years ago? Right after we graduated from high school. You were up in the grown home that Joey and Loulou use."

"Yeah, yeah. Let's stick to the point. You didn't notice when your boss died?"

"His house should have sent me an alarm," said Artie. "But—"

"The house didn't warn you because it was asleep. My friend Loulou, she knows some special nurb maintenance codes. She says the code to them and they go offline."

"Qwet teep is slowing *me* down," said Artie. "You saw Joey zap me with the qwetter last night, right? Qwet teep is why I stayed in bed so long. You're qwet too. I can tell. It's spreading like the measles. I was up all night making love to my wife. We didn't fall asleep till after the sun came up."

"I had a night like that myself," I said.

"Right on," said Artie, briefly cheered. And then his mood darkened again. "I feel lower than squid-shit about Gaven. I should of been checking on him. Whether or not his house was calling me. I screwed up."

"Tough to guard a guy like that," I said, hoping to draw Artie out. "Not likable. I'd say he's been dead less than an hour."

"That's a sick painting on the floor next to him. It's the inner Gaven? I see you brought your rat again."

"He doesn't matter." Naturally Skungy wanted to argue about this, but I shut him up.

Artie and I walked out on the porch and stood there companionably. Artie was my age. Just another guy trying to get by. Gently we merged the edges of our teep. I was still doing my new trick of alternating between cosmic/robotic modes only about every few seconds. Staying sociable, but enjoying my high. Artie fell into the same rhythm.

Moving as one, we walked down the porch steps and away from the nurbs. Gaven's gnats stayed inside, hovering over his body.

"You're not the one who killed Gaven, are you?" asked Artie in a low tone.

"No, man. Of course not. I came to the farm looking for Loulou Sass. You didn't see any sign of her?"

Artie was silent. He wanted to say something, but I could teep that he was scared of being blamed. But then he went ahead and spit it out.

"I don't like to admit this," he quietly said. "But I heard something about half an hour ago. Gaven and Loulou yelling.

And then they stopped all at once. I should have done something—but I was zoned into the teep with my wife. Deep into our humble joy."

"So you heard the noise, you stayed in cosmic mode, and—"

"I felt your vibe coming into Gaven's house, and that finally got me out of the sack. Poor Gaven. He was a jerk, but even so—" Artie trailed off.

Two police spiders were loping up the drive— dark blue, long-legged, with a fluid and sinister quality to their gait.

The lead cop was yet another guy I knew from high-school days. Lief Larson. I even knew his assistant, a hard guy we called Grommet. God, I was getting old. I knew people who were cops.

"Hi, Lief. Grommet."

"Zad dad," said Lief. "The gnat cameras told me you'd be here. They claim they saw you kill Gaven with an overdose of nod spray. They say they have video." He stared at me.

"You're putting me on," I said flatly. "Trying to frame me."

"That's my job," said Lief, backing off a bit. He was an odd guy, with a sardonic, tragic view of life. He didn't take anything seriously. He leaned over and released a particular kind of forensic nurb, a thing called a crawly hand. It began creeping around on Gaven's body. As the name suggested, it resembled a small, pale human hand, only it had nostrils in its thumb, an eye in its palm, a tiny mouth on the back of the hand, and a cluster of slender tentacles where the index finger should have been. Unpleasant to look at.

"The gnats were offline when I got here," I told Lief. "And I doubt they'd make up stories about me. I found Gaven dead, yes. With that weird picture lying next to him? My theory is that he had some kind of brain attack."

"Zad the artist," said Lief. The forensic hand was pushing its flexible tentacle-probes deep into Gaven's nose. Lief gazed at me, a muscle twitching in his cheek. "Next you'll tell me that you gave Graber the bill for this wonderful portrait and he keeled over stone cold dead? Come on, Zad, don't screw with me. What's actually happening here? What's this qwet teep I'm hearing about? What's up with Joey Moon and Loulou Sass? And why did you come out to the farm?"

"I was supposed to start selling Gaven's Slygro products in my store. Pet rats like this one I have here. I came to talk to Gaven about the plan. As for the rest of it, I'm as confused as you. I don't know anything about qwet teep."

"I doubt it. We questioned Ned White after he left your store an hour ago. He was all excited about a qwet teep treatment that he'd gotten from your friend Reba Ranchtree. Talkative guy. He said you'd spent the night with Loulou Sass. Who lives on this estate. And who arrived in Louisville riding a stolen road-scorpion." Lief gave me a long look, then turned to Artie. "How about you? What's your excuse?"

"I'm the security guard. I was asleep."

"You and the nurbs both. The mystery of the enchanted farm. I'll let you go for now, Artie. But Zad, I'd like you to come downtown with me. I'll drive you in your car, if you don't mind. The slugfoot Lincoln. I want to check out the ride. My spider can follow along."

"You're arresting me?" My voice rose in surprise. Teep or not, I hadn't seen this coming.

"*Yeah*, you're arrested," rasped Grommet, getting right in my face about it. He had a broad face, high cheekbones and a trim beard. "That a problem? Want to escalate?" He'd always been a bully. I remembered him rubbing snow on my face. And bragging about forcing sex on girls. A nasty person. I resisted my impulse to whack an elbow into Grommet's eye.

"I'm calling you a murder suspect," said Lief. "I don't like it when people bullshit me. We'll get our judge owl to arraign you. I'll drive you downtown to meet the owl, and then you can see about getting some bail."

Skungy was up on his rear haunches, curiously sniffing at the forensic hand, which had forced some of its probes right through the wall of Gaven's chest. Measuring levels, feeling for clots. And now the forensic hand chirped to signal that it was done. Lief picked it up and held it to his ear.

"The hand reports that Gaven Graber died of asphyxiation,"

he intoned, staring me. "You can see there's no bruises around his throat. Either he was smothered or he somehow stopped breathing. Time of death approximately one thirty this afternoon. And now it's two thirty. When exactly did you arrive here, Zad?"

"Not till two. The gnats called you almost right away. And Artie showed up a little later."

"The house isn't telling me jack," said Lief. "And the gnats are blank for the fifteen minutes before they called us in. Like a professional hit. Are you pro, Zad? Did you smother him?"

"I think it was this ugly picture. It scared him to death. Took his breath away."

"Scare a cold fish like Gaven Graber?" said Lief with a snort. "Yes, I can see that his death expression matches the picture's. Too tidy. It stinks. I'm thinking murder one."

"The picture herded Gaven into a psychotic break!"

"Spare me the fancy bullshit," snapped Lief. "Once we get downtown, maybe we'll pound the truth out of you."

"You guys don't do that anymore," I said, hoping this was true.

"We've still got a back room," said Lief shortly. "Crunch numbers, crunch heads." He stared at me again, still hoping I'd crack. "The crawly hand is done, but I'm gonna cart Garber's stiff to our morgue. Maybe we'll cut him up. Or put him in a cell with you. Get old-school on the case. You mind if I bring Gaven in the back seat of your car?"

"I'm supposed to ride in my car with a corpse and a cop?"

"You'll be handcuffed as well," said Lief, always pushing for a reaction. "And we'll be keeping your car for awhile."

Right about then, Grommet caught Skungy with a net. The nurb mesh tightened, and Grommet dropped the squalling Skungy into his coat pocket. "We can run him through a terminal interrogation," said Grommet. "Or maybe you'd talk to save your qwet rat?"

"Oh, you're really up on the qrude lingo," I blindly challenged. "*Qwet rat.*"

"I might as well tell you that today's investigation is about more than you killing Graber," said Lief. "We've got an inquiry from the big DoG. The Department of Genomics. They want to know more about qwet. We're gonna search this whole farm on the DoG's behalf. They'll cut our department a fat check."

Three more cops arrived, one on a roadspider, the other two in an oversized roadhog van. Lief handed one of them the weird picture of Gaven that had been lying on the floor. "Put this in the trunk of that Lincoln over there."

"The boys and me are gonna comb through this place now," Grommet told me, hefting a billy club that he'd produced from inside his coat. He was such a caricature, such a complete dick. "I'm still waiting to hear if you have any problems."

I stared at Grommet in silence, not wanting to give him any satisfaction.

"And—Zad?" added Grommet, sweetening his voice. "DoG says your nurb reseller's license is revoked. You'll have to close your Live Art store."

Combined with my teep sense of Grommet's gloating hostility, the news hit hard. As I'd done when facing Whit, I took a series of deep breaths and melted far into the cosmic mode. Beyond the pale. One with everything. The world was like a springtime dogwood tree—with Grommet and me like little white flowers, wearing ballet tutus and dancing in the breeze. All a performance, all a show. Nothing mattered.

And now here came Junko Shimano, galloping up the driveway on her pale green roadspider.

"Hi, Zad," called Junko, pulling up next to us. "Gaven's really dead? Bummer, bummer, bummer. I heard about it from his gnat cams. The control of the cams has passed to me."

"State your name," said Lief Larsen.

"Junko Shimano," she said, dismounting from the roadspider. "I'm Gaven's chief engineer. And I brought a lawyer along."

She held out a lawyer head, that is, a blobby nurb that was covered with the squidskin image of one Herb Stork, Esq. About the size of a roast chicken. The counselor wasn't able to make it out here in person on such short notice; he was in his home office, realtime-linked to our scene.

"Cease and desist," said the lawyer head. "*Habeas corpus*. Lacking firm evidence of a crime, you can't do a destructive autopsy."

"I've been tracking the feeds from Gaven's gnat cams on the way over here," added Junko. "I'm up on what's down. Gaven has a notarized Advance Directive form. You can't just go and trash his body, Detective Lief Larsen."

The lawyer head sounded forth. "The Advance Directive specifies that, lacking a countervailing legal order, Gaven Graber's remains are to be placed into his stasis machine for possible resuscitation. As you know, this is a standard practice."

"Gaven has his stasis machine on standby in the farm's old smokehouse," continued Junko—doing a ping-pong routine with her lawyer. "That little gray stone building over there? If you policemen want to do something useful, help us carry Gaven's body. Right away? He's already starting to deliquesce, as I'm sure you know."

Grommet was on the point of barking out some ignorant insult, but Lief waved him off. "We'll be glad to assist," said Lief smoothly. "We know about stasis machines, of course. It's fine, just so the body remains accessible to our forensic nurb hands. And you'll have to inform us if and when Graber is repaired and resuscitated."

"It's quite likely to happen," said Junko. "Gaven set aside a fund for the best in medical nurb ants—just in case something like this happened. We're not done with him yet."

"Let me ask you something, Ms. Shimano. Were you in conflict with the deceased?"

"At times," she said with a shrug. "We argued about business strategy. But it was nothing I'd kill him for. What am I, a suspect now? I can't believe you're arresting poor Zad."

"Do you know of some better suspects?" asked Lief smoothly.

"Oh—everyone," said Junko, leaning over the corpse. "What a horrible face! Gaven had very low empathy, even after he—well, he had low empathy no matter what. None of us at Slygro really *liked* him. What a horrible look he has on his face."

"What about qwet teep?" slipped in Lief. "What do you know?"

"That's under non-disclosure," interrupted Junko's lawyer head. "She can't talk about that."

"What do you know about the picture Garber was looking at when he died?" continued Lief. "I assume the gnat cams fed you my conversation about it with Zad?"

"Yeah," said Junko. "I can tell you that picture is definitely based on one of Joey Moon's constructions. He calls them magic mirrors. They start blank and they stop when they reach a peak. I don't know if Joey's ever shown them to anyone besides Loulou Sass and me. But Joey can't be a suspect. He's locked up in a clinic."

"You need to be checking your facts," said Lief. "Joey escaped from the clinic around eleven thirty this morning. He'd be a *good* suspect, from what you're telling me."

"I doubt it," said Junko, not liking the idea. "But we can't stand here talking. We have to get Gaven into his stasis. If you two officers can get him by shoulders, Zad and I can take his legs."

"Just stand aside, Ms. Shimano," said Lief. "My men can carry him on their own. Lead the way, and power up your stasis machine. We'll let Mr. Graber rest in peace." Lief ran his hands over Gaven's face, smoothing the man's grimace, closing his eyes.

Back when Todd Trask had lived here, he cured a few hams every year. He'd pack hog legs in salt for a month, then hang them up to dry for another whole month in the smokehouse—with a slow, smoky fire burning for all thirty days. The smoke kept flies from laying eggs in the meat before it had developed a moldy, impervious rind.

I tried telling Junko about this while she and I walked ahead of the cops carrying Gaven, but she was too excited to listen. She was amped up about using the stasis machine.

"It's a system of concentric deformed ellipsoids, each of them bearing an increasingly strong bosonic shield," she told me. "Like an invisible cocoon of nested sleeping bags. At the very core, the flow of time effectively stops."

Junko opened the smokehouse's heavy, studded wooden door, releasing the lingering smell of bacon and smoked meat. She reached in and flicked a switch. Pale purple light glowed from one side of the room to the other, intricate webs of bright lines outlining a six-foot-long banana-shaped pod. A virtual hammock, dramatic against the smokehouse's soot-covered inner walls.

The stasis field's generators were a waist-high pair of high-tech lumps fastened to the stone walls. They were utterly silent, powered by a subquantum Maxwell's Demon effect that was said to draw energy from the fluctuations of spacetime foam.

"Flop Gaven into the stasis spindle," Junko told the cops, stepping to one side. "It's like you're putting him in a hammock. The field will hold him up. Be careful with your hands. If you leave your hand in the stasis field for too long, it'll get out of synch and snap off at the wrist. Like on a Greek statue." Possibly she was teasing them. I was having trouble reading Junko today.

With gingerly motions, the bearers did their work. Gaven lay there, gently rocking, a high-tech pod-person. The police went back to the porch, and Junko sent the gnats with them. She and I stood alone by Gaven for a minute, looking at him and vibing each other's teep. Junko was sad, exultant, scared, eager, lonely, sly.

"What next?" I murmured. "Where does this go?"

"Slygro is over," she breathed. "Qwet teep isn't a product, it's a *cause*. I want to start a commune where the local qwetties can synergize."

"A commune on Gaven's farm?"

Junko made a tiny gesture of shaking her head. "Something better. Something luxor. I have a few ideas, and you should work your connections too. Call me in the morning."

There was a rectangular spot of daylight at the bottom of one of the smokehouse walls. A vent. I noticed something moving there. A furry little animal in the vent hole, gazing up at Gaven's spindle. Pale purple light glinted on the thing's eyes and on its—beak? Oh God, a platypus.

Carlo had told me a little more about the two qwet platypuses in Gaven's pond. Gaven's software was waiting in these platypuses—waiting for the time when the man's slightly damaged body would be repaired by a colony of medical nurb ants. These high-priced ant colonies included workers in a full range of sizes—running all the way down to the molecular level. Big suture ants, small inspectors, minute tube-cleaners, and an army of nanoants for the deeper-down nasties. Could they really raise Gaven from the dead? I'd always suspected the concept to be a scam.

In any case, the idea of Gaven's personality being inside this platypus creeped me out. According to Carlo, the platypus could force Gaven's personality onto you even if you *weren't* Gaven. It could overwrite your mind. This wasn't at all an easy thing to do. Your mental essence has its own built-in firewalls. Ordinarily nobody can teep into you and replace your personality with theirs.

But Gaven's tweaked platypuses had a work-around. The spurs on their rear legs excreted a paralyzing drug called a conotoxin. It was like curare, only stronger. The effects only lasted for a minute, but that was enough. The platypus would sting you, you'd keel over like a plank, the platypus would teep Gaven's personality into your head, and when you sat up—you'd be Gaven.

The thought horrified me. I wasn't always that good at winning arguments. A lot of time I'd get shouted down. That's one reason I liked to go off by myself and make art. It made me sick to imagine someone else's personality crawling inside my head and bullying me into submission.

I stayed a good distance from the platypus. I couldn't tell if Junko had noticed it too. I did my best to hide my thoughts about it. This whole scene was starting to feel like an intricate game, and I needed to keep any slight edge I might have.

In terms of edges, it might be good for me if I turned up a mansion where we could crash. Jane's family estate would be a great pick. But, now that I looked, I could see that option was already in Junko's mind. In any case, before doing any further mind-gaming, I had to go downtown with Lief Larsen.

Once we were in copland, a squat little nurb owl judge arraigned me on a manslaughter charge. He was a gray lump of feathers with a brown beak, big eyes, and with his legs growing out of a waxy pedestal of memory tissue. The corpus of the Law. Zero empathy from that owl. He gnawed on a dead rat while he pondered my case.

For a second there, I thought the dead rat was Skungy. But, no, Skungy was in another room, locked in a cage. I could teep his unruly vibes. Skungy and I couldn't make any really specific plans. What with teep being oblivious, I wouldn't remember anything he said. But I came out of our teep with a gut feeling that my rat would make an escape before long.

"The manslaughter charge is to get your attention," Lief told me. "To encourage cooperation. The owl and I know you're holding out on us about qwet teep. And about Graber's death. We're releasing you on bail so can think things over, and nose out info. Once you actually help us—and you will—we'll dismiss the charge. Meanwhile sign here to give us your store in lieu of cash bail."

"Can I still live in the store if I do that?"

"You can't live there anyway," said Lief. "The DoG has quarantined it. Like Grommet told you. You aren't allowed in your store at all. That's part of the fallout from your nurb reseller's license being revoked. And *that's* happening because you're involved with qwet teep. Whatever the hell it is, DoG doesn't like it."

I used the cosmic mode to blow off my anger. And then I robotically signed what I had to. When I got out of the cop station, I walked the five blocks to my store—to see in person what had come down. It was nearly dusk by now, with the sky turning gray, with a cool breeze picking up.

6: Loulou in the Oddball

Sure enough, the DoG had a guard at my front door, a blocky nurb resembling one of Craig Gurky's mover golems, with a stingray nurb for backup. Looking in through my store's windows, I could see the place was trashed. Not only had they melted my retail stock with a biomodder wand, they'd burned my nurb furniture, and they'd scraped the paint off my *Cold Day in Hell* pictures. While they were at it, they'd smashed a few of my Mom's ceramic pots that I had. Nothing left but shards, empty shelves, puddles of goo, heaps of ashes—and my blank, stained canvases. It could have been a funky art installation. *My Career Thus Far*.

"Please move along, Mr. Zad Plant," said the Department of Genomics guard. He had a boxy head with a jutting jaw. "You no longer have legal access."

I walked around the street corner and followed an alley to the rear of my store. No guard here, but the back door was sealed tight with nurb lichen, grown all along the door's cracks. I could faintly see the DoG logo in the lichen's scrolled swirls. And my Lincoln was still with the cops.

But there were two bits of good news. My vat of qwet nurb-paint remained full. And my roadspider Xiz was in the alley—idling around, hoping for some chow, dainty on her long legs. Somewhere along the line today she'd shed Loulou, and she'd come home on her own. Xiz was her old self. Typically for a nurb, she wanted me to feed her before she'd talk to me.

The DoG had failed to ransack the chow shed. Moving as quietly as possible, I got a bucket of feed for Xiz. She ate quickly, hungrily, and while she was eating, I decided to have a shot at what Loulou had been suggesting. I'd try and biomod my vat of nurb-paint. Make it into something that could follow Xiz and me out of here. Maybe something like a dog.

My shop's biomodder wand was long gone or shattered to

bits, but Loulou had insisted I could mod my nurb-gel with my own qwet mind. As she'd been saying, there were two things I needed to do.

First of all, I needed to figure out what exact gene pattern I should use to make a dog—I was thinking of a big, crooked yellow dog with bristly spikes instead of hair. When we were boys, Carlo had a nurb dog like that and I'd always wanted one.

It was easy enough to find generic patterns for dog DNA online, and I was able to home in on something close to what I wanted. But, being an artist, I wasn't satisfied with that. I wanted my own personal stamp on my dog. I wanted to grow a dog like the one I had in my head.

And this is where it might have gotten hard, given that I didn't know jack shit about nurbware design. A genemodder wand would have helped here—but I didn't have one. So I did what Loulou had said. I got in tune with the cosmos and found my genemods with cosmic logic.

It was easier than it sounds. Like reaching out and picking up a coffee cup. Your hand knows where to go in space. Or—it was like poking around in my paints with my palette knife until I came up with the desired hue. Junko Shimano would have said I was letting the universal wave function comb through all possible genemods.

Whatever you want to say, I soon had a wriggly strand of virtual DNA in my virtual hand. And now came the second thing.

I needed to install my genemods into each of the cells in the vat of nurb-paint. This was another cosmic mode trip. A type of teep, but kind of—multifarious. In my head it felt like I was a tornado spawning off sub- and subsub- and subsubsub-tornadoes—all the way down to molecule-sized force fields, tickling the teensy antennae within the cell nuclei, zapping the genes with my news.

"You're a dog now," I told the vat of gel. "Refresh yourself."

It roiled and rolled, spilled out onto the ground, flailed out some pseudopods, tightened up, grew quills and—yeah baby, the job was done.

"*Oof*," said my new nurb dog, grunting from his throat. "*Oof, oof, oof.*" Something about my genemod design had given him a weird bark. In any case, I could teep that he had a fine mind.

"I'll call you Jericho," I said. "Is that okay?"

"*Oof.*"

Jericho was happy to be here, and ready for a run. I fed him a little nurb chow, just to put our relationship on a sound basis.

"Follow me," I told him.

"*Oof, oof, oof.*"

And then I was on my roadspider's back and we three were in the street. It looked like rain was coming—but that wouldn't be a problem. Xiz had a domed transparent carapace she could pop over me.

"So what happened with Loulou?" I asked Xiz when we were a block from my store. I glanced back to check that my new nurb dog was still at our heels. Loping right along, yeah. I felt proud of myself for making him. Things were opening up for me at last.

"Loulou—singing to me," said the roadspider. "Not loud. I carry her to Garber farm. Loulou go inside. They argue. I hear crash. Loulou not singing to me. Loulou gone. I run home. Where we go now?"

"My parents' house," I said, for lack of a better idea. We took off in that direction, with Jericho galumphing along behind. Even though his shape was crooked, he ran smooth. Thanks to cosmic logic, his deformations balanced out.

Dad was drinking a lot these days, but he remained a handsome old man—with a mane of white hair. He was still picking up a few society portrait gigs, mostly from old ladies. That's one thing about being a dissolute artist. The artist tag gives you cachet, and the dissolution tag makes a certain kind of woman want to be your redemptive muse. Or your drinking partner. Dad liked having women in his studio, and even better he liked visiting them in their luxor homes.

Mom was annoyed by Dad's decline, and increasingly bitter about his belles. She herself had abandoned her wedding-planner business. It had ended when she had a very public screaming argument with an overly fussy mother-of-the-bride.

"Enough is enough," was all Mom had ever told me about the fight. "I'm tired of weddings."

Lately she'd had taken up ceramics—making nurb glazed clay pots that she fired in her own kiln. She was selling a few of these around town. I'd had some of her pots in my shop—all shattered in the DoG rampage.

It had been a while since I'd gone to visit my parents. I wasn't being a very good son. But they were always glad to see me. I was a welcome distraction from their chronic bickering. They were proud of my success.

Oh, but wait—I wasn't successful anymore. Not with my art career dead, my wife separated from me and my store closed down. I had no place to live—and a manslaughter charge on my head.

"Murder!" exclaimed Mom, when I started telling her why I'd come home. "Why did you do it, Zad?"

"I *didn't*! God, Mom."

"Well, who died?"

"Gaven Graber."

"Poor boy. Nobody ever liked him. Such a know-it-all. Living on Todd Trask's old farm. Were you doing business with him?"

"I was supposed to sell some of his stuff at Live Art. Smart rats. I went out to Gaven's at two this afternoon, and he was dead. The tests show that he smothered to death. Lief Larson got the judge owl to charge me with manslaughter. Lief says I'm not telling him everything I know."

"Disgusting person," said Mom. "I hate the police. They can go to hell." She was still an attractive woman, and very confident in her blunt opinions.

"That's more like it. Where's Dad?"

"In the barn getting drunk with a slut who stinks of perfume. Your father—he's ready to throw me out like an old dish."

"Oh, Mom. It's that bad?"

"Dreadful. Worse every day." Mom's eyes grew watery.

"I'm glad to have you home. I have a list of chores by the way."

"Okay. What's first?"

"The nurb lightbulbs. They're all too dim, and I can't make them brighter. Maybe I'm going blind. You won't believe who Lennox's new woman friend is."

"Let's not get into the full soap opera yet, okay? Let me fix the bulbs."

Our house had a single great room encompassing the kitchen, dining area, and living room—with Mom and Dad's quarters partitioned off at one end. My old room was in the basement, facing the back, looking out on an empty clearing by the woods. Our barn was in the field on the front side of the house.

Over the years, my parents had fixed up their house to match the luxor country estates of their clients. Old-school walnut tables, leather couches, plaid blankets, overstuffed armchairs, cherrywood chairs. Gilt-framed paintings everywhere—some Dad's, some mine, and some from the twentieth century. A blackened stone fireplace. Heavy bare timbers holding up the high ceiling, and a narrow mezzanine looking down on the room. Oriental rugs and oak floors. Pewter, silver, and porcelain. Two stuffed ducks upon the wall. Brass lamps with cloth shades and—here was Mom's problem, dim nurb lightbulbs.

Outdoors the wind had risen. A thunderstorm coming on, the sky slate gray. The trees flailed their branches, scattering colored leaves. It was past six o'clock, and the lamps were too feeble.

"Have you been feeding them?" I asked Mom.

"Feeding lightbulbs," she sneered. Meaning the answer was no. "Everything's such a big production with these stupid nurbs."

"No wonder they're dim," I said. "They're starving." The nurb chow cupboard by the sink opened for me. I took a few chow cubes, and walked around the room, feeding little bits of the stuff to the lightbulbs. They had toothy little mouths on their sides, and they went *nyum nyum nyum* when they chewed. Problem solved.

I peered outside to see if Xiz and Jericho the mind-made

slime-dog were okay. They'd found temporary shelter in the front door's overhang. They were clamoring for food.

"I should feed Xiz and my dog and send them down to the barn," I said. "I made that dog myself, by the way. His name is Jericho. Don't you think he looks like Carlo's old dog?"

"He's crooked and yellow and his hair is like porcupine quills," said Mom. "I like him."

"Thanks," I said. "He's my first real nurb."

"So break out more Roller nurb chow," said Mom, who'd settled into one of the dining chairs. "Roller, Roller, Roller. I despise Weezie Roller. Old bag."

"Jane's mother? I'm not wild about her myself. With Jane and me separated, I haven't seen her for a few—"

"Weezie is your father's new girlfriend. In the barn with him right now. Like animals. Supposedly he's painting her portrait. Who wants to see it? Her husband's dead, her son's cuckoo, and Jane doesn't give a damn. Jane's always told me that I'm more of a mother to her than Weezie ever was."

I collapsed into the chair beside Mom. "Wait a minute. Mrs. Roller? Dad?"

"Read it and weep," said Mom.

"But—but I'm still hoping to get back together with Jane," I said.

"You *should* get back with her, yes. Apologize. Stop *lolling*. Treat Jane right. Start a family with her. Accept that you're not twenty-five years old. I'm completely on Jane's side."

"As usual," I said, smiling. I kind of liked Mom's loyalty to Jane. "But wait—I can't grasp this. Dad and *Weezie*? She's not going to come in here and talk to us, is she?"

"Their tête-à-têtes last into the evening. And then she flaps home to her Glenview mansion on her custom red flydino. If you look, you can see the dino under the eaves beside the barn. With the long beak and the bat-wings? He's noisy sometimes. I'd like to chop off his head."

"Qrude move."

"After Lady Roller leaves, your fat drunken father lurches in here and yells at me. He yells because he's ashamed of himself. I'm at the end of my rope, Zad. Frankly I'm about to evict Lennox. Before he does it to me. Old fool. I'm glad you're here to back me up. I'll live here in peace and make pots with Petrus. He's my teacher."

"Uh, where does Dad go after you throw him out like an old dish?"

"He can go to hell!" said Mom, and cackled. Talking to me was making her feisty. "My son the murderer can send him there!"

"Not a murderer," I muttered. "Let's have some food."

"There's a nurb horn of plenty on the counter," said Mom. "Ask it for whatever you want. I've abandoned the weary charade of making proper food. Petrus says nurb food is good for you. And have a drink."

"Drink like Dad?"

"Fat drunken old fool."

I fed Xiz and Jericho, and sent Xiz down to the stables where my parents kept their roadspiders. I was a little worried Jericho might run off, so I led him down to my old living quarters in my parents' basement—a bedroom and a bathroom. The bedroom seemed to be full of pottery crap. I herded Jericho into the bathroom and left him there.

"*Oof*," he said. He couldn't even bark right. Definitely a first-draft dog. But I was loath to turn him back into a puddle.

I went upstairs and the storm was upon us—drops rattling against the windows, stuttering flashes of lightning, sharp cracks in the sky. Cozy to be in the house, with the lights on, a glass in my hand, eating supper with Mom.

Except that suddenly, amid the chaos of the storm, I started hearing things. Someone nearby whispered my name. Loulou's voice.

"Zad. Help me."

I looked around, not seeing her. I had a sense of her presence nearby; I could smell her breath and her skin. I reached out my hand and seemed to touch something, but then it moved out of reach. At the same time I was hearing a knocking from downstairs. Before I could process any of this, I heard a wild hooting from the barn. I jumped up from my chair.

"It's Weezie's goddamn flydino," said Mom. "He does this every day. A big baby with a voice like a foghorn. He's hungry, or lonely, or tonight he's afraid of the storm. I'd like to chop off his head. Weezie's too." She was on her second glass of wine. "Sit back down and eat, Zad."

I was far too wound up for that. I heard another sharp tap from downstairs. And there were voices by the barn. Pressing my face to the kitchen window, I saw Dad and Weezie under the barn eaves by the sleek crimson flydino, thirty or forty yards away. Weezie was preparing to depart.

Dad's hair was white and full. He looked lively. Weezie was rubbing the flydino's neck and cooing to the beast. Dad was feeding him a bucket of chow. Had I really heard Loulou's voice a minute ago?

Amidst all my confusion, I was still trying to process the concept of my mother-in-law as a sexually active person. Mr. Roller had been dead for a few years. Old Weezie's features were pleasant enough, and she had a figure a little like Jane's—curvy hips and small breasts. She had the same red-yellow hair as Jane, although Weezie's was certainly biotweaked. She wore tight jeans and a red nurbskin jacket. And now Dad was holding her in his arms and kissing her goodbye. Faintly I heard Weezie's laugh.

And now Loulou was back, her voice directly behind me. "Zad! I'm here. But I'm—I'm in a tube."

I whirled and, impossibly, I glimpsed a flash of her mouth in mid-air.

"I'll wait for you downstairs," said the mouth. And then it disappeared, leaving only a lenslike warp, a swiftly moving dimple in space. And then that, too, was gone.

Stifling a yell, I darted my head this way and that, even going down on all fours to peer under the table.

Mom stared at me, her glass frozen in mid-air. "What's wrong with you!"

"You didn't hear a woman's voice, Mom? Like from a ghost?"

"I don't know. I wasn't paying attention. Too busy listening to Weezie Roller laughing. That whore."

"I heard Loulou Sass. I slept with her last night. She went to Gaven's, and then she was gone. She and Gaven—they left at the same time."

"Are you saying that you killed this Sass woman too?"

I pressed my hands against the sides of my head, frantically teeping for a touch of Loulou. Her aura had faced away—it seemed she had a way of hiding her teep from me. Would I find her floating mouth downstairs?

Teeping towards the basement, the only target I located was—a man in the rain, lurking outside the glass door to my downstairs bedroom. What? I tried to get a fix on who he was—but now he somehow hid himself from me too, compressing his personality into a tiny dark point. Maybe I'd been imagining him and Loulou both. Maybe I was losing my mind.

My only defense was a return to that same soothing cosmic/robotic pulse. I slowed my breath and savored the hissing sweep of the rain on the roof.

I looked at Mom. "If you didn't hear Loulou's voice, did you at least hear the loud knocking in the basement?"

"Oh, that's just my pottery kiln," said Mom. "Cooling off. I don't know if I told you that Petrus helped me move my pottery studio into your old room?"

"I noticed."

"We didn't like working in the barn, what with Lennox hanging around. He's gotten so rude." Mom seemed a little fuddled. She wasn't a heavy drinker, and the two glasses of wine had gone to her head. She pursed her lips and cocked her head, studying me. "Are you really involved with two murders?"

"*I didn't kill anyone!*" I shook my head and sighed. "It's been a wack day. I'll go downstairs and lie down. Use my wristphone to research some things on the web." In reality I was hoping I'd find Loulou down there. Moving slowly and deliberately, I walked back to the dining table and drained my glass.

"Wait and say hello to your father," urged Mom. "I won't

start a scene with him. I don't want to make you crack up completely, poor Zad."

The dino trumpeted once more. Reflexively I went to peer out the window again. At first I only saw Dad, walking towards the house alone, wearing a hooded yellow rain-slicker. But then the lightning flickered *zzzt-zzt-zzt*, and I glimpsed a great winged reptile strobing through the rain-spangled air. Weezie Roller was in a dome on the dino's back, the queen of the night.

Dad clomped inside.

"Zad! Great to see you. Making any art?" Despite Mom's warnings, Dad didn't seem especially drunk. But you could never be sure. In any case he was glad to see me.

"Not much painting these days," I said. "The shop's been eating up my time. And the nurbs. But today the Department of Genomics closed my place and—"

"Zad's charged with two murders!" interrupted Mom, sounding like she believed it. Everything was muddled here, everything a huge, emotional deal.

"Interesting career move," said Dad half-smiling—not taking Mom very seriously. "Do you need to lie low? I'd love to have you working in my studio again. I've lost my stamina. But, seriously, are you in trouble with the police? I have some friends I can call if—"

"You and your *friends*," said Mom, rising to her feet. "You and your slimy, sleazy Weezie Roller."

"You and your *tutor*," spat Dad. The two of them had accelerated from zero to sixty. Like a pair of boxers lunging from their corners for another round.

"Don't you talk about Petrus! He has nothing to do with—"

"At first I thought Petrus wasn't interested in Sally," boomed Dad, talking loud enough to drown Mom out. "I figured I was safe. But then I came up to the house early for lunch, and I saw Petrus in bed with my wife. The tutor earns his pay! I'm thinking I might do a painting of the two of them. Cast it as a classical allegory. *Juno and Ganymede*. I might be able to hang it at the—"

"*Get out*!" shrieked Mom. "*Out out out*! I can't stand you for another second!"

Dad paused, thought things over and made a decision. "It's mutual. I'll move into the barn and sleep in my studio. I'll grab a few things and go down there now."

"You're leaving me?" cried Mom, tacking against the changing wind.

Dad looked at me, holding out his hands to the side. "Yes, we're unhappy," he told me. He wasn't smiling anymore. "Yes, our marriage is over."

Too much. "Talk to you later," I told Dad. "I'm going downstairs, Mom."

Cosmic/robotic, cosmic/robotic, cosmic/robotic. I went down the carpeted stairs to my boyhood bedroom. Upstairs the parents argued a little more, but the force had gone out of it. I heard Dad's footsteps padding back and forth as he gathered his things. The front door slammed and he was gone. Mom's bedroom door slammed as well. I could hear her sobbing. I hoped I'd die before I got old.

My room had indeed become a pottery studio, with a smell of clay and slip. Two old-school kick wheels, a squat nurb kiln, shelves of bisque-fired and fully finished pots, tubs of clay, natural sponges, gray-stained potting tools, jars of glaze—and in the far corner, my old bed—with a dent on it like someone had lain there. I hoped Mom and Petrus hadn't been using it.

Jericho the nurb dog called my name from the bathroom, better than *oof*, but I messaged him to shut up. Silence again. The room was terribly dank and lonely. Why was I even here? It was way too early to go to sleep. I was fond of my parents and I was sorry for them, but the sooner I could get out of here the better. I found a little nurb heater and turned it on. And now, thank god, I picked up the faint scent of Loulou.

Someone rapped on my glass door again. The sound wasn't from a kiln cooling, it was from a thin guy standing there, peering at me through the rainwater running down the glass—just like I'd thought in the first place. He was a teeper, in fact he was—

"Joey Moon!" I whispered as I opened the door. "Don't

make noise."

Joey was soaked and shivering, dripping water on the floor. Teeping his vibes, I felt little hostility and no madness. He was back to his reckless hell-raiser artist self.

"I got all better at the clinic," said Joey. "They gave me a bath. And I fixed my teep. Then I broke a window and stole their roadhog. Loulou told me where all I'd find you."

"Loulou! Can you hear her voice now?

"No, qrude, what you talking about? I called Loulou via my wristphone around one o'clock. I was needing a place to hide. She was on her way to hit up Gaven Graber. Wanted to sell him something she stole. She said I should ditch the roadhog and lie low all afternoon. Then root you out at your Mom and Dad's."

"Funny she knew I'd end up here," I said.

"Loulou's spooky. She's like a spider in a web. Where's she at?"

"Gaven Graber died when Loulou went to visit him," I said. "And she disappeared."

"Loulou offed him?" asked Joey.

"I don't know."

"Did you make it with her last night?" demanded Joey, switching topics.

"You were locked up. I didn't think you'd be getting out."

"I'm back, qrude." Joey studied me, a touch of menace in his eyes. He had spiky colorless hair and a skinny head. A punk hillbilly artist. "And where's my rat brother? Skungy. My little twin."

"The cops impounded the rat. And they arrested *me* for killing Gaven Graber. I'm out on bail."

"Making it real," said Joey with a laugh. "Show you what it's like. You got any dry clothes?"

I found a worn sweatsuit in my old dresser. Once again Jericho grunted my name from the bathroom. I thought I'd closed that door, but it was open. Was Loulou actually down here? Why couldn't I see her? Spooky.

"Here," I said, handing Joey my sweats. He was more

muscular than I'd realized, with the body of a runner.

"So Gaven died," said Joey, draping his wet clothes on the kick wheels. "Big whoop. The man's got a stasis bed and a swarm of doctor ants. He'll be back. It's like trying to kill gophers. Always another Gaven."

"The police say the Department of Genomics wants to close down Slygro," I told him.

"Fine by me," said Joey. "Gaven messed me up with that qwet teep. I been stuck in a loop. Me teeping me teeping me teeping me—like a pair of funhouse mirrors. Last night, on the nod in that clinic, I turned the regress into a dot. Like perspective in a painting, qrude. A point at infinity. And then I was well. Ping! Crown me king."

I liked the sound of this, and I got into a brief teep merge with Joey. It felt like a quick series of dreams. I saw two goldfish swimming in a bowl, one red, one yellow, each leading, each following. The circling pair of fish shrank to a yellow jelly-egg spotted with red dots. I saw a ladder whose rungs came loose and tumbled down, one atop the other, playing a rising arpeggio. I saw Loulou. I saw a heart inside my heart.

"So you're qwet too," said Joey.

"Yeah. I'm learning to control it. I think of it as mastering the cosmic/robotic flip. You can do the merged-with-the-cosmos thing, or the robot-following-logical-details routine. And once you're qwet, you can control that particular shift. Because you have access to your brain's gee-haw-whimmy-diddle switch."

"Gaven's stupid-ass word," said Joey contemptuously. "For that alone, the man deserved to die. What a lamer. He's no kind of genius at all. He's a fuddydud biz man with the mind of a roach."

"It might be one of your magic mirrors that killed him," I said.

Joey shrugged. "Loulou said as how she might use it on him. I had it all set in our cottage on the farm. I'd fixed it so a fella sees himself as very very gumpy. An ugliness regress. The infinite ugly point."

"Technically, Gaven died of asphyxiation."

"But you and me know he was killed by a Joey Moon mirror," said Joey. "Too scared to breathe. I'm whompin' up some kick-ass art, qrude. Better than some feel-good scene of Ye Olde Louisville."

Obviously this was a slur on my work, and I was ready to argue about it. I enjoyed that kind of debate. Like a boxing match, or tennis.

"At least I sell my stuff," I snapped.

"*Used* to sell it," shot back Joey. "And now you live in your parents' basement. How qrude is that?"

"I don't live here," I said. "Jane threw me out, and today the DoG completely trashed my gallery. I'm sleeping here for, like, one night."

Before Joey could fire back, I heard Loulou's voice, very close again. Coming from my bed. Mom hadn't heard Loulou, but now Joey did. Old people missed a lot.

"Don't be so pushy, you stupid gub!" Loulou was yelling. "Get out!"

The covers on my bed twitched and we heard a thud, as from someone whacking something. A small green pig flew away from my bed, no bigger than a football, bucking and thrashing, going *gub-gub-gub-wheenk.* She had floppy triangular ears, and a snout that tapered to a point. Not really a pig at all. More like a tapir. Her legs were mere doughy bulges on her bottom. She bounced off the floor, caromed off the wall and found her way back to the bed, making some use of those rudimentary legs. And then, rebounding off my mattress, she disappeared into a dimple in space.

"Loulou!" called Joey.

"Hey Joey," said Loulou's voice, coming from the spot where the gub had disappeared. Her mouth was visible and one of her eyes. As if she were peeking at us through a tiny porthole. "Hi, Zad. You saw the little green gub just now? Good, good, good. So I'm not going nuts."

"You're in an invisible tube?" I shouted, not sure how loud to pitch my voice.

"I'm in a tunnel. It's so tight. I can't wriggle out to you

guys, and if I go further in, I can see these creepy dragonfly people at the other end."

"How—how'd you get in the tunnel?"

"The oddball swallowed me," said Loulou's mouth. Her lambent eye looked serious. "The oddball has a mind. She's a girl. And she has a tunnel insider her. The tunnel leads to another world. The people up there call it Fairyland. They're hillbillies who look like bugs."

"Wait, wait, wait," I said. "Back up for a second. That little mouth on the oddball swallowed you?" In a dreamy kind of way this made sense.

"The oddball is like the dirtbubble, right?" said Joey.

"Tell me about the dirtbubble," I asked.

"It's this brown ball what Gaven keeps on a pillow," said Joey. "Gaven's been measuring on it. Down in his lab. The dirtbubble showed up after I turned qwet. It's interested in me. It smells like shit and medicine."

"The dirtbubble looks like the oddball, yes," said Loulou. "But the oddball is nice shades of lavender instead of brown, and she has a much nicer vibe. And the oddball doesn't stink."

"So you saw them together?" I asked.

"In Gaven's hall. He had the dirtbubble with him, and I'd brought the oddball to sell him. The dirtbubble and the oddball didn't like each other, they were flying around chasing each other. Gaven and I started arguing, and the oddball scared the dirtbubble off. And then the oddball swallowed me. And then it smothered Gaven to death."

"I want this to be bullshit," said Joey. "A trick." He reached for the scrap of Loulou that hovered above my bed, but she darted to one side. I grabbed from that side, but to no avail. Loulou—or the oddball—was eluding us. And now she was peeping at us from a corner near the ceiling.

"I'm inside the oddball and halfway to the bugs' Fairyland," she reprised. "I *want* to come back to Earth, but I'm stuck. The oddball gets wider inside. She's bigger than you think. I already crawled through to look out the other end. It's not far. But I'm trying to get back to Earth, and the oddball is clamping down."

"And what about that gub?" I asked, totally at a loss.

"Two gubs are inside this tunnel, see. A green one and a spotted one. They crawl up on me, like they want to feel me all over. I hate them."

"What does it look like at the other end?" I probed.

"I see out of something like a giant clam," said Loulou. "With a big shell on the top and the bottom. The other end of the oddball is like a pearl sitting on the soft body of the clam, and I look out of a slit in the pearl. I can see two thin, leathery people sitting in chairs in a ballroom. They have wings like dragonflies. They're like insects. Their faces are brown and small, with weird big eyes. They act friendly. They talk real country. The first time I peeked through, they were, like, *Yee haw, shit howdy, welcome to Fairyland.* And then I scooted back. In case the bug people wanted to sting me."

"When I went all batshit this week, I saw talking bugs and toothless pigs," said Joey, keeping a straight face. "Yaar."

"Don't you make up lies to get in on my glory," said Loulou sternly. "This is *my* adventure, not yours, Joey Moon. And don't make fun of me either. You're the one who's crazy, not me."

"Tell us about the gubs," said Joey. "At least we done seen one of *them*."

"Two gubs inside this tunnel with me, yes," said Loulou. "Smearing all over me like begging dogs. One gub is all these woodland shades, and one is cream colored with tan spots like a cow. The pretty green one is a girl, and the other one is a boy. I'm not exactly sure how I can tell. The gubs have really strong teep, and something like a squidskin web link, but I don't understand their minds at all. Either they're really dumb or really smart."

"And when you peeked out the other end a second time, you could still see the dragonfly people?" I asked.

"*Oh*, yeah," said Loulou. "They're watching the oddball to see if I'll crawl out. They're buzzing their wings and clicking their mouths and being hicks. They act cozy and down-home, but maybe they want to sink their teeth into my musky flesh. I hate them. *And I hate gubs*!"

We heard a solid thud—like someone punting a ball—and here came the second gub. This one was spotted like Loulou had said. Piebald as a Gloucestershire pig, his skin a dirty white color with irregular brown patches. The spotted gub bounced off a pottery wheel, his little eyes glittering with—surprise? Amusement? He was drawing in deep inhalations of air, and squealing on his exhales. As on the green gub, the spotted gub's feet were rudimentary blobs. As soon as he came to rest, he began jumping up and down, trying to get back inside the oddball. I was picking up some thoughts from him, as if via the web, but the patterns were incomprehensibly strange.

"The oddball says she's moving this party to Zad's barn," said Loulou. "Meet me there in a minute, boys. You've *got* to help me crawl back out." The scrap of her face dwindled to a dimple, and the dimple drifted away, leaving the spotted gub on his own.

"What's going on?" called my mother, suddenly silhouetted at the head of the stairs. Her image wavered as the shrunken oddball flew past her and passed invisibly through the ceiling and, I supposed, out into the night. The spotted gub bounded up the stairs and launched itself on a hard, flat arc, shattering one of the living-room windows. Hot on the oddball's trail.

Mom cocked her head, waiting for an answer to her question. "Zad?"

"Nothing's going on here," I told her. Slight understatement. "I have a friend visiting. Joey Moon? He brought that, that hyper pig. He's the husband of that woman Loulou who disappeared."

"Should I call the police?" asked Mom. "Are there burglars?"

"God, no."

"Everything's real fine, Mrs. Plant," said Joey, stepping forward so Mom could see him from the top of the stairs.

"You shouldn't be down there. It's a sty. Would you like a drink, Joey? A snack?"

"Sure thing, ma'am," said Joey, already heading up the steps. "I could definitely use me a jolt." I followed along, and Jericho dogged my heels. He'd been hiding from the gubs in the bathtub

Mom had dried her eyes and composed her face. "I just had a terrible argument with Zad's father," she told Joey. "He's gone now. Help yourself to something. Whiskey, merrymilk, wine."

"I'm sorry about you and Dad," I told Mom.

"Maybe it's for the best," she said. "Who knows. Maybe he'll come crawling back. If I'll take him. No matter what happens, I'm keeping this house. And Petrus is *not* moving in. Enough is enough."

"Tell me about this here yellow dog," said Joey, looking to change the subject.

"I modded him out of nurb-gel," I bragged. "Maybe he's art."

"Ugly enough for that," said Joey.

"The dog is cute," said Mom. "But Joey's pig? He broke my window. Can you patch it, Zad?"

As I covered the broken-out pane with smart nurb cardboard, Joey was sipping at a glass of bourbon, scarfing down crackers and cheese, and looking at the pictures on the walls. "Old Lennox Plant ain't no slouch as an artist," he allowed. "Even if he do paint pictures of rich folks' houses."

Mom rolled her eyes at Joey's uncouthness. And she addressed her next remarks only to me. "I know it's silly to say this, Zad, but I'm a little worried about your father just now. Alone in his studio. Despairing over the collapse of our marriage."

"The man might string himself up like a country ham," suggested Joey. "I had an uncle who done that. Right in his smokehouse. They didn't find him for two weeks, and his skin, it were hard as wood. Uncle Tut. Served him up for Thanksgiving dinner—sliced so thin you could read the Bible through his meat."

"Don't listen to this guy," I told Mom. "He's a qrude freak."

"A fine artist," said Joey. "Like your man and your boy, Mrs. Plant. I'm like Jericho the wonder dog. What you might call esoteric."

Mom wasn't interested in anything Joey said. "Maybe you

should look in on your father," she told me again.

"I think so too," I said, seeing an exit opportunity. "Joey and I could sleep over there. With all the clay in my old room, it's not exactly—"

"Comfortable," said Mom. "Don't worry, I'm not jealous if you'd rather be with your father than with me. I'm perfectly all right on my own. A chipped old dish."

"We'll take off in the morning," I said, sidestepping that one. "And I'll say goodbye before we leave."

"And tell me everything Lennox said," added Mom.

"I can't be taking sides," I said. "It's up to you two."

"You should be on my side," said Mom. "Your father is completely in the wrong. Him and his cheesy Weezie."

"Weezie Roller?" said the irrepressible Joey. "That's rich."

"Sleazy, cheesy, floozy!" said Mom, glad for Joey's interest.

"We've gotta go," I said, and ushered Joey outside.

The rain had stopped. The moon and stars were crisp and bright on high. The air had that refreshing tingle you get after a storm. No wind. I could hear rushing streams. Jericho rocked along behind us, not exactly limping, but with a weird hitch in his gait. Maybe I'd overdone his asymmetry. A first draft.

"You grew up here?" said Joey.

"Yeah. And my dad has his studio in the barn. I was his apprentice after high school, you know. Until I switched to nurb-paint. Dad didn't want to make the change."

"I dig using nurbs for art," said Joey. "But they can be bombs or snails or mirrors or floaty bubbles. Why just paint forever? I've had hella many ideas since gettin' with the quantum wetware."

"Your mental regress points at infinity," I said. "I'd like to use one of those in an art nurb."

"Do what you gotta do. And give me a goddamn show."

"If I ever get my gallery back. Meanwhile we have to get Loulou out of the oddball."

"I don't understand where she's even supposed to be at," said Joey. "I keep thinking this is one of her head trips. Funky fantasies that she's teeping us. Her father was cold and uppity.

So he was like a leathery dragonfly with glittering eyes, yeah. And Loulou didn't dig her younger brother and sister. So they were like pesky little gubs who want too much attention. Being different is important to Loulou. It kind of figures that she'd say she's up an oddball's ass and halfway to—wherever."

"But I think we do have to admit she really *is* inside the oddball," I said. "That's why we only see a little bit of her face."

"Maybe."

We'd reached the barn. Dad was moving around in there, talking to himself, rehashing his argument with Mom, banging into furniture. For sure he was drunk now. No rush to go inside. For all I knew, Loulou might be as likely to find us out here.

"What if Loulou's so-called Fairyland is a hidden reality that parallels the mundane," I suggested. "The same furniture as our world, but with different creatures in it. Freaky, strange fairies with nothing sweet about them."

"Fairyland's just a word that Loulou claims she heard," said Joey, doubting everything.

I thought some more, trying to piece a story together. Thanks to being in cosmic mode, my emotions weren't all that involved. I was enjoying the play of cosmic logic. Loulou said the oddball was inside something like a big shell on the other end? What could I do with that?

"Suppose the oddball is like a tube from a parallel-world mollusk that's hovering above our space," I proposed. "The oddball tube is sucking up whatever it finds. Extracting sand fleas from the sand."

"You're scaring me, qrude," said Joey. My image had gotten to him. He threw back his head and hollered. "*Loulou!*"

"*Wheenk*," came a little voice from the dark. It was that same spotted gub who'd crashed out through the living-room window. He was broadcasting a series of off-kilter web glyphs, stuff like sheaves of curves and galleries of faces. And at the same time he was gazing into the air above us, rapt with attention. He was sensing something we didn't see—

"*Gub gub gubby*," said Loulou's voice, trying to sound both brave and perky. A patch of her face was visible again. Her lips were dark, her eye was bright. "Save your woman, boys. Those dragonfly people are yelling into the clamshell like they're calling a hog. I'm afraid they'll crawl into the other end of the oddball to come after me. And this end of the tunnel is still pinched tight. It's like the oddball is pursing her lips."

"Force your way out," advised Joey. "You need a jolt. How about you kick yourself in the butt? Like you kicked this here spotted gub."

"How would I bend my leg that far, you idiot?"

"You can do it," I said, getting into Joey's idea. "Cosmic mode yoga. Like Joey had when he put his foot onto his shoulder at the pond. Maybe just fold back your leg at the knee and let your heel kick you."

"Put your mind into your leg and let the leg think about a leg, and go into a leg regress," jabbered Joey. "Visualize a bull's eye on your sweet cheeks!"

"Wait." Loulou's face briefly disappeared and then it was back. "Those leathery people are actually crawling down the tunnel from Fairyland. Insect eyes and extra hands!" She disappeared again, leaving only a dimple in space, but we could hear her muffled voice. "*Get away*! *No!*"

I snatched up the spotted little Gloucestershire-pig thing at our feet and shoved him towards the puckered spot in space. "Swallow the gub instead of her," I yelled to the unseen dragonfly-people. I forced the plump little creature into the oddball's tunnel with Loulou.

"Kick!" yelled Joey to Loulou.

I heard a thump and an *eeek*, and here was Loulou, panting, flushed, her curly hair in disarray, her sly eyes bright. Our Fairyland fox. Her leg was still bent back; she straightened it out. My pet nurb dog Jericho backed off, his yellow quills bristling.

The oddball was hovering nearby, her size pulsing from a pinpoint to the size of a cantaloupe, glowing lavender, with that same conical mouth. The two gubs within the oddball let out a series of excited squeals, greeting each other, the squeals very modulated and intricate, almost like words. And, then, for a horrible instant, I seemed to see a leathery face come pushing out of the mouth. A bug-like head from Fairyland, complete with feathery antennae.

"Go away!" screamed Loulou, and blessedly the head withdrew. And now the oddball darted off on its own, heading who knows where. All was still. Just Loulou, Joey and me beneath the mundane moon. Loulou turned away from Joey and gave me a special hug.

"Workin' the crowd as per usual," said Joey, sounding jealous. "Who's it gonna be, Loulou? Zad Plant or me?"

"Don't be a bellowing moose," said Loulou quietly. "Don't butt and lock antlers."

"I'm teeping that Loulou *wants* us to fight," I murmured. All our emotions were on the surface.

"But she only wants a *little* fight," agreed Joey. "To show that we care"

"Maybe I'll keep both of you," said Loulou. "Two artists at my beck and call. Why not? I'll be your shared muse. Everything's going to be different now. Qwet teep will be a huge fad. And this oddball trip I took—wow! I'm so glad I'm back. Is it late at night?"

"Eight or nine," I said. "Why don't the three of us lie down and do some heavy teep, Loulou. So we can soak up the vibes of your adventure. Whatever it was. I never saw Jane's oddball act so lively before."

"She's changed," said Loulou. "As soon as I saw her in your apartment, I had the feeling she was watching. And waiting for—I don't know what set her off, really."

"Let's go into the barn for the night," I suggested. "Lots of couches and rugs in Dad's studio."

"Better than our tenant-farmer grown home on Gaven's farm," said Joey. "The cops are watching that place anyway. But tell us more about the oddball killing Gaven, Loulou. You sure it wasn't my picture what did it?"

"The mirror picture freaked him out, yes, but it was more complicated than that," said Loulou. "First of all, the dirtbubble was trying to eat the oddball as soon as I got there, but the oddball was too smooth and fast. Gaven was yelling he wasn't going to pay me unless I slowed the oddball down. I got mad at him, and I showed him the magic mirror—I'd brought it from our cottage just in case. And then Gaven's staggering back, and he's shouting that the dirtbubble is gonna eat me."

"He was asking for it," said Joey.

"Yeah. And he got it. But not quite yet. First of all the oddball banged into the dirtbubble really hard. Took a nip out of it, sent it squealing out the door. And then air started rushing into the oddball's mouth like water down a drain, and she swallowed me. Like a snake gulping down a mouse head-first."

"What then?" I asked, fascinated.

"Inside the tunnel I could see a dim yellow light from the walls. The oddball squeezed me up higher till I was in a round place where I had some room, like I said before. And down below me, back towards the mouth, I could hear Gaven having a big struggle. I heard his voice really clear—his head was inside the oddball now. But then the oddball was flexing on him, and he got quiet. The oddball suffocated him and she spit him out."

"You didn't go back down there and look out the oddball's mouth?" I asked, trying to figure out what I might tell the cops.

"I was too busy. Those two gubs inside the oddball would pop up out of nowhere and start touching me. And their thoughts are so drifty and strange. Anyway, like I was telling you before, instead of going back towards Earth, I crawled a little way further into the tunnel, where it got narrow again, and then my head popped out into another world from a giant clam, and I saw the two dragonfly people sitting in a ballroom, and they said it was Fairyland."

"Loulou's web of wonder," said Joey. "Stranger than truth? You decide."

"You should be more sympathetic," cried Loulou. "You wouldn't even care if I *did* get eaten by hillbilly dragonflies from another dimension."

"All I know is you've been scaring us half to death," said Joey. "Gaming us like rubes. Hiding behind bends in the air.

Throwing squiggly pigs."

"*You're* the pig," snapped Loulou. "Always mistrusting me. That oddball is magic, I tell you. A tunnel through higher space. Gaven had some other name for the oddball—I forget what. Geek gibberish."

I used my wristphone to comb through the web possibilities, and I started making suggestions. Finally I hit on a winner.

"An Einstein-Rosen bridge—what they call a wormhole?" I said. Loulou nodded, and I kept going. "Gaven might say the wormhole leads to—the Higgs plateau? Or he maybe he called it a brane?"

"A wormhole to another brane, yes," said Loulou. "That's what Gaven said. Two parallel worlds. And the oddball's tunnel runs in between. In a way I liked it inside the tunnel."

"You were screaming for help," pointed out Joey.

"Okay, I was scared, but it was loofy. It wasn't dark in there. It was like seeing through yellow stoner glasses. I just didn't like it when that green gub would glue her sticky little body to me and run her snout up my thigh. I had this weird feeling she was looking at my body's individual cells. Like a genemodder does."

"I surely do relish this happy horseshit," said Joey with a grin.

"Me too," I replied. We started laughing.

"Whoop it up, boys," said Loulou, riled by our glee. "I could have died! And now I'm hungry and beat. Let's go in the barn, yeah. And let's forget about Fairyland if you're going to be all sarcastic and ignorant."

"Jane's still going to want her oddball back," I said. "*Especially* if it's alive. Did you hear that Reba thinks the oddball and the dirtbubble are sex nurbs?"

"Sex is all Reba knows about," said Loulou dismissively. "Gaven said the dirtbubble is the first wave of some big attack. It's a tunnel too, and he's been talking to something at the other end. The dirtbubble voice is promising Gaven power and money."

"Money is all *Gaven* knows about," said Joey. "Maybe it

was my picture that made him stop breathing, but it didn't happen till his head was inside that tube?"

"Don't keep trying to hog the credit," said Loulou.

"It'll be a drag if Gaven rises from the dead," I said.

"I'm waving on this action," said Loulou. "We're on the far edge. Qwet teep, qrudes."

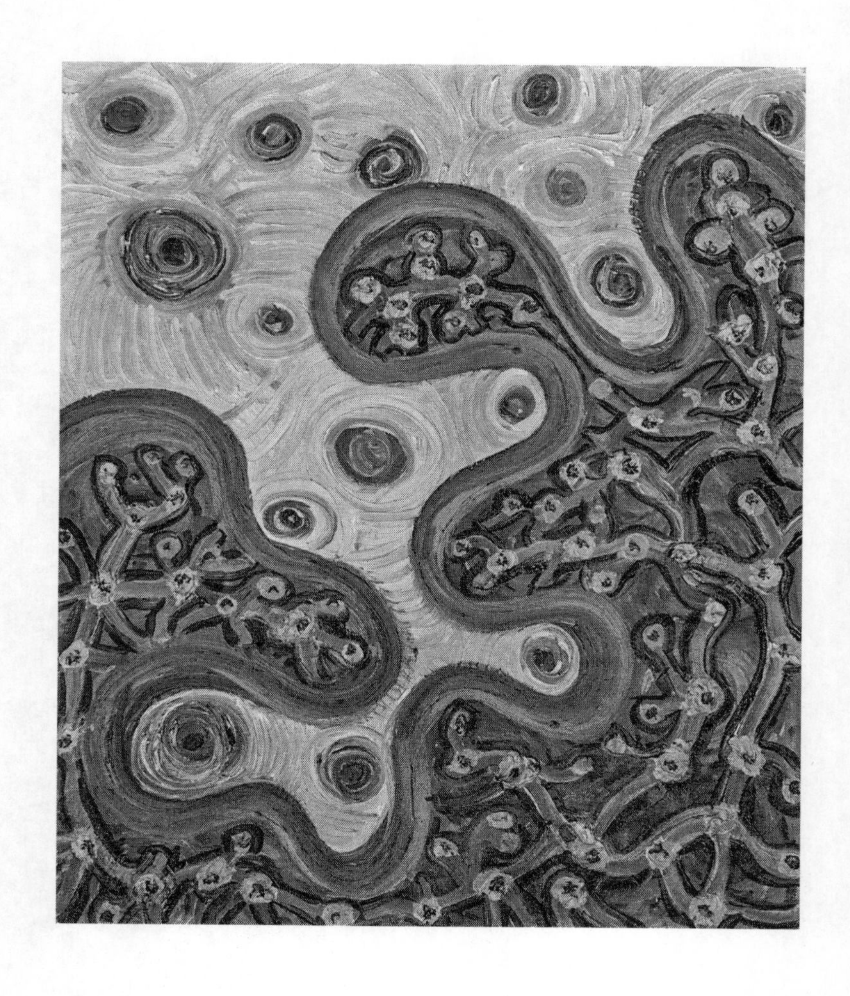

7: Flying Jellyfish

"Junko wants to set up a qwet teep commune," Joey told Loulou as we prepared to go into Dad's barn for the night.

"I know," said Loulou. "We're imagining an old-school psychedelic hippie scene? I guess you guys know that it's Jane's family's house that Junko wants. The Roller mansion. Junko was going to work on Jane tonight. Try and make Jane qwet."

"How come you always know so much?" I asked Loulou.

"Everyone trusts me and thinks I'm small," she said with a tart smile. "People don't realize what a sly-boots I am."

The thought of Loulou being a sly-boots zapped me with a pulse of lust. "The Roller mansion is in fact standing empty," I said, wanting to help. "Except for a bunch of nurbs gone wild. Mr. Roller's dead, and old Weezie moved into the gate house. The crap that lives in the big house was creeping her out."

"Jane's brother Kenny lives in a house balloon tied to the mansion's tower," put in Joey. "With his boyfriend Kristo. Kenny's a wild guy. I used to sell him axelerate buds."

"Like Kenny needs something to amp him up," I said. "Like he's not already a loon."

"Axelerate always cools *me* down," said Joey. "Helps me keep up with my head. Guys like Kenny and me—we're too smart for our own good."

"Too smart," echoed Loulou. "Sure you are, Joey. That's your big problem. Too smart for a job, especially. At least Zad here owns an art gallery. Another reason to keep him around."

"You're out of the news-loop on this one, babe," said Joey. "The Department of Genomics locked up Zad's store. He's a homeless bum. But he don't have no practice at it. He's signing on as my bum apprentice."

"My dad could talk to old Weezie Roller," I mused aloud. But I didn't feel all that good about this particular idea. It seemed disloyal to Mom. On the other hand, living in a commune of teepers in luxor Glenview—

"The wacker, the slacker!" said Joey.

"Means what?" I had to inquire.

"One of Joey's slogans," said Loulou. She put on a sarcastic documentary-narrator-type voice. "In saying this, the ascended master J. Moon meant that the more *frenzied* his surroundings became, the more *relaxed* he would feel himself to be. *The wacker, the slacker.* Words to live by." And now she switched back to her jaded wife mode. "But Joey, yesterday was wack—and you were so far from slack that they hauled you to the clinic and misted you with nod pods."

"Shut your crack."

"So witty, my husband," said Loulou. "Such a gentleman."

"Let's talk to Dad," I suggested.

We went in through the stable where the roadspiders were resting. Jericho came in too. At my command, he curled up on the floor. Dad's studio occupied most of the barn, a lively space with couches and a day-bed, fine carpets spotted with paint, hanging plants, a long bar, a gallery's worth of unsold paintings, a couple of heavy-duty easels with works in progress, and the air fragrant with oil paint. Dad lay face-down on a rumpled day-bed, out cold. I laid a tartan-plaid blanket over him.

Joey, Loulou and I chatted a bit more, still feeling out the possible contours of our three-way relationship. And then we bedded down for the night—Joey and Loulou on couches, and me with some blankets on the floor. Loulou gave each of us a warm good-night kiss. Joey took this in stride. Right now, my main interest was in sinking deep into the cosmic state and spending the night merged with Loulou's mind. Cosmic merge wasn't as good without sex—but even so it was brand new.

We had a wonderful night of teep there—Loulou, Joey and me. It lasted nearly twelve hours. As usual, the teep was oblivious, meaning I couldn't have reliably told anyone what I'd experienced. But I awoke feeling good, and very fond of my two teep partners.

My newly gained mental images of Loulou's experiences with the oddball were surely incorrect in detail, but perhaps they were accurate in vibe. In addition, the long teep session had given me an intuitive understanding of Joey's regresses and of his points at infinity. I had a feeling I could turn Joey's ideas into powerful creative tools. I wanted to try this soon—before my inspirations faded into fog.

Looking around the room, I saw that Joey had made his way to Loulou's couch. Lucky bastard. The two of them were a soft, warm, sleeping lump. A married couple.

Sensing that I was awake, Jericho padded over and hopped onto my stomach. I studied him, purring some fresh mods onto his genes and refreshing his form. A little more red in his spots. A saddle-shaped patch on his back. His legs less ungainly. A nice upward curve into his tail. Floppier ears. A dignified grizzle of white on his snout. Stretch out his body a bit.

Maybe I really could switch from being a painter to being a nurb modder. But at this point it was still like I was only putting makeup on Jericho. For true art, I'd need to dig deeper.

My thoughts wandered back to Loulou. I felt wary of her. She'd gamed me rough yesterday—stealing my roadspider and Jane's oddball. And then that whole drama about Fairyland—could it possibly be true? Be that as it may, I was intoxicated by my two nights of teep with her. I could accept sharing her with Joey, if that's what it took. A second mule in Loulou's stall.

It might seem odd that my primary thoughts were of such mundane and sensual things, what with so many serious problems in play. Day before yesterday I'd become a qwettie, and I still needed to sort out what that meant. Yesterday the oddball had swallowed Loulou and had shown her a tunnel to another world. Gaven Graber was lying dead in a stasis hammock, and I'd been charged with killing him. The cops were planning to harass me until they found out what qwet teep was all about. But, as high as I felt this morning, I was focused on the upsides.

My friends and I were telepathic. We could flip into cosmic ecstasy whenever we liked. We could biomod nurbs with our minds. I just needed to straighten out my sex life with Loulou. And, eventually, to work things out with Jane.

The thing was, I already knew that my affair with Loulou

would be short. She was a rocket ride, a jump off a cliff, an explosion in the sky. Not to mention being very manipulative. And married. I was happy she'd turned up during this footloose interval when I was separated from Jane—but even while I was chasing after Loulou I knew Jane was the haven to whom I longed to return.

I wondered if Junko had met with Jane last night, and if she'd gotten Jane to go qwet.

My eyes wandered past my father's paintings to the blanketed hump of the man himself. I visualized a medieval hill city, with Dad a sleeping giant beneath the hill. A mythic archetype. In some measure my father and I were the same. I spiraled into a vision of me inside Dad inside me inside Dad inside me. And then, Joey-Moon-style, I let the snaky regress swallow its tail and become a wheel, rolling to the horizon and dwindling to a painter's point at infinity.

A loofy head trip. This was the kind of thing I should be using for, uh, *something*. But what? Maybe a way to make Dad qwet—without using Junko's qwetter gun, or spitting on Dad or, god forbid, having sex with him. I wanted something loofy and fun.

Drawing on skills I hadn't consciously known I had, I used cosmic logic to kindle a jive-ass quantum wetware mind-matter routine within my lungs. I tensed my chest, minting macromolecules, enriching my breath with a mist of qwet dots.

Walking to Dad's bed, I leaned over him—and breathed into his face. He snorted, twitched, awoke, and stared at me, startled.

"What's up, Zaddy," he said, just like in the old days. He sat up slowly, carefully, expecting a hangover—but I could teep that he was feeling good. Better than he'd felt in a long time.

"You made him qwet!" exclaimed Loulou from across the room, sitting up disheveled on her couch, breasts bare. "All by yourself. You're a wizard, Zad. Hi, Mr. Plant. Can you feel my mind?"

"Sweet bird of youth," said Dad, in a wondering tone. "Thank you."

"Can you get us into the Roller mansion?" asked Joey,

slipping into his daily routine of asking for stuff. "We want to live there. We want to bring in a whole crew."

"*You want*," echoed Dad, teeping Joey's vibes and not much liking them. He got up and looked out the window, his worldly eyes taking things in. It was sunny again, the wet grass green, and the trees mostly bare, with red and yellow leaves on the ground. Dad edged himself into cosmic mode and stood there with his fingers slightly twitching, as if he were holding a brush.

A minute later he was in robotic mode, and ready to chat. I told him about the mental switch and about the cosmic mode and about oblivious teep. Joey and Loulou began chiming in. We four got a nice vibe going—a mix of Loulou's gestures, my tangled feelings, Joey's jagged vibes, and Dad's disengaged bemusement. His lucid paintings were in the mix as well.

"I like telepathy," said Dad. "And—you know—that cosmic mode makes for a good high. That's a selling point."

"Not *selling*," said Loulou. "Qwet's going out for free. Junko Shimano's gonna be giving it away before anyone even knows. Junko invented qwet, you know. And she's gonna ask Jane Roller if she's okay with making her family's mansion into our base. Like Joey said."

"I don't see you and Jane as friends," Dad told Loulou. He gave me a look, as if amused to see me embroiled in woman problems like him. "But maybe we four can take a ride over there. See what Weezie Roller says. There's been some talk about me moving in with her. I suppose your qrude new pals don't have roadspiders, Zad? That's okay. We've got a couple of extras; they have webs in the trees. Eating squirrels and birds."

Saying goodbye to Mom wasn't as complicated as I'd expected. While we four were mounting our roadspiders, Mom came outside to see what was up. I told her something like the truth. And I offered to make her be qwet like Dad.

"Would Lennox and I get along better then?" she asked.

"Maybe," I said. "That would still up to the two of you. I do think qwet is going to help me as an artist. When I get some time."

"Peace and quiet," said Mom. "What an artist needs. Not

a lot of wild running around. But I'll think about the qwet, okay?" She had clay on her hands, and she was wearing her dusty potting clothes. She looked quite beautiful.

While Mom and I talked, Dad sat off to the side on his roadspider, wearing an expression of disengaged penitence, his eyes focused on the beyond. He'd already picked up on my trick of using cosmic mode to space out when hassles loomed.

"Fat drunken old fool," Mom called to Dad as she went back inside.

We rode off, with Jericho pumping out some of his *oof* barks before following in our wake.

Junko Shimano met up with us on the way to the Roller mansion, riding her own roadspider and dressed in messy exercise clothes. She'd had supper with Jane last night. The bad news was that she hadn't converted Jane to being a qwettie. The good news was that, as far as Jane was concerned, it was okay if a limited number of us camped out in the family mansion. But we'd have to talk to mother Weezie and to brother Kenny. If they okayed it, Jane might eventually come over with her new beau Whit Heyburn and check out the scene.

"*Beau*?" I challenged. "Has Jane gone crazy?"

"She did say beau," confirmed Junko, enjoying the gossip. "Whit was taking Jane out after I had supper with her. She was already dressed. Amazing outfit. They were planning an all-night party at, uh, Kegel Kugel? And then maybe back to Whit's place for breakfast. I think he lives in Glenview too. Jane says she and Whit are working on a business deal."

"*Kegel Kugel?*" I had a brief sense of being the odd man out in a game of musical chairs. "That's the luxor party club in that black ball on top of the Clark bridge. You have to be rich to get in there. Or be a high-end hooker. Jane shouldn't go to Kegel Kugel at all. Not with Whit! He's vicious to the core!"

"Maybe Jane's desperate to get your attention," said Junko. "Maybe this was a deliberate provocation."

"Or...maybe it's *Whit* that wants Zad's attention," put in Joey.

I didn't return the banter. I was worried sick. Being a

fuddydud. But now Loulou flashed me a laughing smile and I felt better. Footloose, right? Before long, Dad, Loulou, Joey, Junko and I were riding up the curving nurb grass avenue that led into Glenview from River Road. The land rose from the river into gullies and knobby hills. Atop a crest on the right was the immense, half-timbered mansion of the Carnarvon family. On the left was none other than the Heyburn family's neo-classical, columned mansion. It was a full-size replica of Thomas Jefferson's Monticello.

If Jane was getting close to Whit, she might very well be at the Heyburns' right now. Whit lived there with his servants; he'd moved his parents into a senior home downtown. Yes, I had a feeling that Jane was looking out one of those windows.

The walled Roller estate loomed ahead of us, fenced all around, and with a solidly built brick gate house—Weezie Roller's domicile. The all-but-deserted main building was modeled on a Norman castle. It had immensely high battlements of sparkling gray limestone, and the walls were pierced by diamond-paned windows and corniced slits. Decorative turrets sprang from each turning; a substantial master tower crowned them all. Besotted by old movies, Jane's grandfather had redesigned the place in the 2020s.

As we passed Weezie's gate house and approached the limestone castle, our roadspiders grew skittish. A giant nurb jellyfish was hovering above the mansion, tethered to the pointed peak of the highest tower. The iridescent medusa was what we called a house balloon—with well-appointed rooms on her lower level, hydrogen-filled bladders on her upper level, and dangling tentacles below. A braid of her tentacles was fastened to the tower.

"Kenny's place," said Joey. "She's called Laputa."

"I know all about her," I said. "Kenny had Jane and me over for dinner a few months back, along with Whit Heyburn and Reba Ranchtree. Kenny and his boyfriend Kristo. Kenny got wasted and tried to push me out through a porthole. I don't know how Kristo puts up with him."

"I've seen Kenny from afar," interposed Loulou. "He's

handsome. That counts for a lot. If you're an *ugly* jerk—forget it. But *good-looking* jerks are romantic and damned."

"Intriguing bohemians," Dad said to Joey and me. "Eh, boys? I guess you'd call yourself an artist too, Joey? I know about those exploding paint-nurbs you made. Redecorate your home in one go. I got paid to restore a parlor where you'd ruined one of my murals. Interesting colors in your bomb—I turned one of your splotches into a butterfly. Here, I'll message the color to you." Dad was enjoying our outing, and happy to be qwet.

A rock thudded into the ground beside us, then another and another. Our roadspiders made herky-jerky evasive moves. Joey lost his seat and fell to the ground. The seeming rocks uncurled to become many-legged gray scuttlers—overgrown versions of those woodlice or pillbugs that you find in rotting leaves. They were staring at us with bright eyes—analyzing our images and searching out info. Jericho nosed at them uncomprehendingly. A hundred meters above us, a maniac laughed.

"I hate you, Kenny!" screamed Joey, shaking his fist.

"Come on up!" called Kenny. His head was a small dot in one of the flying jellyfish's portholes. "Brunch time! Bloody Marys! Zad the loser, broken-down Mr. Plant, crazy Joey Moon, slutty Loulou Sass and—Junko the geek!" A kind word for everyone.

Turning to Loulou and me, Junko tensely asked, "How can that creep instantly decree that I'm a geek?"

Loulou fielded this one. "Maybe it's that your hair's all lank and it's in a high folded-over pony-tail and you're wearing a gray sweatsuit with no bra. Any Louisvillian can see you're not a Collegiate School girl."

"I hate it when people call me a geek," said Junko. "I'm going to get even with Kenny for that."

We parked Jericho and our roadspiders in the stable beside the mansion. Dad walked back down the hill to visit with Weezie in the gate house. And I led the others up the manor steps. I glanced over towards the Heyburn estate again, but I couldn't see the elegant brick mansion from here. Stop obsessing, Zad.

The nurb lock on the Rollers' old oaken doors recognized me as a member of the extended family, and it let us come in.

In my boyhood the castle's interior had been pure old-school—walnut wainscoting, ornate glass panels, dangling brass lamps, Spanish tiles, parquet wood floors, and oriental carpets. Over the years Mr. Roller had added a mad hodgepodge of nurb upgrades. Given that he'd expanded his business from producing nurb chow to marketing the nurbs themselves, he had access to the latest and greatest. Over wife Weezie and daughter Jane's objections, Mr. Roller had evolved the mansion's interior into a bizarre and bustling nurb habitat. Son Kenny had been all for it.

Right in the front hall, Mr. Roller's favorite nurb armchair had recently given birth to a litter of four-footed baby chairs. Normally, nurbs couldn't reproduce, but Mr. Roller had removed the crippleware sterility codes from this one particular chair. He liked giving copies of it to his friends, and by now there were twenty or thirty of them loose in the house. The baby chairs scampered away from us, their woody legs pattering on the yielding flesh of the front parlor's nurb rug. A nurb chandelier thrust a pair of brassy stalks around a corner, peering at us with dim eyebulbs.

At the far end of the hall lay a mound of busted-open Roller nurb chow bags, and beyond that was the mansion's enormous ballroom. I surmised that Kenny and Kristo—or their helper nurbs—were hauling in food to keep the mansion's menagerie alive.

I saw a hungry nurb teapot on the mound of chow, grubbing with its spout. A bendy grandfather clock used its pendulum like a tongue. The newborn leather chairs were rooting into the food, as were their older siblings, not to mention a clutch of slithery rugs. A fat couch bellied up beside them, with a toothy mouth beneath its plump arm. A pair of table lamps fluttered above the lode, their shades pulsating against the air.

Kenny's pillbug nurbs had followed us inside, and now they scooted past us towards the chow. Their excessively numerous feet made an unpleasant skritching sound on the floor.

"Like jungle animals at a watering hole," observed Junko. "See the tendrils running down from the ceiling. It's all covered with nurby growth up there. Colored fungus?"

"Old Weezie hated it when Mr. Roller installed that stuff," I recalled. "He'd always wanted a fancy coffered ceiling like in the lobby of the Brown Hotel downtown. A 1920s movie theater look, you wave, with embossed squares and polychrome flowers and cartouche scenes of dancing nymphs. So he got some hairball in the United Mutations lab to design a nurb lichen that was supposed to emulate all that. But it's not even close."

"Totally fubar," said Joey, his head thrown back. "The shapes are layered like in the motion trails you see when you're good and high. Like solid scribbles. More inspiration, huh, Zad?"

"I'm feeling those rank colors," said Loulou. "They hurt my sinuses almost. For sure I'd wear a dress of that."

"Mrs. Roller got worried that spores were drifting down from the ceiling and poisoning her food," I said. "That's when she moved down to the gate house. A year after that, Mr. Roller died of cancer. Jane said he had some sick growths on his back. Like daffodils and shamrocks."

"Don't want that!" said perky Junko. "A standard way to retrofit this place might be to get some firepigs and flame out the nurbs. Only—a place this infested, the building might burn down." Junko paused, looking around. "Plan B could be to make all these guys qwet—and then do some teep-based biomodding on them, if they'll hold still."

"The nurbs might rebel once they're qwet," I warned, looking around the freaky house. "Skungy the rat is qwet, for instance, and he's known to bite people. Poor Skungy. I wonder if he's still with the cops."

"Plan C would be to set loose some cannibal nurbs to eat the excess nurbs," continued Junko. "Banzai beetles and degenerated sea cucumbers."

"Why not we use our bad-ass qwet rats for the clean up?" said Joey. "I like the rats better than—what was that you just said, Junko? Stink cucumbers and bung beetles?"

"Rare species," said Junko with a half smile. "High-priced. The qwet rats could be fine."

"There's a buttload of my rat brothers in stasis on Gaven's farm," said Joey.

"You know about them, huh?" said Junko. "Gaven was warehousing them. Okay, let's activate the rats and sic them on these scurvy nurbs. Safer than going bananas with my qwetter. Even though—down the line, I predict that every living thing will be qwet. A better world. My goal."

"Did you build yourself a simplified qwetter like you said?" asked Loulou.

"It's in my dyke geek sweatsuit pocket here," said Junko. "I bummed our old design down to ten parts and then I replaced it with a biomodded yam—just like I said I'd do."

"I can make a nurb qwet with my spit," said Loulou proudly.

"I can do it with my breath," I bragged.

"But before we get into all this I want to go up to that flying jellyfish," said Junko. "We'll confront Mr. Judgmental Male Gaze. Speak truth to power. I'll qwet Kenny and his jellyfish house both. Put them in teep contact. I'm betting the big jelly has some grudges against Kenny boy. We'll watch the show."

"Once Cap'n Junk here is done with Kenny he'll be glad to let us live in the family manse," said Joey.

Leaving Kenny's feeding pillbugs behind, we ascended the first flight of stairs. The second floor had held the bedrooms, and was now a dimly lit jungle of wiry bedspring vines, with hairbrushes and hankies flitting through the tangled thickets like wild birds. Rabbity pillows foraged in the undergrowth; fat beds lolled like cows. Three tattered humanoid figures were crawling about, their expressions fixed in vegetal leers.

"Sex nurbs," I explained. "Weezie and Mr. Roller were into them for awhile— before people knew about the sex nurb diseases. They kept these three on, partly as a joke, and partly because Kenny liked watching the sex nurbs do it with each other."

"Eew," said Junko. "I never grasped that you heartlanders

could be so stark. I'll definitely clear out this floor. The qwet rats can gnaw most of it down. Turn it into squeaks. And we'll eliminate those sex puppets, for sure."

"They're lurching towards us like pervy zombies," said Loulou. "I wonder if they're good at what they do."

"I'm better," said Joey.

We clattered up the next flight of stairs. In pre-nurb days the third floor had held Jane's and Kenny's play rooms. A couple of Jane's talking toys wandered over to us—a monkey banging cymbals while he sang, and a high-voiced rhinoceros doll. I'd seen these two before, and they knew my name. They made me miss Jane. Her voice, her gait, her bouncing mop of hair. I walked to the window, but the Heyburn house was still out of view.

Two rival flocks of nurb vegetables interrupted my reverie—it was carrots versus beets up here. In the old days, Weezie had kept a kitchen garden going on this floor, using a drip system and big troughs of dirt. She claimed the light was better on the third floor—woodsy Glenview was shady.

Today the carrots were speeding about like hyperactive inchworms, and the beets ricocheted off the walls. They were vying to press the most foliage to the sunny windows—when they weren't rooting in their wet dirt.

Fungal puffballs slid in the wake of the animated vegetables, buffing the wooden floors. A long-legged feather-duster stalked about, cleaning root-grit off the nurb chairs and tables. And a platoon of tiny flying dinosaurs were ferrying in nurb chow, carrying the nuggets in their beaks.

"I like this floor just like it is," enthused Joey. "It's stone cold perfect."

"What if you wait here and guard our rear," suggested Junko. "Just in case something goes wrong with Kenny and the flying jellyfish."

"Fine by me," agreed Joey. "I'll try and call Skungy and Sissa. See if they've broke out. And don't you go sneakin' off with Loulou, Zad."

A spiral staircase led to the tower room—a round chamber

a few yards in diameter, and fully jammed with the writhing, slimy, translucent tentacles of Laputa the hovering house jelly. Her tendrils were feeding on yet another stash of Roller nurb chow. Several of the strands displayed eyestalks. Laputa was observing us. She had a rudimentary intelligence—but nothing like the intelligence she'd have if we managed to make her qwet.

"Hop on," blubbered a slit mouth in the side of a thick tentacle. "Free ride." The tentacle was festooned with sling seats like bights of rope.

"It's fine," I told the others. "I've been up here before." Not letting ourselves think about it too much, Loulou, Junko and I hopped aboard.

As if on a carnival ride, we were drawn out through a large, open window. The tentacle released its hold on the tower and we swung across the slate roof and into the void. As the tentacle began shortening itself, the castle walls dwindled beneath us in a queasy-making perspective view.

Now I could see Whit Heyburn's home. My eyes hopped from window to window and—there! A blur of white and a touch of gold. Jane looking out! My poor captive wife. It was up to me to free her. Unless, of course, she was perfectly content after an exciting night of play. Was that really her? Hard to tell. Was she qwet yet? I reached out with my teep, and I seemed to feel her lively vibe, but I hesitated to attempt a teep merge. I could have called her on my wristphone of course—but then I'd just be the prying, jealous husband. Bide your time, Zad.

Back and forth we bobbed, oscillating ever more rapidly as we continued to rise. Loulou was moaning. And then—*plurp*—we'd been pulled into a chamber of the giant floating nurb. A comfortably furnished parlor.

"*Willkommen ins Quallenhaus*," said Kenny. "Velcome to jellyfish house."

Kenny was doing the accent because his boyfriend Kristo was German. Kristo had come to Louisville as a consultant regarding some Bayer AG chemical engineering processes that the Roller nurb chow plant used, routines involving krill oil and whey solids. Jane and I had laughed about the concept of krill oil when we first heard of it. Suddenly it was hard to go for more than a minute without thinking of Jane. Her date with Whit was definitely getting to me.

The floating house's parlor had a bar, a horn-of-plenty nurb, and big windows, with shiny, jiggly furniture growing from the floor. We made introductions all around, and Kenny offered us food and drinks. He and Kristo were well into a pitcher of Bloody Marys, with merrymilk toddies and a couple of axelerate buds on offer as well.

The day was warm and pleasant. Great view up here—the elegantly proportioned Heyburn house clearly in sight, sunlight dancing on the Ohio River, the autumn leaves bright beneath the skeletal trees. A fresh breeze wafted in, dissipating the jellyfish's faint smell of the sea. Laputa was bobbing, but not too much—her tentacles were springy enough to damp the vibe.

Kristo and Kenny wore matching iridescent nurbskin suits, one yellow, one green, very tight on their chests and thighs. Both of them were incredibly fit—they had muscle-sculpting nurb leeches living beneath their skins, an experimental release that Kristo had brought from the overseas Bayer labs. Kenny had tried to infest me with the sculptor leeches the last time I'd been here. I'd yelled at him, and that's when he'd tried to shove me out the window. We'd never liked each other much, but never mind, we were in-laws.

"So here's the deal," Loulou was explaining. "We want to set up a qwettie commune in your mansion, Kenny. Nothing's in there now but skungy nurbs."

"You've seen the two love-making nurbs?" asked Kristo. His voice was clear, with little accent, even though his phrasing was odd. "I adore these fellows. So hale and grim."

"We'll be burning them," said Junko. "After our qwet rats kill them." She was acting fairly aggressive. "It's about making this place livable again. Takes a firm touch to clean up a toxic nurb bloom. I'm a retrofitter with a Stanford Ph.D. you understand. And I *invented* qwet."

"That gives you the right to destroy my past?" challenged

Kenny. "To hell with that. And what's all this bullshit that everyone's talking about *qwet*?"

Junko reached into her pocket, itching to zap the obnox Kenny with her qwetter. Loulou waved her back. "Zad can do it," she told Junko. "Watch."

I used a cosmic logic routine to start up some nanoassemblers in my lungs. Like I'd done for Dad. I held my breath, filling my chest with a quantum-charged haze. I grabbed Kenny, hugging him like I wanted to kiss him on the cheek—and breathed my qwetting molecules into his face. Quantum weirdness percolated down into the man's cells.

"I feel you, Zad," said Kenny after the briefest of transitions. His voice was mild and kind. "It's like I've never noticed you were human," he added. "Sorry, man." I myself was feeling some reciprocal empathy towards Kenny. Me at one with the ghastly Kenny Roller! Qwet teep.

"What are you making to happen?" Kristo asked me. He was puzzled, backing away, balling his fists.

"Making you," said Junko. By now she'd drawn out her qwetter—the new version resembled a toy gun that a kid might improvise from a crooked potato or, more accurately, from a bent yam. "My turn." With theatrical flourishes, she fanned her free hand back and forth across a wart on the yam's rear—like a sheriff shooting up a saloon. Not only Kristo, but the entire floating jellyfish became qwet.

"I thank you," said a resonant voice from the room's walls. The jellyfish sounded like a woman with mucus in her throat. "Help me more, Junko. Make me smarter than these ungrateful men. Teep me a copy of your mind."

"Like that's a small thing?" said Junko, shaking her head in wonder. "Casual reincarnation. Why not." She raised her two hands in an ecclesiastical gesture of blessing. "You'll be me, yea, as the Skungy rats are like unto Joey. And I saw that it was good. Lo, a flying jellyfish is become alter ego."

"I well feel Junko's wings of thought," said Kristo. He put his arm around Kenny's shoulders. "And I well feel your mind, my beautiful man. We'll make good fun with our qwet, is not?"

Kristo and Kenny stared into each other's eyes, immersing themselves in a glow of shared teep, temporarily blind to the rest of us.

"I'm like Junko Shimano, yes!" boomed Laputa the jellyfish. "A nurbware engineer. I'm hacking myself free of the United Mutations sterility constraints. I'm fecund! Here we go! Launching larvae!"

Flup, flup—two chunks tore loose from the walls and reshaped themselves into flat wriggly shapes like oval kites. Furiously undulating, the pair writhed off across the mansions and hills of Glenview, crossing the Ohio River, heading for Indiana.

Flup, flup, flup—three more pieces came free—not from the walls, but from the floor beneath our feet. They left really big holes, two meters long and a meter across. Further *flups* were sounding from every part of the jellyfish, frenetic as hail on a roof. Flying jellyfish larvae wheeled about us on every side, some of them the size of surfboards.

"Someone get us out of here!" hollered Loulou, dancing sideways across the sieve-like floor.

"Listen to me, Laputa!" ordered Junko. "Lower us to the ground!"

"You save yourself," said the jellyfish. "I'm multiplying. My fine Junko Shimano mind is in every flying larva. With my old low memories as well. I'm immortal! I want to explode this old body before I lose my precious gas. I'll make a fireball to erase the stink of Kenny Roller."

"Even nurbs hate the guy," I said with a wild, unkind laugh. I'd dropped my sympathy-inducing teep with Kenny. I was throwing all my mental energy into finding the best way out of this rapidly escalating fiasco. If I could catch hold of a dangling tentacle—

"Stand aside!" yelled Kenny, snapping out of the reverie he'd been sharing with Kristo. He shoved past me, climbed out a window and began sliding down a tentacle—just as I'd been imagining. Maybe he'd plucked the plan from my mind.

But the tactic proved not to be a good one—at least not for

Kenny. Laputa the jellyfish hadn't liked Kenny to begin with and now, with her personality enhanced by a copy of Junko's mind, she liked Kenny even less.

"Surprise!" burbled the giant jellyfish, and pinched off the tentacle that Kenny was shinnying down. The poor guy was still at least fifty feet above the ground. So now he'd fall to his death.

Even though I felt weary and disgusted at the thought of aiding Kenny, I did the qwet and empathetic thing. I leapt out of the open window, timing my jump so that I landed flat on the back of one of those flappy jellyfish larvae. Like a comic-book superhero, I steered my flying surfboard down—and scooped the flailing Kenny from the air. I angled off to one side to set Kenny on the ground, then rocketed upwards to save Loulou.

Turned out I didn't need to rescue Loulou. By the time I reached the level of the now-ragged jellyfish, Loulou and Junko were riding larval flying surfboards too, with the bewildered Kristo sharing Junko's board. Junko landed Kristo on the ground beside Kenny. And then as if on a sudden whim, Junko's flying surfboard burrowed one of its ends into the ground, taking root.

Joey was still watching us from the third floor window. For the moment I had the merry, pink-cheeked Loulou to myself. For a lark, we flew skywards together, circling each other in a joyous double helix, fully into the cosmic mode. Drawn in by our vibes, the other flying jellyfish larvae circled us, making piping noises that may have been laughter.

Higher and higher we climbed, up into the cooling air, seeing the sweet Kentucky countryside of Skylight, the gray sprawl of old Louisville, and the gracefully bent Ohio River. The Roller and Heyburn mansions were far, far beneath us. And for the moment I stopped worrying about Jane.

By now the mother jellyfish consisted of little more than her translucent hydrogen bladders and a dangling net of punched-out flesh. Her voice rose faintly.

"Kenneee!" Her vibe was stern. Qwet or not, she had no mercy for my brother-in-law. Feeling a premonition of what was to come, Kenny was already running across the castle's rolling lawn.

Wobbling and farting, the tattered flying jellyfish dropped her elevation to fifteen feet and stayed right above Kenny, dogging his steps. Pale blue sparks danced along the fringes of her scalloped remains.

I had little desire to play the superhero again, but I teeped a strong emotive warning to Kenny. He signaled back that he knew what was coming—and that he could take care of himself. Wanting to be in on this, Loulou and I swept downward, landing at the corner of the Roller mansion.

With a poot and a pounce, the jellyfish ruptured her hydrogen bladder and ignited the gas with her sparking halo. The explosion was anticlimactic—little more than a pop and a sizzle. A puffball of fire enveloped Kenny, but it was weak and watery. The flames scattered upward into the heated air. Kenny was down.

Our group ran across the lawn, converging on the blackened patch of grass where Kenny lay on his stomach. Small flaming scraps of jellyfish flesh lay scattered to every side. But by the time we reached Kenny, he was back on his feet, hollering defiant curses, shaking out the kinks in his arms and legs, throwing back his head and whooping.

"You're a god, Kenny," said the admiring Kristo.

"I used my qwet," jabbered Kenny. "I jacked into my cells and they shrugged off the flames."

"And yet you resemble an overcooked pretzel," marveled Kristo.

Indeed, Kenny's hair and eyebrows had been singed away, his clothes had been vaporized, and his skin was black with soot. But he had no actual burns.

Junko pushed up to Kenny and delivered her punch line: "This is what happens when you call me a geek," she said. "Get it?"

Kenny laughed. Thanks to our qwet, whatever happened felt basically okay. "I lost some good stuff with that floating house," Kenny said. "Like my axelerate buds."

"Don't you get it yet?" said Junko. "With qwet you can stay in cosmic mode until you're as high as you'd ever want to be. Or, if you're good at plant empathy, qwet might help you steer a regular prickly pear cactus into turning Tunisian—so it pops out some of those axelerate buds. But that's enough about grubby druggie schemes."

"I can't believe that big jellyfish killed herself," I said. "Just for a silly grudge."

"None of you understands anything," said Junko.

"Doctor Shimano's on her high horse," said Joey, laughing. "Our Stanford prof."

Junko waved her hand for silence and continued her info dump. "The jellyfish larva that's rooted in the ground over there? It's in polyp mode. Do you know the jellyfish's life cycle? No? The larva becomes a branching polyp like a wiggly tree. New jellyfish bud off from the polyp's chubby branches. If one of those new baby jellyfish gets enough chow, she can grow big in a few days."

"Where's the immortality?" I said.

"Every one of those jellyfish will have the old jellyfish's mind patterns," said Loulou. "Not to mention the patterns that Junko copied onto Laputa right before she went wild."

"Free house jellies and free axelerate," said Joey. "I'm liking this real good. You're gonna back us a hundred percent, right, Kenny?"

"Maybe," said Kenny with a frown. "But if all these new jellyfish are like their bitch of a mother, they'll hate me too. What have I ever done? It's not fair. To hell with jellyfish. Kristo and I will move back into the mansion. If you qrudes can really clean up. I'll take the third floor—it's more or less livable already. I'm going up there for a shower right now." Kenny ran his hands over his stubbly head. "Do I look like hell, Kristo?"

"Good hell," said Kristo. Arm in arm, the lovers headed for the castle.

"You're okay, Zad?" said Dad, coming around the corner with Weezie Roller at his side. "We heard a pop?"

"Kenny!" wailed Weezie, catching sight of her son.

"I'll be fine," said the crispy, sooty Kenny. "Let's have all these qwet freaks live here for awhile, okay Mom?"

"I'm one of them now," said Weezie, smiling at us all. "I'm qwet too." She definitely had the cosmic glow. I could feel a merge settling onto us. "We're going to annoy my snotty neighbors like never before," added Weezie with a silvery laugh. "The crusty Carnarvons and the hyena Heyburns."

"You'll have our entire commune on your side," said Junko.

"Does *commune* mean orgies?" said Weezie, all mock innocence.

"No!" I cried, aghast at the prospect.

Dad burst into laughter. Why was I playing the fuddydud?

"Orgies are halal with me," drawled Joey. "Zad, you hide out in the tower and paint, if you get all prudish. But I do agree those skungy old sex nurbs oughta go."

"No need for things like that anymore," said Weezie, her smile approaching the trillion-watt level. "What with hot young qrudes like Joey and Loulou in our scene. Not to mention the legendary Lennox Plant." She smooched a kiss onto Dad's cheek.

"Reba and Carlo will be coming too," said Junko. "I could go for some Reba. I like that languid Southern thing. Creamy white skin, ladylike, no muscles—*mmmm*. But, truth be told, I'm more of a mind-merge girl than an orgy dog. Demure like Zad."

Weezie gazed at me, her smile drying up and cracking. She'd never really thought I was good enough to be Jane's husband—and now I was picking up the vibe that she didn't think I was good enough to be my father's son. Whatever I did, I was in her way.

"Why aren't you with Janie, Zad? You're letting that horrible Whit Heyburn have free rein. Hop on your roadspider and—"

"Let's talk about us cleaning up the mansion," interrupted Junko.

"I'm teeping for my qwet rats right now," said Joey. "I'm the pied piper, qrude. I can think a weensy-whiny note so high that can't nobody pick up on it but my ratty bros." Silently he opened his mouth all the way, tensing his neck muscles, showing his yellow, uneven teeth. I couldn't hear any sound in my head, but Loulou did.

"Don't *do* that," she said, wincing. "It's like a horrible parasitic worm tunneling through my brain from ear to ear."

A nurb pelican coasted down to the lawn a few minutes later, a delivery bird, too small to carry a person, but with a biggish bill. And riding on his back were Skungy and Sissa.

"Hey, Joey!" squeaked Skungy as the delivery pelican landed. "Heard your call just now. Yo, Zad!"

"You done broke free of them cops?" Joey asked Skungy.

"I made a mental stink that stunned them. They unlocked the doors. In a fog. Couldn't see me at all. And I never bit nobody." Skungy twitched his nose, showing off his yellow teeth.

"Then what?" I asked.

"Little Sissa found me in the alley behind the cop shop. My baby rat who you sold to Whit Heyburn. She cruised down to my alley on this here bird."

"I broke out of the United Mutations lab the hard way," bragged Sissa. "A killer frenzy. A rampage. I'm tough, yeah."

"Did you bite Whit Heyburn?" I asked, not quite sure if wanted to hear a yes or a no. "Is that blood on your fur?"

"Naw," said Sissa with a squeal of laughter. "It's poo. I stank my way out, just like pa. Reeked them folks real good. Someone opened my cage. I gnawed into Whit's office. He weren't there. He'd gone off for a date with Zad's wife." Sissa twitched her whiskers provokingly and now Skungy laughed as well. A grating series of chirps.

"So where'd you get the nurb pelican?" asked Joey.

"Being as how I was in Whit's office, I used his desk to order me up a delivery bird. I saved pa. And by the time you called for us, Joey, we'd fetched the big litter from Gaven's farm, and was homing on you anyhow."

The parcel pelican opened his bill and out scrambled—*whoah*—a dozen qwet rats, squeaking, scritching, scrabbling.

"What's this?" cried Dad, getting confused. "What's this?"

He didn't like rats. They scurried around the Rollers' lawn, looking for things to eat. They worried the charred scraps of jellyfish, sniffed out spilled crumbs of nurb chow—and then they found the shed where the chow supply was stored. In moments they'd chewed through the door and swarmed inside. A symphony of squeaks.

"Rabid rats," said Junko. "They were in stasis on Gaven's farm, right?"

"Yeah," said Joey. "I knew that, so Skungy knew it too. All these rats are me. And ready to clean the castle. Talk about your process art!"

"I don't know about having filthy vermin in my home," said Weezie.

"Think of them as fairytale maids and coachmen," said Junko. "Like in *Cinderella*. They'll polish your palace from the lowest cellar to the highest aerie." She put some heavy teep behind her words, passing her vision to Weezie. "All that dead crud on the ceilings—gnawed away by tonight. No more vines on the second floor. Those pushy beets and the carrots on the third floor? The three creepy sex nurbs? Gone. We'll do the job this afternoon. Then we'll stage a big dinner to celebrate, and the qwet rats will put on a show. I'm sure they're full of song. Right, Joey?"

"Sounds like fun," allowed Weezie. "Kenny can build a fire in the fireplace, once the rats clean the chimney. We'll all be high on our qwet. And drunk on the wine-cellar. And then—*oooh la la*. Orgy time! If not today, then maybe on Tuesday. A big party."

I repressed a groan. Weezie frowned at me—once again wishing me out of the picture. But then she chattered on.

"Lennox, let's go down to the gate house and plan! You can wear my husband's gray silk tuxedo. And I have some darling outfits to model for you. We'll be the lord and lady of the manor. And, Junko, I want to reserve the front bedroom on the second floor for Lennox and me!"

8: *Funhouse*

Thanks to our budding scene, people all over the world would be qwet in a couple of days. And then Louisville would be hit with a plague of ravenous wormholes—all of them connected to a monster up in Fairyland, a thing that we'd learn to call a myoor.

But never mind that for now. At the start, everything was good. We called the Roller mansion the Funhouse. The cast of characters included me, Joey and Loulou, Junko, Dad and Weezie, Carlo and Reba, plus Kenny and Kristo.

We were pretty much high all the time. Life in the Funhouse had the feeling of a joyful waking dream—a three-day dream that seemed to last for weeks.

On Sunday, our first day there, the fourteen qwet rats helped clean out the house, although we humans did quite a bit of work as well. To help with the lifting, I had Craig Gurky send over two mover golems—none other than Gustav and Bonk. In order to improve communications, we qwetted the two golems right away. They didn't mind—in fact they decided to hang around the Funhouse for a few more days, whether or not Craig wanted them home.

The rats gnawed loose the vines and the crap on the ceiling. We pushed the stuff into a heap. Gustav and Bonk hauled it outside, along with a lot of extra crap. The rats were in a kind of cannibal frenzy—they were gnawing on the nurb fragments in the mound. It was kind of disturbing to watch, like a medieval Black Plague scene, especially with those three tattered humanoid sex nurbs on the heap.

There seemed to be no limit to how much the rats could eat, even though they didn't seem to get much larger in size. They moved and thought faster, I guess, or radiated off the extra energy in ear-splitting squeaks. And of course they crapped a lot. Weezie kept complaining about the rats, but naturally Joey insisted the qwet rodents were great guys.

Sunday night, Skungy was the only rat inside the Funhouse with us. Sissa was outside keeping an eye on the two dozen newcomer rats. I let my elegantly crooked nurb dog Jericho come in, also the mover golems Gustav and Bonk.

"Speaking as nurb, I don't think you did good job on dog Jericho," Bonk told me. We were standing in the kitchen.

"Bullshit," I said. "I remodded him this morning. He's crooked on purpose."

"You say," put in Gustav. "Takes practice to get right touch. Nurbs very refined."

"I'm the real biomodder around here," said Loulou. "I could give you more lessons, Zad."

"Sure," I said. Infatuated with Loulou as I was, all her ideas seemed fine.

"But we can do that later," said Loulou. We followed the others to the enormous ballroom at the rear of the house, where everyone was running and sliding across the shiny parquet floor, happy as kids.

Eventually Joey and Carlo banged their heads together, and then sliding didn't seem like as much fun, so we all settled down in the cleaned-up living room. The Roller mansion looked great, like a millionaire's hunting lodge, with fine wooden furniture, leather couches and lush, living rugs—as good as it had been when I was boy. I wished Jane were here with us, although I didn't *quite* want to call her just now. For one thing I still hadn't found her oddball. And for another, well…

Loulou was being very flirtatious, sitting on a soft couch between Joey and me. From the emotions I was teeping, I knew that we three would be having group sex tonight. No doubt about it. I was excited at the prospect—and anxious.

I'd come close to sharing Reba with Carlo after high school, but we'd never closed that deal, at least not that any of us could remember. I was uneasy about getting in bed with a naked man. Homophobia was still quite real in Louisville, at least for some of us.

But this time, with all three of us qwet, I felt I could get past my qualms. Turning my teep on Joey, I noticed that, for his part, he was having jealousy problems. The two of us shared an uneasy smile—and an emotive feeling that Loulou was worth it. Yes, yes, we'd rise above.

The whole gang was sitting around drinking and nodding out, getting deep into cosmic mode. We had a big fire in the hearth—Kristo had done the work for that. Kenny had been busy on the third floor tricking out his new space. Jericho lay near the hearth, and Skungy lolled on the fake dog's back, as cosmic as the rest of us, quite the beloved pet. Even Weezie was starting to think the qwet rat was cute.

We were hungry by now. Weezie had gotten bags and bags of live food delivered from a nurb food supplier on River Road. But nobody had the energy to lay out a formal meal on the baronial dining table in the next room.

"I'll show you some real biomodding," said Loulou, about to make her way to the freshly stocked kitchen.

"Don't put spit on everything," said Junko, and handed Loulou her qwetter yam.

So Loulou qwetted and biomodded the food. The thing about nurb food, it was still alive right up until you chewed it up, like fruit is. But even a nurb loaf of bread or roast chicken was alive. It stayed fresher that way. And you could keep biomodding it up until the last minute.

Loulou's concept this time was to jolt the foods into walking around the living room and offering themselves to us. Dad got wind of the plan and went into the kitchen to work with Loulou, regaling her with a description of an old Flemish painting that showed an imagined scene of endless free eats—it was *The Land of Cockaigne* by Peter Bruegel. Dad had a nice clear image of the painting in his head, old-school painter that he was.

So—following Dad and master Bruegel, Loulou set a roasted shoat to wandering around the living room with a knife tucked into a flap of skin on his back. The young pig's butt was a tasty country ham, nicely cured. The pig was trailed by a scarecrow figure with limbs made of skinny loaves of bread.

When you broke off a chunk, a new chunk grew in its place. A couple of helium-filled roast chickens flew around the room, flapping their crisp wings, and pausing if you wanted to tear off a leg or a chunk of white meat. Baked yams and apples did choreographed routines on pointy little feet.

For dessert, Loulou set a nurb prickly-pear cactus to growing from the floor. Its lobed pads were in fact thick pancakes dusted with confectioner's sugar. Beside the cactus, some living pots of orange marmalade and blackberry jam stood at the ready with spoons in their hands. The pots watched us with bright beady eyes.

The common room echoed with cheers for Loulou's craft. She bowed and grinned, her eyes like happy slits.

"Teach us your trick about breathing out qwetter molecules," Kenny said to me when the meal was done. "The move you used on me in the jellyfish."

So I explained my routine. Wanting to stay in the spotlight, Loulou held forth on her techniques of making things qwet by sharing bodily fluids. And of course Junko insisted on messaging the full gene sequence for qwetter yam to those of us that hadn't already seen it.

"I can go all of you one better," said Joey, after quietly thinking it over for a minute. "I can qwet people and nurbs and animals just by thinking at 'em. Watch those chairs peeking in at us from the side of the door."

Indeed, four of the baby armchairs had been lurking in the shadows of the dining room, peering in at our doings, giggling at the thought that some day humans might be sitting on them. All day they'd been scampering away from us like shy fawns. But now, in the face of Joey's basilisk gaze, they trooped into the living room and let us pet them. Their little backs were sleek and soft; their flexible legs were nimble. Via qwet teep, Joey coaxed the four chairs into doing acrobatics for us—balancing in a column, nesting together in a ball, tossing one of their number back and forth. And then, chortling in merriment, the chairs went to hide behind the dinner table again.

"What you do is make a thought pattern like a loop of ribbon with a quantum twist," said Joey, broadcasting a copy of his design. "Half the time it's a plain ring, and half the time it's a Mobius strip. Call it the *Joey twistor*. It's hypnotic, man. You can't get it out of your mind—even if you're a nurb or, hell, even if you're a frikkin' ant. If you ain't weird yet—Joey's twistor is gonna do you."

I could see the twistor in my mind's eye, and it was indeed enthralling. Like a skeleton picture of a cube that keeps flipping perspective—but the twistor wasn't a cube, it was a ring. Or, no, wait, it was a Mobius strip. Either / Or / And. Loaded with a heavy vibe of quantum weirdness. I could feel the twistor crawling down into my cells and checking things out. Like a night watchman rattling doors. Making sure I was fully qwet.

"How do you zap someone with your twistor if they're not qwet yet?" I asked. "It's not like you can send it by teep."

"Everyone has glints of teep," said Joey. "Remember that regular people are flickering between robotic and cosmic mode at a rate of, say, twenty-four frames per second. Like a movie. You focus your mind's eye on your victim, key on their vibes, pick the right instant, and zap the elixir in on them real hard. Just a taste. One touch of the twistor and — *Today you will be with me in paradise.*" Joey was so Kentuckified weird that he liked to drop Bible verses into his conversation.

"I love this," exclaimed Weezie Roller, admiring the Joey twistor she had in her head. "And it even works on nurbs? Let me have a go. Abracadabra!"

She pointed at a silky nurb pillow on the floor. The pillow was an oversized peony flower. As soon as the pillow turned qwet, she gave a twitch, plumped up—and scrunched two of her spotted petals so they looked like sneaky eyes. A big fold in her middle took on the look of a laughing, toothless mouth.

"Oof," said Weezie. "It felt funny to do that."

"Good hack," Junko said to Joey. "I'll post a web tutorial for any of you who's interested in the physics underlying Joey's twistor." No takers on this offer. We were cosmic. We didn't want to learn. We wanted to play.

Dad qwetted the living nurb clock on the mantelpiece, and

set it to chiming a melody from Bach. Reba shaped a nurb blanket into a boa constrictor snake.

"We enter this new age of do it oneself," said Kristo.

"Wacky nurbs," said Joey. "Where it's at. Don't even need to get high no more. Let your grown home get high instead."

"Let's do an animal," said Dad.

A housefly was buzzing around the room, happy to be out of the coming winter. Fixing the fly with a wizardly eye, Carlo zapped him with a Joey twistor, then teeped into his insect mind. Softly buzzing, Carlo lay on the floor, lying on his stomach with his head raised and his eyes closed. The fly perched on the mantelpiece and began grooming himself, rubbing his forelegs together. Precisely in synch, Carlo entwined his extended forearms.

"Find female," muttered Carlo. "Make larvae." He swept his arms behind his back. "Get Reeeba. *Buzzz.*"

The fly did some loops and rolls, then spiraled down to land on Reba's cheek. Without any conscious thought at all, Reba swatted the thing. The fly fell stunned to the stone hearth beside Jericho.

"*Zzzt!*" went Carlo. He rolled onto his back and quivered his arms and legs—the very image of a damaged insect fighting for his life.

Joey leaned over the hearthstone, examining the fly. "Looky here! He's imitating *Carlo*." Sensing trouble, Jericho and Skungy backed away.

The fly had risen onto his pitifully thin rear legs. Awkwardly balancing himself, he waved his forelimbs and made a grainy buzz that sounded for all the world like—a high, horrible Carlo voice.

"*Save me! Save me!*"

"That's more than enough," said Reba, and stomped the fly flat.

Carlo screamed, went limp. Reba was quite unable to wake him. She burst into tears.

"Sweets," suggested Weezie, piqued by the lively goings-on. "Flies love sweets."

Reba took a spoonful of preserves from the dancing jam pots and dribbled it across Carlo's lips.

"*Spawn*!" cried Carlo, leaping to his feet. Hard to say how much of his routine had been a put-on. Reba let out a chase-me scream and ran upstairs, with Carlo at her heels, buzzing even louder than before.

The upstairs was big enough that we had separate rooms. Kenny and Kristo were hogging the third floor and the tower. Dad and Weezie took the front corner room on the second floor, with Carlo and Reba in the room next to that, and hopeful Junko in a tiny maid's room next to them. Joey, Loulou and I were in a double bedroom along the house's rear side. Our bed was a plump nurb; we'd tweaked it to be larger than king size. My dog Jericho slept in our room as well.

The light rays from our nurb candles gave the room a warm glow. But Joey and I were still uncomfortable about sharing a bed. Loulou had an idea.

"Run a headtrip so you don't see each other," she suggested. "Self-hypnosis. Then Joey won't be jealous, and Zad won't worry about turning queer."

No point trying to appeal Loulou's judgments—after all, she was reading our minds.

The invisibility illusion took a minute to get right, but it wasn't that hard. It was like the way you can ignore the mesh when you're looking through a screen, or ignore the pink blur of your nose that's always at the edge of your visual field. Seen through my eyes, Joey Moon was a pink blur too. Conversely, I was hidden from Joey by a smooth mental warp of his own construction.

Mr. Modesty and Mr. Shy. Two unseen incubi ravishing lady Loulou. She laughed and moaned. Another night to remember. But maybe not such a pleasant memory.

Somehow Loulou was beginning to get on my nerves. Too tough for me, maybe, or too hip, or too grasping.

Monday morning, we three drifted down to the spacious kitchen for food. Carlo, Reba, and Junko were already there. Kenny and Kristo were still asleep, and Weezie and Dad were just coming downstairs too. The kitchen had captain's chairs, a big round table, a couple of couches, and glass doors opening onto the lawn.

There wasn't any sense that we had something special to accomplish this morning. Never mind the police, and let Junko worry about distributing qwet. Everything would take care of itself in due time. We were cosmic.

As it happened, old Weezie Roller had used the web to listen in when Loulou was telling Joey and me about imagining each other to be invisible. And she'd teeped into our emotions when we'd gotten down to our sex. Whatever. Once you and your friends are telepathic, your old notions of privacy drift away.

Anyway, the point is that Weezie had always been very self-conscious about the shape of her chin. And, having heard Loulou talk about invisibility, she'd formed the idea of bio-modding one of her nurb scarves so that its front side displayed images of the room behind it. And she'd wrapped this "cloak of invisibility" around her neck.

"How we doing, gang?" sang Weezie, bouncing into the kitchen with Dad. She was jazzed about having so many houseguests.

Everything was fine, if I could let it be that way. I could see bright blue sky out the kitchen windows, and there were shiny baby house jellies bumbling about in the limbs of the trees. Everything was perfect in every detail.

"What happened to you?" Carlo was asking Weezie. "You're head's floating two inches above your shoulders, Mrs. Roller. Like someone guillotined you."

"Oh, damn," said Weezie. Her hair swayed as she tried to look down at herself. And then she gave up and removed the scarf, returning to full visibility, soft chin and all. She glared at Dad. "Don't you look at me in the morning? Why does a woman even bother about her makeup and her outfits?"

"I, uh, did notice you're wearing pink," said Dad. "Seems like you could notice your invisible neck on your own."

"I don't like the mirror in the morning," said Weezie. "I figured I was perfect now—with one of my ugly parts edited out."

"None of you is ugly," said Dad, finally hitting his stride.

"Atta boy," said Weezie. "Let me at the coffee plant." Maybe Weezie wasn't so bad. Just another human, after all, a human looking for love. It was hard to hate someone if you kept teeping their emotions. Now Weezie's eyes happened to meet mine. I could tell she still didn't like me. Oh well.

"If I seem distracted, it's because of what happened in the middle of the night," Dad announced. "I had a vision."

"Tell all," said Reba, comfortable on a kitchen couch with a plate of ham and eggs, Carlo at her side.

"I heard thumping," said Dad. "Like something bouncing up and down beside our bed. Weezie was fast asleep. I sat up, and I saw a ball hanging in midair. Transcendent, crystalline, charged with numinous energy. And—"

"Jane's oddball!" I put in. "It swallowed Loulou for awhile at Gaven's. And it suffocated Gaven to death. I haven't even told you about all that. Anyway, the oddball followed us to your studio, Dad. And then she must have tracked us to the Funhouse."

"You're talking about the shiny thing Jane found in the woods last year?" said Dad. "Yes, of course. That's the thing I saw last night. I was wondering why it seemed familiar. But it's turned very lively."

"The oddball is a tunnel to another world," said Loulou. "I saw dragonfly people over there who watch us. They call their world Fairyland."

"I sensed something along those lines," said Dad. "Very peculiar. For a minute there, I thought I was dying. Higher world and all. I thought maybe I was talking to angels. But with hillbilly accents."

"What did they say to you?" I asked Dad.

"Hard to be sure," said Dad. "They were like a man and a woman. But kind of—stupid? I got tired of them, and then I began trying to perceive what's between our two worlds. I was seeing it as a living void, dark with light. Like the spaces between my thoughts."

"I'm feelin' this!" said Carlo with a whoop. "It's so good to be qwet. I was *never* this ripped at breakfast before."

Upstairs something was bouncing. But none of us was in a mood to go up there and look.

"When I'm ready, the oddball will come for me too," I said.

"So you're ready to see Fairyland?" said Loulou.

I'm ready to call Jane, I thought, but I kept that to myself.

The moment's freaky energy dissipated when my still rather awkward dog Jericho came gyrating into the kitchen. He poked my thigh with his snout, begging for chow.

"You still don't have that poor nurb's legs right," said Loulou while I fed Jericho. "Not that I like to nag."

"Hell you don't," I snapped.

"*Rrrrowr*!" she said.

"I'm not a photorealistic guy," I told Loulou. "Okay? If you're so smart, why don't you and I have a nurb crafting contest?"

"We'd need equal amounts of nurb-gel to work with," said Loulou, liking the idea of a showdown. "So the contest is fair."

"Here," I said. I focused on Jericho and biomodded him in such a way that he fissioned in two. I added two new dog legs to the rear of his front half, and turned his back half into a cartoon version of an oversized lobster—with big claws and long, waving antennae. "You take the lobster, Loulou."

"*Oof*," said Jericho's front half. He was unsteady on his new feet. You had to feel a little sorry for this misbegotten mutt.

"We'll do this like a Levolver match," said Loulou. "Set a target animal, and we both work for ten minutes. Making a series of biomods and refreshing our critters' bodies as we go along."

"Fine," I said. Somehow I was more and more impatient with Loulou. "I've already made a godly dog and a blobby lobster," I continued. "So let's shoot for something new."

"Make two cute little whales," proposed Weezie.

"How will the whales get around?" I asked.

"That's for *us* to figure out," said Loulou. "Ready, set, go!"

"Down boy!" I told Jericho, and turned the poor dog into a

lump, but leaving his woebegone personality intact. Carefully sculpting his genes, I tapered Jericho into a cone, forking his thin end into flukes. I had a solid mental image of my target whale. Cute and spunky, with a white belly and a blue back.

From the corner of my eye, I saw Loulou's lobster take on the form of a garden slug. "A default Levolver start-up shape," she said. "I won't be imposing top-down shapes at all, Zad. They'll be emerging from bottom up morphogenetic processes. Ontogeny recapitulates phylogeny."

"Gooble gobble," said Joey. "One of us!"

"Do you ever think it might be evil to biomod nurbs?" asked Reba. "Anti-life? Against nature?"

"Nothing evil about cute little pet whales," chided Weezie. "You youngsters are such goody-goodies."

I kept on revising my nurb, paying particular attention to the curve of the new Jericho's back and to the shape of his flukes. I was totally cosmic and quite high. If I made Jericho's underside slippery enough, he could beat his flukes and slide himself around. Special rough spots on his belly would help steer him left and right. A jet-like blow-hole on top could set him to bouncing like a basketball if he pulsed the puffs right. His long, wriggly, lipless mouth could do the work of hands. Yes, yes, this was going to work.

Meanwhile, Loulou was evolving her own nurb, modding and refreshing at a rapid pace. Her blob changed from a slug to a snake, then thickened into a lizard. The feet morphed into claws, then back into fins. The tail turned into feathers that fused together and became a meaty stub that slowly broadened and curved into, oh joy, whale flukes. Loulou's nurb chirped, chittered, growled and boomed—as if giving a real-time commentary on its progress.

"Time's up!" called Weezie, enjoying the show.

"Jericho the toy whale!" I said. He rocked back onto his flukes, waggled his side flippers, bent his long mouth into a winning smile—then fell over on his side and struggled to roll back onto his tummy.

"Presenting the miniature Norwegian *hval* of Loulou Sass!"

declaimed Loulou. Her rather thin whale was lying flat on his belly. “Pet him,” Loulou urged us. I ran my hand across the hval. The nurb had lovely, realistic skin—sandpapery to the touch. His eyes were spritely and alert, and when he smiled, the inside of his mouth was a convincing shade of pink.

“Can he move?” asked Weezie.

“He can fly!” said Loulou, triumphant. A wriggling twitch traveled along the length of the little whale’s body, ending in a beat of his subtly muscled flukes. The hval rose into the air, buoyed, I suppose, by an internal bladder of hydrogen—similar to the ones that the jellyfish houses used.

Loulou was ready to claim her victory—but now Junko intervened. “Smell that?” she said, cocking her head. “Immune system failure.”

“Oh hell,” said Loulou dejectedly. “I put in too many frills.” Coldly I repressed my sympathy for her. Everything Loulou did was annoying to me today.

Her floating hval began to buck and flutter. His body’s internal tensions were destroying his metabolism. The mephitic stench of death filled the room. The dying hval flopped to the floor.

“Open a door to the garden, someone,” said Weezie. “And, Zad, your whale is very cute.” She favored me with a rare smile. “Who says you’re useless?” *Thanks, Weezie.*

“Want legs,” said Jericho hoarsely. “Want to stand.”

I tweaked his form once more, and now Jericho was a walking whale.

“The classic fish-with-legs archetype,” said Dad. “Very fine. It’s good that the legs look human. Gets deeper into your head.”

“*Ong*,” said Jericho, his bark gone watery, his mouth comically big.

“So let’s reset Loulou’s smelly hval,” said Junko, staring at the skinny, dead whale. “No sense wasting the nurb-gel.” One touch from Junko’s keen mind, and the wad of gel was as sparkling and pleasant-smelling as before.

“And now *I’ll* sculpt something,” continued Junko. “It’ll only take a second. A surprise for Reba.” She gave Reba a lingering glance, scooped up the glob of gel and slipped out of the room.

"Look out, Carlo boy," said Joey. "You got competition!"

A moment later, a new form appeared in the kitchen door, with smiling Junko walking behind it. The new shape was a—blanket? A waist-high blue blanket, balancing on her lower edge—surely the blanket was a "she"—with a stylized happy-face drawing on her front surface. The drawing was an *anime*-style caricature of Junko. The blanket had a shiny satin edge. A crib blanket. Before we could properly react to her, the blanket did a bellyflop onto the floor and humped rapidly towards Reba.

"What *is* this?" cried Reba, pulling up her feet.

The blanket was fast. Reaching the kitchen couch, she reared up, mounted the cushions, flowed across Carlo's lap and plastered herself against her target. Reba's lap.

Unexpectedly, Reba released a luxurious sigh and leaned back. Carlo clawed at the insistent blanket, trying to pull her off his partner, but his fingers slid through the nurb's shiny edges as if through water.

Reba was slumped against the couch's arm, quite overcome—as if by cozy nostalgia. And Junko stood to one side, smirking like a proud puppeteer.

"My blankie," murmured Reba, holding the shiny border of the thing against her cheek. "My little-girl baby blankie is back. So cozy. Thank you, Junko, thank you for teeping my deep emotions. Tell blankie to cover me, yes. Wrap me tight. I haven't felt this good in years."

The outré scene lasted for a minute or two, with the rest of us watching in silence—like bewildered peasants and shepherds around a crèche.

"I think Junko can start sleeping in bed with us," Reba told Carlo, breaking the silence. "If she brings blankie."

"But—" began Carlo.

"Oh, you can let me into bed with you and her," said Junko. "You big bristly man. I won't bother you. I just want to be warm. Part of the human tribe."

That afternoon Lief Larson phoned me on my wristphone. And that ended my fantasy that I didn't have to worry about the police.

"So your rat Skungy ran off and he's with you at the Roller mansion," said Lief, his face hovering before my eyes. "Why didn't you file a report?"

"I, uh, I was going to. Yes, Skungy's here. He's hard to control."

"That's a problem with the qwet nurbs," said Lief. "Slygro is too small a company to handle them. The Department of Genomics wants to give United Mutations an exclusive license for anything pertaining to qwet. You'll be helping our cause if you can provide negative testimony regarding Slygro and your friend Junko Shimano."

"Like what?"

"Unreliability, malfeasance, lax protocols, false intellectual property claims—like that." Lief had completely lost the mildly humorous tone he'd been using before. Serious as a heart attack. Biz and big money involved.

"Maybe I can help," I said, playing for time. "I'll see if I can get Loulou and Junko and Joey to talk. I'll record what they say. I'll snoop around." Would I really sink that low? Probably not.

"Just don't try to out-think me, Zad. I can schedule your trial as soon as I like. Did you know we've stopped using human juries? United Mutations sold us a jury nurb last week. Like a twelve-headed dog with a Joe or Jane Shmoe personality in each head. And I can get our judge owl to raise your charge to murder one. A death rap. Sooner than you think. Our system's highly optimized."

"Why not just have Grommet come out here and shoot me?" I snapped.

"We're thinking of that, too," said Lief, every trace of amiability gone. "Resisting arrest. Either way you've got two more days."

Not knowing what else to do, I rode my spider over to Gaven's farm with Skungy in my pocket. Hoping to dig up an exonerating clue. Pin the murder on the oddball.

Loulou and Joey came along. Like I've been saying, I was tired of Loulou, or embarrassed or something. I would have preferred going to the farm alone. My third night with Loulou had been too much. It had pushed me over some kind of edge. Like eating too much of a tasty food. Be that as it may, Loulou wanted to be in on whatever I discovered at Gaven's—and Joey didn't want to let her go off with me alone.

We had our first surprise going up Gaven's driveway. A heavy roadhog limo was pulling out—Whit Heyburn's rig, with the same chauffeur/bodyguard as before. Whit had the passenger compartment's windows set to dark.

"Do I see someone else in there too?" asked Loulou a little cattily. "Is it Jane?"

"Musical chairs," said Joey. "The fuckers and the fuckees."

"Go to hell."

The roadhog made a sound like a blaring horn and accelerated, as if to run us down. Our roadspiders scattered. Whit's limo sped away.

"Can't believe I used to work for him," said Loulou.

"Do you still?" asked Joey. "That's what I'd like to know."

"Don't be so *suspicious*!"

"Let's see if Gaven's still in stasis," I said.

It was dark and quiet in the gray stone smokehouse with the good bacon smell. The stasis cones were turned off; the hammock was empty.

"Whit Heyburn took the body?" I suggested.

"Gaven's risen from the dead," said Joey. He dug at the earthen floor with the toe of his shoe. "See that teensy ant? They used a colony of med-ants to patch the man, sure enough."

I bent over to examine the nurb ant. She was pale gold with surgically precise mandibles. Her antenna were elegant helices. Half a dozen tinier ants sat perched on her back and, for all I knew, these riders carried yet tinier ants for sending inside human arteries and veins. The graceful, purposeful ant was making her way towards a crack in the wall, heading back to her ant hill. Amazing.

"Deep down I didn't really think Gaven could come back," I admitted.

"With a trillion dollar biz deal in the air?" said Loulou. "That'll wake a guy like him for sure."

"So Gaven rode off with Whit," I said. "Alive. *Gaven* was the other person in the car, Joey."

"Maybe there was *three* people in the car," said Joey with a lewd chuckle. "Some folks likes a three-way real good."

"Shut your crack!" I yelled, grabbing hold of Joey and shaking him. Skungy started shrieking at us to stop. If it came down to it, the rat might take Joey's side.

"Boys!" said Loulou, savoring the drama. "Control yourselves."

At this point we were still in the smokehouse. I stepped out into the sunlight and ran my hands across my face. It wasn't a tenable situation to be sleeping with Loulou and Joey. I sincerely wanted to stop, even if it meant no more Loulou. I felt like a dog who'd been rolling in rotten meat. Nor was it tenable to have the cops wanting to execute me. I needed to find a clue on this damned farm. I needed to understand the meaning of the oddball and the dirtbubble.

"The oddball isn't here," said Loulou, peering into my mind and picking up my subvocal mutterings. "And I'm not rotten meat, you ungrateful jerk."

And that's when my affair with her ended. Loulou didn't look pretty to me any more, and I didn't like her voice. Why had she and I gotten so deeply involved?

"The oddball's hiding in the Funhouse," said Joey in a neutral tone. "Remember?"

"I know that," I said, my voice tight. "But I thought I'd have a chance of finding the dirtbubble here."

"Gaven probably took the dirtbubble with him," said Joey, reasonably enough. "But if you want, we can go in his house for a look-see. Maybe I'll see if I can steal something."

"You won't find shit," said Loulou, limp and dejected. "I don't know why I came over here. I'm remembering Gaven dead in the hallway, and that Fairyland trip where I saw the dragonfly people in rocking-chairs on the porch. And meanwhile Zad's thinking nasty things about me. What a stupid drag. I hate you, Zad."

"And I hate you." My emotions were out of control.

"I'm going to ride my spider over to our old tenant cottage on the hill," said Loulou gloomily. "I'll get some of my stuff before we go back to the stupid Funhouse."

"I'll meet you at the cottage in a minute," said Joey, skirting around our argument. "I'll want to fetch some of my things too."

Joey and I went into Gaven's house, with Skungy riding in my shirt pocket. The front door wasn't even locked. The place had been picked clean. No papers in sight, and not much of anything valuable lying around. But Joey took it into his head to loot flatware from the kitchen. Somehow nobody had bothered with that stuff. It's not like it was worth much anymore. It grew on plants. But Joey was stuffing spoons and knives into an empty nurb chow bag.

I went upstairs with Skungy and we examined Gaven's room with the twin beds. I remembered Reba having said Gaven kept his dirtbubble on a little cushion and, yes, here was a pink little pillow under the night table, a pink cat's bed with a soft dent where something had once sat.

Holding my breath, I stretched out my hand and felt the spot—just in case the dirtbubble was sitting there, somehow invisible. I'd noticed at my parents' farm that the oddball could pull back into the higher dimensions and shrink down to a tiny dimple. But, no, the dirtbubble wasn't here. It was with Whit and Gaven and—Jane.

Fuck it. I called her with my wristphone.

"Hi, Zad. What are you doing?" Sure enough, Jane was in Whit's car. I could hear Whit talking to Gaven in the background. Everything was bad and wrong.

"I'm lost," I told Jane. "I feel like I'm going to die. I want you back."

"Getting tired of Loulou? Reba says you're sleeping with Joey too."

"Don't let's be tough with each other, Jane. Let's talk to each other face to face. Or do teep. Have you gone qwet?"

"Can't you tell?" She laughed softly—and I couldn't tell if this meant yes or no.

"I—I know where your oddball is, Jane. She's loose in your family's old house. She's not any of the things that we thought before. She's the mouth of a tunnel that leads to another world."

"Clear as mud. Gaven and Whit have something like it, you know. The dirtbubble. Gaven's arguing with it. Or with whatever's behind it. Gaven's angry that the dirtbubble didn't stop the oddball from smothering him."

"Would Gaven be willing to tell the cops that I didn't kill him?"

"I doubt it. He doesn't like you."

I sighed, trying to sort things out. "And you say the dirt-bubble talks?"

"It has a nasty, sputtering voice, almost like someone having diarrhea. I can hardly listen to it. And it stinks like rubbing alcohol and rotten garbage. It keeps telling Gaven and Whit they'll rule the world. You ambitious little men. Maybe we *should* get together. All of us. See what happens. Tomorrow night? Till then, Zad."

The connection went blank and Skungy squeaked a warning. Something was hissing at us. No end of disasters. I saw a furry little creature with a black leathery beak and with spines sticking out of his heels, like a rooster's spurs. Creeping towards me. Ready to strike. One of the two platypuses containing Gaven's personality.

"He came out of the closet!" shrilled Skungy. He was on the floor within range of the platypus, but he didn't yet have the nerve to attack it. The platypus was maybe three times Skungy's weight. Although his beak wasn't much of a weapon, those conotoxin-loaded spurs were serious. He could paralyze me and overwrite my mind.

I scrambled across one of the beds and made for the door, but the platypus got there before me. And he started closing in on me again—surprisingly menacing for something that could have been a child's plush toy. This was absurd. But I was in grave danger of becoming Gaven. I grabbed a object off Gaven's dresser and threw it. A hairbrush. The platypus dodged and hissed.

Somehow Skungy had scrambled atop the dresser too. There was all sorts of crap on it. A glass, a bottle, a bowl, candy, a vase. Fumbling for something massive to throw, I knocked Skungy into the crack between the back of the dresser and the wall.

"Nurb back there!" squealed the rat, dragging himself back onto the dresser top. "Hidden in a slot."

This was it, the big clue I'd been hoping for. Keeping one eye on the advancing platypus, I located the nurb hidden in the slot behind the dresser, and I grabbed it, even though it made an effort to wriggle away. It resembled a gold watch with a crocodile-skin band. Yes. Gaven's wristphone. Loaded with data, no doubt. In the confusion of his resurrection, Gaven had neglected to strap it on. *Score.*

Skungy shrilled another warning. Ah yes, there was still the matter of getting out of here with my mind intact. The platypus was ramping up for a charge. If he took a flying leap, he'd have a shot at scratching me with his spurs. The way he was set up, he'd have to paralyze me with conotoxin before transferring Gaven's personality into me. Last week's tech. If I could physically avoid him, I'd be okay. But if the platypus stalked me long enough, he'd win. But I was leery of trying to stomp on him.

"Do something!" I yelled to Skungy.

My qwet rat was crouched at the edge of the dresser top, with bunched muscles visible beneath his skin. As the platypus came racing toward me, Skungy leapt like a tiny panther—or no, more like a rabid flying squirrel. Guiding his path with his tail and his limbs, my rat landed square upon the platypus's back.

Skungy sank his yellow fangs into the nape of his victim's neck. The platypus hissed furiously, rolled over, and curled into a ball, extending his dripping spurs—but to no avail. Skungy clung tight to back of his neck, and his jaws were not idle. In seconds he'd severed the creature's spinal cord. For a *coup de grace*, he ripped out the platypus's throat.

Proud of himself, my clever rat squatted by his felled rival for a moment, cleaning himself by rubbing his paws and his snout against the dead platypus's fine fur. And then, with Skungy in one hand and Gaven's wristphone in the other, I galloped down the stairs and onto the porch.

Joey was waiting on his roadspider, about to head for the decrepit little grown home across the way. The cottage where I'd once lived. I'd called her Bel. Already so many years ago.

Joey seemed not to have noticed—or not to care—that I'd just won a life or death struggle. "Loulou just called to say she'd relish a session in our old house," he reported. His smile was more queasy than lubricious. "She's waiting in bed in the altogether. Wants to patch things up."

"It's over," I said, fully realizing this was true. "I'm heading to the Rollers' alone."

"Loofy with me," said Joey, his face brightening. "Thanks, qrude."

"Skungy here killed Gaven's platypus for us," I said. "So you're safe."

"Well—there's *two* of them platypuses," said Joey. "But never mind. I'm guessing Gaven made off with the other one."

Meanwhile I could feel Loulou's teep, checking out my emotions. She was annoyed about me rejecting sex with her. And jealous about my having phoned Jane.

Back at the Roller mansion, Dad was on the terrace outside the ballroom, drinking bourbon and working on a portrait of Weezie, using tubes of oil-paint that he'd found around the house, relics from one of the Rollers' passing hobbies. Dad had managed to turn off his teep entirely, like a hen-pecked geezer taking out his hearing aid.

"More relaxing," said Dad. "Who needs to know what's on everyone's mind? So what? I'm into the light behind everything. See?" Dad gestured at his painting. It was done in shades of pastel, with a halo around Weezie that bled into a pale glow at the edges of the canvas.

"Like I'm a saint," said Weezie, quizzical and proud.

Given that Weezie was breaking Mom's heart, I wasn't into this line of thought at all. My two-legged miniature whale Jericho was nudging my legs, and that gave me an excuse to walk off.

I fed Jericho some nurb chow, and we headed across the lawn to where Kenny and Kristo were fooling with some of the new jellyfish houses that had settled into the trees. The young jellies were the size of horses—iridescent, undulating, their sparkling tendrils in constant motion.

"Kenny vants to convince them he is a good guy," said Kristo, laughing. "But they're all being born with Junko's personality. It disturbs Kenny if so many *quallen* are wanting to kill him."

"While you were gone, I ordered an elephruk-load of nurb chow from the family plant," Kenny told me. An elephruk was an amped-up elephant that had been gene-tweaked so that its rear was a big leathery bin like the back of a dump truck. Elephruks came with diamond-fiber struts in their bones, and they could lug huge loads, up to fifteen tons.

"My jellyfish ratings are on the mend," Kenny continued. One of the wobbly disks drifted down to the ground and allowed him to flop himself onto her—like a kid on an inflatable round raft.

"I love you," Kenny told the jelly cajolingly. "You're not a geek. You're wonderful." Was he sincere? To some extent, yes. Spending so much time in the cosmic mode was polishing away our nasty spikes. The jelly bucked and giggled. Three more of them floated down.

Jericho bit onto a tendril and tugged. The jelly tugged back—and suddenly Jericho was entangled beneath the disk and in some danger of being eaten. Kenny intervened with promises of more chow, and the jelly allowed Jericho to perch himself on her top surface.

Kristo and I got onto the other two jellyfish, and we organized something like a game of tag, wobbling around the lawn like four fingers of a single hand. When we were done, I asked Kenny to order me an elephruk load of nurb-gel from the Roller plant as well.

"If it's easy for you," I added.

"I'm the boss," said Kenny. "I'll call for the stuff right now. Oughta be here tomorrow by noon. It'd be loofy if you make some arty servant nurbs for us to have around the house. With the Zad Plant touch."

"Strolling minstrels?" suggested Kristo. "Like at a Christmas fair?"

"Something like that," I said, biting back a snotty put-down. Please the clients, right?

Yes, I was imagining a new phase in my career as an artist, even with my wife gone, a manslaughter charge on my head, and society on the verge of falling apart. If you're an artist, the career comes first. That's how we are.

9: *Spreading Qwet*

Loulou and Joey showed up at the Funhouse a little later, lugging stuff on their roadspiders. Loulou didn't even look at me. They went upstairs and busied themselves with redecorating their room. Dad and Weezie went upstairs too. As the evening set in, Carlo, Reba, Junko, Kenny, Kristo and I began a soap opera called *Goobers* on a wall-sized squidskin. My mind wandered back in time.

It occurred to me that the worn old squidskin on the wall might be the very same one that Mr. Roller had used for showing us that scary movie at Kenny's birthday party all those years ago. That movie had been about penguins and squid. Jane with her red-gold hair had been sitting between Whit Heyburn and me. When a mean squid darted out at a penguin, Jane had thrown her arms around me. I could still remember her scent, like honey and something salty that tasted good, a scent that locked into my brain for life.

Goobers ended and Junko spoke up. "I want to start giving away qwet tomorrow. It'd be more, like, ethical if we could get people to volunteer. Maybe we need to post an ad. Like, *you need qwet now*."

"At this point qwet is mostly a rumor," said Carlo. "We've been keeping it underground. Although, yeah, lately Jane Says has been orchestrating some leaks."

"And now we're blossoming into daylight," said Junko. "Come on, let's talk about the pitch. What are the marketing points? We used to do this in our classes at Stanford. I'll start. Qwet is free."

"It gets you stoned," said Kenny.

"We don't say *stoned*," cautioned Junko. "We use a code word. *Enlightened*."

"Gives you telepathy," said Reba. "That's the best."

"Telepathy, yes," said Junko. "And empathy and mutual

understanding and, what the hell, *love*. We've got a product to move, people."

"Direct nurb control," I put in, running my hand across Jericho's sandy skin. "It's awesome to biomod a nurb just by thinking at it."

"Cosmic logic," said Junko. "Creativity. *Power*."

"Shouldn't someone say what qwet actually is?" put in Kristo.

"Quantum wetware!" exclaimed Reba.

"But that doesn't even mean anything," I protested. "It's mumbo-jumbo bullshit."

"*Ahem*," said Junko. "It means reprogramming your body."

"That sounds scary," said Carlo. "Take it from a salesman. *Quantum wetware* is fine on its own. Who wouldn't want that? Wetware means genes. Quantum means new and improved. Biology's first upgrade since the dinosaur age!"

While we were talking, Junko had linked into the squidskin on the wall. She was crafting a commercial based on our words, overlaying images of us onto dreamy backgrounds. And now a happy T. Rex filled the screen and let out a joyful roar.

"Be the king of creation!" said Junko's voice, light and peppy. "Qwet. Enlightenment. Love. Power. A free personal upgrade coming to you from Junko—starting tomorrow. Ask for qwet now!" A link symbol flashed on screen, a stylized letter Q within a star burst.

"Nice draft," said Reba. "Let's work on it some more. And maybe you're being a little, uh, *egotistical* saying it's from *Junko*?"

"People like my name," said Junko. "It's fun to say. And I did invent qwet, so there. And, Reba, that's not a draft. I put it up live just now. Behold." Junko set a graphic counter to running in a corner of the screen. A needle was spinning round and round, ever faster. That much response.

At this point Loulou came downstairs with Joey. "Lamers," she said. "You're watching ads?"

"Junko's ad," I said, kind of itching for a chance to argue with Loulou. "Too bad Jane isn't here to work on it too. She'd kick it up a notch."

Loulou scowled. "Mooning over the little woman. You and I are really through."

"We can be friends," I essayed.

"I don't have friends," said Loulou theatrically. "There's the people I'm fucking, and there's everyone else."

"Hot," said Carlo. "Qrude."

"Dumb," said Reba. "Vain. Let's pretend we're the cast of *Goobers* and we'll put our dirty laundry on the screen. I'll be Ella Mae Goober and Loulou, you be Sammy Sue. Everyone else pick a character too. We'll trance out and rip a trip."

Being a cosmic cast of *Goobers* was fun for a while, with Loulou and Reba really going after each other. Basically they were enjoying it—like playing a game. I was cast as a minor background character, but Loulou was watching my reactions. Yes, she claimed she didn't want to be friends with me, but maybe she did. Maybe there was something else she was still hoping to get from me. With Loulou I never knew. But I did know I wasn't going back to her.

After everyone went to bed, I stretched out on one of the living-room couches with Jericho my pet nurb whale. I was totally in cosmic mode. The Funhouse felt like a dollhouse where one wall is missing and you can look into all the rooms from the side. I could see the teep patterns from everyone's minds. The patterns were overlaying each other to make moiré interference fringes like you'd see in old-school Op Art, only the teep patterns were three-dimensional, and they were moving all the time, meshes of dull lavender and dim orange, shaping themselves to fit the corners of the living room's vaulted ceiling. I was qwet and cosmic for true.

Just as I was getting comfortable, I remembered about the cops threatening to kill me. The memory came at me like an epileptic fit, like an airborne moray eel rushing towards my face.

"*Ungh*!"

And then I was back into a tight-ass robotic private detective mode. I took Gaven's wristphone out of my pocket.

My clue. Supposedly this nurb was secure, but I won it over by making it qwet. And then I delved into it, spending an hour tracing through Gaven's message threads, his notes, and his formal reports. Gaven's basic plan had been to pump up the price of qwet-related services, and then to sell his Slygro stock to United Mutations. No big surprise. Reba buying all that stock had thrown a kink into the plans. Gaven had been talking to Whit Heyburn several times a day, still hoping to work something out.

Whit seemed to be everywhere. Loulou was spying for Whit, Whit was in cahoots with Gaven, Whit had bought a qwet rat from me, and Whit was talking about orchestrating a freeware qwet giveaway just like Junko wanted to do.

What I truly couldn't stand about Whit was that he might be having an affair with Jane. It wasn't only about jealousy, I told myself—it was about wanting to protect her. If you'd grown up with Whit, you knew he was dangerous and more than a little unkind. I got so worked up that I tried calling Jane again—but this time she didn't answer.

I dug deeper into Gaven's wristphone files, cracking his feeble secondary encryption codes as I went along. And here I found a possible reason for Whit's new connection with Jane.

I'd always known Jane was careless about contracts and legalese. And I now knew that, as part of the arrangement for the Jane Says agency to handle the Slygro publicity, she'd signed an agreement with Gaven that, oh hell, merged their assets. Even a flaky artist like me could understand what that meant—but not Jane. She probably hadn't even read the contract. And for the crusher, Gaven had turned around and optioned his Jane Says agreement to Whit.

So if Whit took a mind to it, he could take everything Jane owned. He must have told that to her. She was trapped, abashed, uncertain. Should I walk up the road to the Heyburns' house and save Jane right now? Don't be a pest, Zad. Talk to her in the morning.

I flipped back into cosmic mode, watching the room's moiré thought patterns shift and merge. Jericho twitched his legs and smacked his lips, having a whale dream. I had a nagging feeling there was something else in Gaven's files. Something I'd only seen out of the corner of my eye.

Going back into the robotic mode, I rooted around. And there, in the depths of the wristphone, hidden amid some accounting data, I found the outlines of a plan involving the dirtbubble and the oddball.

The dirtbubble had appeared at Gaven's lab soon after he and Junko had started making people qwet. It was connected to an eerie, powerful monster in Fairyland—a thing called a myoor. The myoor wanted Gaven to spread qwet, but he'd been hesitating. Via the dirtbubble, the myoor had told Gaven that, if things went well, she'd take steps to install Gaven as the emperor of our world.

The oddball herself was a separate agent. She was working with the spotted gub that I'd seen at my parents' farm. Apparently the spotted gub was male and he was courting the green gub, who was female. As part of his campaign, the spotted gub wanted Jane and me to do something involving the myoor—something that went against the myoor's natural inclinations.

A tangled intrigue.

Whit was in on Gaven's hoped-for deal with the myoor—and Whit was a take-action guy. It was Whit who'd enlisted Loulou to get hold of Jane's oddball. They'd hoped their team could wipe out the oddball, but so far that hadn't worked out. Not only was the oddball backed by the spotted gub, she was a lively force of her own.

Perhaps Loulou had only slept with me so she could steal Jane's oddball. And—just in case Loulou didn't come through—Whit had advised Gaven about entrapping Jane via the ruse of an asset merge.

I felt sad and sick. I'd spurned Jane for a woman who didn't love me, and now the crooks were cheating my wife out of everything she owned.

In one of his personal journal notes on the wristphone, Gaven confessed that he was afraid of the dirtbubble and the oddball both. He didn't trust either of them. And his fears had been justified. The oddball had killed him.

And all of this meant? I was too tired to sort it out. Nestling into the comfort of the cosmic mode, I fell asleep.

Sometime during the night a thump awoke me. Inevitably it was the oddball, hovering beside my face, as if examining me. She was larger than before, luminous, her pale lavender body the size of a cabbage, the inside of her conical mouth a fleshy shade of dark pink.

I tried to push her away. She didn't move—no, she remained stock still, as if bolted to the fabric of space. Fascinated, like a mouse before a cobra, I ran my hand over the oddball's grooved, mauve skin. Warm. Her mouth stretched open, as if in a yawn.

"No," I implored. "Not yet."

Scared to make any sudden moves, I laid my crossed hands upon my chest, throwing myself on her mercy.

The oddball continued hovering there. Watching me. She'd killed Gaven, and maybe she'd kill me. A breath of air swirled around my head. My hair fluttered, drawn towards the creature's mouth. Desperately I teeped into her—hoping to make a connection—and then a mind began talking through her channel, telling me not to be afraid. It was the voice of the spotted gub. Initially his thoughts were simple, but then his monologue amped up a notch or two. And then a thousand notches. The spotted gub was feeding me a blast of information so dense and arcane that it knocked me unconscious.

Tuesday morning I slept late. When I awoke I lay there for a few minutes on the living-room couch, worrying about Jane and Whit. And then I remembered about the oddball and the voice of the spotted gub.

It was hard to distinguish the teep memories from dreams. The spotted gub had told me to do something involving the—myoor? That same word Gaven had used. I had an image of something huge and flat—a jelly-meat pancake, sprawling across thousands of acres, stretching from Glenview to downtown Louisville. It was—wait, had the spotted gub told me that the myoor would be sending down wormholes to eat us? News from a mind like a sun.

Talk about a trippy dream. One thing for sure, I was gonna help Jane. Keep Whit and Gaven from robbing her and pushing her down. I'd call her this morning. Or this afternoon. For whatever reason, I felt shy about talking to her. In any case, Jane had said that she and Whit might be coming over tonight.

I could hear voices in the kitchen, and I was picking up teep from the other parts of the house. But for the moment I preferred to be here, alone in the living room. Me and the cosmic void and the teep interference fringes.

I could see through the window that it was raining hard outside. We had some dry wood by the fireplace, along with a medium-sized hatchet. I busied myself splitting wood and getting a fire going in the hearth, then slumped back onto my couch with my pet walking whale. I felt like going back to sleep. But now, as if drawn by the warmth, the others drifted in—Dad, Weezie, Joey, Loulou, Kenny, Kristo, Reba, Carlo, Junko, and Skungy the rat.

"Good that we're all together," said Junko. She flopped into an overstuffed armchair near the fireplace. "And good that it's a crappy day. We have some work to do. It's time to start qwetting people. We'll be tossing out Joey Moon twistors like they're lollipops at a holiday parade. We can do it from here."

Carlo groaned and Dad made a grumbling noise. Dad and Weezie had joined me on my long couch by the window. I myself was fully down with Junko's plan. Liberating qwet would defy my enemies—Whit Heyburn, United Mutations, Gaven Graber, the Department of Genomics, and Lief Larson. Fuck them all.

"I thought Slygro would *sell* the qwetting service," protested Reba. She was sitting on a dark green loveseat with Carlo. She had her blue blankie nurb on her lap. "Okay, qwet itself is free, but people should pay to get it *installed*."

"Oh, Reba," said Junko tenderly. "That's not gonna work anymore. The tech is changing every day. The way it is now, if you're qwet, you can pass it on by thinking at someone in a certain way. Thanks to the Joey twistor. It's only fair for us to be sharing that information. We're launching an avalanche that'll cover the world. Like a disease epidemic—but in a good way."

"A cosmic plague," said Joey, comfortable with Loulou on a plump maroon loveseat. "Joey twistor fever."

"What about the money I spent on my Slygro stock!" cried Reba.

"I feel you," said Kenny. "But admit that we rich kids are kind of greedy." He and Kristo were on yet another of the big room's couches, cozily leaning against each other.

Kenny was messing with a qwet floating jellyfish in his lap. He'd brought about ten of them indoors—they were bumbling around the room, cute and shiny. Kenny was using his teep to modify their colors and curves—although not in really interesting ways. Kenny wasn't an artist like Joey or me.

"*Prudent* is the word I'd use," responded Reba, working her Southern accent. "It's tacky to be *greedy*."

"Resell your stock to a tacky greedy company while you can," I suggested. "United Mutations. That's what Gaven was planning to do all along. He's been talking to Whit Heyburn every day."

"I'll sell it to Whit direct," said Reba slowly. "He'll think he's getting a sneaky side-deal. Then *he'll* be the one taking the hit if Slygro tanks. Yaar. I hate Whit."

"Be sure Whit thinks he's tricking you," urged Junko. "Act like a dim bulb belle."

"Pussy's in the well," I said, goofing on the nursery rhyme rhythm. I was punch-drunk from spending so much time in cosmic mode. Everything was funny, and everything reminded me of something else.

"I'll be the go-between," Loulou told Reba, ignoring me. I could have been a squeaky piece of furniture for all she cared. "Whit thinks I'm his spy. I'll tell him that you're about to sell to United Mutations. And then he'll call you for sure. You play coy and tease him into making that private offer. Hang up, and in between I'll fan the flames, and then you call him back. And I get a taste. Ten percent."

"High finance, low crowd," said Reba, who still looked down on Loulou. "We'll see about the ten percent. Maybe less."

Loulou and Reba had a lively half hour then, talking to Whit on their wristphones, flirting and sweetening their voices, reeling in their fish. The rest of us lounged on the couches, holding in our laughs, batting around the jellyfish for fun. At the end of it, Whit had bought Reba's stock for twice what she'd paid.

"I'm a skinny girl *now*!" said Reba, dancing before the fireplace. "I took me a back-alley dump."

"Whit's money is definitely in your account?" asked cautious Junko.

"I can see it," said Reba, gesturing in the air. "Minus Loulou's—oh, call it three percent."

"Stingy cow," said Loulou.

"Slutty pipsqueak. Don't you start with Reba. I'll tongue-lash you till you cry."

"Hey!" interrupted Carlo. "Let's keep our team spirit. Come here, Reba."

"All right," said Reba, very merry. She flounced across the room and settled down on Carlo's couch again.

A fraught moment of silence passed, with Loulou and Reba passing hard looks back and forth, ensconced with their partners on loveseats on opposite sides of the fire. Slowly their hostility died down.

Rain was gurgling in the gutters and running down the windowpanes. The world outside was dim shades of green, broken up like stained glass by the fresh black branches. Our war room was damp, warm, and a little smoky. Skungy lay nestled in my lap and Jericho was propped against me like a cushion.

"Did Whit say anything about Jane?" I asked Reba. "I wish you'd asked him. I'm worried about Jane with him."

"Call Jane yourself," said Reba. "Be a man."

"Oh, I'll do it later," I said. "My energy's low. I was up late looking through Gaven's files. And I saw the oddball in the night. Hear that, Dad? A voice from the other side was coming through the oddball. The voice of the spotted gub. He showed me a giant slug, the size of Louisville. He said the slug wants to eat us all."

"I never should have brought that oddball to Gaven's house," said Loulou, pretty much in a bad mood about everything. "Just at the most basic level, I never got paid for the heist at all. None of you Louisville snobs *ever* pays a debt, so far as I can see."

"No need to be rude when you're a guest in someone's house," said Weezie frostily. This was shaping up to be a bad day.

Junko clapped her hands once for attention, rose from her armchair and got back to pushing her plan. "Time to spread qwet!" she exclaimed. "One prob. You'll be touching the minds of strangers. As soon as you qwet someone, you'll have teep contact with them. And for that one instant, you're connected by deeper kind of teep than usual. It goes under your mental firewalls. It's a clone-capable link. Very risky. For that single fraction of a second, you can overwrite them or they can overwrite you."

"I thought nobody could overwrite your mind unless you're paralyzed," I said. "Isn't that why Gaven's platypuses have conotoxin poison in their spurs?"

Junko lifted her eyebrows like I'd raised an interesting point in a grad-school seminar. "You *are* paralyzed during the moment that you're laying a Joey Moon twistor on someone. And so's the person you're treating. You're totally merged and open. Like one person. But that wears right off."

"How do you know all this?" Loulou asked Junko.

"I was thinking about it all night," said Junko. "After Carlo and Reba fell asleep." She looked a little abashed. "I was too excited to sleep myself. So I did some research and some experiments. And I realized that if you use the Joey twistor to qwet a horrible, super-hostile person, they might possibly wipe your mind. So you need to be aware of that, and to move very fast. Like you're walking along the wet sand at an ocean's edge, and darting away from breaking waves. Be alert."

"Alertness isn't always enough," said Kenny, bopping one of his jellyfish against Kristo's head.

"Exactly," said Junko. "And that's why you'll need a way to make a backup of yourself before you start. So that if some freakazoid overwrites your brain, you can bounce back. I figured out the final steps this morning when the sun was coming up. What an amazing night."

Dad made a sour face. "Talk about your flipped-out zealots. Junko here doesn't see a mind-wipe as a dealbreaker. Just a minor bump on her road to world domination."

"Reinstalling yourself from a restore point is like a jump-cut in a movie," continued Junko, pretty much ignoring Dad. "Your personality flows across. Psychic continuity is an illusion anyway."

"New day, new me," said Kristo.

"Yes!" said Junko. "You wake up and look at your memories and you arbitrarily assume you're that person. You're used to doing this. Restores won't feel unfamiliar. I'm gonna do a demo now. I made myself a restore point forty-five minutes ago when I walked into this room. And now I'll jump back to that. Watch."

Junko twitched, blinked at us and resumed speaking. "Good that we're all together. And good that it's a crappy day. We have some work to do. It's time to start qwetting people. We can do it from here." Her pronunciation was exactly the same as it had been before.

"You're jiving us," said Carlo. He was tired of Junko. He didn't like that she'd used her blue blankie routine to push into bed with him and Reba.

"Huh?" said Junko, who, as a result of the restore process, had forgotten the past forty-five minutes of conversation. "I'm telling you that we'll telemarket qwet. Only there's a catch. You'll be teeping into the minds of strangers. So first I want to show you how to make a full and eidetic backup of your mind. It's like time travel almost. Watch. I'll—"

"You just *did* that," said Loulou. "Assume that you've already said everything that you're about to say. Move on with the rest of us."

"Oh," said Junko. "Right. So you've seen that my backup process works."

"Where did you store your backup?" asked Reba.

"In my lean, shapely butt," said Junko, her voice rising towards a giggle. "No lie. I use the muscle memory of my gluteus maximi. Latin plural there. Two nicely entangled skeins of neuromuscular junctions. One cheek for each half of my brain. It's like remembering how to ride a bike. And I'm the bike."

"So you save yourself into your muscles, and then you can chance any soul-destroying stunt you like," said Kenny, getting interested. "*I seem to be a pain in my ass*. How will I know to run the restore if I'm, like, weaving potholders in a rehab room?"

"Maybe you'd be better off weaving potholders in rehab," said Junko tartly. "Maybe you'd be nicer to be around." She still wasn't any too fond of Kenny.

"She hides her true answer," said Kristo, closely watching Junko. "There is no automatic restore. One of your friends would need somehow to trigger it. But really, Junko, the restore should be automatic. Like a dead-man's switch? Triggered if the client's mind is too distant from his or her stored template. I suppose you know that one measures distances in personality space via Sheckman's fractal Hausdorff metric?"

"Oh, kiss my ass," said Junko. "I'm talking about a beta release that actually works. Yes, I'm working on a dead-man's switch. And, yes, for the time being, one of your friends needs to invoke your restore by saying your name three times. Like in a fairy tale. Do you want to know how to do a personality backup or not?"

I won't reprise the details of the words and images that Junko used for teaching us her arcane maneuver. It's enough if I describe how it felt when I did it.

Slouching on my couch, I unfocused my attention and entered a meditative mental state. I imagined I was setting out Zad-attracting treats on a big oak table in a dim castle hall. Things I liked to look at, foods I enjoyed, toys I loved to handle. The Zads came down the balustraded staircase, out of the wainscoting, up from beneath the table, down from the embossed ceiling, and out of thin air. Soon we were all present, all of us Zads—little boy, lonely ghost, messy painter, happy humper, deep sleeper, sly lurker, rowdy rider, hearty eater, the goof who stares at clouds. My remembered selves were like skins I'd shed and like dusty paper masks, piled high upon that big oak table. *Tkk*—I lit a match. The skins and masks burst into wild flame. I was in the good old white light then, me and my Zadlings, our tiny voices singing out our secret thoughts. We rose with the smoke, then whirled into a twirl that touched its tip unto my royal ass and—*yee-haw!*—we pulsed in a lightning-jolt of Zadness, thereby vaccinating the physical meat me against ever never forgetting who I am.

Like that, you wave?

Saving my personality gave me a bouncy, rubbery lift. Ever since the frantic scene with the platypus in Gaven's bedroom yesterday, I'd been worried about someone overwriting my soul. But now I was safe.

Meanwhile Dad and Weezie hadn't even tried backing themselves up. Maybe they'd reached their weirdness limits. But everyone else was trying the new trick. Reba was flapping her arms and whooping like crane; Kenny and Kristo were crooning a Mongolian throat-song duet; Joey was crawling on the floor with Loulou riding his back; Carlo had his face buried in his hands. Even little Skungy was making a backup of himself, storing a copy of his mind into his long, hairless tail.

Slowly things quieted down. We were awed at what we'd done. We stared at each other with slack grins, rocking back and forth, like a group of people gathered under a dripping awning after a monster storm.

"Right on," said Junko. "Now we rock the Joey twistor far and wide."

"Wait, wait, wait," said Dad. "I don't like this. You're talking about changing the biology of every person on Earth. On a whim. What if it's not a good change? What if it's hell?"

"Lennox is right," chimed in Weezie. "Being qwet is fun,

but we don't have to shove it down everyone's throat. We hardly even know what qwet *is*."

"Qwet is a happy dinosaur," said Loulou. "Haven't you seen Junko's fabulous ad?"

"Look, I'm sure I can find a way for people to undo qwet," said Junko. "In case they don't like it. I'll figure that part out when I have time."

"But right now, no, you don't know how," said Carlo. "I'm feeling iffy about this campaign. Can someone remind me what's the freaking rush?"

"For one thing, I'm worried about being arrested," said Junko. "I got some calls from the Department of Genomics about my ad. I took the ad down, but they want to bring me in for questioning."

"How does starting the qwet campaign change that?" Carlo asked.

"I have all the local DoG honchos on my to-qwet list," said Junko. "Also the top cops. We'll change their ways of thinking, you bet. Before they can give us a hard time."

"Sly," said Loulou, enjoying this.

"Any other reason to rush?" asked Carlo, still not enthused.

"I want to beat out Gaven and United Mutations," said Junko, setting her jaw. "I know they want to do this too. It's a race."

"Oh, *that* makes sense," said Dad. "Like you're racing to be the first to drop a hydrogen bomb. Or the first to unleash the bubonic plague."

"Old Lennox and his tearful violin," said Loulou. "*Crunch*! Oh my, I seem to have stepped on your precious antique instrument. Might as well dance on it now! *Crunch, crunch, crunch*!"

"Let's launch," said Kenny.

"The caravan barks, the dogs move on," said Kristo, not knowing what he was talking about.

Thinking back to this moment, it's a little hard to recreate our state of mind. Thanks to cosmic mode, it was as if we were stoned. And we thought of qwet as a very good thing. And we planned to be selective about whom we qwetted. And, trivial as this seems in retrospect, it was a rainy day and we were bored.

"I promise I'll work on the roll-back option tomorrow," Junko said. "Or later today. But I really do want to beat the others. I'm telling you that universal qwet is going to happen. Both Gaven and United Mutations see it as a key marketing strategy. But they're likely to screw it up. They'll put advertising hooks in it, or a backdoor control, or they'll lock in some cheesy terms of service. I'll do it right. Clean and clear."

"How do we pick our targets?" asked Joey. "Other than the DoG and the cops. Do we call random goobs and ask them if they want qwet?"

"I've got a humongo list of volunteers from my ad," said Junko. "The ad I posted last night? Oh wait, you were upstairs with Loulou. Do you ever check the web, Joey? Except when you're ego-surfing for your own name?"

"Everybody's so raw today," said Joey. "Tell you one thing—we can't zap people much beyond Louisville. You try and teep more than three miles, and my Joey twistor gets lost in the, uh, quantum babble of white noise."

"How would it be if that was the last phrase you ever heard," said Dad, who'd managed to get himself a bourbon by now. "*Lost in the quantum babble of white noise.*" Incongruously he laughed. "Pass me a splinter of my shattered violin, Loulou. I need a toothpick." We were all getting into that spirit of—whatever.

"You'll be my call wallahs now," said Junko. Seeing our blank faces, she amplified. "Like in India the person who brings you tea is the chai wallah? Hello, Kentucky. Anyway, I've put my volunteer list on the web for you, and I just now filtered out anyone who's more than three miles away, so work your way down, picking the ones that nobody's picked yet. And we'll take care of those nosy nervous Nellie bean-counters at the DoG."

I studied the list in my mind's eye. It was absurdly long. We'd never get this done. But the mechanics of the process intrigued me. So I got to work.

The first person I contacted was an old guy calling himself

Johnny Nonesuch. I used my wristphone for the contact, and I saw Johnny's face floating before me. He was a weathered Louisville qrude with streaked, shoulder-length hair. He wore a T-shirt with a picture of a skinny Tunisian cactus with glistening purple axelerate buds.

"Y'all calling from Junko?" he asked, knowing her name from the ad.

"Yeah. You want your qwet now?"

"What does it do? The ad showed a roaring dinosaur and it said I'd get wisdom, power, and love. Thass nice." Johnny Nonesuch ran his hand over his T-shirt. "Far as it goes. But will qwet get me high? Some dry times lately."

"Best high ever," I said. "Hold still and calm your mind. Qwet's coming in."

I let my teep flow out along the web path to Johnny Nonesuch. Even though he wasn't actively a teeper yet, I could feel the pulse of his personal vibes, steadily alternating between robotic mode and cosmic mode. I came in on a cosmic peak and hit him with the Joey twistor.

It wasn't an entirely pleasant feeling. Like Junko had said, sending out the qwet-teep pattern gave me a fleeting sense of being paralyzed. At anyone's mercy. Like a surgeon who falls under the sway of his own anaesthetic.

Johnny Nonesuch was paralyzed for a moment there himself. We were as close as lovers. But then we bounced apart. Johnny Nonesuch was qwet and feeling the power. He teeped his gratitude and we were done.

The next volunteer was an intense young woman named Laraine Dunkle.

"I saw the ad," she told me. "I want love. My men are always skanking away. Even when I treat them good."

"I'll give you the power of telepathy," I said. "And you can pass the power to them. And your souls will be in harmony."

Same as before, I shoved the Joey twistor into the new user's head. The mental quantum Mobius strip did its thing, and Laraine was qwet.

This accomplished, I used the wristphone to communicate a

concrete fact. "Hang onto that pattern I sent you. And message it to the men you want to get close to."

Laraine answered with a teep-pulse of exultation. Like a whoop on graduation day.

Next came Jim Cheeks, a bristly, muscular guy.

"I'm a nurb housing contractor," he told me. "Getting these big old seeds to sprout the right way. Sometimes biomodding them before we start. And listening to the customers bitch, always. I been using a biomodder wand on the nurbs, but I think your ad said this qwet stuff will give me a better way?"

"Teep programming," I said. "A sensual, emotive path. So the nurbs understand what you dream and feel."

"Great day in the morning," said Cheeks.

Zip zap—another satisfied qwet user was born.

Carlo was the first to hit a bad one. A little ironic, given that Carlo wasn't at all enthused about our recruitment campaign. When Carlo installed qwet onto this one particular user, the guy surged across their teep link and overwrote Carlo's mind.

Carlo let out a wild scream, his voice high and thin.

"I owe a blood oblation to the Lord!" he cried, looking wild-eyed around the room. We dropped whatever we were doing and backed away. Carlo was possessed by the soul of a psychotic hillbilly

"Carlo, Carlo, Carlo!" I yelled, wanting to invoke the restore routine like Junko had said. But Carlo didn't properly hear me. He grabbed the hatchet by the fireplace, the one I'd been using to split wood.

"I wonder if maybe Junko *should* have implemented that dead-man's switch," said Dad, all poker-faced and sarcastic. He and Weezie clambered over the longest couch, getting it between them and Carlo.

Kenny sicced three of the little flying jellyfish on Carlo. They plastered themselves to his face, covering his eyes, nose and his mouth. Carlo was still waving the hatchet, but a minute later he was out of steam. He dropped the hatchet and began clawing at the jellyfish on his face. He couldn't breathe.

"Carlo, Carlo, Carlo," screamed Kenny at the top of his

lungs, his mouth only a couple of inches from our possessed friend's ear. The restore routine kicked in.

Carlo thrashed his arms as if in the throes of a seizure. Their job done, the three jellyfish peeled themselves off and floated away. Carlo made a sizzling sound in the back of his throat. I almost imagined I could see a sinuous thread of vapor drifting from his mouth—the departure of an evil spirit.

"What a burn," croaked Carlo, slowly looking around the room. "I was Vaughan Henry from the Shively part of town." He looked down at the hatchet by his foot. "What's this doing here? Ah yes. Sorry, guys."

"Time for a break," said Reba. "Food, coffee, like that."

"Color me gone," said Carlo. "Tender my resignation." He and Reba headed for to the kitchen, with Dad and Weezie in their wake.

"Keep at it," Junko urged Joey, Loulou, Kenny, Kristo and me. "We need momentum. I promised free qwet in my ad. And we absolutely have to qwet all the local cops and DoG staffers—whether they like it or not."

"We've only done sixty-seven people so far," protested Joey. "And I'm seeing twelve hundred on your list. Twelve hundred just from Louisville. And the list is growing. I ain't gonna sit here for weeks and months bein' no frikkin' *call wallah*. And every half hour somebody comes after me with that goddamn hatchet."

"We can store the hatchet outside," said Junko.

"Feeble," said Kenny.

But Joey did take the hatchet outside, with Skungy the rat riding on his shoulder. Looking out the window, I saw Joey standing in the rain talking to the rat, making gestures. Joey was in a weird mood. He raised his arm and threw the hatchet across the yard with all his strength.

The hatchet struck a beam on the side of the nurb chow shed and stayed there, quivering. Sissa and the twelve new Joey Moon rats ran out of the shed. Joey hunkered on the lawn, smiling and jabbering to his posse, very animated. The rain was running down his face and matting the rats' fur. None of them seemed to care. They were into some very high-bandwidth communication. I tried to eavesdrop on their emotive teep, but I couldn't decipher it. The rats and Joey had such similar minds that their teep was like an idiosyncratic private language.

"Don't like this," said Junko, standing by the window next to me. "That freak is up to something."

"*You're* not a freak?" said Kenny.

Joey and the rats came inside, dripping water on the parquet and the rugs.

"I'm saying we let these little guys be our wallahs," said Joey. "Our telemarkeeters. My rat pack. I done coached them."

"Did you teach them my trick for making a backup?" Junko asked. "No? Too time-consuming? Too complex?"

"Aw, hell, if a rat freaks, we just kill it," put in Kenny. "Stomp it."

Of course this launched Skungy into one of his paranoid, hysterical rants—just as Kenny had known it would. I calmed Skungy down. And now Junko taught the backup method to the rats. She liked teaching things. A born professor.

"These rats are all just copies of Joey Moon anyhow," grumbled Kenny. "I honestly don't see why losing one would be so bad."

"Each of these rats has hours or even days of unique personal experience," said Joey. "Each moment of each life is incalculably precious."

"Each green leaf is sacred," intoned Loulou, very sarcastic. "Every insect is god. This is why bug wallahs sweep the paths before me when I wander my temple garden in walking meditation."

"Oh relax, you guys," said Junko, wanting to quench the steady bickering. "I do think Joey's had a good idea. We'll let the rats do our calls."

Just for a goof, I tore off a chunk of Jericho's nurb-gel so I could sculpt a call center for the rats. Jericho roared and thrashed his tail but I managed to cool him out with chow and with promises to give him even more gel when the Roller elephruk arrived with his load.

Then I knelt on the floor and modeled a little oval conference table that dolls might have sat at. I made fourteen little chairs just the right size for our rats, with holes in the backs of the chairs so their tails could wave free. The rats took their seats, looking proud of themselves, their whiskers twitching with curiosity. To complete the setup, Joey overrode the nurb reproduction block on his wristphone, and coaxed it into spawning off fourteen mini-wristphones with screens the size of pinkie fingernails. Joey presented these to the excited rats, who zealously strapped them to their tiny arms.

"So cute!" said Loulou, finally seeing something she liked this morning. "Like the first day of school."

"Thing is, I don't dig rats," said Kenny. "If I haven't made that clear." He and Kristo went to join the group chatting in the kitchen. This left Junko, Joey, Loulou and me to oversee our new call wallahs.

"Git on it, y'all!" Joey told the rats. "Do it like I told you."

The rats began squeaking to their tiny wristphones in low tones.

Almost immediately Junko and I sensed something wrong. Rather than showing images of individual people, the rats' squidskin screens were tiled into tiny dots.

"They're calling multiple prospects in parallel?" asked Junko.

"Hell yeah," said Joey. "I taught em to fork their processes. You not the only one knows how to be a cyberfreak, Junko."

Uneasily we watched for another couple of minutes. The rats' squeaks had risen to a frantic twitter.

"How can the clients even understand them?" Loulou asked.

"Don't need no small talk," said Joey. "No *Mother may I.* Rats call folks up and they're qwet."

"I'm really having trouble monitoring this," said Junko, mentally fumbling around in her web space. "My list is—wait! The rats aren't even *using* my list. And they've qwetted—are you crazy, Joey? *Seven thousand people*?"

Joey stared at us in silence, savoring our dismay. "You doin' good," he said, leaning over the rats' table. The rats peered up at him, their eyes bead-bright and full of mischief.

"We're cookin' alright," said Skungy. "Making a mark."

"They've been systematically calling every single person in reach!" wailed Junko. "And—am I getting this right? They've been telling their converts to do the same?"

"What I told em," said Joey, his expression defiant. "Joey Moon process art. The bi-ass chain-reaction avalanche you was jawin' about."

Even though it was way too late, Junko was finally having second thoughts. She yelled at the qwet rats and threatened to throw them into the fire. Skungy and Sissa bared their fangs and made Junko back away. Meanwhile the twelve younger rats fled outside. Of these, four hid themselves in the foundations of the nurb chow shack, two of them rode off on Kenny's roadspider, two of them flapped away on Reba's flydino, and four hopped aboard the floating jellyfish that were continually drifting away.

"Telepathic Rats Beam Mutation Rays From Sky," announced Joey, peering out the window at the wobbly house jellies amid the clouds. "This shit is apocalyptic!"

With a final volley of defiant squeaks, Skungy and Sissa ran out to the chow shed as well. Junko, Joey, Loulou and I were the only ones left in the living room. The others were eating or upstairs—feckless, zonked, obliv. They'd lost interest in our game.

"With each transfer, the zone of contagion grows," said Junko, her voice tight. "It's going exponential. It'll reach New York this afternoon. Thanks to *you*, Joey Moon."

"You're welcome," said Joey.

Junko sighed. "Okay, deep down I wanted this to happen. I think even Gaven wanted it. But we wanted control."

"Hell with control," said Joey. "No such thing."

"The crazy thing is this seems at all reasonable," said Loulou, her voice slow and calm. "Being in cosmic mode for days on end is, like, the strongest drug trip you ever had. You get this deceptive sense of lucidity. As if you're thinking more clearly and logically than ever before."

"And I know I'm always right," added Joey. "I'm the Lord of Rats."

No, we weren't lucid at all. We were slushed.

Junko had a temper tantrum around then. She jumped up and down on the little chairs and table that I'd crafted for the rats—smashing them to bits. The fragments of gel relaxed into sticky puddles. I scraped up the stuff and patted it onto Jericho's belly, like applying plaster with a trowel. Jericho was glad, but not fully assuaged.

"It was mean to break the rats' cute chairs," I told Junko.

No answer. She was slumped silent in her easy chair now, her attention in the web.

Meanwhile Loulou and Joey were hugging each other on the maroon loveseat, possibly on the point of making love. Conceivably Loulou would ask me to join in. Don't do it, Zad.

I went out into the drizzling rain, with Jericho tagging along. He was insistently talking about the extra nurb-gel I'd promised him from the upcoming delivery. He wanted to get fat and to spawn a baby whale.

As if on cue, a snuffling honk sounded. It was the elephruk, splashing up the Roller's mossy driveway. The leathery gray nurb bore a glistening mound of gel, really quite a bit. Noticing me, the elephruk messaged her name: Darby. I'd seen her before. In the old days, she'd sometimes come to the Rollers to entertain us kids at Jane's birthday parties.

Trumpeting a fanfare, Darby strode onto the lawn. She came to a halt in a great puddle, peering at me with her tawny gold eyes.

"Okay if I drop the load right here?" she asked. For an elephruk, her speaking voice was very clear. "I just now got qwetted by a rat on a flying jellyfish," she added. She stretched out her trunk and softly felt my face. "You're qwet, too. Have we met? You seem familiar."

"Yeah," I said. "The hayrides at Jane's parties. Put the gel in the barn, would you? You can have some chow and dry off if you like."

Darby had always been a comfortable presence. Her vibes

were big and wise. Rocking from side to side, she ambled into the weathered wooden barn. It had stables and straw and wooden columns holding up the ancient metal roof. Darby sat back on her butt and tilted her back. The gel slid off like a giant slug. About fifteen tons.

"Awesome," I said. "I'm an artist, you know. I'm planning to sculpt creatures from this stuff. Like this pet whale. Come here, Jericho. I'll fatten you a little more."

"You're a genemodder," said Darby.

"That's right," I said, amplifying Jericho's curves. "I use qwet to figure out the genes for the shapes I want. Once I have a nurb's body right, I program its mind. Are you glad to be qwet?"

"Too early to say." The elephruk picked up a sheaf of hay with her trunk and swept it into her loose-lipped mouth. A moment later she spat it onto the hard dirt floor. "Old and dry. This place isn't a real farm at all. I'll eat some of that chow I carried here yesterday."

"It's in the shed," I said, pointing. "Six qwet rats in there with it. Are you scared of rats?"

"You think I'm a screaming fat lady lifting her skirts?" said Darby. "I made friends with one of those rats when I brought the chow yesterday. Skungy. I can teep that he's there now." She lumbered to the shed, opened the door with a butt of her head, then dragged a laden pallet of chow into the barn. "This is more like it," she said, grinding up the tobacco-smelling nuggets of feed with her great yellow teeth. "Stop hiding, Skungy."

"Busted," said Skungy, emerging from beneath one of the feed bags. "Hey, Darby. Glad you got qwet. We're profound, baby. On a cosmic high."

"Elephants are profound all the time," said Darby. "Thanks to having big brains. No offense."

"So I'm miniaturized," said Skungy. "A mean and cringing rat. It's good." He turned his attention to me. "Some wild shit with that global qwet campaign, huh Zad? Has Junko calmed down?"

"She's grimly viewing with alarm," I said. "Joey was crazy

to let you rats do the qwetting. We're in for a whole world full of scatter brained freaks."

"Is that bad?" asked Skungy.

"Qwet's got a cost," I said. "All the Funhouse gang is snapping at each other today. It's as if we're all coming down, even though we're still up. But the high doesn't feel as awesome as it did yesterday."

"What's that thing floating over there?" asked Darby. She had her trunk stretched out like a pointing arm.

A lumpy sphere was hovering in one of the old stables. Drab brown, with a smell of horse liniment and decaying meat. The dirtbubble. Its pink mouth was open, ready for action. It drifted out of the stable, moving towards us. A breeze began to blow. Straws tumbled end-over-end across the pounded-earth floor.

"Look out!" I called, already backing away.

Skungy scrambled up Darby's leg and onto the top of the elephruk's head. The rat was like a naive tourist seeking a vantage point. He didn't grasp what was coming. He assumed the elephruk and I could keep him safe.

"The dirtbubble wants to swallow us!" I yelled. My feet were slipping across the plank floor. I grabbed onto one of the free-standing wooden beams that supported the roof. The wind was like a hurricane; the air was full of dust. Everything happening too fast.

Skungy lost his footing atop the elephruk. Squealing a desperate curse, he went tumbling into the dirtbubble's maw. Poky, dull-witted Jericho bounced across the floor in his wake. I was safe for the moment, plastered to lee side of the beam.

And now—oh my god—Darby fell into the ball, trunk first. Her stubby legs skidded across the dirt, she lifted into the air—and the gentle beast's fat body disappeared trunk-first into the dirtbubble's nightmarishly dilated mouth. All of Darby gone save for one leg. The leg wouldn't fit.

The gale dropped. For a moment the grotesquely inflated dirtbubble wobbled and floundered above the ground, a brown balloon the size of a truck. Darby's leg protruded from its mouth like the twitching butt of a cigar. With a crunch, the dirtbubble pinched the leg off, and it thudded to the floor. I could hear Darby's frantic trumpeting from within.

The dirtbubble began shrinking, as the elephant-sized bolus moved away from our space and up towards Fairyland. The trumpeting faded away. The severed leg lay on the barn floor in a pool of nurb slime. The leg was the size of a bale of hay.

The satiated wormhole hung pulsing in the air. I stood there frozen, fascinated, peeking around the wooden beam that I still hugged. The dirtbubble swelled a bit and its mouth twitched—something coming back our way. A foul belch that carried a whiff of iodine. The bedraggled Skungy popped out.

The qwet rat screeched and rushed at me, blind with panic. He scrabbled up my leg so fast that his claws dug into my skin, and he only stopped when he'd reached a spot of shelter inside my shirt.

The dirtbubble dimpled down to near-invisibility and moved on.

10: Weezie's Party

"What's all the noise out here?" Carlo had appeared at the barn door. "You celebrating because your nurb-gel came?"

"Celebrating?" I echoed hollowly. "The dirtbubble just swallowed an elephruk. You remember old Darby? Look at that leg. Nothing else of her left."

"Wow." Mellow with cosmic mode, Carlo wasn't particularly worried about anything, not even this.

"I think all of the wormholes besides the oddball are going to be man-eaters," I fretted. "Like the dirtbubble. Hungry mouths, Carlo. Feeding tubes from—from the myoor."

"Gobble frenzy coming up," said Carlo. He nudged the oversized leg with his foot and laughed.

I didn't feel good about this at all. I was deep into the worrywart robotic mode. Following Carlo's example, I switched back to cosmic. Better. I was like, let it come down, qrude.

I slipped my hand inside my shirt and started petting Skungy. Slowly our heart rates returned to normal. But I still had my concerns about Jane.

"You're a business guy, right?" I said to Carlo.

"Used to be."

"I was digging around in the records on Gaven's wristphone last night. Jane signed a crazy agreement that merged her assets with Gaven's. And Gaven optioned that agreement to Whit. Does that mean Whit owns Jane's stuff?"

Carlo shook his head. "Gaven died—at least for a little while. The moment you dip your toe into the River Lethe, all of your partnership agreements are null and void. It's even better than a bankruptcy. The smart guys do it all the time. Buy a med-ant colony and die."

"So Whit can't threaten Jane?"

"Not with that particular piece of paper, no. Why are you flailing yourself? Talk to Jane in person, qrude. What is fucking wrong with you? You know she's staying in Whit's house. Two hundred yards from here."

"I'm—I don't know. Maybe she doesn't want to see me. She said we were done."

"Offer her the elephruk bone. A token of your manly prowess."

"Oh leave me alone, you slushed freak."

"I'm here for you, brother." Ignoring the rain, Carlo capered across the lawn and leapt high in the air to snag a newborn jellyfish the size of his own body. He wrestled the jelly to the ground and began using it like a toboggan, sliding across the wet grass as if he didn't have a care in the world.

"The dirtbubble was squeezing us," said Skungy from inside my shirt. "It was wet and it made me numb."

"Like venom?"

"I think it mummifies you. I was lucky to escape. I had to fight to stay awake. I bit and clawed and wriggled my way back to the mouth."

"What about Jericho?"

"Jericho? If you're gonna make nurbs, make them funky, Zad. Give them some soul. Folks want strong, sick art—not talking dolls. Jericho was a piece of crap and I'm glad he's gone." This was the Joey Moon personality talking.

Me, I'd thought Jericho was pretty cool. I pulled Skungy out of my shirt and tossed him through the barn door onto the lawn, throwing him maybe a little harder than necessary. This was the qwettie short temper. I calmed myself with a little more cosmic mode and then I called Jane.

"Zad?" She looked lovely.

"Hi Jane. Have I told you I miss you?"

"You told me." She smiled, appreciating the attention.

"We're meant to be together, darling. Don't hang up, I also have some important advice."

"Like a telemarketer? Offering an immortal loaf of wendy-meat, a blade from an artisan knife-plant, and a farm-grown skillet? Plus the greatest musical squidskin hits of the twenty-first century—all rolled into one eye-poppin' dirt-cheap

Tunisian cactus bud."

"I'm serious, Jane. Are you alone?"

"Sort of. Whit Heyburn's in the other room with Gaven. Channeling web news. They're all excited about their deal."

"Numberskulls," I said. "You know you want me back. The advice: I was looking through Gaven's records, and I have a feeling that you might think Gaven or Whit have some kind of legal power over you. Because of that agreement you and Gaven signed? Merging the Slygro and the Jane Says assets?"

"You're nosing into every tiny corner of my life?" said Jane, very annoyed.

"Please don't get huffy. Listen. Any agreement you signed with Gaven is void because he died."

"Really. Wow." Jane paused, thinking this over. "Even though he's come back to life? Even though he's here with Whit?"

"Doesn't matter. Carlo said so, and he's biz. What are Gaven and Whit up to anyway?"

"Jabbering about qwet going viral. That dirtbubble thing was here talking to them a little while ago. It says the myoor is glad about the qwet. Whatever that means."

"I saw the dirtbubble just now in your barn here, and it didn't talk."

"Maybe you don't rate." Jane laughed. "Not that it's fun to listen to. I think I told you it's like a talking butthole. The voice all burbling and thick. Just awful. It keeps telling Whit and Gaven that they'll rule our world."

"Sure they will. Come be with me instead of with those losers. I'm right here in your family mansion, you know."

"Of course I know. We're coming to the big sex party tonight."

"Sex party?"

"Mom's invited a hundred people. She's calling it a cotillion, but I can tell she's hoping it'll degenerate into an orgy. She's out of her tree. Thanks to being qwet and living with your father. I'm not sure qwet is a good thing."

"You're qwet too?"

"I am. I caught it via an anonymous call from a rat. Or maybe it was someone from Indiana. A telemarketer. Like you."

"I want to give you one more jolt of info. A warning and a fix."

"You're husbanding me? Loulou's definitely out of the picture?"

"Completely out," I said. "The warning: Gaven still has that platypus with his personality on it. He might try to overwrite your mind. That's a real risk when you're around complete sleazebags."

"*Ugh*," said Jane, looking over her shoulder towards the other room. "I can almost see that happening. These guys are the worst. What's the fix?"

"Junko showed me how to make a backup copy of myself. It's pretty simple..."

So now I explained Junko's moves to Jane, sending the words and images over wristphone, going over and over it until Jane finally had it straight. She did a backup while I waited, and I helped her check that she'd gotten it right.

"Dear Zad," said Jane. "You care." Mentally reaching out, I could teep some of her vibes. Cozy.

"Why don't you come over here right now?" I said. "If the boys try to stop you I can help."

"Oh, let's just wait till the party. I can handle these two creeps. I'm still hoping to snoop out the details of their big plan. There might be an angle for me."

"Be careful, Jane. Things are changing so fast. I guess the qwet explosion's all over the news?"

"They say it's reached Nashville, Indianapolis, and Columbus. Maybe DC and Manhattan this afternoon. And there's no way to stop it. I'm kind of surprised the local cops and the DoG haven't come down on you."

"Junko zapped them," I said. "They're qwet now. All mellow. Or maybe freaking out. Lost in their personal psychodramas." It wasn't likely that Grommet or Lief Larson or anyone else would be coming after me today.

"I can't believe you're not channeling the online news,"

added Jane. "On a day like this. You're lost in your artist dreams. As usual."

"Pretty real here right now," I said. "I told you I saw the dirt-bubble, right? It swallowed that nice elephruk. Darby. Look."

I angled my wristphone towards Darby's severed leg. To make the sight worse, Skungy had skulked back into the barn, and he was gnawing at the nurb flesh along the leg's monstrous shin.

"Oh god. Is this the end of the world, Zad? Is everything falling apart?"

"Let's face it together, Jane. Whatever it is. Come now."

She looked at me, her gray-green eyes glowing, her tawny gold hair mussed. My beloved wife. Focusing on her, I could teep her warm vibe even more clearly than before. And she was feeling me too.

"Yes," said Jane at last. "I'll be right there."

I went into the Roller mansion and hurried to the tower to stare at the Heyburn house. Rain pouring down. A dippy little dome atop the red-brick home. Four white columns in front. Neo-classical, Palladian, Jeffersonian—I wanted to crush the place into rubble.

But now, *yes*, Jane stepped out the front door, her hair a bright flag, and her red umbrella poised. She was heading down the granite plinths of the steps but—oh hell—that goddamn Whit was at the door, calling to her, getting her attention, gesturing with his hands.

And now, *don't do it*, Jane furled her umbrella and went back inside. Maybe just for a minute? For five and then ten and then thirty minutes I stood at my tower post, watching and waiting. Nothing. The Heyburn house in the steady rain.

I tapped my wristphone and called Jane. She looked the same. I could see Whit in the corner of my visual field, also Gaven. Sitting in chairs.

"Hi again, Zad." Jane sounded normal.

"I thought you were coming right over!"

"I changed my mind. The boys are finally explaining their big plan to me. It's fairly loofy. They'll let Jane Says do the

PR, and they'll cut me in. Please don't worry about me, I'm *fine*. See you at the party tonight. We'll talk then."

Jane shut down the connection, and when I tried to call back, she didn't answer. It made me mad. What to do? Cosmic mode, qrude. Let things ride. Jane'll be here before long. Don't act like a jealous fool.

"Vanting voman," observed Kristo, peering up the tower stairs from his and Kenny's room on the third floor. Exaggerating his German accent was his idea of a joke. Not that he was a bad guy. I could teep that he empathized with my emotional turmoil. He felt it was nothing that some hugs and kisses couldn't fix. He took a step up the stairs towards me.

"Kenny is under our bed," Kristo told me. "He has some nurb-gel that he makes into veird ants. His fun just now. Will you play?"

"I'm going back to the barn," I said, squeezing down the steps past Kristo. "Biomodding nurbs of my own. Big sex party here tonight, did you hear?"

"Orgy, *ja*." Kristo pumped his arms back and forth to mime wild party behavior. Invitations to Weezie Roller's posh, louche gala would be all over Louisville by now. A free-for-all. My thoughts stalled when I tried to visualize the scene.

On the second floor, Carlo and Reba were curled up inside a ten-foot house jelly that Carlo had managed to fly into their bedroom. They waved to me as I walked by, giggly lovers in a magic bower.

Downstairs, Weezie was pacing the hall jabbering through her wristphone, lining up still more action for her party tonight. She'd tweaked her hair into the same perfect gold/red shade that Jane naturally had.

Dad had set up his easel by the open front door. He was humming to himself and working on a painting of the rain, the brush rapidly pecking, putting in every single drop of water.

In the living room, Junko, Joey and Loulou were entangled on the couch by the fireplace, channeling weird shit from the web. They were naked. Qwet gave you stamina. And, at least for this afternoon, Junko had taken my place in the ménage a trois.

"Qwet's spreading like wildfire," reported Joey, noticing me. He sat up and pulled on his jeans.

"Lots of fighting," said Loulou. She and Junko were donning their shirts. Even in cosmic mode, having me there made the three of them self-conscious. "With qwet, people pick up on mockery and disdain," continued Loulou. "And they blow their tops. Not always fun to see yourself as others see you." She wagged a finger at me. "Mr. Judgmental. Mr. Cold As Ice. Mr. Better Than You."

"Am I the only one who's noticed how ill-humored we're getting?" I asked. "That's a typical thing with stoners, you know."

"I'm not ill-humored," muttered Junko, combing out her hair with her fingers. "I'm *worried*. About things going so wrong."

"It's not all bad," said Joey. "Did you see about those people starting a house-jellyfish commune downtown? The jellies are stuck together like frog eggs. They call it Wobble Manor. And there's a city-wide music jam going on. Everyone teeping into this hive-mind beat they can feel in the air." Joey beat a ragged tattoo on the couch.

"Fine, but what about the murders in Shively," said Junko. "Vaughan Henry, the same guy who infested Carlo's mind? He's copied himself onto twelve so-called apostles, and they're running amok. That kind of stuff is happening all over town. Meanwhile the police aren't answering calls."

"People will figure out how to protect themselves," said Loulou. "They'll learn your backup routine. And if we really need to, we'll kill the killers ourselves."

"Easy to say," remarked Joey.

"More of us than them," said Loulou. "Like healthy cells neutralizing tumors. No need for cops. They're all about helping the rich."

"I wouldn't mind seeing some cops around—like when the culties and looters show up at the Funhouse," said Junko. "I'm worried about Weezie's party. She's trying so hard for an edgy crowd. She *actually wants an orgy*. A woman her age."

"Sex never hurt nobody," said Joey. "Me, I'm wondering about what happened in the barn. I was snooping, and I saw some of it through your wristphone, Zad. That little ball swallowed a whole damn elephruk!"

"I'm worried that's only the beginning," whispered Junko. "We might see hundreds more wormholes like the dirtbubble. Or thousands. Roaming around and swallowing us." She paused, staring at us, her eyes a little wild.

"Going inside the oddball didn't hurt me a bit," said Loulou. "She was a tunnel to Fairyland. Kind of fun."

"I think the wormholes like the dirtbubble are different," I said. "I don't think they're tunnels that you waltz through. I think they lead to pouches inside the myoor. Stomachs, or maybe gizzards with teeth."

"And it's worse than that," said Junko, her voice still a whisper. "The wormholes—they can find you better when you're qwet. Especially if you're making yourself cosmic. Gaven and I figured this out. And then I went and spread qwet anyway. I'm a horrible person."

"Bad Junko," said Joey, too high to take anything seriously. "Bad, bad girl. Loulou and Reba are gonna give you a bare-bottom spanking. At the big party tonight. In front of everyone."

"Gaven noticed that the dirtbubble was twitching whenever a person went by," said Junko, shifting uneasily in her seat. "He started making measurements. Pretending to be a scientist. He used a laser-bug."

"I remember him doing those tests," said Joey. "I liked the laser-bug."

"We calibrated the dirtbubble's reactions," continued Junko. "Its reaction was about a thousand times stronger around Joey. Because Joey had wedged himself into full-on cosmic mode."

"Can you undo qwet?" I asked Junko. "This morning you said you'd find a way. Get on it!"

At this point her composed face began to quiver. "I was wrong about that," she sobbed. "Once your wetware molecules learn how to be qwet, that's where they want to stay. It's a minimum energy configuration. Impossible to dislodge."

My mind felt like a kaleidoscope turning too fast. We'd unleashed qwet upon the world. I'd seen a wormhole eat an elephruk. The wormholes might eat us all. Jane was huddling with Gaven and Whit. Qwet was irreversible. And we were facing Weezie's party tonight—not as bad as the other news, but something I wasn't looking forward to at all. I needed a break. I needed my art.

I pushed out into the calming rain once more. And made my way to the barn alone. My new pile of nurb-gel was still there, although Skungy was nibbling at it. He was done with the elephruk leg. He'd gnawed the whole damn thing down to the bone.

"You're always eating, but you never grow," I said.

"When I eat, I vibrate faster," said Skungy. "Makes me *profound*. I'm spinning visions, qrude."

"I'm glad that killer dirtbubble isn't here right now."

"I can see wormholes snarfing people off a busy street," said Skungy, looking up from the nurb-gel. "I see them crashing Weezie's party like anteaters on an anthill. I see long dark tongues snaking up the stairs and down the corridors. Everyone screaming and running away. *Phht, phht, phht*!" Skungy giggled. A ragged, grating sound. "Did you notice that the dirtbubble's mouth is like a disembodied asshole?"

I didn't answer. Maybe somehow I'd be a hero and find a way to save the world. But right now all I could think about was crafting some nurbs. I frowned at the rat on my mound of nurb-gel. "Don't get in my way, Skungy, or I'll stomp you. I can move a lot faster than you think." Yes, I liked him, but I had that qwet irritability thing going on.

Skungy moved around to the other side of the gel. With a sigh of pleasure, I dug my hands into the mound. The gel smelled good to me.

It wasn't out of the question that my nurbs might help against the alien wormholes—but mainly I was being driven by the crack-brained notion that if I made some loofy nurbs for the party, people would get excited about my art again, and I'd reboot my career. I could still come back.

My art-career dreams were weirdly disconnected from the very real possibility that demonic wormholes might soon be devouring us. I mean, who goes shopping for art when the Apocalypse is in town? But, no, I wasn't thinking about that. I was thinking about making some really great nurbs. Jericho had been bland and dull. I'd work at a deeper level now; I'd make nurbs that personified core emotions and psychic archetypes.

Eager to get rolling, I qwetted the whole mound of nurb-gel, and gave it a personality based on my barest animal functions. I wanted the flubby nurb to be like a one-ton amoeba. So I modded it to have a matrix of internal protein-chain springs. The wobbling of the springs would let the amoeba move around.

I biomodded the mound's color-producing functions as well. The gel had been sparkly to begin with, but I gave it some of the properties of nurb-paint, and I added in a phosphorescent glow. The mound now had branching bright threads visible within. Its colors were sour and tasty in the barn's rainy-day gloom.

"Hi, Blob," I said.

Blob made burbling noises by swallowing and forcing out big gulps of air. At my wristphone-transmitted behest, Blob bulged out some pseudopods and started poking Skungy until the rat stopped making his inroads on the big nurb's flesh. Skungy squealed an insult and scampered off through the rain to check the action inside the Funhouse.

I stayed with my art. I was intrigued by the way Joey Moon had mapped a full copy of his personality into Skungy. Although the idea of duplicating myself made me uneasy, it would certainly be a strong move. After all, that's what a lot of art is about—immortalizing the artist.

I didn't want my double to be something lowly like a rat. I'd have him look exactly like me—*some* of the time. But to give the act another dimension, I'd have my nurb double's appearance fluctuate. He'd be qwet, you understand, and he'd be cycling between cosmic mode and robotic mode. And I'd let his appearance change with his mode. It would make a nice objective correlative for my own ever-shifting psychic state.

Also I'd have my double be more outspoken then me. Ruder.

He'd have no filters; he'd say just about anything. That was another motivation for making art—you could indirectly tell people what you *really* thought, without having to say it straight out and get your ass kicked.

Using a rusty metal pitchfork, I pried a chunk off the glowing Blob, a piece the same size as me. I did some preliminary biomodding to mold the thing into a humanoid blank, a doughboy lying on the barn's dirt floor. And then I gave it a nice set of muscles.

And then, gathering my courage, I made the big move. I got into a teep resonance with the nurb and vibed in my full personality, memories and all. Like making a backup. To complete the process, I did a tweak to remove most of the nurb's inhibitions—blanking out what they used to call the superego.

"Hi, Zad," croaked my copy, sitting up. "What's my name?"

"SubZad," I said. "Sub for subliminal, subconscious, and subordinate."

"Subordinate to who?"

"Me?"

"That'll be a cold day in hell," said SubZad, just like I would have said to Dad. He looked down at himself in the watery late afternoon light. "What about that fluctuating appearance you planned?" he demanded irritably. "Do that too. I want to be more than a clone."

"Here we go. Fine. Stay blank for a minute." The changes that I now made were, I suppose, the truly artistic touch in my process.

I thought of the cosmic mode as water, versus the robotic mode as ice. I thought of the cosmic personality as smooth and mellow, versus a robotic personality that's quirky and tight. Using my cosmic-logic-designed biomods, I found a way to actualize these distinctions within SubZad's metabolism.

And, for a really original touch, I gave SubZad some abilities to biomod his body in real time. He'd be a bit of a shapeshifter. Shapeshifting wasn't something that people ordinarily did, as biomodding your genes on the fly was a good way to kill yourself. But thanks to cosmic logic, I was able to find a way to give SubZad access to a safe and limited set of internal controls.

I watched my adjustments take hold. SubZad had been alternating slowly between cosmic and robotic, perhaps once every five or ten seconds. And now you could see it happening. Yes!

Just now SubZad was in robotic mode, and his face looked like whittled wood—a brittle, many-faceted pattern that moved in abrupt twitches. But he was melting towards the cosmic. His features softened, and he reached a middle zone in which his face looked completely human—like skin and flesh, a mirror image of me. The softness ripened, and SubZad's face seemed to rot. He developed patches and streaks of color, like a loosely expressionist painting. Quite lovely, in a way, although certainly it was unsettling to see my face deliquesce.

Growing still more cosmic, SubZad smoothed into a generic cartoony form, like a doll or a balloon-animal. And then, for a brief time, he became a mildly glowing angel of light. And the angel amped back down into a cartoon, an expressionist painting, a photorealistic copy, a tensely chiseled model, and—at the bottom range of the robotic mode—a flaking polyhedral mesh.

"Wavy," said SubZad. "I'll enlighten people. Teach them the deep rhythm of life. But, Zad, am I the best you can do? Make another nurb too. Get loofy, qrude. Go all the way out! Build a nurb that makes no sense. Not just another me. Another you. Another me."

"You want to help?" I asked him.

"Two heads are better than one," said SubZad, a trapezoidal streak of green running down one side of his face, and a burst of orange on the bridge of his nose. "Especially if you're confabbing with a Dynaflow personality like mine."

"Love it," I responded. "I wouldn't have said exactly that. You're already diverging from me. So, yeah, let's make another nurb."

"I'll pitchfork a fresh hundred and fifty pounds of gel off of Blob," said SubZad.

Blob heaved and blubbered and flashed an angry shade of magenta. I didn't like losing any flesh. But SubZad got a chunk loose and we set to work on it. For the first time since

Jane had left me, I didn't feel one tiny bit lonely.

SubZad's mirroring of me had turned my thoughts to Joey's raps about vanishing points and artistic perspective.

"Let's make a man who's an endless regress," I said. "But he has the default normal-nurb personality."

"Yaar," said SubZad, in a cosmic mode state where his face resembled a yellow smiley cartoon. "And call him Mr. Normal. If you have a regress on display—it hints that there's no final answers. It hints that reality is a house built on sand."

To sharpen the jape, I let Mr. Normal's infinite regress take the place of his head. That is, Mr. Normal looked like a man, but instead of a head, he had a little man standing on his shoulders. And the little man had a smaller man on his shoulders and so on, with a dwindling centipede of arm-waving figurines converging to central zone where I conjured up an extremely small and bright nurb lightbulb, held in place by unbreakable nucleonic threads. Designing the genetic code for all this would have been quite unfeasible—but I had the benefit of qwet cosmic logic.

"Mr. Normal burns with a hard and gem-like flame," I said, gesturing at his tiny, savagely brilliant bulb.

SubZad studied my new nurb in silence for a moment, his expression robotic and strict. And then shook his head. "We're outsmarting ourselves with the regress, qrude. Nobody but you and me and maybe Joey will ever understand what the fuck they're looking at. All those little legs and arms—they're disgusting. Get rid of that crap and have Mr. Normal be a man with a head that's a lightbulb. Nice and simple. A big bulb, and not too bright, so it doesn't kill your eyes to look at it, and to show that Mr. Normal isn't all that smart. You could actually sell some copies of a Mr. Normal nurb like that."

"Commercial gold," I said, not quite seriously. But I didn't mind taking suggestions from SubZad. He was almost me. I remodeled Mr. Normal's genes, taking out the recursive regress complication, and setting a foot-high nurb lightbulb on his shoulders, pointy on top, and with the sketchy glow of a filament within.

A remembered image rose in my mind, and I matched the image by making Mr. Normal's body more robotic-looking, with horizontal bars for his shoulders and pelvis, and with visible hinges for his elbows and knees. Fitting in with the same theme, I reshaped Mr. Normal's hands to look like lobster claws—a tweak that could also be useful if we had to face an invasion of wormholes,

"Little Bulb," said SubZad, fully cognizant of my art-historical memory associations. "Gyro Gearloose's helper in the twentieth-century Duckburg universe of the transcendent master Carl Barks. Little Bulb doesn't talk, no. He blinks and he makes gestures with his eager arms."

"Yeah, baby," I said, enjoying Mr. Normal's flicker flow. He was strobing his light in subtle rhythms like visual music, and clacking the pincers of his powerful hands.

"Fuckin' A," concurred SubZad. His appearance was jittering around in the cartoony/expressionist transitional zone. "I'm keying on the wave too," he said. "Mr. Normal thinks he knows where we're at. He's normal, so he gets most of it completely wrong, but it's fun to riff off his misapprehensions. Like skateboarding down stone steps."

Spooky to be hanging with these two bizarre nurbs in the dim barn. Was Mr. Normal dangerous? As planned, I'd given him the default normal-nurb mind—had that been a mistake? Worst case: Mr. Normal might physically drag me to the cops' lair downtown. But, nah, he wasn't like that. He was a quirky construct, a work of art, my Little Helper.

As for SubZad, he felt like a brother, which seemed good. But—my worries wouldn't stop— nurbs were subject to code errors and to malware attack. And SubZad was much stronger than me. What if he went rogue and killed me so he could take my place?

"I won't kill you," said SubZad, fully in synch with my emotions. "Don't be pissing your pants, qrude. But maybe I'll kill Whit Heyburn."

"You the man."

Blob, still piqued about the loss of mass, showed some signs of wanting to slime over here and to reassimilate SubZad and Mr. Normal. But Mr. Normal had found a flicker rhythm that kept Blob away. Mr. Normal was showing emergent capabilities of his own—which was what I'd hoped. Good art makes you surprised.

I was tired. I found a mound of dry straw and fell asleep with my arms around SubZad, holding him close, comfortable with his oscillations, like the brother or sister that I'd never had. Mr. Normal sat beside us, keeping guard, his mind a tangle of social trends and wiggly nonlinear waves.

When I awoke it was night. Still raining, with a steady rhythm of drops on the barn's metal roof. Music as well, squonk music from the mansion—Weezie had hired a good band.

Guests' voices were lifted in revelry. A fuck-ton of them here already. I could teep their vibes in the ballroom, with more of them slogging up the rain-soaked drive.

Peering out the barn door I studied the arriving qwetties. Most were in sodden fancy dress, and they wore nurb accessories. Qrudes from all over town. Everyone was high on cosmic mode. Reaching for the big aha. It was like a Mardi Gras parade, or a dream, or a psychedelic festival.

"A zoo," said SubZad, who was squeezed right up against me, also watching the crowd. His face was cosmic, degenerate, slack. "I wish this qwet wasn't making me empathize with everyone. It's much easier to mock them or to hate them. I wonder if any of these human women would ever fuck me. I'm so much more than a toy."

Mr. Normal amped his strobe light up to a twitchy flicker that drew a pair of the arriving revelers our way. Like moths. They were happy to catch their breath in the shelter of the barn's overhang. The guy was wearing a giant dick molded from nurb-gel—it was three or four feet long.

"Dig the native bearer," said SubZad, pointing to a tiny figure beneath the penis.

Yes, the man had a little nurb assistant whose job was to hold up the tip of the penis with both hands lest it dig into the ground. The penis owner was coarse-looking, with thinning hair, and his partner was a florid, plain-faced woman with six breasts tiered into three lacy black brassieres.

"We're Sam and Suze," said the woman.

"Party's in the big house," I said. "In the ballroom in back. I like how you two dressed up."

"Does that dick work?" asked SubZad, all polyhedral and doctor-like.

"Try me," said Sam, who came across as a low-rent redneck. "Bend over."

"Trundle that thing in to Weezie Roller," replied SubZad. "The hostess. She'll want a taste. Tell her Zad Plant sent you, and that Zad says she needs a better lay than his father."

"Take it easy," I cautioned SubZad. "You don't have to say every single thing that pops into your head."

"Oh, you're afraid you'll look bad and lose your free crash-pad?" said SubZad. "Worried that Weezie will tell Jane you're a crass horndog?" Maybe, from his perspective, SubZad thought he was joking. Or maybe not. He was still in robotic mode, with the facets of his skin glinting in the light. He seemed more like a psycho than a jester. It was unpleasant to see that side of myself.

"That's a loofy lightbulb man you have," said Suze, kindly changing the subject. Her face was electrically alive in the flickering glow.

"I made him just now," I bragged. "Mr. Normal. I made my loudmouth subliminal twin here too."

"Your twin's a nurb?" said Suze, turning away from the strobe light and jiggling her breasts at me. "All six of these are me. I had my genes modded." She glanced around at the looming walls of the Funhouse, the festively lit jellies adrift on the back lawn, and the twinkling Blob in the recesses of the barn.

"I've never been to no party in Glenview before," added Suze. Thanks to teep, I could taste her and Sam's emotions—a mixture of pride, longing, shyness, and resentment. "I heard this is supposed to be an orgy?" Suze asked.

"Let's get inside before—" began Sam, but then he let out

a yell. "Oh no! There goes my smart dick!"

The giant penis had pulled free. It was speeding into the barn's gloom like a hyperactive inch-worm, with its tiny nurb porter running in its wake. The porter's voice grew shrill as the penis slithered into a slit that Blob had opened for it. And then the penis was gone.

"Sorry to bust your chops," I told Sam.

"Shit fire," he said. "Fella likes to walk into an orgy with some *heft*, you know what I mean?" He gazed down at his now-bared privates. "It's not like I'm no Needledick the Bugfucker, but all the same—"

"You'll do fine, Sam," said Suze, putting her arm around her man's waist. "We've got my fancy boobs for bait. Meanwhile, let's just zip you up, so's your meat and potatoes can pop out later when there's some eyes."

Their little helper nurb ran out of the barn, shinnied up Suze's leg and found a perch in her second-highest decolletage. Like someone settling into the balcony at a show.

SubZad and I left Mr. Normal in the barn and walked around to the back of the Funhouse. We entered the ballroom via the terrace door. I recognized many of the guests from around town, including the usual Louisville society crowd that Dad catered too, plus the new generation that had gone to school with me.

Given that we were in the Rollers' ballroom, this might have seemed like one of Jane's prom parties, or like a Todd Trask Derby bash—but, no, it was different. A bunch of random outsiders were in the mix. Also, everyone was totally loaded on cosmic mode. Plus I had the odd SubZad at my side, acting out the antics of my inner self.

The squonk band on stage was called Bag Stagger. I'd vaguely heard of them around town—two men and a woman named Skeezix, along with menagerie of tuneful nurbs. One of the guys, his name was Dharma, was blowing into a mockingbird nurb, whose samples formed a filigreed wall of sound. And he was rocking polyrhythms from a belly-beater as well. The other guy, Kink, was man-handling a nurb bagpipe nearly half his size; it was a hideous beast with eyestalks, drone pipes, and mouths like floppy saxophones. The spiky-haired dark-skinned Skeezix stood in front, flickering like a flame, wielding her gitmo nurb like a crunchy electric guitar. All three of the musicians were performing vocals—syncopated jive, harmonized choruses, and the occasional psychotic rant.

Weezie and Dad danced up front near the band. No doubt it had been Weezie's idea that the two of them dress as a can-can dancer and a top-hatted toff. They were having big fun, and smiling into each others' eyes—which I found intensely irritating. I was still bugged about my Mom.

"Fuddyduds," said SubZad, staring at them. "Deeply lame." I fully agreed, but I wouldn't have said it that flatly.

"Hey there, Zad," said Reba, slinking up to us. She was wearing a tight maroon nurb gown whose long skirt flowed to the floor. "Did I talk to you yet?"

"I just got here," I said.

"I've been resetting myself over and over?" said Reba, raising her voice to be heard over the Bag Stagger sound. "I made a backup while I was floating in that jellyfish in our bedroom with Carlo. It was *so* romantic, Zad. I keep wanting to revisit that moment again." She noticed SubZad. "Since when do you have a twin brother? Ooh, his face is changing. Is he sick?"

"You look hot and jiggly," said SubZad. "Ever done it with a nurb?"

"Not lately," said Reba dismissively. "Not soon." Her eyes roamed. She tended to notice a lot more details than me. "Look at poor Junko trailing after Loulou. I hate Loulou. Of course she had to go and seduce Junko this afternoon. Junko's supposed to be in love with *me*."

"Loulou's fun," I said, unable to resist defending her. "She's smart and full of life. And if she's a little selfish, it's because she's seen hard times."

"Oh please," said Reba. "Don't let her reel you back in. Dig it—there's Kenny and Kristo trying to pick up on two guys from the west side." Her voice rose to a raucous caw. "Teach them German, Kristo!" Her eyes kept moving, taking stock. "There's poor Craig Gurky dancing with his mover nurbs.

Gustav and Bonk? I can't believe Weezie invited Craig. And all these other goobs. Who are they? Oh wow, look at Joey Moon slobbering over the tacky woman with six tits. She's got to be fifty years old. I guess Joey needs a mom. And can we talk about Weezie's outfit? Those ruffles on her legs? Like a clown suit. This is some flop of an orgy, Zad. Isn't anyone gonna *get down*?"

"Won't happen," shouted Carlo, who'd appeared at Reba's side, joining our huddle amid the dancing throng. "I don't foresee a dogpile fuckathon at all."

"The problem is empathy," I said, fitting my voice into the spaces between the Bag Stagger sounds. "Cosmic empathy gets in your way. If you want to get orgiastic with strangers, you need to forget that they have emotions and minds."

"Zad's holding forth on his vast sexual experience?" yelled Loulou, joining us as well. She was wearing the same tired pants and blouse she'd had on this morning.

"If you mock Zad, I'll throw you out," said SubZad, momentarily wearing his knobbly robotic look—all corners and edges.

"Oh, great," cried Loulou, not at all intimidated. "Zad's made himself an art-school bodyguard nurb. Hey, before I forget, I just realized something about this ballroom. I saw a copy of it—up in Fairyland. When I traveled through the oddball? The other end of the oddball was a big pearl sitting inside a giant clam right in the corner of this exact room. Anyway, this band is great, aren't they? Skeezix is so qrude."

Reba was coldly looking Loulou up and down. "You don't have any nice party clothes at all?"

"I don't think Reba has empathy," said SubZad.

"Oh yes, she does," said Carlo. "You're Zad's copy, huh? Reba has empathy, but it's S&M empathy. She savors people's pain while she's being mean to them, you wave? And I'm her boyfriend, god help me."

"Qwet's blanketed the world," announced Junko, standing at the edge of our little group. "I just checked the web. Europe, Asia, Africa, South America—all covered. Those rats and flydinos went wild." Junko was triumphant, terrified, full of wonder. "No sign of a wormhole invasion yet. Fingers crossed. Maybe everything's wonderful."

"Junko's been worrying we're all going to die," put in Reba. "That's why she dipped all the way down to Loulou this afternoon. Like she had nothing left to lose."

Bicker, bicker, bicker.

All around me, people were writhing to the dissonant, jigsawed bleats of the Bag Stagger sound. Over by the wall, two people actually *were* preparing to screw—a fez-capped man on all fours above a supine woman whose limbs were coated with a nurbskin of gold.

Where the hell was Jane anyway? I stepped onto the terrace, found a spot under an awning and called Jane on my wristphone once more. This time she answered.

"On our way!" she sang. She was wearing makeup and a silky green party dress. But something was wrong on her left cheek.

"Is that a black eye?" I demanded.

"I walked into a door," said Jane, too quickly. "Pre-party pump-priming. We'll be there in ten mins."

Half an hour later, Jane, Gaven and Whit came walking across the Rollers' back lawn, their airy nurb umbrellas faintly aglow and with raindrops springing off the bells in tiny bursts of spray. Whit and Gaven looked trim and confident, assholes that they were.

The pale purple oddball and the dull brown dirtbubble were in the air behind the trio, repeatedly darting at each other, like birds competing for a perch. The scene looked choppy and cinematic—thanks to Mr. Normal doing his strobe routine by the barn.

"Jane," I called, starting across the lawn. "Are you all right? Did these guys hurt you?" Her only answer was a stiff wave of her hand.

I hurried to her and got under her umbrella. She really did have a black eye. And her vibes—she wasn't like the Jane I knew.

"Back off," she said in Gaven's voice. "I'm driving this car."

For a wild instant I hoped Jane was kidding me. But no, Gaven had overwritten her. He'd used his goddamned platypus.

"Want a quickie?" said Jane, switching to a falsetto. "I'm ready. I just did Whit while Gaven watched."

Gaven and Whit began laughing like hyenas. They smelled like bourbon, even in the open air. I couldn't let myself explode. I had to take this one step at a time. Cosmic mode, Zad. I focused on the party noise from the house, on the hiss and ping of the rain, on the festive glow of a floating jellyfish.

"This way," I said, steering Jane, Gaven and Whit to the awning on the terrace. "We have to talk."

Jane stood still, quietly regarding me. I felt like I could see her real self behind the callow, geeky expression that dominated her face.

Overhead, the dirtbubble ball made a razzing noise. A smell of sewage and gasoline. Maybe it was gearing up to eat someone. But the oddball kept nudging it, distracting it, keeping it from settling down. As if it wanted the dirtbubble to go somewhere else.

"Panic time coming," said Whit, staring at me, his face blank and insolent. "You should work with us, Zad. You've got some skills. Maybe we can get Jane's personality back for you. Unless you prefer her like this. I do."

Instead of answering, I leaned in close to Jane and said her name three times. "Jane, Jane, Jane." Whit didn't know about our new restore routine. I only hoped it would work.

And, thank you dear world, it did. Jane smiled at me, shaking out her bright gold hair. Whit started to protest, but she cut him short.

"*Fuck* you!" she said, clawing his face, gouging scratches with her nails. And then she backhanded Gaven with a return swing, having clenched her fingers into a fist. "*Jerk*!" The men were stunned, off-balance, half-drunk.

"I can't stand seeing them," Jane told me, talking fast. "I'm going inside. Get rid of them. Then come to me. I've missed you." And with that, she was across the terrace and heading through the ballroom door. The oddball followed her.

So now it was me against Gaven and Whit. I messaged the Funhouse crew for support, but, at least for now, they were into their own trips. The party was raging; they were high; they were sick of my dramas. Only SubZad and Skungy responded. They came out the ballroom door as Jane went in. She seemed only slightly surprised to be passing my shifty double. Anything was possible tonight.

The Bag Stagger squonk band had dropped into a hip-hop beat, with the gitmo wailing, and the bagpipe honking like a baritone sax. Skeezix and her guys were rapping staccato rhymes, shouting the last syllable of each line. The terrace flickered with Mr. Normal's flashes, seemingly in synch with the beat.

Skungy was on my shoulder. The dirtbubble was sputtering overhead. Whit and Gaven were glaring at SubZad and me. Showdown.

Something skittered towards me across the terrace, the party lights glinting off its fur and eyes. The poison platypus that carried Gaven's personality.

"I'll get this one too," said Skungy, preparing to leap.

"My turn," said SubZad, his face dreamy. He swung his arm in a circle, meanwhile doing some kind of internal biomod, so that his arm mutated into a wobbly rubber limb that was six feet long. SubZad's hand landed precisely on the platypus's back and, with a single squeeze, he reduced the thing to scraps of gel.

"You want me to kill Gaven and Whit?" asked SubZad, restoring his arm. "I'd be cool with that." His face had a chiseled look. Like a professional bodyguard.

"Not Gaven," I said. "He's—" It was hard to describe exactly what Gaven was. Geeky, greedy, awkward, and with low empathy—but not exactly evil. Misguided? Lost? A fool? "We'll see about Gaven later. But Whit? Yeah. Rub him out." Hard to believe I'd reached this point.

"Keep away!" barked Whit. He'd already deployed his nurb stingray. It was hovering in front of him, gently rippling its wings in the damp air, with its long poison spike curled up from the rear. For his part, Gaven was clutching a flame-thrower firepig nurb. The firepig was a sausage six inches long, and with four stubby legs. He could exhale methane and strike sparks with his teeth.

SubZad might have been able to snatch away their weapons. But I wasn't liking our odds. That stingray thing scared me. But now, finally, some help from my so-called friends arrived. It was Carlo, carrying, of all things, a metal sword.

"Went to get this off the den's wall," said Carlo, striking a pose and flourishing the blade. "That's what took me so long. Dig the stingray. Aren't those illegal, Whit? Sic him on me, why don't you. Snotty chickenshit creep."

Fully into the moment—almost too much so—Carlo inched forward, making tiny circles with the tip of his outstretched sword. With an abrupt flap, the stingray rose up high, meaning to come down on Carlo from above. But Carlo was quick. His blade swept through the air, and now the floppy nurb lay in two pieces on the ground, its tail furiously lashing. Wearing a face like a garbageman nurb, SubZad plucked out the tail's stinger with another move from his rubbery arm—and he buried the stinger in the dirt.

Skungy squealed a cheer. Carlo continued inching closer to Whit, his sword still outstretched. Cautious little Gaven hung back to one side, still clutching the firepig, but not wanting to risk defending his partner.

I was just starting to rejoice. But then everything changed.

For the first fraction of a second, I mistook the desperate, full-throated screams for a part of the Bag Stagger sound. But, no, the band wasn't even playing. The guests were wailing, crashing to the floor, breaking things, sending out horrific vibes. The ballroom's glass French doors bulged, then shattered. I smelled a swampy odor of decay, laced through with a sharp scent like turpentine. Six or seven dark wormholes were in the ballroom, eating people.

The wormholes were lumpy dark-brown balls like the dirt-bubble, frantic as chickens pecking cracked corn. A ball would flatten itself, then spring forward, opening a sagging, irregular mouth—formless as a hole in the ground. The hole would catch onto someone's head and shoulders, pinch closed, and rock back and forth, frantic with greed, swallowing the struggling victim right down to the feet. And then the wormhole would wobble in wild triumph, forcing the captive into some unseen higher-dimensional tunnel that lay within the ball. After that the wormhole might disappear, or it might cast about for another victim.

Terrified and unbelieving, the guests were struggling against each other, their fine party clothes torn and awry, their shoes skidding on the floor as they pushed their way through the jagged openings of the French doors, heedless of cuts on their bodies, uncaring of their fellows who were being trampled underfoot.

I noticed Dad and Junko in the panicked mob. Jane and my other friends were nowhere to be seen. But maybe—

Careening past me, the woman with six breasts knocked me off my feet. Whit was standing over me, yelling to the dirtbubble.

"Get Zad!"

The icky brown ball came for me, and the torrent of people parted to flow around us. Whit was smirking, thinking he'd won. The dirtbubble's wide, disgusting mouth was almost upon me.

And then, as if by a miracle, one of Craig Gurky's mover golems came to my aid. It was the one called Gustav, doing his trick of curling up like a ball. He bounded over the heads of the crowd and struck Whit directly in the chest, knocking him to ground.

In the second that remained before the stinking dirtbubble swallowed me, I threw myself onto Whit, wrapping my arms around his chest. The lips of the dirtbubble's toothless mouth fumbled around us—and it began swallowing us as a pair, like a boa constrictor eating two rabbits at once. Whit cursed and struggled; I held him tight. Our heads, our shoulders, our chests were within the dirtbubble's maw.

It was dim in there, but not pitch-dark. The dirtbubble's flesh gave off a dank glow. The stinking slime within the dirtbubble stung my skin. My tense muscles relaxed. I was picking up some teep from the myoor beyond the dirtbubble—the myoor had a mind like a primordial sea teeming with chains of life. But the slime was making me too dumb to focus. I was thinking I could sleep in here, I could sleep for a long time. My grip on Whit was going slack.

People were pulling on my legs. I slid down the length of Whit's body. Down—and out of the dirtbubble's mouth. SubZad and Carlo had hold of my feet. I'd escaped. I was on the terrace, lying on my back, with rain sprinkling my face. Whit's feet were inside the dirtbubble. I was numb, and filthy all over. I didn't care.

The dirtbubble's lively lump flexed—and then it was small once more. Maybe it would come for me again? No, it drifted out across the lawn. Carlo and SubZad were shaking me. Junko was leaning over me, too.

"*Robotic*," she kept saying. "*Be robotic!*"

I could do that, yes. It had been a while. I slipped out of cosmic mode. And now I remembered what Junko had said about the wormholes keying in on people who were qwet and in a cosmic state of mind.

"You be robotic too, Carlo," warned Junko, giving him a nudge.

"Hate like hell to come down," drawled Carlo.

"I hear you, qrude," echoed SubZad, his face blurred.

"You two think it's a *joke*?" said Junko. "A hundred people must have died here. Loulou, Joey, Reba. Our friends. They got Jane's mother, too. It's the same all across town."

"What about Jane?" I croaked. "And Dad."

"Your Dad's okay," said Junko. "He's upstairs. As for Gaven—he's nowhere to be seen. I have a feeling he escaped too. Gaven always takes care of number one. But..."

"Jane?" I repeated. Junko shook her head.

11: *Fairyland*

I got unsteadily to my feet and peered into the ballroom. It was empty in there, with scattered food, broken chairs, shattered glass, splashes of blood. All the people had fled outside, or to the other parts of the Funhouse. Looking across the rainy lawn, I could see the faintly glowing wormholes, still hunting, still swallowing people at will. I couldn't believe that Jane and my friends and Jane's mother had been eaten. Jane's brother Kenny seemed to be okay. I could see him inside a floating jellyfish with Kristo. Apparently his wooing of the jellies had paid off. He could ride in them again. I noticed that Kenny and Kristo were hardly projecting any vibes at all. Robotic mode was the way to go.

Some of the surviving guests were clustered around the blinking nurb I'd made. Mr. Normal. Maybe his flashes were keeping the wormholes at bay. My lifesaving pal Craig Gurky was with this group with his golem movers. I gave them a grateful wave.

And, weirdly enough, that elephruk was standing there too. Darby. The dirtbubble had spit her out? Maybe the thing had decided it only liked swallowing humans. Not only had Darby recovered from the myoor's paralyzing poison, she'd even regenerated her missing leg. She was tooting a little tune, giddy with joy over her return.

But the main thing was that Jane was gone. And I was going to find her. I found a hose outside the house, and rinsed off the smell of the dirtbubble.

Going back inside, I scanned the ballroom one more time, and finally spotted what I was hoping to see. The lavender oddball, hovering in a dim recess of the ceiling—as if she were waiting for someone. Waiting for me.

Of all the wormholes, only the oddball seemed like she might be a friend. I strode across the ballroom, allowing myself a touch of cosmic mode to make sure the oddball noticed me.

"Zad," she said, twitching her conical mouth. Speaking aloud. Her voice was high and sweet, with a trace of a lisp. "Come to Fairyland. Jane's inside me. She wants you to join her. You two can move the myoor."

Did I believe this? I had no other choice. I went and stood stock still beneath the oddball.

"Swallow me," I said through clenched teeth.

"Don't be scared," fluted the oddball, widening her mouth. "I'm not part of the myoor. I'm gentle."

"But you smothered Gaven a couple of days ago."

"Gaven's our enemy. He's for letting the myoor run wild. Maybe Gaven doesn't realize this, but the myoor wants to swallow every single person on Earth. The spotted pig and I aren't for that at all. The myoor doesn't need to swallow everyone. She only needs the two right people. And do remember—I was nice to Loulou when she was inside me. I'll make sure you have air. So here we go." The oddball sank towards me.

I slid in as smoothly as a penis into a vagina. The walls didn't sting. They smelled like musk and honeysuckle. Although it was tight in the tunnel, I could breathe fine. Mauve light filled the walls, light from the flesh of the oddball.

Two gubs were in here, the same ones I'd seen before, the ones we'd been talking about, the green gub and the spotted gub, romping like a pair of lovers. I thought of my overwhelming encounter with the spotted gub last night—his teep reaching down to me through the tunnel of the oddball. But seen close up, he still looked like a little pig with a pointy snout. By way of greeting me, the two gubs began rubbing on me like friendly dogs.

The gubs were putting out squidskin web signals as well as teep. The teep showed me their moods, and the web signals hipped me to specific images. Not that they made any more sense than last night. The info from the green gub was like the feed from, say, a worldwide botany study whose images had been randomly cut and spliced, all of this pervaded with a watery, root-twining vibe. The spotted gub's output was more restrained than last night. He was displaying abstract and chaotic imagery, vaguely mathematical. I had a sense that, if I wanted to understand them, I'd need to process every single one of the screwed-up glyphs at once.

Losing interest in so much inscrutability, I pushed my way past the gubs. Jane was only a little way ahead. She was waiting for me in a spot where the tunnel widened to form a soft, glowing cave.

"Oh, Zad," she said, embracing me. "What's happening? My poor mother's dead. And Reba too." Her eyes were wet.

I told Jane what I knew, and what I'd been speculating. Meanwhile, on the teep level, she and I were sharing a heavy vibe of—love?

"You've certainly made yourself interesting again," said Jane. She held me out at arm's length, examining me. "That flashing Mr. Normal nurb you made—I noticed him. He's good. A strong, simple concept. He would sell." Again I noticed Jane's black eye, and she sensed me seeing it. "So did you kill Whit?" she asked, trying to sound casual and tough.

"I tried. I got the dirtbubble wormhole to swallow him. That thing almost got me too. Its slime is some kind of anaesthetic. I'm thinking the wormholes might just *paralyze* people—without actually killing them. Like a spider wrapping flies in silk. Whit could still come back. And Reba, too. And your Mom. Maybe we can bring everyone back."

"And *Loulou*?" said Jane, still jealous about the other woman. "Seeing her get swallowed was the only good part about tonight."

"Oh, can't we get past Loulou, Jane? Can't we start over?"

She sighed, rubbed her face, and sat silent for a awhile. "Oh, why not," she finally said. "I mean, this could be the end of the world, right? Let's love each other like we used to. We were happy then."

"Dear Jane." We hugged and kissed some more. Jane had the same old pleasant smell. Salt and honeysuckle. The two gubs were in this hidden chamber with us now, alternately nosing at my leg and at Jane's. Not even bothering to try and analyze their mental imagery again, I just nudged them away.

The oddball wanted us to move along. She was inching our cave towards the Fairyland end of her tunnel.

And then, *whoops*, we slid out. The spotted gub popped out with us, and the subtly shaded green gub as well. The four of us were standing on the bulging pink body of a giant clam within a pair of wavy shells. A little like Botticelli's *The Birth of Venus.*

The top shell was open, and a soft, dimpled pearl rested upon the clam. The pearl was the oddball, and the pearl's mouth was puckered shut. That's where we'd come from. The upper half of the clam's shell rocked forward, nudging us. We stepped onto the wooden floor; the heavy shell swung down.

It was night up here, and we were in an empty ballroom that looked very much like the one in the Funhouse. A pair of four-foot-long dragonfly people were sitting in arm chairs, studying us. Their bodies were thin and leathery, their faces small and wry. They had fuzzy antennae on the tops of their heads, and long, gossamer wings that hung over the backs of their stuffed chairs. Each of the creatures had four arms and two legs. Their hands were clad in little white gloves, and they had rounded yellow booties on their feet.

"How-do," said one of the Fairylanders. "I'm Stanky, and this here's my man Jeptha. We's talkin' down-home style to put you at your ease."

"I'm quite sure that's not necessary," said Jane, very proper. "We're not hillbillies. We're Jane Roller and Zad Plant from Louisville."

"Don't need to put on no citified airs," said Stanky. "We're plain folks like you." Her voice was low and raspy, and she vibrated her veined wings as she talked. She had a shiny nut-brown face with a thin-lipped mouth, up-turned nose, and almond eyes.

"Right pleased to meet you two," put in Jeptha. "Hold on."

At the first sound of Stanky's voice, the green gub and the spotted gub had begun moving across the ballroom floor towards the outer door. They proceeded in little hops, pushing off with their stubby legs and bouncing a few feet at a time. They weren't exactly scared—it almost seemed like they were deliberately baiting the dragonfly creatures into an attack.

And then, with a sudden snap of his long body, Jeptha launched himself from his chair and skidded face-down across the ballroom's wood floor with his wings trailing. I guess you'd call it a pounce, not that there was anything graceful about it. Be that as it may, Jeptha had snagged the lackadaisical gubs. The little creatures gave out some of their wild, complex squeals—to no avail. But, as I say, it wasn't clear that they really wanted to get away. Perhaps the squeals were a kind of laughter. Jeptha clamped the spotted gub under an arm, presented the green, botanically-minded gub to Stanky and crawled back to his chair.

As he reseated himself, Jeptha gave me a friendly, comfortable wink, as if he were a burgher hoisting a stein of beer. "The gubs and us does this all the time," he said. "The spotted fella's been comin' around for a year. We call him Duffie. He's got an interest in Jane and you."

"And that pretty green one comes here to play with him," said Stanky. "They's more important than they looks. Duffie's in love with the green gub. But he's got a rival. The dark gub. He tryin' to win the green gub for hisself."

Uncurling a proboscis from beneath his tongue, Jeptha sank the tube into the spotted gub. Stanky did the same with the forest-green one. The gubs sat unprotesting on their captors' laps, dwindling like leaky balloons.

Somehow oblivious of all this activity, Jane was sniffing the air and peering into the hallway off the ballroom. "You're sure it's safe to breathe here?" she asked me. As if I knew. "I don't understand why this place is an exact copy of my parents' house. Stanky and Jeptha are—bugs?"

"We ain't bugs," said Stanky, smacking her narrow lips and wiping off a milk-mustache of creamy gub juice. "Use your noodle. We live in Fairyland, and we're *fairies*. Or dragonfly goblins, you might could say. And you folks are what we call bumpfs. Two worlds. The green gub tells us it's easier to make two universes than just one. Start with nothing and make a plus one and a minus one. So we's the minus and you's the plus. You the roots and we the flowers. We don't never break a sweat. Down there you bumpfs do all the work."

Jeptha emitted a wet buzz that might have been a laugh.

"Is my mother here?" asked Jane.

"She's inside that dang myoor thing out there," said Jeptha. "Swallowed up. In storage. Like she's asleep."

Finished with the spotted gub for now, Jeptha cast him aside. Far from being weakened, the drained gub was livelier than before, his mind awash with higher-dimensional shapes and outré patterns of numbers. He bounded towards the terrace door. Stanky released the plant-obsessed green gub, who caught up with the spotted one. Duffie. The gubs paused at the threshold, exchanging their weirdly intricate squeals, as if having a lively discussion.

The unseen myoor outside bleated and made a noise like the opening of a large, wet mouth. Once again I felt a touch of teep from the myoor's mind. Like a fermenting vat of living organisms. The gubs tittered like school children hearing a dirty joke and then—they disappeared, vanishing from tail to head, off into the Nth dimension or some such place. All was calm.

Jane had further questions for Stanky and Jeptha. "This place looks just like my family's house," she said. "I know you said Mom's inside the myoor, but is there a fairy copy of *me* that lives here? A Jane who looks like a bug?"

"No call to keep saying we're bugs," said Stanky. "We're folks like you."

"You're *not*," cried Jane, her voice breaking. "You're gumpy and fubbed."

Jeptha made more of the damp, grating sounds that stood in for laughter. His long wings quivered in bumpkin glee. Our situation was so outlandish that I almost felt like laughing myself. Picking up on this, Stanky pointed a thin arm at me.

"Zad's horrible and gumpy and fubbed," she said, twisting her body in mirth, and making that wet hiss of fairy laughter.

"You fairies don't look like us one bit," insisted Jane, as if reassuring herself.

"Bumpfs and fairies don't have no kind of one-to-one match a-tall," Jeptha reassured her. "It's the *rest* of Fairyland that's a copy of Earth. The glens and dells, the snails and shells, the homesteads and the country hams."

"Yeah, but our ballroom is trashed, with broken glass and spattered blood," said Jane petulantly. "Not like yours." She had a way of getting very stubborn and precise when she was upset.

"The Fairyland version of Earth do have some lags and what you'd call discrepancies," allowed Stanky, cocking her head in an odd way, as if she had extra joints in her neck. "But looky thar! Them window panes is melting away. And, yep, I see jaggies of glass blooming on the floor. Might be the update is spotty and slow on account of the myoor being outside."

"Or haywire from Jane and Zad being here," said Jeptha. "We don't normally see live bumpfs in Fairyland. You like two things what crawled out of a carnival mirror, ain't you?"

"Not that human beings is unknown to us," added Stanky. "Should I tell em, Jeptha?"

"Go ahead."

"Once in a while my husband and I uses the oddball to sneak down and pilfer doodads," said Stanky. She held out one of her clawed fingers.

"That's my grandma's engagement ring!" cried Jane. "You stole it? Mom wouldn't stop talking about it, and I searched for days."

"We're collectors," said Stanky with a motion like a shrug. "Jeptha's got Zad's shoehorn, too. And a couple of old Lennox Plant's paintbrushes. And one of Zad's mother's pottery bowls."

"You're horrible and—" began Jane.

"You already said all that," said Stanky. "You're our guests. So let's keep it friendly-like."

"I ain't never touched no live bumpfs before," said Jeptha by way of changing the subject. "When we goes out collecting, we don't never let no bumpfs get near. Let me have a feel of you, Zad."

And with that he flicked his wings and skimmed through

the air my way. I flinched, but already he was upon me, buttonholing me with his four gloved hands. He smelled spicy and dry. Like cloves. Gently he ran his delicate antennae over my head, exploring the shape of my face.

"Having these two up here is gonna turn things all catawampus," said Stanky. "I could tell Duffie's happy. Even though he didn't say nothing."

"That spotted gub's been fishin' for these two for a year," agreed Jeptha. "And we helped make it be."

"So okay," I said. "What the fuck are you talking about now?"

"Wal, last year Duffie talked us to setting out our tunnel clam's oddball where Jane would find it," Stanky explained. "Like bait. Tunnel clams is exceeding rare, you understand. Jeptha and me lucky to own one. Can't collect doodads without no tunnel clam."

"Let's get to the point," interrupted Jeptha. "That spotted gub has been fixin' to get you two up here so you'd understand about movin' the myoor down to your side. For to outfox the dark gub. Too bad Stanky here had to go and blab to the dark gub about the plan."

"It don't really matter," said Stanky. "Even now that dark gub don't understand about the two sheets. He thinks you bumpfs are mythical dreams or some such. The universe that the dark gub comes from is flat as a pancake. That gub can't really think about space at all. But the spotted gub, our Duffie, he knows the score. Even if he do come from a peculiar place that's like a twisted wad of baling wire."

"Duffie's smart, and that dark gub ain't," agreed Jeptha. "He never laughs, won't listen to nobody, always wants his way. Like a preacher, almost."

"He ain't good enough for that pretty green gub," said Stanky, sounding almost tender. "And that's why we's helpin' the spotted gub."

The two dragonfly creatures looked at us, perhaps expecting a mutter of agreement, but by now Jane and I no longer had any real grasp of what this conversation was about.

"I expect I oughta back up and tell about the myoor," said Jeptha with a sigh. "She's a meat blanket that's made up special by the green gub. And it's our bad luck that the green gub set down the myoor right here. The myoor's sizable, she runs all along the river into town. The first you saw of her was that one wormhole. The one you was callin' the dirtbubble? The dirtbubble was the myoor's advance guard. Her scout."

"And now the myoor's pushin' down wormholes all over your Louisville," said Stanky. "Swallowing people and paralyzing em, looking for the two special best bumpfs that the green gub's gonna want for eggs. A myoor's natural instinct is to collect every single bumpf on a whole planet, just to be sure that the green gub gets the widest choice. Louisville today, and then onto Indianapolis, maybe, or Cincinnati. And New York City, natch. Paris, Istanbul, Rio, you name it. She'll sweep your Earth clean."

"This is about eggs?" I asked, more and more confused.

"The myoor is the green gub's womb," said Stanky. "The green gub's lookin' to spawn two babies. She's gonna pick two bumpfs, run some mods on them, and let her mate wet em down with a squirt of gub sperm. Could be either the spotted gub or the dark gub what does *those* honors."

"You're gonna bewilder these folks," said Jeptha, shaking his odd little head.

"I can't hardly understand how the green gub can even look at that dark gub," continued Stanky without a pause. "The way he's flat and all. It's gotta be the spotted gub who wins. And—like we been sayin—that's what all this la-de-da is about. Jane and Zad gonna close the deal for the spotted gub! That's why the spotted gub done lured you through our dang oddball!"

"I—I can't handle any more of this crazy jabber," said Jane, leaning against me, her knees wobbly. "I need to lie down."

"You're not being good hosts," admonished a nearby voice. I saw an aethereal figure like a young woman, nearly transparent, faintly blue, with long hair and a flowing gown. She was floating in midair, lying languidly on her side. Her hair's tendrils waved with each faint current of air. "Shame on you, Stanky and Jeptha," she added, her voice like a sigh. She had no trace of a hillbilly accent.

Looking around the ballroom, I realized there were some other air fairies in here as well. It was easy to overlook them.

"Lenore with her fancy manners," grumbled Jeptha. He glared at me. "So, fine, you two bumpfs want some clabber and cornbread for supper? A roast sparrow? No? Well, go on and get your sleep. Can't rightly do much till daybreak nohow."

"Can we find a quiet bedroom upstairs?" I asked. "Or is the whole house teeming with you people?"

"It's tight just now," said Stanky. "What with the elves and gnomes and the air fairies. Refugees from the myoor."

"Not that me and *Stanky* needs a bed," said Jeptha, kind of bragging about it. "We prefers to sleep outside, upside-down, holding onto any sizable branch of a tree."

"But the myoor's putting a hurt on our trees," continued Stanky. "So we headin' for the barn's rafters tonight." She turned to the air fairy named Lenore. "How about you be the one to find Zad and Jane a bed, if you so wild about playing the lady."

"I shall," said the hovering air fairy. "Come along, dear bumpfs."

Jane and I followed Lenore to the living room, which was an exact replica of the one in the Rollers' house. Except there were about fifty fairies. Two dozen of them were elves in natty green caps—fine-featured little folk telling tales and singing rounds. Half a dozen dragonfly fairies like Jeptha and Stanky were fastened to the walls. Something like a merman and a mermaid were lolling in an enormous cut-crystal punch bowl, along with a goggle-eyed cuttlefish fairy. Four hard-faced gnomes were gathered beneath a table, playing cards. One of the gnomes seemed to be the leader; he was distinguishable by his jutting beard. His fellows called him Blixxen. Five blazing imps were entangled in the fireplace, continually twining their forked limbs.

One last fairy resembled a worm with a mortarboard hat, a

round starched collar, and a pair of spectacles with heavy black frames. I was curious about that one. Sensing my interest, he sought to open a conversation.

"I'm Professor Wriggle," he said, inclining his smooth and featureless head. His voice was a whistling drone emanating from a tiny hole at his body's anterior tip. "Tell me, is cannibalism common among you bumpfs? When I was but a pinworm, Nurse used to scandalize me with tales of your race. Might I have a peek at your deadly fangs?" Professor Wriggle's glasses were held in place with an elastic strap in back. But he didn't seem to have eyes. Nor did the glasses have any lenses.

I would have been glad to talk with the fairy worm, but I became distracted because the draft from the chimney was dragging our airy guide Lenore towards the hearth. At the last moment, she twirled her translucent body in such a way that she flowed over the mantelpiece, slid across the ceiling and rejoined us by the door.

"Do take a pew!" Professor Wriggle was urging me, all set for a long talk.

But Jane waved him off, and Lenore led us upstairs—to the same room that I'd shared with Loulou and Joey on our first night in the Funhouse. Going up the stairs, we had to step over a number of tiny fairies sleeping on the steps.

Once in the bedroom, Lenore allowed the breeze to take her where it would—and she swept out the open window and into the continuing rain. Something out there was bellowing. A damp, unpleasant sound. And again I teeped a mind like a primordial soup of life. The myoor. I wasn't ready to look at her yet. I closed the window.

A dozen elves lay mounded on our bed, but Jane and I moved them to a pair of pillows on the floor. Their delicate, sleeping bodies were feather light.

Finally in a bed together, Jane and I embraced—relishing our shared warmth, our mingled scents, the contact of our skins. Salt and honeysuckle. We merged our minds via teep and sank into slumber, sharing a dream of a vast, green mind that filled all of Fairyland—and all of Earth.

In the morning I was awakened by a dozen thumb-sized toy soldiers parading back and forth along the mattress, right beside my face. They were executing a drill. One of them was singing out orders, and two others were piping and rattling a matchstick fife and a thimble drum.

Catching the flicker of my eyelid, the leader strutted closer to my face, saluted, and addressed me in this wise.

"Sergeant Cobble at your service! We're sent to you by Colonel Jeptha and General Stanky, requesting your presence for a breakfast briefing."

Jane made a waking-up noise and spooned against my back. My beloved mate, with me in my blanket burrow.

"What are those things?" Jane asked, peeking past my head. "Nurbs?"

"Toy soldier fairies!" said Sergeant Cobble with another snappy salute. "We live in a Christmas stocking beneath the stairs."

"Please no," said Jane. "Too weird and twee. I was hoping we'd wake up in my apartment by the river."

"Still in Fairyland," I said. "You can go now, Sergeant Cobble. We'll be down in a few minutes." Looking around the room, I saw that the elves who'd been sleeping on the pillows were gone.

"At ease!" shrilled the Sergeant Cobble. He and his fellows leapt off the edge of the bed and buzzed off with abandon, each of them frantically beating a pair of insect wings. They were funkier and livelier than any nurbs I'd ever seen. Fairies were a whole different thing.

"So Jeptha said that the people inside the myoor are alive," said Jane, thinking things out. "In stasis. And it's all so the myoor can turn two of them into gubs."

"Let's finally have a look at this myoor," I said, getting out of bed and walking barefoot to the window. "Wow."

The rain had finally stopped, and it was a sunny day. But the sun was bringing to life the myoor's fetid smell. Instead of a lawn, the mansion and barn were surrounded by the creature. It formed a rippling landscape of dappled beige and yellow skin, like a giant mollusk, stretching as far as I could see. Glinting eyestalks projected upwards here and there, and the myoor's skin was slit with toothy mouths.

One of her mouths opened to unleash a peevish bellow, and a nearby mouth responded in kind. A relay of sour bleats flowed down into the gully and up over the hill, past the Heyburns' neo-classical mansion, past the Carnarvons' timbered lodge, and onward towards town. The myoor was a pool of life— but a dissatisfied one. She was obsessively worried that she might not find the two perfect people for the green gub's reproductive needs. Hadn't found them yet. And, like Jeptha had said, if she kept right on looking, she might end up swallowing everyone on Earth.

"The myoor reminds me of lava," said Jane, standing at my side. "The way she flows around the houses and barns. And she's killing the bushes and the trees. See there?" Right behind the barn, the flesh carpet had humped itself up high, and a pair of its mouths were chewing a maple to a ragged rack. "She smells so bad."

"Jeptha said the myoor already stretches from here to downtown Louisville," I said. "Supposedly she'll grow and grow. All just to find two people for modding into gub eggs."

"What about all the people she's already stored?" said Jane. "Do you think we can see them through her skin?"

"Maybe," I said. "There'd be a bunch of them near the ballroom, right? I see some bumps in the myoor's skin down there."

"We should save those people right now," said Jane, backing away from the window. "But I'm so afraid. I act strong, but I'm not. I'm horrible."

I put my arm around her waist, wanting to calm her. "First we'll have breakfast with Jeptha and Stanky."

"What stupid names they have," said Jane, twisting away.

"You'll feel better after we eat."

"I'm not eating a thing," said Jane. "Don't you remember the old fairy tales from when you were a kid? If you eat the fairies' food, you can't go home."

"I don't know that these are the exact same kinds of fairies as in those old books."

"Sure they are," said Jane. "The old tales—they're racial memories." She nodded, agreeing with herself, something she liked to do. And maybe she was right.

The whole house was bustling with fairies. I saw them everywhere I looked. Some were the size of houseflies, some nearly as large as people. Briefly a group of wee sprites circled Jane and me, no bigger than hummingbirds. They looked like bathing-beauty angels, carefully coiffed and trailing specks of pixie dust that glinted like tiny gems. Tinker Bell fairies, you might say.

A loose-lipped loitering gnome ran his hand over my shirt, as if wanting to steal it off my back. He didn't smile at me, nor did he meet my eyes. A female elf sniffed curiously at Jane's leg.

Professor Wriggle's voice was whistling in the sun-splashed living room. Things weren't going so well for the Professor just now. He was arguing with two gnomes, Blixxen and another one. They were calling the big worm a cheater, and Blixxen had snatched the worm's mortarboard hat. The Professor was piping that the gnomes shouldn't get so excited over a gentlemanly game of cards. He said they were behaving like troglodytes, fit only to live in an underground cave.

We edged past them all, and went into the kitchen, where Stanky offered us an oversized steamed beet that was filled with something resembling cheese. "Real good eatin!" she exclaimed, cutting off a couple of fat slices. "That's curdled gub juice inside. I spit up some of what I drank last night. It's a seldom treat."

"Just some bread and water will do," I said.

"Don't rightly have no bread," said Jeptha, offering us a yellow shelf-mushroom the size of a steak. "This roast fungus is what we got. Them gnomes brang it up from their cave. It lights up at night."

"We have golden apples!" piped a pair of elves, watching us from the kitchen door.

"*No food!*" said Jane, giving me a poke.

"We'll just have some water," I agreed. "You think that's okay, Jane?"

"Maybe. I'm dying of thirst."

"Okey dokey," said Jeptha, carefully pouring us two glasses of water and holding his long wings out of the way.

Looking into the glass before raising it to my lips, I noticed motion in the water. Something like whirlpools, but more substantial than that. Thread-like serpents, translucent squid, miniature merpeople—nearly invisible, definitely there in my glass. Thirsty Jane was on the point of drinking when I stopped her.

"What?"

"The water, Jane. It's full of fairies."

"Oh hell. And I'm parched. We need to get home."

"Let's get to the dang point of your visit," said Jeptha. "We want you bumpfs to get rid of our myoor."

"How are we supposed to do that?" I exclaimed. "How big is she exactly?

"A mile wide and seven miles long," said Jeptha. "A monster."

"The spotted gub wants you to lure the myoor down to Earth where the dark gub ain't so likely to find her," confided Stanky once again. "You do recall that it's all about them two wanting to fertilize the green gubs' eggs, right?"

"We fairies want to get the myoor outta here any way we can," added Jeptha. "She's tearin' our place up. Once she's on your all's home turf, I reckon you savage bumpfs might even kill her. Most of us fairies ain't all that bloodthirsty, see. Except for the gnomes."

"What if we forget all this weird crap and say to hell with you?" said Jane, clearly fed up with it all.

"Do nothing, and the myoor's gonna keep on swallowing bumpfs till Earth's a ghost world," shot back Stanky. "And it'll serve you right."

"Maybe we can learn to hide from the myoor's wormholes," I proposed. "The myoor and her wormholes can barely see us unless we're in a special state of mind, right? We could avoid getting into that state."

"And what state is that?" said Jeptha, as if he already knew, but wanted to hear us making fools of ourselves.

"Ecstasy," said Jane, practically spitting the words in Jeptha's face. "Joy. Cosmic harmony."

"So Zad's plan is that you bumpfs stays dull and flat a hunnert percent of the time forever?" said Stanky. "Boy, that's a winner."

"Or maybe we just evacuate Louisville," I said, grasping at straws.

Jeptha shook his brown little goblin's head. "We've had space fairies tell us what the green gub and her myoor's done on other planets. Every time the green gub is fixin' to hatch a new litter, she whomps up a myoor, see? And the myoor slimes all over a planet, sucking up bumpfs. Sometimes that green gub is mighty particular. She might let her myoor stay at it for centuries if that's what it takes. The longer it goes on, the worse things get. So we asking you to rustle up the gumption to kill off this here myoor, or maybe you offer up a pair of bumpfs that the green gub happens to like."

"Why don't Zad and I go home through my oddball and think this through?" said Jane brightly. As if she were brushing off an undesirable client. "I need food and coffee and a glass of water before I kill someone. And that someone could be you. *So*, Jeptha, tell me—my oddball—it still works?"

Stanky and Jeptha exchanged a glance. "It *would* work," said Stanky.

"If we could find it," added Jeptha.

"The oddball's a pearl inside that giant clam in the ballroom!" I exclaimed. "Clams don't go anywhere."

"Wal, a clam might go somewhar if someone was to carry it," said Stanky cautiously. "It's them all-fired gnomes. The air fairies saw two of em making off with our tunnel clam last night."

"What!" cried Jane. "I knew it! You're complete fools."

"The gnomes took it down to their big cave," said Jeptha calmly. "That's how those dang critters are. Thieves. I expect it's up to you two to fetch the oddball back."

"Jeptha and I don't mix with gnomes if we can help it," explained Stanky. "They're a crooked bunch."

"Crooked!" I exclaimed. "You two are burglars yourselves."

"Oh, we're just collectors," said Stanky. "Them gnomes are criminals. And they worship the dark gub."

"There's a door to the gnome cave in the barn," put in Jeptha. "All you need to do is pick your way across the myoor without getting bit."

"I'll help ensure their safe passage," said Professor Wriggle, poking his pink head into the kitchen. "I'm well loved by all and one."

"Lord take me now," said Jane quietly. This was one of her and Reba's ironic lines. They'd been saying it ever since high school.

"Is that a—prayer?" inquired Professor Wriggle, writhing the rest of the way into the room. "I'd enjoy making a study of the bumpf—religions? Quite colorful and outré, I'm sure. We know so little of your race's customs, Jane. I wonder if I might transcribe a series of interviews with you while you're here? Perhaps we could produce a monograph."

Jane didn't deign to answer. The gnomes had snapped the stiff top of Professor Wriggle's mortarboard, and it hung down rather pathetically on either side. He was still wearing his empty-framed glasses.

Raising the front third of his body over the edge of the kitchen table, the professor rubbed his underside across a slice of the steamed, gub-juice-stuffed beet. A corrosive fluid oozed from the fairy worm's skin, turning the food into a purple puddle. Professor Wriggle began slurping up the liquid through the tiny hole at his anterior tip, dribbling bits onto his stiff white collar.

"A once-in-a-lifetime treat, Stanky," he whistled between inhalations. "Superbly prepared."

"Is the worm blind?" asked Jane. "Those aren't real glasses at all."

"I'm all eye, from head to tail," said Professor Wriggle.

"That is, my entire surface is photosensitive. The glasses are a prop, a distraction, a yuk. The gnomes weren't taken in. They sussed out that I can see with the skin of my tail. So they accused me of cheating at their pawky game of cards. I quite reasonably observed that only a fool plays fair with gnomes. And then Blixxen broke my mortarboard."

"*Jeptha's* the fool," said Jane. "*He* lost my oddball."

"Indeed," said Professor Wriggle. "I took the liberty of eavesdropping on your recent conversation. If you venture towards the gnomes' cavern, you'd do well to travel in the company of a sly old snake like me. And bugger this fancy dress." With an impatient twist of his body, Professor Wriggle cast aside his collar and his mortarboard. But he retained his fake glasses, which were now the sole decoration on his long, mauve-pink body. "Shall we embark?"

"I'm not going down in any cave," said Jane. "*You* get the oddball, Zad. And hurry."

"What if we lose each other?" I fretted.

"I'll be waiting here. In my family's house. Or, no, it's the Fairyland version of our house. I'm so hungry and thirsty I can hardly think. Just go."

"Can I bribe the gnomes?" I asked Jeptha. "What could I trade them? Gold?"

"You might offer them your clothes," said Jeptha. "Bumpf pants. A good sight rarer than fairy gold."

"It pleases Jeptha to jest," said Professor Wriggle in a lofty tone.

"He ain't funning!" said Stanky. "Jeptha knows his gnomes."

"I know the gnomes rather well myself," said Professor Wriggle, putting on an air of wounded dignity. "I am, after all, a fairy worm from the subterranean kingdom."

"Whatever," I said. "Let's find that hole in the ground in the barn."

The five of us made our way to the ballroom door. Jeptha and Stanky buzzed along with their dragonfly wings, Jane and I followed after them, and Professor Wriggle slithered at our side.

The myoor's body reached right up to the terrace outside.

As soon as we approached her, a fresh eyestalk sprouted and a slit mouth opened. That same ghastly stench wafted forth. And once again I felt the aura of the myoor's teep. A steamy, tangled vibe, as if from a jungle.

"The myoor don't mummify folks with her mouths on *this* end," warned Jeptha. "Just does that with her wormholes down below. When she swallows someone up here, she flat out chews them for chow. Poor ole myoor might catch a bellyache from eating Zad. When she's got her mouth all set for a horrible gumpy fairy." Jeptha and Stanky released a fizzy buzz of laughter.

As I've already mentioned, the myoor's skin was light brown, with irregular patches of pale yellow. Seen close up, the yellow areas were somewhat transparent, with the sun lighting up the myoor's jellied inner flesh. Her body wasn't more than a foot thick, and the preserved people within made lumps. I could glimpse part of the face of one of the stilled human forms—but it wasn't someone I knew. Or maybe he was the husband of the woman with the six boobs. His face was stiff and weird.

The myoor mouth near the terrace door made a sound, a quieter version of the sour bellows I'd heard before. The myoor wanted to eat us. Up here in Fairyland, when the myoor swallowed you, she chewed you up for food, as opposed to paralyzing you for possible use as an egg. The myoor could see us with her stalk eyes, and she was vibing us with her teep.

"We just glad that ole myoor don't crawl inside our houses," said Jeptha.

"Yadda, yadda," said Jane impatiently. "How's Zad even supposed to get across to the barn? Will you and Jeptha fly him there, Stanky?"

"You bumpfs is awful heavy," said Stanky. "We fairies is made of finer stuff. Don't reckon we could carry him."

"Zad can zoom!" said Professor Wriggle. "Spring and twist, slip and slide, nimbler than the sluggish myoor."

"You'll zoom too?" I asked the worm. "You'll show me the way?"

"I'll, ah, burrow," said Professor Wriggle. "Do you see that little hole in the dirt between the terrace flagstones just here? That's my back door. I can make myself exceedingly slender, you see. I'll slip through and await you in the barn."

"Zad's gonna run across like a hog on ice," said Stanky. "I want to watch this."

"You two are the biggest jerks I ever saw," said Jane, glaring at Stanky and Jeptha. "Stupid hillbillies. Gumpy bugs. I bet you gave the gnomes my oddball on purpose."

"Don't listen to Jane," I quickly said. "She's upset."

"*Yeah*, I'm upset. That lump in the myoor right there is probably my Mom. And I bet the one next to her is my best friend Reba. And now Zad's about to get chewed into a myoor-burger! Look at the big flat teeth in that disgusting mouth. And it smells like—I don't know what. A bloated dead cow floating in the river."

"We's glad you hate the myoor," Stanky told Jane, unfazed by her insults. "You and Zad gonna be the ones to drag her down to Earth. You gonna be a Fairyland hero, girl. And the spotted gub's gonna be your pal. Now step aside and let Zad make his run."

"Bumpf man bump!" cheered Jeptha.

"I'll be back for you soon," I told Jane. What with the stench in the air, we weren't up for a kiss, but we gave each other a tight hug. Jane's body always felt like the perfect fit for mine. Balm to my senses.

I backed off some distance, then took a running jump across the myoor's first open mouth. The myoor's hide was slicker than anticipated. I immediately lost my footing and fell on my ass. The nearest stalk eye focused on me, and—oh no—the tough skin beneath me was opening up a slit. Postponing any effort to stand, I crawled hurriedly towards the barn on all fours, moving at, it felt like, about fifty miles an hour, my arms and legs a total blur. Mouths and eyestalks threatened from every side. I was lunging and gliding, bopping and jiving, too fast for the myoor's traps.

But then I hit a transparent patch of the myoor's skin, and I saw something that threw me for a loop. It was the once-vibrant Loulou in there, pressed against the underside of the myoor's hide like a frozen match girl peering through a window, her open eyes glazed, her face stilled in an expression of sad surprise. Blindsided by grief, I lost my focus. What if the myoor turned Loulou into a gub? And she'd hated the gubs so much...

Behind me a myoor mouth caught hold of my foot. Galvanized, I pulled away and managed to stand. I began moving even faster than before, shuffling my feet like an Olympic cross-country skier, finishing my final sprint in world record time.

Safe on the barn's homely plank floor, I turned and waved to Jane, Jeptha and Stanky, who were cheering me from the ballroom's terrace door. And now the dirt by the barn's entrance shifted—and here came Professor Wriggle, writhing out and plumping himself up—a naked four-foot-long pinky-brown earthworm, with annular ridges all along his length. He felt around with his lively, twisting front end, sensing the sounds, the smells and the—sights.

"Where are your glasses?" I asked.

"I parked them in my nest. I'm traveling incognito."

"And the tunnel to the gnomes' cave?"

"Third stable on the left."

We pushed aside some straw and, yes, there was a capacious hole. Once I'd crawled in a few yards, the sloping tunnel opened up enough for me to walk erect. Professor Wriggle wormed ahead of me, speaking aloud and with his body faintly aglow, officiously guiding my way.

We progressed downward for ten or fifteen minutes, and then Professor Wriggle came to a halt.

"Their cave's around the next turn," he told me. "If it's all the same to you, I'd prefer to wait here. I've never actually been inside."

"Are you scared of the gnomes?"

"Very much so. They're known to stomp on worms. Indeed, Blixxen was threatening to do precisely that. At the close of our argument about our card game."

"But Blixxen won't get here before us," I said.

"I wouldn't be so sure of that," said the worm. "The gnomes have many tunnels. They build for the glory of the dark gub god."

"Gub god?" I echoed.

"Hasn't anyone told you that the gubs are gods?" asked Professor Wriggle.

"How do you mean?"

"The being who created Earth and Fairyland—that's the green gub goddess, born in an entirely different cosmos. The spotted gub and the dark gub are male gods from yet other worlds. Esoteric unseen aspects of reality abound, dear Zad. But, getting back to the matter of Blixxen…"

Just then a hairy, barefoot figure dropped from a hole in the ceiling of our tunnel. It was Blixxen himself, lit by a glowing crystal suspended from his neck. Although only waist-high, the sturdy Blixxen projected a convincing aura of menace.

"*Stomp the worm*," he said in a deep, raspy voice. His beard bobbed with his chin.

Professor Wriggle emitted a shrill whistle and collapsed, his body twisting in frantic loops, his posterior end dribbling waste, and his anterior end moaning for mercy.

"You looking for the big clam?" Blixxen asked me, ignoring the abject worm.

"Yes," I said. "But don't crush the professor."

"Not worth getting my feet dirty," said Blixxen. "I want to show you our cave. We'll settle our troubles. The gang's expecting you." Blixxen ran his callused hand across my face. "Soft and pink. You're like a worm yourself."

"Shall I come as well?" asked Professor Wriggle, suddenly perking up.

"Don't want you," said Blixxen. "You're a crook. If you're so damn curious, you can peek through a crack. Like you always do. Have a look at what happens to trespassers."

"Be careful, Zad," warned the worm. "The gnomes are brutes." Increasingly uneasy, I bade the professor farewell.

12: Spotted Gub

The gnomes' dim, dank cave was like the interior of a cathedral, but without a cathedral's symmetry. Flowstone had bedecked the walls with frozen gray draperies. The rolling floor was set with squat stalagmites like drip-castle spires, reaching up towards the stalactites hanging like knobbly icicles from the limestone ceiling, abloom with popcorn-like growths. Glowing shelf-mushrooms were everywhere.

Perhaps fifty gnomes were in the cave, males and females, all barefoot and garbed in drab colors. Many of the little men had beards, and the women wore kerchiefs. A flock of hammer-headed birds were rapping on the sides of the stalactites, sounding deep gonging tones. The slow, solemn music was endlessly elaborating a simple theme.

I noticed a stream of luminous aquamarine water running down one of the wall's motionless cascades of stone, and I thought of how thirsty I was. The water flowed into a turquoise pool, whose deep, intense shade showed it to be fantastically deep. Stanky and Jeptha's tunnel clam rested upon a hummock of stone beside the eerie pool. The clam's shell was partly open, and I could see the oddball within. Three gnomes stood by the clam, staring into the pool, their lips moving as if in prayer. One of them was a muscular priestess, and the other two were her acolytes. The priestess wore a glowing crystal like Blixxen's.

"You're just in time to see us offer up the clam's pearl," grated Blixxen, still at my side.

"Wait, wait! My wife Jane and I need the pearl to get home. Do whatever you like with it after that. We call it the oddball? It has a wormhole tunnel inside it."

"So he wants the oddball," sneered one of Blixxen's fellow gnomes, stepping forward. This fellow was thicker-limbed and lower-set than Blixxen. He'd been at Blixxen's side when they'd been arguing with Professor Wriggle this morning. "I'm Staark," the gnome told me, giving my hand a painful squeeze.

"I'll trade you my pants for the tunnel clam's pearl," I offered. "I can throw in my shirt as well."

"Fancy material," said Staark, feeling my clothes like a tailor. "But no dice. The dark gub wants that oddball. He wants to use it for contacting Earth in case he needs to. So he sent us up to the house for that oddball clam last night."

"A gub told you to steal the oddball?" I exclaimed. "Look—gubs are crazy pests that make no sense. Even if you and Professor Wriggle think they're gods. I *am* taking that special pearl, guys. Whether you like it or not."

"Nix," said Staark. "You're through." He and Blixxen were blocking my way.

The two gnomes may have been acting like thugs, but I was double their size, and my teep powers gave me the ability to throw them off balance with an unexpected mental jolt. I zapped them, bonked their heads together, and hurried past. My plan was to dive directly into the oddball's slit, and to take things from there.

Meanwhile, the priestess and her two acolytes had raised their voices in an urgent chant. "Great gub! God gub! Dark gub!" In synch with the chant, the gnome cave's funereal marimba music was rising to a crescendo.

I reached the edge of the pool, and the clam with the precious oddball was nearly within my reach. But just then all of cave's glowing mushrooms went dark. The sole illumination was from the gnomes' necklaces, and from an aquamarine shaft of light beaming vertically from the pool.

With a smooth and sinister motion too quick to follow, the dark gub rose from the water and into the air, blocking my way. His darkness was velvety, as if he were absorbing light. He was larger than the gubs I'd seen so far. Portentous. As imposing as—a god. Yet when he turned sideways, he all but disappeared. He was as flat as a sheet of paper, with a single eye set into one edge. All around me the gnomes joined in the priestess's chant.

"Gub of gubs! All-knowing gub! Mighty flatness!"

The dark gub was as big a bull. The silhouette of a bull, that is. He gave me peremptory shove with his snout, pushing me away from the pool. He was flat, but there was considerable force behind his gesture. There was no way I could get past him to the oddball.

"Can you talk to me?" I asked the dark gub. "Can I explain?"

The dark gub curved his body and cocked his head to one side, as if wondering at my temerity in addressing him.

"Indeed I can speak," said he, his voice a sinister whisper from his flat snout. "Get thee hence, foul phantom."

"Why call me phantom?" I protested. "I'm real. I come from Earth. It's on the other brane of this cosmos." I held my hands palm to palm, few inches apart. "Two parallel sheets of space? Do you understand space at all? The oddball is a tunnel."

"A delusional fancy," said the dark gub. "I wit that any cosmos must be, *a priori*, a unitary and undivided whole. The most proper form is an endless plane." He twitched his snout towards the oddball. "Yon sphere is a scrying orb, akin to a sorcerer's crystal ball. You are a baseless fragment from a soothsayer's fantasia."

The big gub's glittering eye was devoid of empathy. My audience with the Great One was over. With a self-satisfied grunt, he balanced the oddball on his snout and sank into the abysses of the glowing pool.

Jane and I were screwed. Marooned in Fairyland. Could things get any worse? Sure they could. Coming up on me from behind, Blixxen and Staark kicked my legs out from under me and seized my arms. Their minds were in a blocked, impervious state, and I had no hope of zapping them.

"All right," I began. "You've all made your points. The dark gub is god. And I'm nothing. So let me go and I'll leave you alone. I'll walk back through that dirt tunnel to the barn. And, hey, you can keep my shirt. Okay?"

This wasn't going anywhere. The priestess gnome was leaning over me, a curved knife in her hand. A scimitar.

"The dark gub wants your unnatural life to end," Blixxen

hissed into my ear. "An oblation. We'll spill your blood into his pool."

"What are you *talking* about?" I cried. "I'm no harm. I don't even exist!"

"You're making trouble," said Blixxen, his breath hot and meaty. "The dark gub wants to father the green gub's children. He doesn't want you helping the spotted gub with sneaky plans."

The mushroom lamps had amped back up. All the gnomes could see the show. The harder I struggled, the tighter Blixxen and Staark held my arms. The priestess's two acolytes had taken hold of my feet. And the priestess herself stood at the ready, flexing her powerful arms, her scimitar raised. I sensed that the plan was to decapitate me as soon as my captors had leaned me over the pool—or had at least gotten me reasonably close to the edge.

As long as I kept struggling, I could postpone the climax. The priestess was kept dancing around me, preparing for the *coup de grace*, and then I'd manage to roll over, flinging myself this way or that and, with luck, rolling a foot or two further from the glowing blue water.

The gnomes watching our struggle were cheering and enjoying themselves. Mad with terror, I had the strength of three men. But I couldn't shake loose the four gnomes holding me. They were raining blows on me with their free hands whenever they had a chance. I was starting to fade.

Somewhere nearby I heard a faint whistle. Professor Wriggle's voice, from a tiny crack in the ground beneath my ear. Staark was punching me in the stomach with one of his fists, trying to soften me up for a final push.

"Hang on, Zad," the professor seemed to say. "Help is on the way." Was I imagining this? Was the voice the pipe-dream hallucination of a dying man? In any case, it gave me strength. With a savage final effort, I raised my arm high, and flung Staark away. Maybe if I dove into that pool I'd find a submerged passage to—

"End it now!" the enraged Staark yelled to the priestess

with the curved blade, and she darted towards me, very poised, very powerful—

"*Gub, gub, wheenk!*" cried the spotted gub, bouncing into the gnome's cave like a cartoon Gloucestershire hog. He was larger than before, easily the size of the dark gub. Not that I could see him very well. My eyes were puffed to slits from the beatings.

Filled with superstitious awe, the gnomes panicked and fled, taking my clothes with them, leaving me bare and bloodied on the smooth stone near the glowing pool with the now-emptied clam to one side.

In a trice the spotted gub was upon me. His body split open along the seam of his gut. For some odd reason I thought of a carnivorous pigskin change-purse, and it made me laugh, although the laughter hurt my bruised lips.

"Zad!" called Jane, now visible inside the gub. "Get in here with me! It's safe. Hurry, darling."

I was too banged up to stand, but the spotted gub crouched over me, lipping me with the rounded edges of his split belly—and then I was ensconced in there with my wife.

"He's taking us back to Earth," Jane said as the spotted gub's stomach-slit sealed over. "He's our friend. Oh, Zad, what have they done to you!"

No way to see where we were going. And I was on the verge of unconsciousness. The spotted gub was feeding me images of parallel sheets with tubes connecting them. Like two soap films with a connecting bridge. Some kind of analogy. Patterns sliding across the films and through the smooth throats of the tubes. Too much to think about just now. I relaxed into the spotted gub's kindly aura. A few minutes later, his stomach opened up again. Jane slid right out, then reached back and gently pulled me free. A moment later she was holding a glass of water.

"Dear Zad. Those gnomes almost killed you." She dribbled water into my bloody mouth. It was the best thing I'd ever tasted. "I'll get some medical nurb ants," continued Jane. "I keep a colony here."

"Where—where are we?" I was so bruised and exhausted that I didn't have the strength to look around.

"We're in my apartment, thank heavens. Wait right here. And remember to stay robotic. We have to worry about those wormholes now that we're back on Earth." I heard Jane's footsteps padding across her floor—and everything went black.

The nurb ants did their work. An hour later I was my old self, safe in Jane's round housetree condo, with cozy light filtering through the living walls, glowing on the antique wooden furniture and oriental rugs.

But I couldn't fully bask in the pleasure, given that I had to stay robotic—lest I provoke a renewed wormhole attack. Conversing with Jane in this state felt stiff.

"Should we have sex?" I asked, as if discussing a traffic route. "Now that we're together again?"

"You're moving in?"

"If you let me."

"You haven't begged enough," said Jane, then laughed, her red-gold hair flashing. "Oh, of course I want you back. It'll be wonderful. But no sex just yet. I'm still freaked about the nasty stuff with Gaven and Whit. And maybe we're too rational just now. We're like…like grown-ups." Jane laughed again, a happy sound, filling our beloved apartment.

"If...if we get back together..." I began.

"Yes?"

"We could finally start our family," I said. "If you're still up for that. All this running around and nearly getting killed—it makes me think. I mean what's it all for?"

"Life's great and subtle wheel," said Jane, her eyes soft. "I know what you mean. I'm glad you're going to be okay. We'll talk about all that stuff later."

"Loofy med-ants," I said, touching my face. My bruises were gone. "So what's going on in Louisville anyway? What day is it? You've checked your wristphone's news feed?" In the back of mind I was intensely thinking about the vision the spotted gub had shown me, and about how I might use it against the myoor.

"Today's the day after Weezie's party, just like up in Fairyland. Everyone's in panic mode. Thousands of people have been swallowed. Qwet's all over the world, but the wormholes are only here in Louisville. You and I know that's because the myoor only reaches from Glenview to downtown. People have been streaming out of the city like they're leaving a war zone. Take a look off the balcony."

As always, the view was stunning—the living buildings, the lacy bridges, the Ohio and its irregular ledge of falls—everything preternaturally sharp and clear. A perfect fall day once again, crisp and sunny, everything washed clean by yesterday's heavy rain, and all the leaves off the trees. The streets were empty, other than a few wandering nurbs. The myoor wasn't bothering with the nurbs.

But, wait, if I looked harder, I could see some people down there after all. Skulking along the edges. They were into their self-protective robotic modes, and their vibes didn't jump out at me, but they were there. Hardcore downtown-scene folks—artists and craftspeople, bums and grifters, qrudes and the poor. People with no place else to go.

Jane leaned on the balcony railing, thinking things over. "The clean wind," she said after a bit. "It was so horrible in the gnomes' cave. Were they really planning to kill you?"

"They were into a trip about the gubs and the myoor," I said. "It's complicated. How did you end up inside the spotted gub anyway?"

"He popped out of nowhere in the ballroom," said Jane. "He started talking to me."

"Talking out loud?"

"Yeah. If you pay attention, you can hear that the gubs put words inside their squeals. Like the qwet rats, only more so. The spotted gub began talking to me like an excited kid trying to say a lot of different things at once. And he was sending me a bunch of glyphs. Like with a web connection. Clearer than teep. He wants to make babies with the green gub. But I'm confused about the rest of it."

"Supposedly the gubs are gods," I said. "The green gub

made our universe, all of it, including Earth and Fairyland. The spotted gub and the dark gub are competing to mate with her. And the dark gub thinks I'm on the spotted gub's side. So he told the gnomes to kill me."

"A god wants you dead?" said Jane, oddly amused. "That's so Zad. The ultimate outsider."

"The artist's fate," I said, glad to have Jane making this funny. "What else did the spotted gub tell you?"

"He says the green gub is stalling and playing hard to get," said Jane. "Being too fussy about where she'll lay her eggs. I happen to remember the spotted gub's precise words. I've been, like, pondering them in my heart. Want to hear?"

"Sure."

Jane made her voice high and squealy. "I take missy past air-bite mouths we get Zad Zad before throat slit very fast we wow beauty green gub whoops to Louisville drool dazzle green gub's myoor we use holy man and woman I picked. I drip drops we make gub babies for hatch next cosmos and wheenkity wheenk to the dark gub."

"A rigorously precise plan," I said, smiling now myself. "I like the drool dazzle. It's giving me more ideas. Where's the spotted gub now?"

"In our bed. Did I forget to tell you? That's another reason we might not want to have sex yet. The spotted gub is in there, kind of wallowing around. He's made himself small again. He's interested in my knickknacks and my underwear and my jewelry. Touching everything with the pointy tip of his snout. You can go talk to him yourself. For whatever good that'll do."

"In a minute," I said. "Right now I'm happy to look at normal things. Robotic grown-up that I am."

"Did I tell you that I really liked your Mr. Normal nurb?"

"You told me. It made me glad. My nurb SubZad, he helped me design him." We sat in silence on the couch for a minute. I longed to melt into cosmic mode and share some teep with Jane, but I didn't dare. Instead I put my arms around her. Smelling her salt and honeysuckle. Almost as good.

"My poor Mom," said Jane against my shoulder.

And poor Loulou, I silently thought. I felt bad that Loulou and I hadn't parted as friends. She'd looked terrible inside the myoor.

"I don't see how we're supposed to handle the myoor without Junko and Joey to help," Jane was saying.

"I wonder if Gaven's going to be working against us," I said.

"I heard on the news that he's been arrested. They're blaming the qwet and the wormholes on him. He's locked up right here in Louisville. With everything in a panic, they don't have a way of moving him out. Serves him right for helping Whit. Stupid turd."

I didn't want to think about Gaven. "We might get busted, too, now that we're back," I said. "We have to work fast. Jeptha said something about us luring the myoor down to Earth. And I have an idea—I guess I got it from the spotted gub. The myoor's wormholes—they run from Earth up into pouches in the myoor's body in Fairyland, see. If you got some kind of weird momentum going, the myoor might dribble down to Earth through her wormholes."

"Fountains of stinky meat," mused Jane. "And even if the myoor survived that, we'd have her on our own turf. And maybe we get the army to attack her."

"I don't trust the government," I said. "The Department of Genomics trashed my store, and the Louisville cops were going to kill me. The spotted gub and us qrudes should take care of the myoor ourselves. And we'll have to free the people who the myoor swallowed."

Just then the spotted gub called to us from the bedroom. At first I heard his voice as a curly squeal, but then, prompted by Jane, I began picking up on the words within the sound.

"Cosmic Flip Trip zonk bomb fest," the gub was saying. "I heard Zad thunking the myoor falls in her fishing hole. Good catch."

Jane and I went into the bedroom. The spotted gub was resting with his fat end on our bed, with his snout sticking up like the root of a turnip. Jane's little possessions were scattered around him. His body had made a yellow stain on our sheets.

"How long do you plan to stay here?" I asked. "You're ruining the bed." We might be allied with this bizarre, possibly divine being—but he didn't have to share our apartment.

"Myoor see big crowd at Cosmic Flip Trip wacky wack leans too far and falls out seven hundred and seventy-seven windows eeek," said the gub, his dark, shiny eyes twinkling. He seemed to be having a good time.

"Cosmic Flip Trip," echoed Jane. "I feel like the gub found that phrase in my head. Can you see what's next?"

"Yes."

"Tell me."

I marshaled my thoughts. "All the qrudes in Louisville go into cosmic mode at once, see? And when the wormholes come swarming, we snap into severe robotic mode, and the baffled wormholes are fumbling around, and we yank on them with ropes, and the myoor breaks into pieces and we're dragging her through the holes. Maybe she gloms back together down here. But, *hmm*, what then? How do we free the people she's swallowed? How do we eliminate what's left of the myoor when we're done? Spotted gub, can you show us more?"

The gub let out a twirly squeal that set a stream of images to blooming in my head. Aha. Our path was a little less foggy than before.

At this point the spotted gub wanted to get back to chasing after the green one. The creator of our cosmos. The spotted gub wanted to fuck god. Go for it, qrude.

Still sitting upright our bed, the gub made his pointed snout disappear, and then his sloping shoulders and then his dirty-white brindle-spotted butt, and then he was entirely gone. Off in some higher dimension.

Jane got into some immediate and practical housekeeping concerns. "I can't even look at those stains on the sheets. Good thing the bed's a nurb. I'll have it run its self-cleaning routine. No use trying to order a new bed nurb, what with everyone leaving town."

"You're down with my battle plan?" I asked, sending her some images of what I had in mind.

"Ready to roll," said Jane. "Def! I'll work out the campaign for the Cosmic Flip Trip, and I'll get the ad online in less than an hour."

"We won't actually tell people that they'll be bait for the myoor, will we?"

"Duh! We tell them it's, I don't know, a civic reclamation ritual. A transdimensional squonk fest. Social healing. At Churchill Downs. Free beer and chicken. Whiskey and ham. I'll get Skeezix and Bag Stagger to play. Or maybe Tawny Krush."

"Bag Stagger is perfect," I said. "They already conjured up the wormholes once, right? At the Funhouse party."

"We don't stress that aspect at *all*," said Jane, and shifted into announcer mode, making her voice low and urgent. "The Cosmic Flip Trip. Win back your soul. Get as qrude as you want to. And raise the dead. Come on home, Louisville. It's party time. Brought to you by Jane Says."

"When is this party going to be?"

"Tonight," said Jane with a shrug. "Why dilly dally? We're facing the—what's the word? Judgment Day. Apocalypse. No time to lose."

"You can organize the Flip Trip that fast?"

"I'm Jane Says. I've got this town wired, Zad. You know that."

"I'll get cranking on the tech prep," I said. "I want to make some special nurb vines for pulling down the myoor. And a thousand copies of Mr. Normal, ready to flash. The biggest strobe-light event of all time. We'll use the flicker to corral the myoor in one spot. On the track. And then we'll find a way to deal."

"Love it," said Jane. "Let's build the yanking vines and the Mr. Normals downtown—instead of way out at the Funhouse in Glenview."

"We'll use Craig Gurky's shop," I proposed. "It's huge, like a warehouse. We'll need—sixty tons of nurb-gel? Can we get that from the Roller plant?"

"If anyone's still in town. How big is sixty tons?"

"Maybe four elephruk loads? Darby and one of the elephruks can do it. Did I tell you the myoor spit her back out? After that first wormhole swallowed her in the barn? And Darby made herself a new leg."

"Good old Darby," said Jane. "Remember we were riding on her back at my eleventh birthday party, and I wanted you to hold my hand, and you were sneezing because of the hay?"

"I was pretending to sneeze," I said. "I thought it was funny."

"You were very immature."

"I'll hold your hand now."

"That's nice. And you'll call Kenny about the gel, and I'll work up my ad. By the way, I already said hi to Kenny while you were on the nod and the ants were patching you. Kenny and Kristo plan to keep living in the Funhouse."

"Not pushing his luck with the jellies, huh? I'll ask him to meet us at Gurky's place. He can bring my Mr. Normal and my SubZad. And meanwhile Darby starts hauling gel. I hope everything clicks."

"It will," said Jane. "It's fated. Written in the sands of time. I get the feeling that the spotted gub already knows everything that's going to happen."

"Magic pig that he is," I said. "I can't believe the weird shit that's come down the last few days."

"A kaleidoscope roller-coaster," said Jane. "And wait till—" She paused and made an encouraging gesture. We intoned the tag line together. "*Cosmic Flip Trip!*"

I called Craig Gurky on my wristphone. It was reassuring to see his wide, homely face. "You still in your shop?" I asked.

"Sobbing, elated reassurances to you as well, Zad. I'm here, but Mom skedaddled to Aunt Effie's in Chicago."

"Jane and I are coming over right now, okay? And probably her brother Kenny. We want to use your space for, for—oh, it's complicated. You'll like it. I'll tell you the rest in person."

"Jane and Kenny? Ooh la la. I'll put on nice clothes."

"See you soon. Stay robotic, qrude."

I checked in with Kenny, and he said that there were still a few people at the Roller plant, and that they'd send thirty tons of nurb-gel over to Craig's, with thirty more to come. Like the rest of us, Kenny was ready to try anything.

"Zing!" said Jane, looking up from her wristphone. "I'm releasing my ad. It's rough, but rough is more convincing. And it'll evolve."

"You already lined up Churchill Downs and the food and all that?"

"More or less," said Jane, making a languid, high-society motion with her hand. "As long as enough people come—something'll happen. It's not like they'd be using the track for races today, with the city a disaster zone. Skeezix and Bag Stagger will be down with performing for sure. So let's stride."

On the way to Craig Gurky's we saw Ned White from the jewelry store get eaten by a myoor wormhole. It was terrible. Some people had looted Ned's jewelry store on their way out of town, and Ned was drunk, standing in the empty street with a pumpkin of whiskey, yelling that he was the last man standing, and that Louisville was still his town. He looked over at us with a unhappy, open-mouthed grin, holding up the pumpkin, offering to share. The air got a little wriggly. I thought it was the alcohol fumes, but then a ball of leathery meat formed behind Ned.

Somehow he knew the ball was there—he heard it or teeped it or felt a breeze. He ran towards us, dropping the pumpkin. It split open with a splash. Just as Ned passed us, the myoor mouth caught up with him; it opened wide and clamped over his head. Ned fell awkwardly to his knees. Jane and I tried to pull back on his legs, like the others had done for me on the terrace last night. But the wormhole was determined. With two or three jerking gulps it swallowed him whole. Like a rattlesnake eating a mouse. And then the clenched myoor mouth disappeared.

I heard a grating voice from a second floor window. Two short men were up there, half in the shadows. One had a beard, and the other, even shorter than the first, had unnaturally thick arms. Blixxen and Staark from Fairyland. Blixxen crooked his finger at me, beckoning. He was trying for a friendly smile, but it wasn't working. Staark made a broader come-on-up gesture. The gnomes wanted us for something. A deal? After nearly cutting my head off?

"Those are the gnomes from the cave!" cried Jane, standing stock still. "How can they even be here?"

"Let's not find out," I said, taking her by the arm and urging her forward. I was half-worried the gnomes would leap down from the window and come after us. But when I glanced back at them, they were just watching us, with Blixxen's beard moving as he murmured something to Staark—whose lips were twisted in a nasty smile.

Staying robotic, moving stiffly, walking as fast as we could, jumping at every sound, Jane and I made our way down the block to Gurky Movers.

"Stupid greeting!" exclaimed Craig as we walked into his echoing, empty warehouse with its ancient brick walls. Craig was amusing himself with one of his metalanguage routines. "Brave and humorous aside. Unrealistically hopeful speculation. Stout affirmation of solidarity. Lewd sexual innuendo directed at your mate."

Jane and I looked at each other and laughed—a little hysterically. We were so glad to be away from Ned getting eaten, away from the sinister gnomes, and here with our harmlessly weird old friend. We'd made it to Craig's and we had a chance of saving the world.

"You're a virgin, aren't you, Craig?" said Jane, just to be talking. "Why don't you ever find a woman to date?"

"I'm not really interested in women that way," said Craig, suddenly serious. "I've been living a lie. For my mother's sake."

"She's gone now," I said, eyeing Craig to see if he was going to crack. I was in a wild, abandoned mood. "Mom's in Chicago. Go wild, qrude. Shed your character armor. Let yourself ooze."

"It's Kenny that I crave," murmured Craig. He stared at Jane and me, his expression blank. "There. I've said it."

And then Kenny arrived, along with SubZad, Mr.

Normal—and Skungy the rat. They'd ridden from the Funhouse on three road spiders.

"No Kristo?" said Craig, his eyebrows twitching out of control.

"Kristo figures there's more wormhole danger downtown than out in the country," said Kenny carelessly. "And maybe he's right. The myoor has a way of focusing her attention on crowds."

"We're right here," said Craig, moving closer to Kenny. "You and I."

Kenny looked Craig in the eye, assessing him. "Did you wave on Zad's Mr. Normal yet, Craig? He has a completely average personality, but with a blinking lightbulb in place of a head. Kind of like you." Kenny paused, smiled. "You never told me you were queer."

"I'll compose my response," said Craig, backing away.

Meanwhile Jane and I were greeting my nurb twin SubZad. "Glad to see you," I told him.

"Likewise, qrude. Can you tell us apart, Jane?" The question was kind of a joke, as the excited SubZad was cycling from robotic to cosmic and back, now like a whittled carving, now like a Galaxy-Z slime-mold man.

Jane smiled. "I think Zad's skin is warmer, right?"

"What about me?" shrilled Skungy, crawling up my leg. "Aren't you excited to have me back?"

"Sure I am," I said. "I could have used you in Fairyland."

"Next time take me along."

"Where were you when I went into the oddball?"

"Hiding."

Darby and a fellow elephruk arrived and they dumped out the first thirty tons of nurb-gel we'd be getting. I led Mr. Normal over to the two piles of gel and I set him to crafting copies of himself.

It was safer to let my nurb helpers get into cosmic mode and do the genemodding. The myoor wasn't attracted by *nurbs* who were in cosmic mode. But if I risked cosmic mode, a wormhole would be likely to appear almost immediately.

I told SubZad about the luminous whips I wanted us to use against the wormholes, and began crafting those, using biomodding to grow them from the gel. The whips were slender, incredibly strong vines, fifteen or twenty feet long, reinforced by monomolecular protein filaments. Each whip had a handle on one end, for pulling. And the business ends had curved thorns, for catching hold of the wormholes' flesh.

Jane was steadily monitoring the reactions to her online ad, repeatedly tweaking the ad as it reproduced and spread. To pass the time while she did this, she rode Darby back and forth between Craig's place and the Roller plant while the elephruks fetched the second load of nurb-gel.

Jazzed about having company, and about having more-or-less revealed himself to Kenny, Craig was pacing around his big space, alternately rubbing his hands and scrawling on a paper with an ancient pencil. Craig's four-foot-tall mover golems Bonk and Gustav strode the old stone floors with their owner, mimicking his hand gestures and the abrupt, quizzical motions of his head.

By the time we were done crafting our army the sun was going down. A squadron of a thousand Mr. Normals stood in formation, a twenty by fifty array, bulb after bulb lined up, like in a carton of eggs. I'd rigged it so the bulbs acted as eyeballs too.

To bring them up to maximum power, we got one of the Roller elephruks to bring in two loads of Roller chow, filling the warehouse with the smell of fine, Kentucky tobacco. Skungy ate as much of it as he could, but he was no match for the thousand Mr. Normals. With their green-glowing whips in hand, the Mr. Normals were kind of scary.

While all this was going on, we were doing our damndest to stay robotic. No spacing out, no staring into the distance, no merging into a comfortable vibe with your pals. Everything strict and precise, and everyone at an arm's length.

I wanted *some* kind of kicks, so I got the Mr. Normals to start flashing. No two of them were exactly in synch, and they dialed their strobe speed up and down the frequency scale until they'd located a maximally corrosive vibe. Disco fever. Craig Gurky dug it, indeed he started dancing a hip-hop jig. But Kenny started yelling he was worried he'd have a seizure. And Jane said the strobes might zone us out and turn us cosmic. So out went the lights.

"We are *so* ready to herd that myoor," said Kenny. "Right, Craig?"

Craig offered a courtly bow. He hadn't uttered a word for several hours.

"Plenty of people at Churchill Downs already," said Jane. "A few hundred, anyway. Every qrude who's still alive and still in town is heading there. They knocked down the racetrack gates and they're inside. Bag Stagger's starting to play."

"Is there food for the people?" I asked. "Free beer and chicken? Like you said?"

"Don't be so petty," said Jane dismissively. "I just said that for flash. And then I changed the party to a potluck. People have whiskey pumpkins and beer dogs and horns of plenty. Everyone's looted all sorts of crap."

"End times, qrude," said Kenny. "Let's hit it. Jane and Zad, you can use the two spiders that the nurbs rode over on. And, Craig, you can ride on my spider with me."

"I'd like that," said Craig, beginning to relax for about the first time in his life. "Here." He handed Kenny the square of paper he'd been revising all afternoon. Kenny studied it, smiled slightly, and put the scrap in his pocket. I never did find out what it said. Maybe it was a love poem. Or, who knows, a hopeful drawing of Craig and Kenny hugging each other.

But I had no time to think about this. We heard people outside. I went to the door with Jane and SubZad. Golden Louisville twilight. A heavy automobile had pulled up in front of Gurky Movers—my slugfoot Lincoln convertible, the one the cops had impounded. And, yes, Lief Larson and his bullying deputy Grommet were in the front seat. Gaven Graber was riding in the rear, seemingly at liberty, but I had the feeling Grommet would shoot Gaven if he tried to run away.

"I'll front for you," said SubZad, pushing past me, wearing a face of stone. "You hang back. Make a new copy of me one of these days. Or not." Nurbs didn't care as much about dying as people do. SubZad started towards the Lincoln, head held high.

"Freeze!" yelled Grommet, jumping out of the car. Grommet and Lief were qwet like us, but they'd gotten over being mellow. They were back into being cops. Grommet held a leadspitter in each of his big hands. The leadspitters were tweaked bombardier beetles that shot metal pellets—like old-school pistols.

"Why bother us now?" said SubZad. He walked up to Grommet, getting right in his face. "Your scene's done. Asshole." Grommet was holding his leadspitters leveled at SubZad's gut.

"Easy now," said Lief, as much to Grommet as to SubZad. Understand that, at this point, Lief thought SubZad was me. SubZad was holding his face still, and was sending out a pretty fair approximation of my vibes. "Gaven tells us that your crowd spread the qwet," continued Lief. "And that you brought in those alien eater things. So now you're charged with treason and mass murder, Zad. Put your hands on the car so Grommet can frisk you. We have to take you in. Even if Louisville's falling apart."

"No," said SubZad. "No time for your tired bullshit. We're on our way to Churchill Downs to kill off the alien invader. You should be grateful to us, Lief. You should be down on your knees sucking my dick."

Lief just looked at him.

"We know about the Churchill Downs scam," snarled Grommet. "Another qrude party. Like that's going to fix anything. Promoting a riot. Gaven told us he knew where to find you, and he was right. Hands on the car."

Jane stepped out of Gurky's door into a low shaft of light from the setting sun. "Give Gaven to us and go away," she commanded. Gaven was cringing in the back seat of the Lincoln, his eyes darting from side to side. I was still in the shadows of Gurky's shop, a few feet back from the door.

"You're under arrest too," Grommet told Jane, his teep

vibes like knives. He pointed one of his leadspitters her way.

With a blindingly fast move, SubZad stripped the leadspitter from Grommet's grip, tearing a wound into the man's hand. Reflexively Grommet fired his other leadspitter into SubZad's stomach. SubZad staggered backwards for a moment. But the leadspitter was tuned for working on human flesh, not on the doughy bodies of nurbs. SubZad regained his balance and came lunging back. He released his careful control over his expressions. His face was that of a decaying graveyard ghoul.

Grommet's leadspitter clattered to the sidewalk as SubZad clamped his hands around the man's thick neck. Grommet was pounding on SubZad with his fists—but to no avail. Struggling and grunting, the pair dropped to the ground, Grommet on top, but with SubZad still choking him.

Lief was out of the car and yelling—he wanted to intervene. He understood by now what SubZad was, and he had a firepig in his hands, but he couldn't find the right angle for flaming the nurb without blasting Grommet.

Suddenly Grommet went limp. SubZad hadn't stopped at strangling him. He'd broken his neck.

Perhaps, from the point of view of the myoor, Grommet's dying brain flickers were akin to being in a cosmic mode. A wad of flesh appeared, flexing like an evil sock puppet. A wormhole. It opened its crooked jaws and swallowed the dead cop as handily as a radish.

Lief pressed in with his firepig, covering SubZad with layer upon layer of flame. The doomed nurb beat his arms against his body and rolled to and fro, but Lief stayed on him until the flames were irreversibly out of control. SubZad dwindled to a sticky patch of ashes on the ground.

While this was happening, I mustered my troop of Mr. Normals. Gustav and Bonk appeared as well, not that we needed them. The one thousand Mr. Normals streamed out the Gurky Movers door carrying their thorned whips, and they crowded around Lief and my Lincoln in a rough circle, six or seven nurbs thick. Jane and I pushed inside the circle, with Skungy perched on my shoulder once again.

One of the Mr. Normals pointed his hand-claw and shot a crackling high-energy spark—a chaotic zigzag ten feet long. It knocked the firepig from Lief's grip, then sparked again, fusing the firepig into a twisted scrap. Further sparks destroyed the other weapons that Lief and Grommet had brought.

Gaven chose this moment to step from the Lincoln with his arms held high. "I'm sorry!" he cried. "Forgive me."

Jane walked over to Gaven, evilly swaying her hips. Lief and I watched to see what came next. Kenny and Craig were peering out from Gurky Movers as well.

"Do you love me, Gaven?" said Jane, her voice raised as if she were on stage.

"Yes, yes! I do!"

"I'm not feeling it," sang Jane. "You're jagged. In a frenzy. Make yourself calm, Gaven. Merge into the One. Teep with me."

"But, but—"

"Do it for just a second, Gaven." Jane's voice grew low and caressing. "Show me you can be nice."

So Gaven slipped into cosmic mode, just for that one second, and then, *yorrrk*! The myoor popped out another wormhole and wolfed the man down, with Gaven kicking and screaming all the way.

"Whoah," said Lief, oddly unafraid. "Enter the Dragon Lady."

"I didn't know you could be so ruthless," I murmured to Jane, kind of appalled.

She gave Lief and me a calm look. "You have to remember what Gaven did. He overwrote my mind. He helped Whit rape me. I won't stand for that." She paused, thinking. "And, Zad, if your theory about the myoor is right, then Gaven isn't really dead, not even now. He's in suspended animation. He's one of the myoor's candidates for making into a baby gub."

"And we might still bring him back," I had to add. "When we drag the myoor down here and pull her apart."

"So maybe we'll have to eliminate Gaven again," said Jane with a shrug. "The treat that never grows old. Let's go to

Churchill Downs."

"What about me?" said Lief, kind of smiling. "I'm supposed to be the one in charge here."

"Oh, right," I said. "How could we forget? You want to come out to the track with us, Lief? Help save the world?"

"Not my bag," said Lief. "I'm just a cop. You save the world. You're the artist. And forget all those bullshit charges against you. Clean slate."

"Can I keep my car?"

"Sure, qrude."

Lief made a gesture vaguely like a salute, and headed off down the street on foot.

13: Churchill Downs

So we rode the slugfoot Lincoln convertible to Churchill Downs. I was in the front seat with Jane. Skungy sat on the dashboard. Kenny and Craig were in back. Our squadron of Mr. Normals marched behind us, each of them carrying a thorned whip. We found an open gate at the side of the track, and we rolled in there like royalty, with Skeezix and Bag Stagger wailing on stage. Far off to one side, there were still some horses in the racetrack stables.

Skeezix spotted Jane and announced us. The qrudes in the grandstand and on the track began cheering. The crowd looked skimpy amid the huge oval of Churchill Downs, but there might have been a thousand of them by now. They all knew about Jane and me—thanks to qwet teep and the Funhouse party fiasco. And they were counting on us to repair the damage.

I took Jane's hand and we stood up in the car to wave at the crowd. The slugfoot slimed along nice and slow. The Mr. Normals were brandishing their luminous whips, etching pale green figure-eight motion trails against the deepening dusk. It was awesome.

When our car stopped beside the stage, Jane and I bounced up a flight of steps to join Bag Stagger. Craig and Kenny stayed in the car, but good old Skungy was on my shoulder.

"*Yeeeeeek!*" yelled Skeezix, bopping sideways towards us with her gitmo in her hands and her mic nurb wrapped around her neck like a snake. She smelled like decaying fruit, but in a good way, like an apple orchard.

Her mic and her instrument were linked via wristphone-style signals to speaker nurbs all across the Churchill Downs grandstand running along one side of the track. Two humongous squidskin concert speakers were draped over the edges of the stage as well, pulsing with thuddy bass.

Skeezix put her face right up against Jane's. She seemed

stranger to me than before, but Jane was used to her. Her chestnut skin was papery, and she had a funny way of pulling up her top lip. She had nurb worms on her scalp that propped her curly hair into excited stalks, like antennae. Skeezix was definitely having trouble keeping herself in robotic mode. She was a full-on musician.

Her backup guys Kink and Dharma came shambling in her wake, clearly jonesing for qwet merge as well. Big bearded Kink had his arms around his enormous nurb bagpipe like it was a besotted friend, with the slippery bagpipe squonking fierce and gnarly. It had three loose-lipped, puckered-out mouths—nasty.

By way of greeting us, Kink leaned his slimy bagpipe against Jane's bare shoulder. The thing pressed one of its mouths against her skin, kind of slobbering, and it blared a welcoming squeal.

The third musician, skinny dark Dharma, was working a bird-shaped nurb that he held clamped between his teeth. It was his nurb mockingbird, spewing out sick scraps of sound from the man's mental Akashic records. For a rhythm line, Dharma was slapping chaotic rhythms from the fleshy belly-beater nurb affixed to his gut.

Meanwhile Skeezix's gitmo was chiming skewed arpeggios of god-chords while she shrieked a song.

Ye godda ye godda ye godda!
Runnin dry
I know why.
In my head
Myoor meat bed.
Ye godda ye godda ye godda!

Dharma's metamockingbird made a sound like a choir of throat-singing monks. "*Brother Zad Zad! Dormez vous?*"

"*Co cosm, co cosmic, co cosmic flip!*" went Skeezix. "*Trippity trippity trip trip trip!*"

Her snake-like mic uncoiled its tail from her neck and

wriggled along her outstretched arm to drape on me, with its little head just below my chin. Skungy curiously sniffed at it, daintily twitching his whiskers.

Kink made a sudden, savage gesture with his sodden instrument and—just like that—the band's avalanche of sound came to a full stop.

"Testing," I said into my mic, like a complete goob. My voice echoed across the terraced stands by the track. I was stiff with stage fright. And now, making the scene even more like an uncomfortable dream—I saw my parents in the crowd. Mom and Dad, standing side by side, not holding hands or anything, but together. Sally and Lennox Plant. Looking at me. My lips began working, with no words coming out.

"We need help, Zad and Jane!" hollered someone in the box seats. A coarse, bullying voice. Oh oh, it was Blixxen the gnome. "You'll help the dark gub! Or die!" A gnome's notion of proposing a deal. I shook my head at him.

He glared and pointed at me as if taking aim. His sidekick Staark was holding—oh god, what was that? A leather sling? Scimitars dangled from both their waists. Clambering onto Blixxen's shoulders, Staark began swinging the sling in a circle around his head. Where did these guys think they were?

Staark's rock very nearly hit my head. It could have knocked me unconscious or even killed me. Skungy squeaked for help, and in seconds a Mr. Normal was on the case. Bulb flickering, he vaulted into the stands. The unsavory gnomes from Fairyland melted into the restive throng, crouching low to conceal themselves behind the rows of seats.

What exactly did they want? No time to think.

"Time for the *Cosmic Flip Trip*!" cried Jane, leaning into me to use my mic. "Time to be high again, qrudes. Our thousand lightbulb men will catch hold of any wormholes before they can hurt you. It's party time!"

No response from the crowd. Anxious glances. Grumbling. "You go first!" hollered someone, and others took up the cry. "Zad and Jane first! Zad and Jane show us how! Zad, Jane, Zad, Jane!"

I should have seen this coming. But I was so into my own plans that I'd only been thinking in terms of me coaching the assembled qrudes into going cosmic, and of me directing my army of Mr. Normal nurbs to save the crowd when the wormholes showed up.

"Zad, Zad, Zad!" chanted the crowd. Yeah, they were sparse amid the grandstand's rows of seats—but they were plenty loud.

All right then. I held up both my arms, calling for attention. "I'm doing it," I cried. And if I ended up inside the myoor—oh well!

Two Mr. Normals were on the stage behind me with their whips, like some crazy dictator's personal guards. Skeezix fired up her gitmo and began strumming a tension-building ostinato rhythm, sliding up the scale. Kink and Dharma chimed in with nurby bleats and groans.

I squeezed Jane's hand and went for it. Slammed myself into full cosmic mode. The objects around me took on a fine, honeyed glow. I could teep a sea of emotions there—fear, lust, excitement, and the simple joy of being in a crowd. For the first time since yesterday or maybe the day before, I wasn't worrying. But that didn't last long.

I heard a whisper behind my head. Something in the air. Oh fuck, a wormhole, dull brown, with that same smell of bad medicine. Moving towards me. But then—*whip*! And *whip*!

My two Mr. Normals had sunk the thorns of their whips into the meat of the myoor wormhole and they were pulling on it like mad—crouching, bending their knees, falling off the edge of the stage and pulling some more. The wormhole neck was getting longer and longer. At first it was like the siphon of a clam, and then it was like a strand of dough flowing into a mound on the ground. There seemed to be no end to how much myoor meat the Mr. Normals could pull through.

"*Me me me!*" sang Skeezix. Her face was happy; she'd flipped to cosmic mode too. *Grunk*, here came a greedy wormhole—but, *whip*, a new Mr. Normal caught this one as well. Skeezix danced ever more wildly, singing her heart out, exhorting the crowd.

Get a Mr. Normal and step outside your mind
Everybody loofy cause it's myoor whippin time!

And thus began the avalanche. It was a humid twilight scene, lit by the Mr. Normals' bulbs and their eerie green whips—taking control of the wormholes as fast as they turned up. The qwet and increasingly confident crowd waxed ecstatic. People had brought reefers, whiskey pumpkins and streamlined purple axelerate buds. Everyone was cosmic by now, and they were freely sharing their stashes around. The rougher hillbilly-biker-type Kentucky qrudes stripped off their shirts to display their living tattoos.

Everywhere you looked, the wildly flickering Mr. Normals were hauling down larger and larger mounds of myoor meat, the stuff giving off a sewer stink that people pretty much ignored. Bag Stagger was jamming a bluesy raga that rose and fell, never quite coming to an end.

Meanwhile Jane and I were still onstage, qwet and teeping, hugging each other. Skungy was dancing on our shoulders, hopping from one of us to the other, letting out tiny, cheerful squeaks. Craig and Kenny down on the track, standing next to the Lincoln, bopping with a crowd of men. And now Mom and Dad came onstage to join Jane and me.

Our wristphones and teep links made it possible for us to talk, after a fashion—despite the chiming frenzy of the band and the roar of the crowd as, all across the grandstand, the thousand Mr. Normals continued hauling away at their strands of myoor.

"You're friends with Dad again?" I asked Mom. "And you're qwet?"

"I got qwet yesterday morning," answered Mom. "Like everyone else. It helped me throw a wonderful pot. The best bowl I ever made. No need for more, really. But now we have those disgusting wormholes gobbling people. As for your father—yes, we're on speaking terms again. He's moving back in, right, Lennox? And you-know-who is gone." Mom smiled in a relieved kind of way, and it was good to feel her emotions.

"You-know-who was my mother," said Jane sharply.

"Weezie might come back," I quickly put in. "She's still alive. Inside the myoor."

"Nothing against Weezie at all," Dad told Jane. "Weezie is a wonderful, vibrant woman. But I missed Sally. Did you hear her say that maybe she's thrown her last pot? Well, after I went home to her last night, I painted what could be my last picture. The clouds around the moon." Dad gave Mom a soft look. "We're ready to join our muses on Mount Parnassus. However we get there."

"You've always been my favorite," Mom told Jane. "It's so nice to see you back with Zad." She paused, glancing around at the hundreds upon hundreds of wormholes being stretched out like giant snakes. "What's this racetrack party about? We heard your ad and of course we came. You two are trying to fix the—"

"Oh, wait, we have to tell them about the little men," interrupted Dad. "The ones who threw a rock at Zad?"

"The gnomes?" I said, more than little distracted by everything that was going on around us. The band was still playing, the thousand Mr. Normals were hauling away on their thorned vines, and the crowd of onlookers were on the verge of a riot.

"Nasty little thugs," said Mom, still talking about what she and Dad had seen. "Foreign. With curved swords. I heard one of them talk about kidnapping Jane. We thought you should know."

"The gnomes are obsessed with that oddball thing that Jane used to have," I said, not wanting to think about this. "But—"

"Oh my god!" broke in Jane. "Your plan is working, Zad."

The legion of wormholes in the stadium had become floating fountains. It was the tipping point I'd hoped for. All this time the thousand Mr. Normals had been continuously pulling down taffy-strands of myoor flesh from Fairyland and now—now they didn't have to pull.

It was like when you suck on a hose to get a siphon started, and eventually the water begins flowing on its own. Huge stinky lava gouts of myoor-flesh were rushing through the wormholes—with the occasional paralyzed human tumbling through like a sodden log.

Dismay and repulsion in the crowd. They were backing away, shoving each other over, moving higher and higher in the stands. Meanwhile the cascading myoor flesh was running down past the rows of seats and puddling on the track, rising like Ohio floodwaters. As always, the myoor was giving off teep vibes of protean, teeming life.

As per my earlier instructions, the Mr. Normals fanned out to the edges of the mass and kept the myoor's outward flow confined, zapping her with megawatt sparks and pinching deep into her flesh with their heavy-duty lobster-claw hands. Rather than reverting to the form of a seven-mile-long slug, the myoor was being forced to pile up deeper and deeper upon the grounds of Churchill Downs.

The myoor was restoring herself, pushing her eyestalks and her dangerously toothy mouths out to her surface. Beneath her skin I could see the translucent flesh crypts in which she stored her sedated human captives from last night's and today's raids.

By now the Bag Stagger stage was an island in a lake of myoor, marooning the band along with Jane, Mom, Dad, and me. Stubbornly and even maniacally, the three musicians were continuing their onslaught of sound. Kink's bagpipe sounded like an alligator tumbling down an endless flight of stairs.

Looking over at the stands, I saw a zonked hillbilly lose his footing, fall onto the myoor and get himself bloodily chewed in half. Much worse than being swallowed by a wormhole.

Overhead, the wormholes were spewing out still more myoor meat, and the monster on the ground was getting thicker all the time. She'd be lapping across the stage before long. I felt uneasy about us trying to scamper across the myoor's mouthy skin to safety.

But, oh good, Craig and Kenny were in my slugfoot presidential-assassination-type Lincoln convertible, riding the surface of the myoor, driving over myoor mouths and past the translucent patches covering the myoor's comatose captives.

The boys were plowing into eyestalks, skidding around like old-time teenagers in a stolen car doing doughnuts in an empty parking lot. Kenny was at the wheel. Craig was whooping and giving everyone the finger, occasionally hopping in and out of the car. He was excited about having an adventure with qrude, sexy Kenny.

I did everything possible to attract them, making repeated and extravagant gestures, trying to message Kenny on my wrist-phone, sending Craig please-help-us vibes via teep. Finally they slimed over to us at high speed. At the last possible moment, Kenny slewed the Lincoln to one side so it skidded sideways onto the bandstand. Bag Stagger fell silent. It was occurring to them that they needed to flee the stage as well.

"Don't like that tooth soup out there," said Skeezix.

"Getting lonely?" Kenny called to me, very devil-may-care. "This would be a good time to have a flying jellyfish, huh?"

"Take us over to the grandstand, okay? These myoor mouths, they're no joke."

"I saw the spot where Mother is," Kenny told Jane, turning serious. "Were you watching? Craig got out and tried to hack through the myoor's skin. To save her."

"I always carry a blade," said Craig, displaying a hunting knife that, for whatever paranoid loner reason, he kept strapped to one of his calves. "I couldn't make a nick in the myoor's skin. And that skin has a temper. I was poking away and it sprouted a tentacle, yanked my legs out from under me and sent me skidding across the slime towards one of those mouths. You guys didn't see that?"

"I managed to rescue Craig," said Kenny. "This is a good car. Even if he didn't get Mother out, at least I know where she *is*. Zad's girlfriend Loulou is right next to her. By the finish line near the far edge of the grandstand. But how do we get Mother out if we can't cut a hole?"

"I have this idea for using the Mr. Normals," I said, wishing Kenny hadn't mentioned Loulou in front of Jane. "But first get us off this stage."

So Craig and Kenny ferried us to the grandstand. Skeezix,

Kink, Dharma, Dad, Mom, Jane, and I rode in the Lincoln convertible with them—the nine of us were piled into the ample cockpit, pinching and grab-assing. We couldn't stop laughing. Hysteria? The cosmic mode?

The mood was edgy in the stands. The qrudes may have been in cosmic mode, but they weren't chill at all. They were scared. To further harsh the vibe, the myoor's mouths had begun bellowing.

Nobody knew how much higher the myoor meat might rise. And they were as stranded in the stands as we'd been on the stage. Working your way down to an emergency exit via the betting parlors beneath the stands wasn't an option—because the myoor flesh had filled in those crannies. A few desperadoes had made a hole in the wall behind the highest rows of the grandstand, up near the iconic Churchill Downs towers. They were trying to rappel down the outside wall. But one of them had fallen and broken his neck.

On every side, the floating wormholes continued gushing. The reek was overpowering. Like being inside an old-time sewage treatment plant.

"The Hanging Gardens of Babylon," said Craig, lifting a pinky. "The Seventh Wonder of the ancient world."

"You fuckers brought us here to die," a guy with long matted hair yelled at me, making himself heard above the myoor's roars. He grabbed hold of Craig and started shaking him. Somehow Craig was always the first one in our group whom strangers attacked. It had been that way ever since high school.

"You don't want to mess with us," warned Kink of Bag Stagger. He was cradling his gross nurb bagpipe as if it were an alien bazooka. "See the mouths, you gunjy hairfarmer? You ever heard about the *kiss of the bag*?" The nurb instrument released a nasty, burbling squonk. "I'm gonna count to two," intoned Kink. "One—"

One of the hairfarmer's buddies raised his whiskey pumpkin, ready to crack it over Kink's head, but just now the gushers of myoor began dying down, and the men got distracted from their fight.

The myoor-flow stopped and, one by one, the hovering, knotty wormholes smoothed over and were gone. Everyone was cheering in relief. This phase was done. The whole damn myoor had drooled through hyperspace wormhole tunnels from Fairyland to Earth.

"Myoor's not gettin no deeper no more," I brightly told the matted-hair guy and his friends. "Kick back, qrudes."

Just in case they still wanted to argue, Skeezix strummed a venomous sound on her gitmo, kind of a maraca noise, like a rattlesnake buzzing its tail. The hairfarmer crew backed away.

The myoor had maxed out at something like fifty feet deep, all across the track and infield of Churchill Downs and bulging partway towards the barns beyond the track. And my Mr. Normals were keeping her corralled like the hardest-ass cowboys you ever saw.

"Can you rescue my mother now?" Jane softly asked me. "You said you would."

I got into wristphone contact with the Mr. Normals, sent a bunch of them to the spot where Weezie lay, and set them to blinking like crazy. I had a notion that it might be possible to precipitate the myoor into something like premature labor. Given that a strobe light can drive some people into seizures, it seemed like wildly flashing lights might make the myoor twitch so hard that she'd birth out her human captives.

For a good measure, I set all thousand of the Mr. Normals to strobing wild jagged rhythms for half an hour. Oddly inspired, Kink set his big bag to tootling along. Any folks in the stands who were prone to seizures—or who, at this point, felt like they *might* be—they covered their eyes and waited for the brain-breaking lightshow to stop.

But the effort was a false path. The myoor ignored the flickering—lobster pinches and electric sparks were the only things that got *her* attention. Jane's mother and the rest of them were still immured.

The myoor had her own agenda. She was settling in here, preparing to spawn. She wasn't even trying to flow out of the gates anymore. She was consolidating her body mass, withdrawing it from where it had been lodged under the grandstand, making herself a little deeper. And, as the myoor tightened herself up, her smell was damping down. Her vibes were more focused than before.

The myoor had abandoned any overzealous plan of swallowing every human on Earth. Although there was no sign of the green gub or the spotted gub just now, it might have been that they were messaging the myoor from N-space. The myoor was ready to hatch some gub eggs whenever those two arrived.

With the back exit stairs open, many of the qrudes were leaving. After all, we'd accomplished much of what we'd come here to do. The Cosmic Flip Trip! We'd lured down the myoor. And now we qwetties could be as cosmic as we wanted to—without the myoor's mouths pouncing on us from the fourth dimension.

Not everyone was bailing. The more hard-core elements of our crowd settled in for the night. The party continued. Bag Stagger got into meditative, wee-hours jazz. Some of the qrudes looted liquor from the racetrack bars, not that you really needed that, when were as deep into cosmic mode as we all were.

The looters went ahead and busted up the nurb wood chairs and tables in the track's fancy restaurants, using the scraps to build a couple of bonfires in the stands. There was a sense that, at least for now, the old rules didn't much matter anymore.

Now and then someone would throw a flaming stick down onto the myoor, just to hear her bellow in surprise. And then the myoor would grab the stick with one of her tendrils and throw it back up at us. Or crunch it to bits with one of her mouths.

Jane and I were sitting with Mom and Dad, talking things over. We could see everything pretty well—it was a clear night, and the moon was three-quarters full. A little ways across town I could see the conglomeration of glowing house jellies that they were calling Wobble Manor.

Craig Gurky was still with us, but Kenny had gone back to the Rollers' place to be with Kristo, taking my Lincoln with him. Skungy was snuggled in my lap. Now and then someone would stop by and thank us, or congratulate us. Like we were stars.

A few people asked me what was going to happen next, and I told them we'd probably see two flying gubs by morning, and maybe the gubs would fertilize some gub eggs inside the myoor, and maybe then the myoor would release her captives, and maybe then...well, that was hard to know.

Really, I wasn't even sure why the gubs hadn't been here all along. Maybe they'd been watching from N-space, with the spotted gub telling the green gub that we were doing a good job.

"Change after change," mused Dad. "Never a final answer." He was very clearheaded tonight, not really drinking at all.

"There's always the big aha," said Mom. "Remember, Lennox?"

"My old slogan," said Dad.

"I was never sure what it meant," I said. "But I think about it a lot."

"For awhile Lennox said the big aha was everywhere," Mom recalled. "Back when he was painting those very loose landscapes. With a palette knife. Beautiful, delicate shades."

"They didn't sell," said Dad.

"Too much aha?" said Mom, smiling. "The bowl I made yesterday has big aha. A bulge in one side. A perfect goof."

"Zad knows big aha too," said Dad. "Even if he doesn't know he knows. My son the artist."

"When I'm working, I'm outside of time," I said. "That feels like big aha."

"Vast," said Jane. "It's good sitting here."

"Waiting for the end of the world," said Mom. "I haven't stayed up so late in years."

"Love the moon," said Jane.

"Gibbous," said Craig Gurky, who been quietly listening. "That's a real word. A gibbous moon resembles a butt sticking through a hole in the sky. Why don't you two guys paint that?"

"You paint it, Craig," said Dad. "And we'll be furniture movers."

"Look down there," interrupted Mom, pointing. "Two

people on the myoor. Crazy drunks. Or are those the—"

"Gnomes!" I exclaimed.

Little guys in the slanting moonlight, casting long, puddled shadows. Blixxen and Staark, fifty yards apart, calling to each other in guttural tones. I saw glints of metal.

"They're cutting into the myoor," I said. "With Fairyland scimitars. Sharper than anything on Earth."

Moments later, two newly freed men were standing on the myoor beside Staark and Blixxen. They looked wobbly, stunned, pale. The gnomes took the men's hands, and skipped across the surface of the myoor with them, weaving past the mouths, heading towards other side. Somehow I knew the men were Gaven and Whit.

"Oh no," said Jane, sharing this realization. "That's all we need. And nobody can free my mother?"

"I'll keep trying, but—"

A ball of green light burst on the scene. It was the green gub, aglow and aflutter. I could teep her mood—she was pleased with how the myoor had settled in here. She was impressed by our labors, and she'd decided to be satisfied with the relatively small sample of humanity that her myoor had bagged.

Another burst of light, mostly yellow, and the spotted gub popped out of the aether as well. The pair of gubs circled above the myoor, calling to each other like birds with a nest. They were bigger than ever, the size of trucks, and shaped like legless pigs with pointy snouts, tiny ears, and bright black eyes.

The spotted gub levitated over to us. He stretched down his waggy saggy snoot and released a juicy *wheenk*.

"Duffie says that the dark gub can't figure out how to get down here," interpreted Jane. "Duffie's really glad about that."

"Duffie?" said Mom.

"That's what they call the spotted gub in Fairyland," said Jane. "He's ready for sex with the green one. He's just hoping that the green gub and her myoor can decide on which two people to use for gub blanks. The spotted gub has two people in particular in he's pushing for."

For a long minute the spotted gub hung there, wobbly and

piebald, studying us four with his bright glassy eyes.

"Don't even *dream* of using Jane and me!" I said, making a shooing gesture with my hands.

"I think the gub-blank gig sounds—interesting," said Dad softly. "A new existence. A step beyond. Perfect for an old man."

"Hush," said Mom. "That gub is listening to every word."

The coarse voices of the gnomes drifted up from the track. Whit and Gaven were gone, but the gnomes were back. They were busying themselves near the spot where the finish line was buried. It seemed they'd extracted another of the myoor's captives. Jane's mother? No, no—it was Loulou, pale and bald.

She crawled a short distance across the myoor and into the stands. She still had her teep, and she homed right in on me. Moments later, Loulou flopped down into a seat at my side. She kissed me in a familiar way. She was still wearing her same unglamorous pants and blouse from Weezie's party. She smelled like mold and rubbing alcohol. Jane made a sound of distaste.

"Thirsty," said Loulou blearily. "How long have I been out?"

"Here," I said, handing her a pod of water. "You missed a day and two nights. It's nearly dawn."

"What about Joey?"

"Still inside the myoor. We've got her corralled right here at Churchill Downs, see. I think the gubs will use the myoor to make two babies pretty soon. And I'm hoping the myoor will be releasing everyone after that."

Loulou shook her head, recalling her just-ended ordeal. "Being paralyzed inside the myoor—it was like being gone for a million years. At first I was into the myoor's mind, if you can call it a mind. A slime-pool of life. I tuned out of that, and then I was a speck inside my body, tooling through my veins. Like roads. I had this hallucination that I'd been invited for a tiny sit-down dinner inside every single one of my body's cells. As if they were apartments, and the cell nuclei were the hosts. It was boring. All we ever talked about was DNA." Loulou cast a sideways glance at Jane. "I can't remember if we're mad at each other or not."

"I'm still mad," said Jane. "About you and Zad."

"Like he's such a prize?"

"Look out!" said Mom. Blixxen and Staark had jumped into the stands. They were running up the steps towards us with blades in their hands. Everyone was scooting back, making way for them.

"Need to talk to you, Jane," puffed Blixxen. Seeing the fear on our faces, he slid his scimitar into his belt. "The deal is that, if you like, we can free your mother for you. Weezie Roller, right? Just come down with us to make sure we carve out the right bumpf."

"Why would you suddenly be helping me?" asked Jane.

"It's about your oddball," said Blixxen, making his voice sound exaggeratedly frank and honest. "We're having trouble using it. If you'll help us, we'll help you. And don't worry about Zad. He just wants to be with Loulou anyway."

"Not true!" I cried. "Don't go with them, Jane."

"Oh, yes I will," she said, jumping to her feet. She'd lost her temper again. If only Loulou hadn't kissed me.

Oh man. I was too worn out to respond. Did I even want Jane at all? She was so much trouble. Always asking for something more. Dejectedly I watched her flounce down the steps. Let her go, Zad. Hell, if Weezie was entombed where the gnomes had cut out Loulou, then Jane would be in sight anyway. I could run and help her if something happened.

"Do I look horrible with no hair?" Loulou was asking me, running her hands across her bare scalp.

"You look great. Especially for someone who's been dead for a million years. You'll always look good to me, Loulou. You're smart and you're qrude. I'm glad we had our time together."

"I can't remember why we broke up. Did the three-way thing bother you that much?"

"Oh, it was more that I missed Jane. I can't believe I'm saying this, but Jane is really nice to me. When she's not mad about—about nothing."

"You ought to go down there and keep an eye on her," said Loulou. "I can teep that's what you want to do. You're like a compass needle pointing her way."

"Loulou's right," chimed in Mom. "Go."

"I'll help you," squeaked Skungy.

"All right," I said, pulling myself together.

It goes without saying that, by the time I'd clattered down from our perch in the stands, the gnomes had kidnapped Jane. They'd clamped their cave-dweller mitts onto her arms and legs, and they were carrying her across the expanse of myoor. She was screaming and struggling.

Meanwhile the Mr. Normals were so hung-up on containing the myoor, that they weren't doing anything about Jane. For the moment I didn't care. I thought it would be qruder to save her on my own. I wasn't thinking very clearly—what with my fatigue, my raging emotions, and being in cosmic mode.

Setting out after Jane, I paused for a moment at the near edge of the myoor, trying to map my pursuit path. So many mouths to dodge. And goddamn Kenny had taken my car.

"Ratview!" chirped Skungy.

He'd flattened himself atop my head, with ears cupped, whiskers outstretched, nose twitching, and eyes upon the prize. He was still wearing his tiny wristphone, and he offered me a link. I gladly took it, and the rat's sensory inputs overlaid themselves upon mine. Via ratview, I was alert to every crevice and declivity in the myoor's hide, sensitive to every tendril of stink, in tune with smacks of the myoor's lips. I set off in pursuit of Jane, weaving past the hungry mouths, graceful as an ice-skater, gaining ground on the short-legged gnomes.

But I lost sight of them when they slid down the far slope of the myoor. Two Mr. Normals were standing there, fully fixated on the myoor. I asked them which way Jane and the gnomes had gone, and they pointed towards the mazy lanes amid the moonlit horse barns. Fearing an ambush, I persuaded the two Mr. Normals to accompany me. Before long we'd lost our way amid the silver moonlight and the flat shadows of the barns.

I turned to teep. Jane's unseen presence was a warm presence in my mind. I followed the psychic glow to a barn near the edge of the Churchill Downs property, and bade the two Mr. Normals to wait outside. I was worried the kidnappers might turn vicious if I pushed them too hard.

A pair of horses were in the barn's stables, shifting in their sleep, at ease, streaked by moonbeams, surrounded by the dusty smell of hay. A pale mauve light glowed from a hatch in the ceiling. The hayloft. I climbed a wooden ladder toward the light, and I found Jane there—with Whit, Gaven, and the gnomes. The light was from Jane's oddball, hovering near the hayloft's peaked roof.

"Zaddie boy made good time," said Staark. He was standing behind Jane, one arm around her waist, and with his scimitar poised against her throat. They'd been waiting for me.

"We make our deal and nobody gets hurt," said Blixxen, standing between Staark and me. He had a blade as well. He made a cautioning gesture with his free hand. "Sit down, Zad. Don't yell for those lightbulb men. Or Jane gets hurt."

Whit and Gaven were lolling against the wall, hairless and with flaking skin. They smelled of the myoor's preserving fluids, and were still in their party clothes, very rumpled by now. They seemed to have their infuriating self-confidence intact.

"We win again," said Whit. "Eat shit, Zad."

"Put down the blade," I told Staark, speaking to him across Blixxen's head. "We can talk. If you hurt Jane, you aren't getting out of here alive. My Mr. Normals will crisp your ass to cinders."

Slowly Staark lowered his blade from Jane's throat. But he kept a tight grip on her waist. Downstairs a horse nickered. One of the Mr. Normals sent a squidskin signal, asking if I needed help. I signaled back that Jane was a hostage, and that they should wait.

"The gnomes came here through my oddball," Jane told me, talking fast. He voice went up high and broke on the last word.

"Here's the story," said little Blixxen. "We're gonna show the dark gub how to use the oddball's tunnel like a guide rope, see? On account of he's having so much trouble making it to your brane. Our great god—he's not the brightest gub that ever lived. Staark and I came down here to make sure one of you guys tethers this end of the oddball for us, Zad. Meanwhile we want to go back to Fairyland and tell the dark gub that his path is set."

"Fine. Go back to Fairyland."

Blixxen glanced up at the bobbing oddball. "Problem is, we're not used to this crazy clam-pearl of Jane's. We don't know how to get inside and crawl to Fairyland. And the oddball doesn't much like us."

"Gaven and I are going to Fairyland as well," said Whit, his voice as languid as if he were discussing a tropical vacation. "We've worn out our welcome in Louisville."

"If all you want is for the oddball to open for you, that's easy," said Jane. She made a gesture, and the oddball dropped down, already widening her mouth.

"We forgot to tell you two something," rasped Staark. "Jane gets inside the oddball first." He dropped his scimitar and lifted Jane with his powerful hands. She landed a kick on the side of his head, but it didn't seem to matter to him. He only squeezed tighter and held her higher. "Whit and Gaven want Jane in Fairyland. For entertainment."

By now I'd signaled for the two Mr. Normals to come in, and I could hear them in the stable. But the oddball's mouth had opened all the way. She was settling onto Jane.

"Easy, Zad!" cried Blixxen, his sword raised high in the air, still in a position to slice Jane across the belly. "Don't be a fool!"

The Mr. Normals were coming up the ladder. Whit sprang across the room and threw a heavy wooden hatchcover across the hole in the floor, holding it in place with his feet. The hatch door danced and smoked with impact of the Mr. Normals' sparks, but for the moment it was holding.

The glowing lavender oddball was holding Jane sideways, like a dog worrying a doll. Jane's head was free, and a leg and an arm. She managed to clamp onto the oddball in such a way that the thing couldn't quite swallow her. And meanwhile

Jane's lips were moving, as if she were mentally rehearsing some plan.

Buying time, I kicked out at Blixxen, knocking his sword from his hand. But now Staark had hold of his sword again and—damn him, he really was going to cut into Jane. And now, as her last-ditch gambit, Jane sang out a measured, choppy squeal—she was imitating the voice of the spotted gub.

The barn's peaked roof split open and the gub's snout was in our midst. The terrified horses whinnied; their hooves pounded against the stable walls. The now-flaming hatchcover flew across the hayloft and landed where Whit and Gaven sat by the wall. One of the Mr. Normals' heads poked through the hatch. Gaven and Whit were fruitlessly stamping on the flaming hay. In another moment this would be an inferno.

But now the tip of the spotted gub's snout vibrated and—*wow*. The air was clear and the fire was gone. And—*huh?*—Staark was gone as well. And then Whit, and then Blixxen. The gub wasn't smashing them to bits—no, he was *erasing* them. Rubbing them out of the picture. Like mistakes in a pencil drawing.

Gaven was rushing around the hayloft in a wild panic. He ended up flinging himself into the mouth of the oddball. This would be his third time getting swallowed. The gub made a questioning squeal and Jane shrugged.

"Oh, let him go," she said.

The oddball flexed and pulsed. No more Gaven. The spotted gub waited for a minute, giving the man time to slide on through to Fairyland. And then the gub zapped the oddball with a spark of dark energy. The troublesome tunnel shriveled and disappeared from our world.

With a debonair wave of his snout, the spotted gub withdrew from the hayloft, squealing an intricate "See you later." And flew back to the track to resume his mating rituals with the green gub.

The Mr. Normals went back outside, dimming their bulbs. Jane climbed down the ladder to the stables to calm the horses and to refresh their hay and water. Skungy went along with her, perhaps to cadge some oats.

Jane returned to the loft alone, and we two flopped down on a shiny mound of straw, catching our breath. The moon was low; a pleasant shaft of its light was angling in through the pierced roof. The smell of smoke was gone. Jane and I were together, and alone.

We began hugging and merging our minds. I loved her curves, her responsive touch. We were like a voice and its echo, a yin and its yang, a pair of puzzle pieces finding their fit.

"It's finally time?" I asked.

"Time to make it real."

14: Big Aha

"We weren't using protection at all," remarked Jane. "This could be it." We lay comfortably naked on the hayloft straw, passion spent.

"I know you know I know."

"I'm glad," said Jane. "I hope we do have a baby soon. I could keep working, but maybe less. We'd have a nanny nurb. Maybe with my personality in her. Can you pull out of your doldrums now?"

"Bumble my way to a happy ending," I said. "So what if the Department of Genomics trashed my store and locked the doors. I bet they'd let me start again now."

"Once they realize we're heroes," said Jane.

"I hope. With the store, I was thinking I might get a bigger space and restock. Maybe partner with Craig Gurky and share his warehouse. He owns that place outright. We could sell Mr. Normals. Customized flying jellyfish houses. Copies of Gustav and Bonk. Personal nurb doubles—like SubZad. And I'm thinking about a line of nurb wigs that look like a little bit like gubs. Zad Plant's Cosmic Pig Wigs! Wigs will be big this fall."

Jane looked down at her bare breasts and playfully cradled a hand against them, the curled hand like a baby's head. "Nyoo-nyoo," she cooed. "Drink your milk." She shot a glance at me, happy and shy. "All you have to do now is get rid of the gubs and the myoor—right, Superartist?"

"I'm on it," I said. We kissed a little more and then we dressed.

Down in the stable, I asked Skungy if he wanted to come back to the grandstand with us.

"Naw," said the tweaked rat. "I'm digging it with these two horses. Basically a horse is a rat, you wave? An equine rodent." Skungy was perched on the back of one of the thoroughbreds.

The horse didn't seem to mind.

"You don't know what you're talking about at all," said Jane. "You're not even a genuine rat yourself."

"A gene-tweaked rat with quantum wetware," said Skungy, drawing himself up to his full height. Maybe six inches now. He'd really been eating a lot. "A higher rat."

"Are you teeping with the horses?" I asked him.

"I fed them that Joey Moon twistor pattern," said Skungy, proud of himself. "Squeaked it into their ears. We've had us a meeting of the minds. Once their trainer Geegee comes back from wherever she's hid, I'll propose a deal. I'll be her assistant. The owners might even let me be a jockey by and by." He bobbed up and down as if mounted on a galloping steed.

"So this is goodbye?" I said. "We'll stay in touch, right?"

"I'm not going nowhere," said Skungy. "Everything's gonna be fine."

The myoor was still out there, fifty feet high, a grisly, forbidding lump. The sky above the myoor was a damp luminous gray. But the eastern horizon was edged in pale yellow. Birds flew back and forth, perching on the barn gables, calling each to each. A gentle breeze was flowing towards the river.

Instead of doing another mad panic dash across the myoor, Jane and I rode piggyback on the two Mr. Normals who'd helped us at the barn. The big, lightbulb-headed nurbs crackled out admonitory sparks whenever the myoor tried clamping onto their feet.

There were still a fair number of hardy partiers in the grandstand. The green gub and the spotted gub were hovering in one particular spot halfway up, absorbed in a conversation with—my Mom and Dad. Loulou and Craig Gurky were still at their side.

"Your father is volunteering to become a gub egg," Mom told me as soon as Jane and I were within earshot. "I think he's out of his mind. But the spotted gub has been pushing for your father, and the green gub likes him too. Apparently the spotted gub was planning this all along. He sent down the oddball last year to get things started."

"If you want to hatch baby gods, you need artists," said Dad. "Right, Zad?"

"Joey would agree with that," said Loulou softly.

The green gub let out a liquid squeal that I couldn't decipher, but Mom understood.

"You're asking *me* to be a gub egg too?" said Mom, looking flattered and a little alarmed.

I cranked my mind up to a sufficient level of alertness to decipher the gub's skirling answer. "God and goddess," she said. "Sally and Lennox. The spotted gub's pick. Sally, you'll create a universe as wry as your crooked pots. Lennox, you'll someday spark my grandchild-gubs. They'll be as iconoclastic fantastic as your landscapes, an eye in every bower. Jump into my myoor. I'll exalt you."

"But—jump into the myoor?" protested Mom.

"Myoor is me," reiterated the green gub. "You know this. My womb. Sweeter than she seems. You'll gubify. You'll drink the knowers' knowns. Your friends will run free, you'll stay we, and my mate will spark you. You'll ripen. In three months, you hatch as glory gubs, a he and she. Sally-gub spawns a cosmos of her own and sets her own myoor within. Lennox-gub seeks to fertilizes gub eggs where and when he can. Luck of the raw. Life's great and subtle wheel."

Hearing that last phrase, Jane nudged me. She'd said it yesterday herself. No wonder. The green gub had made our world. Everything we thought or knew was part of her patterns.

The sun had risen, a yottawatt disk laden with a day's heat. Mom and Dad were gilded by the low light, transfigured, their soft gray hair alive in the airs of dawn.

"We'll do it?" Dad said to Mom.

"It's death," said Mom.

"With afterlife guaranteed," said Dad. "Otherwise—what? We decline, decay, lights out."

"But this is death *today*," said Mom. "I'd like to wait and see some *human* grandchildren."

"You can come back here for visits," slipped in the green gub. "I'll show you a shortcut through the Nth dimension.

Come be a goddess now. You were meant for it, Sally."

"I always thought so, too," said Mom, a smile playing across her face. "What the heck."

With a great wallowing motion, the myoor mounted the terraces of the grandstand, scattering the qrude partiers and the Mr. Normals. Loulou screamed and ran several rows higher into the grandstand.

A huge gout of the myoor came to a rest before Mom and Dad. The surface was indented with two shallow tubs like— open graves. Weeping, cheeks wet, Mom kissed Dad goodbye, then me and Jane. Dad embraced us as well. And now, in slow solemnity, my parents laid themselves down in their ill-smelling flesh tombs. The myoor closed over them, leaving a pair of translucent patches in her hide.

Dimly I saw my parents fold their hands on their chests, settling into hieratic poses. And then they were quite still, slight smiles upon their dear, pale, frozen faces.

The myoor withdrew her pseudopod, bearing Mom and Dad to a more central location. Jane, Craig, Loulou and I followed along, watching, as if in the wake of a hearse. Already Mom and Dad were changing, melting, becoming gub eggs.

Flying above the infield, the green gub and the spotted gub wove the figures of a wild dance, humping against each other, entwining their doughy bodies, puffing out their rear ends, shuddering with passion.

Having reached an orgasmic high point, the spotted gub flopped onto the myoor, making a thunderous slap. With the heedless brutality of overweening lust, he thrust his pointed snout *one-two* into the spots where my sedated parents had lain.

"Hot stuff," said Loulou, who was standing at the grandstand railing beside Jane and me. "Gub sex."

Craig Gurky giggled.

"Show some empathy, you two," snapped Jane. "Those eggs were poor Zad's parents."

Suddenly a frantic squeal tore the air.

It was the dark gub, tumbling into our space at a strange angle. He seemed quite unable to right himself. In Fairyland he'd been a flat silhouette, but here on Earth he was a jagged black line. Although he was too late to woo the green gub, he may have hoped to abort the ripening of her eggs.

Fully in control, the spotted gub blasted the dark gub with a bolt of negative energy. A sizzle ran up and down the creature's flailing zig-zag, chewing away at the two untethered ends. The dark gub dwindled to a single point. And now, with a chagrined *wheenk*, this final remnant returned to the unseen plenum of N-dimensional space.

Refulgent with joy, the spotted gub and the green gub hovered above the myoor, gloating over the fertilized eggs. The myoor's surface was pistoning up and down in lumpy waves. A firework-like cascade of twinkling eye-candy burst forth, blanketing the leviathan with visions: animations, photos, holograms, sounds, and knots of emotion—all linked together by a lacy network of curves.

"Those must be the thoughts of the other people she swallowed," murmured Jane. "The myoor's copying the info into the baby gubs. *You'll drink the knowers' knowns.*"

Yes, swirled and twirled as if by twin tornadoes, the flocks of thoughts funneled into the fertilized embryos that been my parents, enriching the nascent gubs with a few thousand people's memories and experiences. This would give the new gubs a running start towards godly minds. After birth, they'd build from there.

"Do the also-rans escape the myoor now?" asked Loulou. "I want my Joey back."

As if in response, the myoor began expelling the captives from her flesh—all of them save for my parents. *Pop-pop-pop*, hundreds and then thousands of human figures appeared upon the myoor's surface—wan, befuddled, bald. They sprawled and shuddered, they crawled to the edges of the myoor, they pulled themselves into the grandstand, they stood wobbling on their legs.

Joey, Carlo, Reba, Junko, and Weezie—they were back and fully alive. Right here beside us.

Loulou, Jane, Craig and I embraced them, and we sat in a

happy group amid the grandstand's box seats. All around us other reunions were in swing. The grandstand filled with a joyful human buzz.

Our little group talked and teeped and messaged, catching each other up on what had been happening for the last day and half. At first Jane and I did most of the talking. And then we slowed down and our group got into a more typically meandering mode.

"A rough trip," mused Joey, sitting with his arm around Loulou. He paused to breathe in a deep draught of the morning air. "I thought I was living in a comic book being read by a bug-eyed monster. A comic about teenagers in high school. That part lasted for a billion years. And then I saw your parents, Zad. They were Egyptian priests, high in the sky, asking me to confess my sins. So I did. I was beaming out thoughts like a lighthouse. And then I was getting born—back here. With a boner." Joey ran his hands over his bare scalp. "Whit and Gaven are really gone?"

"I'm going to stay high on cosmic mode for, like, a month," said Reba, studying herself in a mirror from her purse. "I need sun. And lots of fruit. I'm literally a corpse."

"It's a good look on you," said Craig. "You could host a squidskin channel."

"Literally means actually," Jane chided Reba. "If you're speaking proper English. And you're not *actually* dead."

"What the fuck, schoolmarm Roller," said Reba in a crabby tone. "You've gotten out of practice at being my friend. Keep it giggly."

"I can get you some nurb silkworms for weaving a wig," Junko told Reba.

"I've got a better idea for—" I began.

"I want a wig too," interrupted Weezie. "I'll be trolling for a new man. With Lennox gone. Is he dead, or what? I don't understand that part, Zad."

"My parents are still inside the myoor," I said. "They're gub embryos. They're going to hatch out as gods. Gub gods."

"I sure hope your mother doesn't hold a grudge," said

Weezie. "If she's going to be a god. She didn't always have the best sense of humor. After they hatch out, will the myoor go away?"

"Did anyone make any promises about that?" asked Craig Gurky, turning to Jane and me.

"Those hillbilly dragonflies in Fairyland told us the whole gub life-cycle," said Jane thoughtfully. "It was like a biology lecture. *The Intrepid Liver Fluke.* But I don't remember about the myoor leaving."

"Ask the gubs," suggested Loulou.

"They're too excited," I said, looking up at the green gub and the spotted gub flying loops around each other. "And they don't always answer our questions. Compared to them, we're like germs. Or electrons."

"All I know is that I don't feel safe with that myoor around," said Weezie. "After my clusterfuck of a party, I don't even feel like going back to my house. But I don't know where else to live."

"You can stay in my apartment for a week or two," said Jane.

"We'd strangle each other," said Weezie. "And teep only makes it worse. I love you—*but*."

"I was thinking that Jane and I might move to my parents' farm," I said. "At least part-time. I mean if my parents are—" My voice caught and trailed off.

"I'd like living in your family home," said Jane, patting my hand. "I always liked it better than my parents' place. More sincere."

"My house isn't *sincere*?" said Weezie. "What's that supposed to mean?"

"Nothing," put in Carlo, who'd been drinking whiskey and slowly gathering his forces. "Language is an empty symbol-game. What I *do* know is that bald will be big this fall."

"I'm trying to tell you guys that I've got plans for some wig-hats already," I said. "It'll be one of my new Live Art products. When I reopen my business. Need to talk to you about that, Craig. About teaming up in your space?"

"Art nurbs and mover golems," said Craig. "Feasible match.

But you don't move in with me."

"Don't worry."

Carlo interrupted, holding up his hands like a blind man feeling his way towards a light. "That company we were all working for—what was it even called?"

"Slygro," said Reba. "I own it. Is that bad?"

"The realtime approval ratings for qwet are quite high," said Junko, briefly doing her staring-into-the-web thing. "The economy crashed yesterday, but now the news of the Churchill Downs liberation is out. People want to adjust and move on. You know how it is. Even an apocalypse only rates a couple of news cycles."

"Adjust to being high," said Joey. "It's a wonderful world. If we let it be. Why was everyone so uptight for all those centuries? Why did we ever think that anything mattered?"

"I'm still seeing something about a treason charge?" said Reba, mentally scanning through the recent news. "Treason and mass murder?"

"Louisville Socialite's Grisly Bash," intoned Weezie, reading unseen headlines. "Glenview Genocide. But, hey, did any people actually die?"

"Not hardly," I said.

Carlo gestured at the thousands of myoor survivors in the grandstand. "We're gutsy heroes, right? We spent a day and a half as hostages inside an alien pod. We have post-traumatic stress. Society can't fault us for anything we've done."

"We might still be blamed for the people having bad reactions to qwet," said Junko, still sifting data from the web. "Fights and murders. Personality takeovers. Negative feedback loops. I could try pushing out a fix. Qwet 2.0."

"Don't water this down because of a few goobs," said Joey. "*Ye have the stupid turds with you always. But a good high ye have not always.* Thus saith the Lord."

"It can be Gaven who takes the blame for anything bad," I suggested. "The scapegoat."

"Where is he now?" asked Junko.

Craig and I exchanged a smile. I'd let him watch via my

wristphone when we'd had the big fight in the hayloft. "Long story short," said Craig. "Gaven's in Fairyland."

"If I never see that man again it'll be too soon," said Reba, returning her attention to her makeup mirror. "Maybe I should grow some nurb lichen on my scalp, Junko, what do you think? Instead of a wig. An Art Deco look. Kind of butch."

"You're butch now?" said Carlo, amused.

"Whatever you and Junko like," said Reba archly. "Remember, we're a threesome. You like us better than Joey and Loulou, right, Junko? A girl like me needs a lot of attention. Let's go to my apartment and firm things up."

The rising sun was putting a nice glow into the myoor's flesh, but she still had all those toothy mouths.

"I do wish I knew how long we have to keep an eye on the myoor," said Junko. "I'm worried that if Zad's Mr. Normals let down their guard, the myoor will slime across the city on another rampage."

"Remember that the green gub is controlling her," I said. "And the green gub pretty much wants to be nice to us, now that her myoor is pregnant."

"Three months till Zad's parents hatch out as gubs," added Jane.

"*Ta daaa!*" said Loulou, and made snorting noises. "I'm a gub!"

"The myoor will get hungry," fretted Junko. "What if I set up a symbiosis thing? Have a grove of tweaked nurb plants take root on her. The plants can feed the myoor with nodules on their roots. Peanuts, yams, taro, potatoes."

"Loulou and I can help tweak the flower and leaf designs," said Joey. "To make the plants look loofy. Really do it right. Everyone's gonna be watching."

"Let's call it a Slygro demo project," said Reba. "Great PR. It could save my bacon."

"I want bacon," said Carlo.

"First you take a shower," said Reba, tossing her bald head. "You smell like calving day in the cattle barn."

"I'll get my Tailthumper skin scent colony going too," said

Carlo, quite unfazed.

"Let's all three of us go to Reba's apartment," put in Junko. "Showers all around. And I'll fix you up with a new blue blankie nurb, Reba. We can worry about the myoor's nurb plants tomorrow."

"Fine with *me*," said Loulou, snuggling up to Joey. "We two won't miss the rest of you at all." She turned to old Weezie, putting on her sweetest smile. "Do you mind if we two keep living in your house, Mrs. Roller?"

"For a few days," said Weezie. "Less than a week. Kenny's still living there, and I'll be back in January."

"We might switch to a jellyfish house," suggested Joey. "Those things are way qrude. Maybe we could anchor ours on Zad's farm?"

Jane tensed at this—Loulou didn't want more trouble.

"We'll take our jellyfish to that new commune downtown," said Loulou with an easy smile. "Wobble Manor."

"Perfect," said Jane.

There's not much more to tell.

The green gub and spotted gub stayed in the sky for three months, waiting for their twins to be born, and vigilant against any harm to the myoor.

Junko, Loulou and Joey planted nurbs all over the myoor, and the plants bloomed into a Boschian jungle, alive with tendrils and translucent spheres. The myoor was happy and well nourished. She let her skin smooth over; her hungry mouths were gone. She was like a memorial garden, with the tombs of my parents near the center, the remains dimly visible through a layer of translucent skin. Not that Mom and Dad looked at all human. They were gubs, with finer details forming on their bodies every day. The Mom gub was a dark warm color, and the Dad gub was a cooler shade with pale spots.

With the myoor at peace, the Mr. Normals no longer needed to fence her in. Far from spreading, the myoor was shrinking. Feeding the substance of her body into the growing gub embryos. Freed of their duties, the Mr. Normals roamed around town, taking on the role of low-key deputies, cooling out any qwet-fueled fights that popped up. Top cop Lief Larson approved. He and I were on good terms now, if not exactly friends.

Jane and I were happy, mostly living on Mom and Dad's farm, sometimes using Jane's apartment in the city. Weezie had calmed down, and she'd moved back into the Roller mansion gate house. Jane was running her Jane Says business, doing promo and design. I was making art, gearing up for a big show to relaunch my Live Art gallery and its new annex in Craig Gurky's warehouse. The DoG had given me permission to re-open.

All through October, Jane postponed finding out for sure if she was pregnant. She didn't want to push it or jinx it. And then, one crisp morning in November, I woke and the bed was empty. Dawn. I went outside and found Jane on the back deck smiling. The trunks of the trees were lit by the rising sun. Jane's eyes were soft.

"I'm having a baby," she told me. "I finally looked inside myself. It's really true."

It was one of those moments when I could understand that this is all there is. The here and now. Jane and me in the world together. The big aha.

So, wait, what's the big aha? Nothing complicated about it. All you have to do is to pay attention. Or not. The big aha comes just the same. It's everywhere.

As December came on, the myoor's pregnancy approached full term. And Jane would be having our baby in June. And my parents were inside the myoor. It all fit.

I got into the habit of going downtown to look at the myoor garden every few days, sometimes with Jane along. Other visitors were prone to wandering the myoor's now-fragrant grounds as well. Some tweaked yam plants on the myoor came into bloom, with masses of white blossoms.

The myoor was much, much smaller by now, ten feet deep and a hundred feet across, with the two big pregnancy bulges in the center. Overhead the spotted gub and the green gub continued their watchful circling, standing guard over their nest.

As it happened, Jane and I were in the myoor garden when the new gubs were born. It was noon on Christmas Day—sunny and bitter cold. A holiday outing.

"Do you hear them?" said Jane as we two reached the center of the garden and its twin mounds. The myoor was shaking, the plants were warbling, and the unborn gubs were cheeping from within the myoor's flesh.

In the most casual way imaginable, the myoor hide split open, releasing the pair. They wriggled out and floated free. A delicately shaded red gub, and a dark blue gub spangled with yellow stars.

The green gub and the spotted gub dipped down to nuzzle their babes, the four gubs conversing, a chorus of wheenks.

A crowd of onlookers had gathered. Not liking this, the spotted gub prepared to take the little ones to someplace quieter. But it seemed that, at least for the moment, the green gub would remain. The baby gubs piped tremulous farewells to her, and then the spotted gub pushed them into the Nth dimension, nudging them with his snout, prying them up from our space.

I don't know if the newborn gubs ever noticed me. Certainly they didn't say goodbye. They weren't my parents anymore at all.

The green gub didn't like having her family out of her sight. With quick, smooth motions she did her cleanup work—gathering what was left of the myoor and absorbing it into her flesh.

Jane and I and the others were left on the bare dirt of the Churchill Downs track. The nurb plants that had bedecked the myoor were scattered about like discards from a winter garden.

Drawing very close to us two, the big green gub chirped a farewell. No telling what she said. She dwindled into the sky, then disappeared, joining her family in N-space. Someday, somewhere, she'll revisit our universe, *her* universe, returning to spawn her next pair of baby gubs.

And here on Earth we have our qwet. We've settled into it; people like it. Jane and I are living with the new baby on Mom and Dad's farm. She's a girl. It's like seeing my life start all over.

Afterword

In this afterword, I want to tell you a little about the origins of *The Big Aha*, give some information about the book's illustrations, say a bit about becoming my own publisher, and inscribe an honor roll of my Kickstarter contributors.

I'm tempted also to include a detailed explanation of the hyperspace wormhole geometry that underlies a myoor's wormhole mouths, and to explain how the myoor could in fact be siphoned down to out plane of reality via the wormholes. But, wait, you can look that up in my ancillary work, *Notes for The Big Aha*. The *Notes* are actually a bit longer than the novel. Look for the March 30, 2013, entry.

You can find free online versions of the *Notes for the Big Aha* on my novel's website, or you can order the *Notes* as an ebook, paperback or hardback.

`www.rudyrucker.com/thebigaha`

Regarding the origins of *The Big Aha*, one of my basic inspirations was that I've always felt like the psychedelic revolution of the late Sixties and early Seventies didn't last long enough. I wanted to revive that time's spirit in the context of an SF novel set in the not too distant future.

My stylistic model was William J. Craddock's little-known novel of the Sixties, *Be Not Content*. The book features deeply funny interactions among the early acidheads of the San Francisco Bay area. I first read it in 1972, shortly after its initial publication.

For years I chuckled fondly to myself about Craddock's masterpiece. But by 2012 the book was all but unfindable. I took it upon myself to republish it—to clean off the master's grave, you might say—and thus my publishing enterprise Transreal Books was born.

In writing *The Big Aha*, I wanted to reproduce Craddock's

spaced-out, off-kilter, irresponsible glee. But, these being post-modern times, I didn't want to do it in terms of drugs. Drugs have been done to death. So I turned to quantum mechanics.

My Boulder Creek friend Nick Herbert was the one who initially hipped me to the psychedelic potential of quantum mechanics. I've known Nick since moving to California in 1986. As well as being a freaky, giggling mountain hermit, old Nick is a genuine physicist with degrees, a dusty job resume, and excellent popular-science books to his credit, including his 1985 magnum opus, *Quantum Reality.*

Nick has a lifelong dream of finding direct ways to experience the paradoxical nature of quantum reality. Nick terms this a quest for *quantum tantra*. He suggests that one step along this path might be to look into your own mind and to notice that quantum and classical processes are both at work. I ran with this idea, and my *Big Aha* characters talk about being in the cosmic versus the robotic mode.

In order to make my novel be more of a thrilling wonder tale, I beefed up quantum tantra by tacking on a second SFictional trope, that is, *wetware*. And thus I arrived at *qwet*, or quantum wetware, which also gives people telepathy, which is another long-term interest of mine.

I put a kink into my qwet teep by hewing to Nick Herbert's scientific dictum that, logically speaking, people must forget whatever they learn via telepathy. Otherwise they might be exchanging information faster than light! Oblivious teep is a nice metaphor for intimate human communication. "Yes we made love, but I don't remember a word we said."

In planning *The Big Aha*, I decided to set it in Louisville, Kentucky. I grew up there, and I wanted to reminisce a little about my youth, and about my parents. My brother Embry lives in Louisville, and I visit him from time to time. I'm always struck by the fact that he's still seeing the people whom he went to gradeschool or even kindergarten with. After so many years together, they speak to each other very openly and with little concern about being polite. In other words, they're free to be completely crass and rude. I find such unstilted dialog amusing, and I wanted to write some characters who talked that way.

Why did I publish *The Big Aha* myself? I probably could have sold the book to a commercial publisher—but that's been getting less rewarding over the last few years, with longer waits, more anxiety, less actual editing by the publisher, less proofreading and smaller advances. Less fun. Publishing is undergoing a phase shift, a transition from one era to the next. The thuddy dinosaurs are losing ground to the nimble mammals. So I'm morphing into a qwet rat.

As an older writer, I felt hesitant about starting my own publishing enterprise. But survival is a matter of doing whatever works in our continually mutating postsingular world. And once you accept self-publishing, there are some advantages to it.

One nice thing, for instance, is that I can include images of my paintings on the book cover and as illustrations at the heads of the chapters. A commercial publisher might balk at doing that. And I'm free to publish the hardback edition with the illos in *color*.

Regarding my paintings, a number of them were made especially for *The Big Aha*. These days I often paint images of what I'm writing about, or of what I'm *planning* to write about. Previsualizing my scenarios in paint has become part of my creative process. And I'm painting more all the time. Riffing off this, I went ahead and made Zad and his father Lennox be artists.

Here's a list of the titles of the paintings that I used here. I put asterisks after the titles of the paintings that were done specifically with *The Big Aha* in mind. The others are older works that seemed like a good fit. I do tend to think about more or less the same kinds of things year after year.

Cover: *Gubs and Wormholes.* *

1. Qwet Rat: *Loulou and Skungy.* *
2. The Coming of the Nurbs: *Louisville Artist.* *
3. Loofy Picnic: *The Lovers.* *
4. Oblivious Teep: *A Night of Telepathy.* *

5. Scene of the Crime: *Thirteen Worlds.*
6. Loulou in the Oddball: *My Parents* [Edited].
7. Flying Jellyfish: *On My Home Planet.*
8. Funhouse: *He Sees the Fnoor.*
9. Spreading Qwet: *God's Eye.* *
10. Weezie's Party: *Fractal Skate Posse.*
11. Fairyland: *The Two Gods.* *
12. Spotted Gub: *A Gub On Her Bed.* *
13. Churchill Downs: *The Mr. Normals vs. The Myoor.* *
14. Big Aha: *Dawn.*

If you want to know more about my paintings, see my paintings website, which has links for my art catalog *Better Worlds*, available free online and as a paperback.

wwww.rudyrucker.com/paintings

Coming back to the topic of publication—when you do it yourself, there's a missing part of the equation . You don't get a pre-publication cash advance.

I'd heard of people turning to crowd-sourcing, that is, asking the public for support but, again thinking as an older writer, I felt uneasy about this. My son and the young writer Tim Pratt encouraged me to go ahead, so I took the plunge and ran a Kickstarter fundraiser.

And it worked well. I raised an amount of money that, although not huge, was more than any of the publisher's advances I've gotten for my last five or six books. Heartfelt thanks to my supporters!

Here's a list of their chosen names, alphabetized by the first letters of each name.

@brunoboutot, @NeuroKit, Adam Kreidman, Adam L Crouse, Adam Rajski, Adrian Briggs, Adrian Magni, Adriane Ruzak, Alan Chamberlain, Alan Kurtz, Alex Baxter, Alex McLaren, Alex Schoenfeldt, Amy Denniston, Andi Hechtbauer, Andreas Winterer, Andrew Beirne, Andrew Lindsay, Andy Valencia, Anthony McDonald, Aram Morera-Mesa, Aris Alissandrakis, arjan brussee, Arthur Murphy, Austin Trunick, Baba Z Buehler, Ben Gansky, Ben Jones, Benjamin H. Henry, Benjamin

Owen, Benoit Hamelin, bnewbold, Bob, Bob Schoenholtz, Borgel, Brad Omland, Brett Camper, Brett Gurewitz, Brian, Brian Anderson, Bruce Evans, Bruce Yarnall, Bryan Helm, Bryce J. Eastman, Calvin L. Stancil, Carl F Nielsen, Carlos Pascual, Casimir Couvillion, Charlie Lee, chootka, Chris Mihal, Christel e^x Davies, Christopher G. Brown, Chuck Ivy, Chuck Shotton, Cliff Winnig, Clytie Siddall, Cooper Speers, Dan Cohen FCP, Daniel Martin Diaz, Darwin Engwer, Dave Bonner, Dave Bouvier, Dave Gauer, David & Diane Shaw, David Golbitz, David Holets, David Johnston, David Pescovitz, David Rains, David T Kirkpatrick, David Wahl, Davide carnovale, Dennis Donley, Dieter P., Dino Morelli, Dirk Materlik, Don and Harriet, Doug Bissell, Doug Smith, Duncan Stewart, Ed Friese, Eileen Gunn, Emilio Rojas, Emma and Jake, Eric Gorski, Eric Hartwell, Eric Poulsen, Evan Rattner, F. Jerrell Schivers, Fenrar Eterovich, foldl, Fred C. Moulton, Fred Kiesche, Gabe McCann, gamme TAKIGUCH, Gareth Branwyn, Garth Kidd, Gary Lee Denton, Georgia Rucker, Gordon F, Gregg Morris, Guy Marsden, Harry F, hugo truyens, Ian Chung, Ian Mond, Isaac 'Will It Work' Dans, Isabel Rucker, J. Kulavis, J. Mark Hamlow, J.D. Dresner, Jacob Gertsch, Jacq Jones, James Grahn, James Green, James Reid II, Jan Brands, Janusz Leidgens, Jas Strong, Jason Norris, Jay Munsterman, Jeff Aldrich, Jeff Mel, Jens Finkhaeuser, Jeremy Alston-Follansbee, Jeremy Goldstein, Jeremy John Wakeman, Jeromy G. Murphy, Jetse de Vries, Jim & Paula Kirk, Jim Anderson, Jim Cavera, Joe daLuz, Joe Sislow, John A, John Alan Simon, John Didion, John Green, John K., Jon Cook, Jon F Nebenfuhr, Jon Lasser, Jon Pruente, Jonathan Baron, Jonathan Rosenberg, Jonathan Thomas, Jörg Kleinpaul, Joshua Gates, Juan Miguel Expósito, justnathan, kall, Karl J., Karl The Good, Karl W. Reinsch, Karl Wieser, Karl-Arthur Arlamovsky, Karl-Heinz, Keith P. Graham, Ken Haase (beingmeta), Kerriann Piccione, Kevin Freeman, Kevin Hogan, Kevin J. Maroney, Kris Verbeeck, Kunal Prakash, Kurt Adam, Kyle "Fiddy" Pinches, Lang Thompson, Laura Starrs, Lawrence Wilkinson, Lee Fisher, Lee Poague, Leon Marvell, Leonard Lin, Libbi Rich, Lindsey Nelsen, Little Aha, M. Starnes, Madeleine Shepherd, Mait Uus, Manuel C. Piñeiro Mourazos, Marc Laidlaw, Marc Majcher, Mark Anderson, Mark Dery, Mark Frauenfelder, Mark Gerrits, Mark Himmelsbach, Mark Hughes, Mark Sherman, Markku Lappalainen, Martin James Ford, Matt Geis, Matt Mets, Matthew Brabbin, Matthew Cox, Mayer Brenner, Michael Beverley, Michael Carychao, Michael Duda, michael strum, Michael Weiss, Micky Shirley, Mike Bonsall, Mike Cornelius, Mike Fuchs, Mike McConnell, Mike Perry, Mike Reid, Mike Rende, Mitchell Yang, Mykel Alvis, Nancy Wu, Nathan Glaesemann, Neil Clarke, Nicholas Hansen, Nina Frey, Noah "bibulb" Ramon, Omar Hakim, Operator99, Owen Rowley, P.F. Smith, P.G. Six, p9000, Paul Cutler, Paul K. Gayno, Paul

Leonard, Paul Warren, Peter Goulborn, Peter Young, Phil Binkowski, Phillip J W, Pienaru Adrian, Pope Phil Monty, Rachel Mizsei Ward, Rich Warren, Richard Kadrey, Richard Klibaner, Richard Murray, Richard Stevens, Richard Stokotelny, Richie Bielak, Rik Eberhardt, Rob Eickmann, Rob Messick, Rob Staenke, Robert Stern, Rod Bartlett, Ronan Waide, Roy Berman, Rudy Rucker Jr., Ruth Coy, rwbogy, Ryan Anderson, Ryan Olson, S. Blain, Sandra Schneiderman, Sarah J Brown, Scott Call, Scott Morrison, Scott Steinbrueck, Shannon Ellery Hubbell, Simon Bubb, Simon Travis, skout, Skylar L. Primm, Stefan Schmiedl, Stephen Fenton, Stephen Tavener, Stephen Wolfram, Steve Davies, Steve Gere, Steve Giovannetti, Steve Lord, Steven Hager, Steven Sweeney (sween), Stewart Cauley, Stuart Broz, Susan Sutton, Tedd, Thanks Name, Theron Trowbridge, Thomas, Thomas Gideon, Thomas Hunt, Thomas Klose, Thomas Lockney, Thomas Lynge, Tim Conkling, Tim Pratt, Todd Fincannon, Tom Warin, Tony Tibbs, Troy Whitlock, Walter F. Croft, William Dass, Wojtek Sal, and Yaron Davidson.

And thanks also to those supporters who chose not to be listed. In closing, I'll remind you of the novel's website.

`www.rudyrucker.com/thebigaha`

And if you enjoyed *The Big Aha,* be sure to check out some of the other Transreal Books titles, including my *Complete Stories*, *Turing & Burroughs*, and *Collected Essays*–as well as William J. Craddock's *Be Not Content*, the book that started this whole project.

`www.transrealbooks.com`

Yours in the big aha…

Rudy Rucker
Los Gatos, California
November 19, 2013